Molly Bates: The Leader of
Two Dozen Very Ugly-looking Brigands

Richard V. Hamilton

MOLLY BATES,
THE LEADER OF TWO DOZEN VERY UGLY-LOOKING BRIGANDS

A historical fiction novel based on the screenplay *Molly Bates, the Leader of Two Dozen Very Ugly-Looking Brigands* © 2000 by Richard V. Hamilton.

Published by Enders' Family Publishing

ISBN 0-9719837-0-4

Acknowledgements

My appreciation to Dave Enders – friend, author, patriot, as well as the president of the most promising and intriguing publishing company in the Republic today without whose kind guidance and suggestions this novel would not have been written.

Thanks to my agent Kate Garrick who very conclusively proved to me that originality in literature can and will be appreciated.

Thanks to all those valiant souls who have read my works in manuscript and appreciated them for what they are.

Godspeed.

To Dawn
who is my ideal
reader.
Best wishes.
Affectionately,
Rolul V. bulley

Table of Contents

I. Pietas

II. Verplaca

III. Praxidice

Part One

Pietas

ONE

Miles Crawford's Attitude

Because there could only be one King, one Empire, and one brand of patriotism, Miles Crawford was yanked rudely out of bed – a bed he was pleasantly sharing with a very pretty, jovial and vivacious woman. Because some pranksters lead by a brewer had tossed a quantity of excellent tea overboard half-a-world away, Miles was dragged through the streets in only his boots and undershirt – the two items of clothing they had graciously allowed him to put on. His hands tied uncomfortably behind his back, his face and ribs bruised, his knees skinned and hurting like hell, he was deposited into a dungeon to starve because back in the Colonies, where his estranged wife resided, a sulky lot of local landlords had decided it was high time to get angry about some of His Majesty's unseemly practices.

There were, of course, other reasons.

No matter.

Miles' relatives, most of whom were wealthy and influential, could have stepped in. But, since Miles was scheduled to inherit a little here and a little there, he proved a dangerous rival; and, being a free spirit, he could easily undermine the family's clout. Otherwise, they would not have hesitated to rush to the rescue like lions.

As soon as they dragged Miles out of the cozy and warm house in which ambers still smoldered in the fireplace, and into one of those damp, unsympathetic, utterly ruthless London mornings, he made a brief appeal to his captors. He was as eloquent as could be expected, considering the early hour, and even cited Magna Carta, a document stating, among other things, that barons in England had some basic rights when dealing with the King. His efforts were in vain. One of the soldiers, an educated fellow in his own right, pointed out that while the document did in fact mention barons, it said nothing about dukes. Miles Crawford, being a duke, tried to recall loopholes but, alas, could not think of any without consulting a readable copy of said document. He asked for one. The reply was that, regrettably, such a copy could not be obtained.

Miles spent three days in a cold, damp, inhospitable cell. Twice a day he was dragged out, questioned, threatened, re-questioned, and thrown back in. Each time, he checked for possible irreparable damage and was happy to find that, so far, there was none. Water was available. Food was not.

Benjamin Carlyle, the Secret Service's pride and joy, came calling once.

"Gustave's buttocks!" Benjamin exclaimed, barging in and regarding Miles with mock astonishment. "Lord Crawford himself! Who would have thought!"

"Where's Carol?" Miles asked.

"Don't worry about Carol," Benjamin boomed. "She's in our pay, Crawford. Gustave's buttocks, the entire department racked their brains for a year, figuring out who the great spy was! Let me tell you, Crawford, I suspected you from the start. But there was not a scrap of evidence. Then someone got the idea of sending the lass to you. Three days, Crawford! Gustave's buttocks, three days was all it took!"

He laughed coarsely and obnoxiously and bragged some more. He called Miles names. He mentioned that, had it been up to him, he would have broken Miles on the wheel a long time ago, evidence or no evidence. Eventually, he left, grunting contentedly.

At the end of the three days, Miles was exhausted and disgusted, and generally in a bad mood. Four soldiers came for him. He offered no resistance. He wondered whether he was going to be hanged or shot. Both possibilities struck him as repulsive. Mustering whatever still remained of his mental strength, he made a lengthy and eloquent speech in which he promised the soldiers riches beyond imagination if only they set him free next to a tavern, and if one of them had a pound to lend him – perfection. The soldiers were too accustomed to this kind of speech to take it seriously, and the fact that Miles was far more poetic than any of the previous orators failed to make an impression on them.

They dragged him through the streets with his hands tied behind his back. The area reeked of equine and human excrement, rotten produce, and who knew what else. Some pedestrians stared blankly at Miles and his red-coated, black-booted escort.

In this fashion, they reached Windsor Castle, of all places.

"Hey," one of the guards on duty asked, "where are you rascals dragging *that*?" pointing at Miles.

One of Miles' guards produced a scroll, unrolled it solemnly, and held it under the inquisitive sentinel's nose.

"His Majesty's personal orders," he added for emphasis.

"Suit yourself."

The guard stepped aside.

Windsor Castle was a notoriously cold place.

His Majesty King George III was a tall, lean man of thirty-seven. His contemporaries thought his behavior was eccentric. He was a sound thinker, an expert in matters artistic, and could make conversation with just about anyone in a country so firmly and rigidly divided into groups and classes that the number of one's peers never exceeded two dozen souls.

It was raining outside. The windows of the King's study were enormous, yet the candles in all the chandeliers were lit. Morning in London. The King was formally dressed. When a servant announced they had just brought Miles Crawford over, the King sat at his desk, picked up a large quill, and started making leisurely use of it by doodling on Lord Chamberlain's memorandum regarding the recent tax hike. His Majesty did not raise his head when two soldiers dragged in Miles.

"Your Majesty!" one of the soldiers said in considerable awe.

"One moment, gentlemen."

The King finished drawing the profile of his Versailles cousin, regarded the caricature with some satisfaction, and laid down the quill. He gave Miles a long appraising look. Lord Crawford was thirty-four years of age and a handsome man. Black-haired, hazel-eyed, slender. He appeared to have been beaten brutally, perhaps tortured. His hands were tied uncomfortably behind his back. The King rose slowly.

"Well, well, well, if it isn't Miles," he said, not unkindly. "Our old and very faithful friend. The Empire's greatest and most valiant defender. Would you care to sit down, Sir Miles? Release him, gentlemen."

They did so. Immediately, Miles' strength left him. He fell on his knees.

The King walked over and said ironically, "That's not necessary now, Miles."

Miles, whose sense of humor was exactly like the King's in many ways, wished he could laugh. He was much too exhausted and in pain. A silly grin on his lips, he swayed and fell slowly on one side. After contemplating him for a moment, the King turned to the soldiers.

"Gentlemen, please leave us alone now."

"Your Majesty," they bowed almost to the ground and withdrew.

George III stood towering over Miles. He pondered. Eventually, he shrugged, leaned on the edge of his desk, and picked up the memorandum again. After attempting to roll over, Miles looked up in astonishment.

"You don't look well," the King observed.

"Sire..."

"Would you like to tell me what happened, exactly?"

"Sire," Miles said with some difficulty, "I'm going to faint, I'm afraid. Hope Your Majesty doesn't mind."

"Not at all," the King replied civilly. "Go ahead."

"Thank you, Sire."

Miles fainted. King George picked up the bell from his desk. He studied it for a while, looked at Miles again, and then at the windows. He shrugged. He sighed. He rang. Almost instantly, a servant entered.

"See if there's any pudding left from breakfast," the King told him. "Bring it here. Also, while you're at it, pick up a pitcher of milk."

"Yes, Sire."

The servant left. George squatted beside Miles and rolled him over onto his back. He slapped Miles' cheeks lightly. Miles opened his eyes.

"Let me help you up."

He lifted Miles to his feet. His elbow touched Miles' ribs.

"Ouch!" Miles exclaimed.

"I'm sorry. What?"

"My thigh!"

"Sorry."

"Please be more careful, Sire."

"Yes, certainly. I apologize."

Gently, slowly, he helped Miles to a chair. The servant came in carrying a tray with pudding, a cup, and a pitcher of milk.

"Thank you, James," the King said.

It's Alexander, Your Majesty."

"I really don't give a shit," the King explained. "You may go now."

"Very well, Sire."

The King opened a desk drawer, produced a finely designed silver spoon, and wiped it clean with a silk napkin. He poured milk into the cup and brought the cup to Miles' lips. Miles sipped.

"Thank you, Sire."

"Don't mention it, my friend."

Standing beside Miles' chair, the King picked up a lump of pudding with the spoon and carried it to Miles' mouth. "Open," he said. Miles obeyed. The King shoved the pudding in. Miles started chewing. "So," the King said, picking up more pudding with the spoon, "why don't you tell me all about it."

"Well," Miles continued to chew appreciatively. "There was this woman..."

"I already know that part. You can never trust a woman, Miles. I thought you knew."

"Well..."

"Don't argue with your mouth full. It's quite unseemly. What made you become a spy?"

"Well, it was sort of like... I don't know..."

"Do you hate your own country, Miles?"

"Uh, no," Miles was puzzled. "Of course not... uh... some milk, please, Sire?"

"Certainly."

He raised the cup to Miles' lips. Miles sipped. King George resumed the feeding process.

"I don't remember ever being much of a politician," Miles explained apologetically. "But they approached me...."

"The rebels?"

"Yeah. Said, listen, you were born in the Colonies, and your wife is a fine American woman...."

He swallowed. The spoon stopped in mid-air.

"Yes," the King prompted. "Go on."

"Well, you know... The people are suffering... The farmers..."

The King winced. The spoon moved forward. Miles chewed.

"Nonsense," the King said. "You divide your time between headquarters and the palace. What would you know about the farmers."

It was not a question.

"You're right, Sire," Miles said. "Not a thing. Perhaps I should."

"I don't know much about them either," the King said pensively. "Although I daresay I know more than you ever will. They're a nasty heathen lot... Anyway, tell me, why did you become a spy?"

"I don't know. I sort of drifted into it. After which they arranged my... uh... meeting with... Jefferson."

This caused the King to raise his eyebrows.

"What kind of person is he? Milk?"

"Yes, please."

The King brought the cup to Miles' lips. Some of the milk dripped on Miles' chin. His Majesty wiped it off deftly with the napkin.

"Well? Jefferson. What kind of person?"

"He's... sort of..." Miles was trying to remember the details. "Well, kind of tall... a sharp dresser... for the Colonies, anyway. Clever. Well-read, I think."

"I see."

"So that's just it. Sort of. I sort of just drifted into the whole thing."

"And then," George said thoughtfully, "you had to tell a woman all about it."

"Well, Sire..." Miles observed philosophically, swallowing his food. "We all make mistakes."

"Precisely. The destiny of the Empire was entrusted to you, and you just gave it away."

"Yeah. Kind of silly, don't you think, Sire?"

"I suppose it was. There's so much hate everywhere, Miles, so much loathing, deep and ancient. Kings come and go, their deeds are soon forgotten, but the hatred stays. The regal locksmith across the Channel..."

He suddenly fell silent and appeared to be lost in thought. Miles became concerned. He did not mind the silence very much, but, when the talking stopped, so did the feeding.

"Yes?" Miles prompted. "The regal locksmith, Sire..."

Staring into space, the King said absently, "The Frog Prince... He's fond of locks.... makes his own locks... has a workshop. You'd never think he's a king; well, at least not the king of France, Louis XVI. Locks. Knows nothing about politics. In a sense, he's not a king at all, just a debonair something or other, a good-natured idler... Except for one thing – England is the enemy! That part he knows very well. And he acts on it! Do you imagine they'd ever think of rebellion in the Colonies if it weren't for the Frog's gold? Frog... Frog Prince... You know? He's only been king a year. He has a peanut for a brain, and compounded in that peanut is the age-old hatred for this here island. This little... Now, how does it go? This little... uh... jewel set in silver seas. Or some such. Yeah."

A fresh spoonful finally found its way to Miles' mouth. Miles chewed. The King looked at him, wincing, the way an intelligent, well-read and reasonably advanced person does at a shallow glutton interested in nothing but food.

"Does the name Gallic Faction mean anything to you?" asked the King suddenly.

Miles pondered.

"I'm sorry, what kind of faction?"

"Gallic. Gallic Faction."

Miles pondered some more. "Not really," he said at last. "It does ring a bell, though."

The King laughed unhappily and shook his head.

"You know," he said lucidly and deliberately, "for the first time in history, Russia and Sweden are of the same mind; and their respective fleets are ensuring safe passage for the Frogger's vessels carrying gold and gunpowder across the pond. It's England versus the world, Miles. It's fascinating. The greatest challenge a country ever faced. And to think the world's destiny changed its course virtually overnight, between your damp sheets, during a casual fuck.... Don't you think it's fascinating, Miles?"

"Sure is, Sire."

"Milk?"

"Yes, please."

George III emptied the cup over Miles' head.

"I don't blame you, Miles," he said, setting the cup on the desk. "Politics, the destiny of the Empire – those are just too abstract for you to take seriously. I mean, the stuff may be amusing enough to gab about; but once something concrete turns up, a new comedy at the theatre, a chance to get laid, or whatever – you just go overboard. Naturally. And, like the hell of a fellow you are, you just spill the beans. Not knowing that she's a spy too. She was also having a pleasant night, I suppose; but day broke, and the lovebirds went about their business. You, to pass information to the rebels; she, to denounce you to the authorities. I'll miss you, Miles. Do you prefer to be shot or hanged?"

Miles had to think about this. The King picked up the napkin and wiped Miles' head and face as best he could. He threw the napkin on the floor.

"Well, sire..." Miles said thoughtfully, "To be absolutely frank with you.... I'd rather go on living."

"Sorry I did that to you," the King told him apologetically. "Nerves, you understand. I've been very impulsive these past few months. Anyway, what did you say?"

"I'd rather..."

"Now, do be sensible, Miles. How can I let you go on living now that it's been officially established that you're a spy for the rebels? I don't mind your being a spy, goodness gracious, no, I mean, one is entitled to be what one likes in this life, but really, you should not have embarrassed yourself like that."

"You could let me slip away quietly, Sire," Miles suggested. "Sort of, like, announce that I've been shot and then just let me go."

For a while, the King seemed to be considering Miles' offer. Miles fidgeted, clearly uncomfortable.

"Your wife lives in the Colonies," the King said at last.

"Yes, Sire."

"You'd go home and join the rebels."

Good point. Now Miles had to convince him he would not, if set at liberty, join the rebels. This was tricky. The King knew Miles too well.

"I don't think I'd want to join anyone at this point, Sire. I've had enough of political games to last me a century and a half."

George picked up the bell and rang. "I don't know, Miles. I can't promise anything. I don't think I can afford to risk you inadvertently embarrassing me and yourself a second time."

A servant entered.

"Call the guards," the King told him.

The servant bowed and left.

"Well," the King went on. "You'll be shot or not shot two days from now. In the meantime, do some thinking, man. Like, please?"

Two guards entered the room and bowed to the King.

"Take him back," George III said calmly. "No torturing, and let him have something to eat from time to time. Good-bye, Miles."

"Good-bye, Your Majesty."

TWO

The Ballroom Affair

It was the first truly cold night of the year. The chill reminded everyone that the season was nearly over. Soon everyone was going to depend on the savings they had managed to put up over the summer, and also on chance lodgings and the market. Many of the men around the campfire were hoping that tonight's venture was going to be their most rewarding one yet.

The party consisted of twenty-three old hands and one newcomer – a large, burly, ruddy-faced man with a curly mane of greasy black hair and a pair of eyes like two black olives in a mawkish Dutch painting. His nickname was Mongoose. His reputation was shady. His attitude was a mixture of arrogance, self-complacency, and astonishment at the incompetence of his fellow human beings, the latter being a feature characteristic of all natural leaders whose plans include claiming their proper place in a new milieu.

The fire crackled merrily. The oldest of the brigands, a wiry middle-aged man called Throaty who wore a perpetually morose expression, lit his pipe and blew a cloud of smoke over the fire, casting a long expressive glance towards the log cabin positioned strategically between two large oaks. The great forest seemed to be crawling with such huts. All of them had been constructed two years ago by the Mistress' decree. Molly was fond of bathing all of her flesh before business; it was a whim of hers no one dared question.

Molly's authority among the brigands was absolute. For two years, their activities had been consistently successful; only two men had been killed;

only one wounded; and no one in Molly's gang ever went hungry or was ill clad. They were better off than most of the country – than most of the world, in fact. No one wished to argue with that kind of success.

Mongoose the newcomer was aware of all this. Still, he was going to see to it that things changed soon, in his favor. He was an ambitious, enterprising spirit. He was not satisfied with the situation.

"Now, what's the wench doing inside?" he asked loudly.

Everyone looked up. Some shook their heads. Others shrugged noncommittally.

"She's bathing, Mongoose," Throaty said. "You know. Washing herself."

Mongoose looked around, inviting everyone to share his bafflement.

"Is that why everybody's sitting outside, doing nothing?" he asked after a rhetorical pause.

"Yes," Throaty confirmed, blowing a ring.

Mongoose grunted, appealing to everyone's common sense. He did not like the brigands' reaction. Well, he decided, let's try a different angle, then.

"She's good-looking, isn't she, though?" he said playfully.

The brigands seemed suddenly embarrassed.

"Yes," Throaty confirmed. "She is. Look, fellow, you just got here."

"Yeah, so what," Mongoose demanded defiantly.

"You'll learn," Throaty promised him.

The others grinned. Mongoose looked around again, noticing with some concern that everyone was trying to avoid looking him in the eye.

"Look, what's the matter?" he asked.

"Her name is Molly Bates, man," Throaty said, nodding sagely.

"Yeah, and?"

"No one can hurt Molly."

The old man was not cooperating. He obviously had some clout here.

"Who's talking about hurting anyone?" Mongoose asked incredulously. Again, he appealed to all of them at once, "Did I say I wanted to hurt her?" He shrugged and explained to Throaty as if the latter were a child, "She's young and good-looking. What's wrong with a bit of lovemaking before business?"

The remark made others giggle. Throaty remained impassive, smoking his pipe.

"What's funny?" Mongoose demanded.

"She's married," Throaty told him.

"Yeah?" This was news to Mongoose. But it was too late to pipe down. He had a reputation to uphold. "Well, what's she doing being here with us, in the middle of a forest?"

"Keeping her husband's estate together," Throaty explained, smoking calmly.

Mongoose heaved a sigh, grinned, rose slowly to his feet, and, without any unnecessary haste, sauntered towards the hut's entrance. The others watched him curiously.

Inside the hut, the fireplace was lit. there was a quantity of hot water in a number of wooden vessels. The whole interior was a washroom, really.

There were two persons inside, one male, the other female.

The woman, known for hundreds of miles around as Molly Bates, was the one bathing. She was a robust, broad-boned, small-breasted, tall blonde. Her features were not particularly striking, neither fine nor crude, merely regular and not unpleasant. Her body was more aquiline than curvaceous. Her hair was shoulder-length. She was very ordinary looking – when she was not smiling.

It was her smile that made all the difference. It always began with a slight twitch of her nose. Then the corners of her mouth would begin to quiver very slightly. Then, her eyes would open wide and sparkle, like the reflection of two Nordic stars in a champagne glass. Her lips would part, baring the upper teeth – and suddenly Molly's entire being would radiate warmth, magnanimity, kindness, sincerity, and good nature.

She also had a different kind of smile – icy, ominous, and frightening. She kept it for very special occasions. There were not too many people along the East Coast who had seen that smile – and those who had wished they had not.

Molly was twenty-four.

The other person in the room did not belong there. His features resembled Molly's somewhat and, accordingly, he claimed to be her direct descendant. He was medium-height, thin, russet-haired, about twenty-eight. His attire was puzzling, belonging to no epoch Molly was familiar with. Molly was perfectly happy to think of him as a figment of her imagination and to leave it at that. No one else could see him; she never told anyone about him. On his part, the young man claimed to be a ghost from the future, which was, in Molly's opinion, astoundingly stupid.

He never told her any stories about this future of his, and she never asked him for any. He did, however, seem to have a great deal of insight where it came to today's politics. Thus, he had very correctly predicted who was going to be present at the Continental Congress; what England's reaction was going to be; and where the initial battles of the Rebellion were going to take place. Once, at the dawn of her career as a brigand, Molly had taken his advice to her advantage, staying away from Lexington. Some of his other prophesies, however, did not make any sense. It was plain silly of him to mention, even jocosely, that the rebels – poorly clothed and ill-trained, their army consisting mostly of men who could not find any other work – were going to defeat His Majesty's professional, business-like, matter-of-fact regiments.

"Now please don't look," Molly said, getting out of the tub.

"Oh, come on, Ruth," the man shrugged, and then giggled. "I can't even touch you. Besides, we're related."

"That's what you say. Stop calling me Ruth please."

"I am your descendant whether you like it or not."

"I told you a thousand times, I can't have any descendants. I'm barren. I can't conceive."

"Still, here I am."

"You're just a fantasy. You don't really exist. I've made you up."

This amused him even more. "You must have one hell of an imagination, then," he told her, inclining his head. "The portrait's title reads, Ruth Josephine Crawford, of Maine. Maine is where you were born. As for Molly Bates, there's a statue in the square; the woman doesn't look anything like you. Shorter, more curves, and far less vital."

"A statue, really?"

"Bronze. The pedestal is limestone, I think."

Tactfully, he did not mention that, according to the legend on the pedestal, Molly was going to die next year while fighting on the rebels' side.

Molly wrapped herself in a sheet, smiled, and became unspeakably beautiful.

"Don't you think I'm pretty?" she asked.

"You're stunning. Someone's coming, I think."

"Never a dull moment. Who?"

"Must be the newcomer."

"Oh, bummer. This is going to be messy. Big fellow, isn't he?"

"Yes. Should I stand aside?"

"Yes, do. Don't leave, though."

"I wasn't going to. I love watching you beat up those idiots."

The door swung open and Mongoose entered, casting a haughty glance at Molly and smiling lasciviously.

"Hello, Molly," he said condescendingly.

"Hi. What do you want?"

"I'm fond of seeing a beautiful girl like you washing herself, know what I'm saying?"

"That's a start," she said. "Go on."

"So why don't I just make you happy tonight."

"Oh," she sounded interested. "How do you propose to do that, may I ask? Are you going to become intelligent all of a sudden?"

"No," he said, frowning.

"Pity."

"I'm going to show you what a real man can do," he declared proudly.

"Oh. You're going to build a house? Or save your country from utter destruction? Raise a son? Present a woman with a dozen tea roses?"

"No."

"I thought not."

"You're going to feel like you've never felt before."

"I can't wait."

"Come here."

He stepped forward. She was very good-looking right then, and he figured that this was not going to be at all unpleasant. Becoming the leader of a successful gang while getting a pretty mistress in the process – things were definitely looking up. A strong woman, too. He expected some resistance. This pleased him as well. He looked over his shoulder to make certain no one was storming in to thwart his plans. No one was.

Outside, the men were listening.

"Now, I think," Throaty said.

"Not yet," said one of the men who had managed to place a wager, taking three-to-one odds that Molly would take more than two minutes to throw Mongoose out.

"I trust Throaty's judgment," another man said. "He has a good sense of timing. He's part-Redskin, that's why."

"Well..." the contestant said doubtfully.

"When Throaty says now, now it is," another man insisted.

Suddenly, a great clatter resounded from inside the hut. Furniture and various other accessories were being wrecked. Then everyone heard Mongoose's wild shrieking. It stopped as abruptly as it started.

"Told you," the first speaker said. "Throaty, he knows it all."

There was more noise inside. A horse neighed nearby.

The gambler complained, "To hear you morons talk about Throaty, he's some kind of prophet or something."

The door of the hut swung open. Mongoose came out staggering. His shirt was in tatters; there was a large shiner under his left eye; he clutched his ribs, stepped forward, reeled, relaxed, and fell flat on his face.

"He seems all right," someone said.

"Splash some water on him, somebody," Throaty ordered quietly. "Or the poor moron will be out all night."

"Throaty knows," said Throaty's loyalist.

Throaty did know.

He was an odd, taciturn man with an odd, taciturn sense of humor. He was the son of a Buckingham and a Cherokee girl. Had the two been married at the time of Throaty's birth, he would have been a duke now. His mother had abandoned him shortly after his father abandoned her – Throaty was not yet five. A mean and cruel Virginian farmer adopted him, and he ran away when he was fifteen, traveling extensively and switching professions before landing, finally, a position as a butler in a wealthy household. He liked a good drink, never read any books, spoke only one language, and seemed considerably wiser than he really was.

His devotion to Molly was unquestionable. Perhaps he could do better by finding another job. Perhaps. Kindred intellects? Paternal sentiments? He had no idea.

The Viscount's New England estate featured a large garden, a greenhouse, a paved road leading up to the junction of two major highways, a fountain, and a mansion whose sheer sumptuousness prompted the Vicount's guests to dub it *our answer to Versailles.*

Every year, from May through October, the Viscount gave two or three extravagant balls a month, and whatever nobility and gentry could be found along the East Coast never missed their chance to come calling. The Viscount employed four French chefs; the servants were so numerous, their master himself was never certain how many of them he had. New musicians were brought over from Europe every season in order to please the guests' refined ears with the most recent and sweetest of opuses.

The Viscount, utterly comfortable in the fiftieth year of his life and married to a very pretty woman twenty years his junior, was a man of high ideals. Considered to be the most influential person in the Mappensville vicinity, he upheld his reputation by making certain that the profits were steady, the population quiet and reasonable, and England happy. The local peacekeeping force was paid very well.

The sumptuous ballroom was brightly lit. A string quartet made pleasant background noise on a carpeted dais. The guests were numerous, buoyant, and very elegantly dressed.

From his chair positioned not too far from the entrance the Viscount regarded his guests contentedly. Margaret, the Viscount's better half, searched the crowd and soon spotted last year's debutante, Mildred by name, whose marriage to Baron John McLachlan was regarded by everyone along the East Coast as a misalliance. The Viscountess approached the Baroness.

"Mildred?"

"Oh, hello, Margaret."

"How was your trip?"

"Oh, just lovely. Italy is so different in the winter. The peasants are so much friendlier and so much more amusing than the riffraff you see here."

"Did you encounter many peasants, then?"

"Oh, two dozen, at least. They laughed and hooted as we rode past them in our carriage. John explained it to me. It's supposed to be a form of Italian peasant greeting, or something like that."

A tall, dark, lean man in an indigo coat materialized beside them, glass in hand. He wore no wig. His blue eyes sparkled with wit and just a touch of purely artistic madness. He wore a short beard. Mildred regarded him with some discomfort.

At the opposite wall, a young robust fellow who, like Hector, was too fond of his hair to wear a wig, but, unlike Hector, was platinum blond, seated himself beside the Viscount.

"Hello, ladies..." dark-haired Hector said suavely.

"Ah, Hector!..." the Viscountess exclaimed as if noticing him for the firset time, whereas in fact she had been carefully monitoring his progress from across the room. Baroness Mildred gave Hector a fresh apprehensive look and once again turned her gaze on the blond man seated next to the Viscount. Artistic Hector was definitely not her type.

With mock pedantry, Hector informed the Viscountess that there seemed to be an amazing new composer in Europe. Knowing Margaret's love of music, Hector figured he would oblige her. Smiling coquettishly, the Viscountess struck his shoulder with her fan. "Oh, Hector, you shouldn't have, whatever it is."

"My acquaintance sent me this tiny piece. The fellow's surname seems to be Gluck." Pronouncing the composer's name, Hector rounded his eyes and lowered his voice conspiratorially.

"What a comical name for a musician," the Viscountess observed.

The Baroness furrowed her brow.

"Oh, and, Hector," Margaret went on, "I believe you and the Baroness have not been introduced."

Hector regarded Mildred with some amusement. She averted her eyes immediately, which amused him further. He spoke quietly, as if disclosing a great secret, "Indeed, I think not. Baroness, permit me to introduce my ugly self. Hector Eriksson, amateur of arts, builder of elegant-looking ships, aged thirty-five." Bringing his lips close to the Baroness' ear, he half-whispered, "Also, I have a very large…"

With genuine horror, Mildred turned to the Viscountess, who was trying hard to suppress a string of giggles, "Margaret, that word, what does it?…"

"It doesn't mean anything," Margaret assured her promptly. Seeing Mildred's horrified expression, she could not help laughing. "All dear Hector wants is to seem original."

Hector inclined his head, excusing himself, and went off. He crossed the room diagonally. Each woman he passed turned to look at him.

Soon Mildred was able to compose herself. Once again, she glanced across the room at the blond man conversing amiably with Margaret's husband.

"Margaret," she said. "Who is that man?"

"Which one?"

"The one with the golden hair."

Margaret peered, soon spotting the fellow. She knew him slightly. He was, in her opinion, unimaginative, dull, and too pompous for his age.

"Jerome? He's just a youngster. Ignore him."

"Oh, I'm sure you don't mean that," the Baroness shook her head, astonished.

Margaret believed the Baroness to be downright stupid – or else, she might have been very clever indeed. Either way, unless Hector was currently involved with someone, Margaret did not care much. *Was* he involved? Was the little Baroness having an affair? The way they had looked at each other a moment ago – she, without blushing, he, without blinking once – was there anything between them? Was Mildred's silly attitude and Hector's theatrics a disguise?

"How do you like Hector?" Margaret inquired dryly.

"Hector? He's… very odd."

"Odd?" Margaret was genuinely puzzled. "Well, he is part Danish, I believe, if that's what you mean by odd."

No, there was nothing between Hector and Mildred. Nothing at all. Margaret sighed. She could, then, go after him if she wished – if she dared. Did she? Risk her prosperity and good name? How would he respond?

"But," she added slyly, "don't you think he's more interesting than Goldie Locks over there?"

"You can't possibly mean that! Could you? Introduce me?"

"To Jerome? Are you sure?"

"Yes. Well?"

Margaret was having a good time. She felt light-headed and mischievous.

"Mildred, you've only been married a year."

The Baroness gave Margaret a huffy look. "Are you reproaching me? Surely you don't suppose I have designs on him? Gosh, I just want to be introduced. Really, Margaret!" She sounded indignant.

"How old is your husband?"

"John? Oh, I don't know. I'm not sure. About fifty, I guess. Or sixty."

"I see."

"Why?"

"For someone as naturally bored as you, a witty lover can be a great consolation at times."

Mildred decided to become indignant at this, which made her look very pretty, freckles and all. There is something inexplicably alluring about women who still maintain a great deal of their adolescence in their twenties. They are especially charming in evening clothes: like children pretending to be grownups, yet with all the grownup advantages. Margaret had an idle urge to pat the brat's cheek.

"Well, I'm faithful and I mean to remain so for quite a while," Mildred declared.

"Of course. But if I were you, I'd rather remain faithful around Hector than Goldie Locks."

"You don't think he's handsome?"

"I don't think he's amusing enough to risk a scandal."

An elderly gentleman attempting a minuet with one of the younger female guests suddenly fell down, losing his consciousness. Some sympathetic souls rushed to him, while others were disinclined to do so, the idea being that they were here to have a good time, not to revive old fools who did not have the good sense to stay home.

Hector, managing to say hello to everyone he knew in the room navigated cautiously towards a very tall, yet very charming woman of twenty-five whose name was Clarisse and who had taken similar measures against unwarranted interruptions and was now waiting for him at the enormous fireplace. Hector was a tall man, but Clarisse was taller still.

They had not seen each other in months and now were naturally shy and cautious. Clarisse, who had not expected to encounter Hector tonight, was self-conscious. Her shoes and stockings were impeccable, she knew. Her mauve and white dress was, she thought, a year out of date. She should have put on a new wig. She had ordered one recently. It was exquisite.

They conversed quietly, trying not to smile too often.

"You can't imagine, my dear Hector, how we all missed you," she said, blushing.

"Clarisse, you're as delightful as ever."

"You know, I wrote you a letter, except I had no idea where to send it. How are things in England?"

"Shhhh. King George..."

"Oh, King George! ... Yes?"

"He's a bit mad, I'm afraid, though rather pleasant to be around. Very witty."

"Did you get to speak to him?"

"Of course. That's part of the etiquette. Also, I saw a number of excellent new ships."

"You and your ships! All you can ever think of is the shipyard."

Their dialogue was bound to get completely incoherent and absurd in another moment. Fortunately, the old electricity was working marvelously, and after only a few minutes together by the fireplace, both were keenly aroused, so much so that all Clarisse had to do was indicate with her eyes the balustrade encircling the main hall. Hector was off in the direction of the staircase in an instant. Clarisse stayed behind.

She passed into an adjacent room that was also full of guests and found a spiral staircase located purposefully out of everyone's way. She removed her shoes and, holding them in one hand, ascended quickly on tiptoe.

Up on the balustrade, she kept close to the wall and, unseen, passed two closed doors before slipping through a third one that was ajar.

It was a guestroom, recently dusted, illuminated by a lone candle. Clarisse noted that the bed was covered with an ornamented silken sheet. She had doubts. She was about to slip out and make sure this was the right room when the door closed behind her and Hector's sword fell on the floor.

They were all over each other immediately, he, kissing her wrists, neck, cheeks, lips, she, undoing his buttons, hooks, and straps, and then her own. Using the bed would have been too dangerous – and, perhaps, too time-consuming. Besides, beds can mess up one's dress and wig something awful. Without further ado, Hector lifted his impetuous mistress and seated her on the massive oaken dresser. Slipping inside her, he bit his lip and winced, annoyed and embarrassed.

"No, no, no, no, no, not yet," she whispered hotly in his ear, sensing that things were getting out of hand too early.

He stopped moving. He stopped breathing. He wished the world would stop as well.

Downstairs, Margaret, who had observed and understood everything, was heartbroken. Pale, taciturn, her smile gone, she rejoined her husband, sitting beside him and placing her hand over his. The Viscount was deeply touched by this token of affection from her. He beamed.

Outside the mansion, the first cold night of the year was getting colder still. The drivers of the guests' carriages were fast asleep on their boxes, except one. After helping himself to one of his master's cigars, the fellow jumped off the box, contemplated for a while the row of carriages, frowning at the common injustice of a world in which some people danced and ate delicacies, while others waited for them outside like a bunch of fucking dogs, and walked off to urinate under a tree.

After relieving himself, he gazed at the stars, wondering, as was his habit, why some of them were positioned just so. When he lowered his head again, he was shocked to notice that the muzzle of a pistol was pointed at his nose.

"Hello," Throaty said suavely, his hand steady, his expression calm. "I'm here to ensure that you make no movements of any kind. Whether you accomplish this in a vertical or horizontal position is your own affair and not mine."

Hector was able to control himself. They waited some more. Eventually, Clarisse started moving again, very slowly. He bid her to stop.

"What is it?" she asked impatiently.

"Hush!" he said.

"No!" she said. "What are you doing?"

He released her, passed to the window and looked out tentatively. He whistled softly, reached for his sword in the corner, pulled up his trousers as best he could, adjusted his vest, and pulled the sword out of the scabbard.

"What is it?" she whispered furiously, burning with frustrated desire.

"Danger," he said, pressing his index finger to her lips. He slipped out of the room.

The great entrance doors of the mansion swung open. Molly entered wearing a mask and was followed by her matter-of-fact, calm, and also masked brigands. The hum of voices died down. An eerie silence ensued. Everyone looked at Molly.

The fact that she was a woman, the numerousness of her associates, the sheer brazenness of her entrance told them who she was. Most of them still refused to believe it and preferred to imagine that this was merely a practical joke, a charade, a diversion of some sort – or, at least, that the masked woman's name was not Molly Bates.

Robberies of this nature were not very common, but when they did occur, they were oftentimes botched by the perpetrators' incompetence. The victims sometimes managed to escape with some of their valuables and most of their dignity intact. Molly Bates was known to be very thorough. The masked woman standing in the middle of the ballroom, pausing for effect, could not possibly be Molly Bates. It would be too unfair.

"Good evening, ladies and gentlemen," the woman said, not too loud. "My name is Molly Bates."

The silence was so complete that even the Viscountess' half-whispered shcoked remark, meant to be private, was distinctly audible, "What an obnoxious woman." The Viscount laid a hand on his wife's arm, but it was too late. Molly walked over to the Viscountess, sword in hand. Margaret backed off – her second mistake of the evening. Molly grabbed her by the hair. Margaret shrieked.

"Ladies and gentlemen," Molly continued, inflicting just enough pain to keep Margaret from trying to twist free, "we have a problem. Do I have everyone's attention? Yes, I do. Good. It's been a bad year for the farmers in this area. We had a cold winter and a dry summer." She let go of Margaret's hair and pulled a pistol from her belt. "The English want their share. Fine. We give it to them. Old George can afford to have his palace dusted every day. Now, you. All of you. We asked you nicely to go easy on the taxes. We told you some of our people were starving. We explained that our houses were falling apart; our cattle dying; half the laborers had run away to Massachusetts, others had joined the rebels' army out of despair. But you wanted your share just the same. So that you could all gather here and talk a lot of nonsense about the weather and the new playthings you smuggle in from Europe. So, here we are. Some compensation is in order, then. We'll appreciate all and any voluntary donations. Valuables, bank notes – anything."

The guests exchanged frightened glances. The Viscount rubbed his chin. Calm and composed, if just a little pale, he said, addressing the leader, "Excuse me, my dear lady, but don't you think you're going a little too far? If only your husband knew..."

"I don't have a husband, Viscount," Molly replied quickly and authoritatively. "Or do I?"

She aimed her pistol at him. He blinked, putting up a palm in a placatory gesture.

"No, of course not," he agreed. "What was I thinking."

Molly nodded. She turned around and addressed the crowd again. "Donations, ladies and gentlemen." Then, turning back to Margaret, she observed, "That's an excellent-looking necklace you have. Kindly hand it over to me," She extended her hand.

"Margaret, you will not do any such thing," the Viscount cautioned.

Like everyone else he had heard of Molly Bates. For a man of fifty, however, accustomed to being obeyed, it is sometimes difficult to accept the fact that his authority is not universal. Set in his ways, he still believed illogically, hoping against hope, that a few well-chosen, stern words were going to clear it all up and that the brigands and their insolent wench of a leader would thereupon leave his house, their heads hung in shame.

Molly inclined her head, smiling ominously. The Viscountess removed the necklace.

"My dear lady," the Viscount said to Molly. "Would you kindly..."

She interrupted him. "Nice ring, Viscount. But not nice enough to die for."

A slight, gentle ripple of fear passed through the Viscount. He suppressed it. The fear returned, and was stronger now. They stared at each other for a moment. Molly won. One of the brigands immediately rushed over with an open leather bag. Molly threw the ring into it.

"Now," she said, "uh... Margaret?"

The Viscountess threw the necklace in the bag.

"The rings?" Molly prompted.

"Now, I must insist..." Margaret protested.

This was ridiculous. The male guests outnumbered the brigands five to one. It was a matter of just one person standing up to the ingrates, one person putting up some resistance – a woman! – before the intruders were pounced upon, overwhelmed, tied up, charged, tried, and sent to prison. A few years later one could visit this brazen masked slut there and alleviate some of her acute, though well-deserved, suffering with some soul-cleansing talk, a leather-bound prayer book and a few delicacies.

Suddenly, Molly made a sweeping motion with her sword. The Viscountess' dress opened in the front, cut top-to-bottom. Pressing the dress together with her elbows and choking on anger and fear, the Viscountess began to remove her rings.

Observing the events from the balustrade, Hector was fascinated, hugely amused, and somewhat alarmed, not necessarily in that order. He knew he was not about to rush down to defend anyone. He was not entitled to do so. No matter how incomplete the results, no man who only moments ago had sexual intercourse with a woman can help feeling just a little responsible for her well-being. He slipped back into the room and closed the door as quietly as he could.

Downstairs, the rest of the brigands began to approach the guests with open bags.

Baroness Mildred, who had managed to engage Jerome's attention earlier and now stood close to him, was about to faint. Seeing this, Jerome said, "Never fear, Baroness. They will not dare touch you."

His courageous remark reached Molly's ear. The leader turned around and, with a brief glance, established who the speaker was. She approached him.

"Hello, dearies," she said patronizingly. "Oh, you look gorgeous, both of you." For a moment, she wavered. Then, "All right, pay time," she announced.

Placidly and with ringing distinction, Jerome said, "Keep away, you slut."

The great silence intensified. All heads turned in their direction. Everyone in the room, including the brigands, feared an outburst. Having resigned themselves, more or less, to giving up their valuables and hoping that the brigands would leave after appropriating same, the guests resented Jerome's interference that might annoy the brigands and cause them to do more damage than originally planned. The brigands wanted to finish their business and clear out.

"I may be a slut," Molly said calmly, "but just now I happen to be the hottest fucking thing around, charmer. Cross me, and I'll make sure that my name is mentioned in your obituary."

Shielding the Baroness with himself, Jerome drew his sword. Instantly, ten pistols were aimed at him. Molly raised her hand.

"The brave fellow wants his chance. Oh, you daring son of a gun, you. Oh, you handsome boor."

She stepped back and threw herself on guard. "Come on," she invited, "Show me you can fence, pretty boy."

Jerome lunged forward. Molly drew back abruptly. He made another thrust, and this time she countered.

"Oops. Lost a button, handsome," she observed.

Jerome looked down. Using this brief opportunity, Molly disarmed him. His sword hit the floor with an ominous clatter.

"Young idealists are easy to trick," Molly observed. "Do you write poetry? Well, don't just stand there. Pick up your sword, you wild creature you."

He did, and rushed at her. She did not budge. For a while they fenced, he frantically, she calmly. Then, jumping backward, she kicked a chair towards him. He tripped over it and lost his sword again. The brigands laughed.

"What's the matter," Molly asked, concerned, "why do you keep dropping your sword?"

"Slut!"

"Stop teasing me. You know I turn you on. Do something about it."

Jerome picked up the sword and sprang to his feet. He was livid. He attacked again. Molly drew back. The guests backed off, giving the duelists more room. Jerome made another frantic thrust. Molly stepped aside, letting momentum carry her adversary past her and into the wall. He fell.

Mildred gasped.

Upstairs, in the guestroom, Clarisse was mostly dressed.

"What's going on?" she asked again.

"Not to worry," Hector said, smiling. "The place is being robbed by about two dozen very ugly-looking brigands. We have twenty minutes to finish what we were doing before they start raping the women and beating up the men."

This frightened her. "Oh, Hector," she whispered.

Fumbling with his coat, dropping and picking up some scrolls and diagrams and shoving them into his inside pocket, he said, "Just kidding. It's Molly Bates. According to rumor, she never allows anything remotely indecent unless absolutely necessary. Puritan mentality and all that. Come."

He dashed to the window, dragging her along. Opening it with some difficulty, he looked down.

"The ledge is very wide. See that haystack?"

She saw. She wished she had not. The haystack was slightly to the left and very far down. Was Hector kidding? Was he nuts? No. He was in earnest. He was sane. He was calm. She closed her eyes for a moment.

"Yes," she said. "But I can't leave without my husband."

"He's very busy right now. This is no time to ask his permission. You'll tell him later you had a headache and had to leave early."

He stepped out onto the ledge and moved laterally, giving her room. Clarisse placed one foot on the ledge, grabbed Hector's hand, and with a single violent effort was outside, ripping the bottom of her dress in the process. They moved further along the wall, away from the window. Hector jumped, landing in the haystack. He spat some hay out and whispered urgently, "Come on, Clarisse!"

She balanced on the ledge, hesitating, suspecting this was her finest moment yet. She took a deep breath and leaped forward, thinking courageously and tragically that she was as good as dead. He caught her by the waist, breaking her fall, and both collapsed into the haystack. They recovered and giggled nervously.

"Are you all right?" Clarisse was first to ask.

"Yeah. You?"

"My foot hurts," she reported unenthusiastically. "And my knee, also."

"Yeah, that's great. Come, my intrepid one," he said, rising and winking at her. At least she though he winked, it was too dark to be certain.

Out front, two brigands with muskets watched the carriage drivers. Hector and Clarisse emerged from around the corner. Hector scanned the surroundings and, indicating that she should do as he did, moved soundlessly towards the first carriage, trying to keep himself out of sight. For the second time that evening, Clarisse removed her shoes and followed Hector in her stocking feet. They reached the carriage. Delicately, Hector opened the door and whispered, "Get in. Try not to shake the carriage too much. Lie down on the floor."

Clarisse, who, despite the very obvious danger, was beginning to enjoy the adventure, complied. Hector closed the door, braced himself, hopped onto the box and, grabbing the whip, lay a stinging lash across the horses' backs. They started off at a trot.

"Hey! Hey mister! Stop!" one of the brigands shouted.

Frightened by the flurry of lashes and the musket shot that knocked off Hector's tricorne, the horses broke into an enthusiastic, life-affirming gallop. The brigands considered following the carriage but changed their minds.

Hector drove rapidly into the forest. The road leading to the shore was narrow, too narrow for the luxurious carriage, but he never once reined in the animals. After about fifteen minutes of frantic galloping, he looked over his shoulder from the box. Satisfying himself that there was no pursuit, he slowed down.

The forest ended. The road continued along the shore. Less than an hour later, Hector drove into the harbor and stopped the carriage. Jumping down, he opened the door. Clarisse was not lying on the floor anymore. Sitting up bravely, she smiled at him.

"We dead yet?" she asked.

He bowed gallantly, offering his hand.

"We came close a couple of times," he said.

Leaving the carriage behind, they continued leisurely on foot, soon reaching a pier docked at which were two newly built ships of unusual design. Hector passed his arm around Clarisse's waist.

"I designed those two and supervised their construction. Beautiful, aren't they?"

Clarisse smiled uncertainly, looking fondly at Hector, who was three inches shorter than she, and turning her eyes on the ships again.

"What will my husband think?" she asked with melancholy.

He paused, swallowing her tactless indifference towards his creation. Women can never grasp the big picture right away, it has to be introduced to them slowly, bit by bit. In the meantime, they will continue chattering about their husbands and clothes and other trifles. Sooner or later, Clarisse was going to appreciate a good ship, he was certain.

"You'll tell him you slipped away and waited in the forest until you thought it was over."

"We should have stayed."

"We would have been robbed. I can't stand being humiliated."

"What kind of man are you, anyway?"

She freed herself and drew away from him, pouting. This further annoyed him.

"What was I supposed to do – fight twenty armed brigands for your amusement?"

"You've never even fought a duel. Ever. You told me so yourself. Everyone duels these days."

"So they say."

"All you're really interested in is ships."

"Yeah, I know. You already told me."

He drew her towards himself. She bent down slightly. They kissed. The ocean was like glass. Hector offered Clarisse his arm and led her up the gangplank on board his creation. There was a cabin packed with blankets and clean sheets through whose porthole the stars shined mysteriously and cozily on the two lovers. The ship rocked ever so slightly. They were no longer in a hurry. They undressed and made love slowly, savoring every moment.

They fell asleep almost immediately afterwards. Hector was not certain whether the words *I love you* in his ear were whispered by Clarisse or suggested by Morpheus. He was suddenly as happy as he had ever been in his life. At dawn, they resumed their lovemaking. Later, dressing and straightening their clothes as best they could, got out from under the blankets, walked on tottering legs to the carriage, and rode into town. Upon arrival, they had a long argument. He wanted to have breakfast. She did not wish to be seen for fear of being compromised. Incensed, she left. "Good," he thought.

THREE

Peacekeeping Procedures

No one had been physically hurt.

Most of the guests had had to part with some jewelry and cash.

The brigands had further ransacked the house, although not very thoroughly.

The slut called Molly Bates had enough sense, hopefully, not to attempt further raids.

Ostensibly, there was no good reason for the Viscount to be overly concerned with what had happened at his mansion. A little humiliation, but, surprisingly, his morale had not suffered much.

But there was another issue, a far more important one, that made the Viscount get into his carriage and order the driver to take him down to the Police Commissioner's house. The ballroom robbery was a good excuse to get back at someone who had caused the Gallic Faction more trouble than any other adversary in the two centuries of the group's existence.

The Commissioner lived in the very heart of Mappensville. Upon arrival, the Viscount found out from the butler that the Baron was already at his City Hall office one block away. The Viscount grunted and, telling the driver to have breakfast at one of the inns nearby, walked the rest of the way.

Mildred's husband was younger than his twenty-year-old freckled wife imagined. Baron McLachlan was forty-three. He had an estate in Essex, England, but for many reasons, including his somewhat seditious temperament, two duels, and a dossier on George III's desk stating flatly that the Baron was a spy for the French, he preferred to dice with fate along the American East Coast in the capacity of acting mayor and police commissioner of Mappensville. The furniture and tapestries at his City Hall office suggested that the Baron was not above accepting modest gifts from the population provided the act did not entail high treason.

The Baron's visitor was not here to offer gifts.

"McLachlan," he said sternly, "I believe you're doubly responsible, since you're both our Police Commissioner and acting Mayor."

"Won't you sit down, Viscount?"

"No."

"As you please." Twirling an unlit cigar between his thumb and index fingers, the Baron studied his visitor's expression. He was tempted to tell him he was too busy right now, but decided he would hear him out first. He said, "The Mayor hasn't graced us with a visit in seven years. Someone has to perform his duties. As for the matter at hand, you suggest, then, that I should just drop everything and fight that wench for you? Her activities are outside my jurisdiction. You should ask your sheriff."

The Viscount winced. Asking the sheriff, who, like the Viscount, was affiliated with the Gallic Faction, was a very unpleasant matter.

"She's very shrewd," he said, studying the Baron pensively. "She attacks suddenly, she leaves quickly, and afterwards no one can prove a thing. She calls herself Molly Bates, which I suspect is not her real name."

The Baron smiled. These romantic aristocrats; inclined to see mystery everywhere!

"Do you know her real name?" he asked, beginning to have fun.

"I think I do," the Viscount said seriously, raising his eyebrows.

"Would you mind telling me?"

"Ruth Crawford."

The Baron rose and stared at the Viscount. Did the visitor have any idea what he was talking about? "Do you know what you're saying?" He dropped the cigar and stooped to pick it up. "Lady Crawford, the wife of.... oh, no. You're mad, my dear fellow."

"Her husband has been away for three years now," the Viscount pointed out.

"She's still his wife. The Mayor's been away for seven years, and yet..."

"He's in England."

"The Mayor?"

"Leave the Mayor out of this!" the Viscount exclaimed impatiently. "Ruth Crawford's husband is in England. Which is all the way across the ocean. Now, the problem is..."

"Stop," the Baron tossed the cigar on his desk and leaned towards the Viscount. The cigar rolled off the desktop and fell down on the floor. "Even if Lady Crawford and Molly Bates were one and the same... which I'm sure they are not... but even if they were, we couldn't just go and arrest her at her own house."

"Why not?"

The Baron shrugged. "We would have to prove that she is Molly Bates, for one thing."

"Very well. The Duke of Buckingham is a friend of mine. I'm going to write him a letter."

The Baron understood. It was not Molly Bates the Gallic Faction was after. Miles Crawford was their true enemy. Imprisoning – maybe executing – his wife was a good way to put him in his proper place.

The idea was unfair, monstrous, and hardly decent. And yet… The political situation in the Colonies was very unstable. The standing army had been surprised a number of times by a bunch of ill-trained rebels who made up for what they lacked in formal training with their ferocity and anger. The rebels' general, inexperienced and oftentimes incompetent, astonished the professionals with unconventional methods, unexpected tricks, and an unprecedented amount of luck – some suspected Divine Providence. There was civil unrest in Boston, while in Philadelphia representatives of all thirteen Colonies convened for what they called their First Congress. Arresting the wife of one of the King's personal friends just might pass unnoticed. The pressure from the Gallic Faction was getting on McLachlan's nerves. He had to throw them a bone, and if the bone was to be Lady Crawford – so be it.

In the meantime, the Viscount approached the bookshelves, picked a volume at random, and leafed through it.

"All right," the Baron said, uneasy about the Viscount's browsing through Figaro's Marriage, which was viewed as subversive literature across the world. "We could, of course, arrest and prosecute her as Molly Bates. Not Lady Crawford. Molly Bates."

That was the safe approach. The Viscount was, in all likelihood, wrong about the woman's true identity. However, like the Viscount, McLachlan doubted that Molly was going to strike again soon. Not in this area. Certainly not this year.

"How?" the Viscount looked up from the book. He sounded interested. "She only becomes Molly Bates at night, once in two weeks."

"We'd need to lure her away from her customary surroundings. There will be a ball at old Usher's house in Philadelphia next week. Let's send her an invitation."

"Good. What then?"

McLachlan pondered. Sitting down dejectedly, he said, "Well. I suppose we could make sure that she's really Molly Bates by..."

"By?"

"By making her confess."

"Surely you're not going to torture a woman of gentle birth?"

"No, of course not. There are other means. Once we have our evidence..."

"Yes?"

"Ruth Crawford...uh ... vanishes, and Molly Bates goes to jail."

"And how will we explain Ruth Crawford's sudden disappearance?"

"Why do we have to explain it? Women disappear all the time. They become nuns or get kidnapped. Or they elope with penniless adventurers and then kill themselves when the adventurer leaves. Come to think of it, we could accuse Molly Bates of murdering Ruth Crawford."

The Viscount was impressed. The Commissioner was perfect for his job.

"Very clever, sir. Very clever indeed."

Taking all of the responsibility, however, was not part of McLachlan's plan. "I'll need the Faction's full cooperation," he said coldly.

"You'll have it."

The clouds hung low over Mappensville. The fresh wind blowing across the continent avoided the city for the time being. The Empire could no longer control all of its parts. It had grown prematurely old in the hands of unimaginative administrators, it had become sluggish and vacillating, it attempted blindly to ignore crisis after crisis that befell its metropolis. Still it insisted obnoxiously, obstinately, and absurdly that its vast American component whose territory was several times greater than that of the *precious jewel set in silver seas*, must continue to respect, and pay tribute to, the overseas potentate. The natural political weight and geography of the Colonies were too much for the King and Parliament to handle. As a democracy, England was too old and too stagnant, and badly in need of reform. As a monarchy, it was laughable. Parting company with the Americans would give it the much-needed shakeup, would restore some of its strength. But it is the nature of all established governments to resist change. It was going to take a succession of defeats at the hands of the Continental Army, directed by an insightful commander and assisted by the French Navy and gold from various other monarchies, to make the English see reason.

FOUR

The Battle Of Mappensville

It was a cold November night. The streets of Mappensville were deserted. No sound came from the dark colonial houses, the City Hall, or the Mayor's mansion. The clatter of hooves produced a great echo throughout the city streets. The echo annoyed the horseman.

The lone horseman, his blue uniform concealed by a large and heavy black cape, galloped through the city and reined in his charger at the porch of Baron McLachlan's house. Alighting, he tethered the horse to one of the two decorative pillars that pretended to support the miniature pediment over the door, and, getting hold of the massive hammer, knocked several times, powerfully and authoritatively. Soon, the sound of steps was heard inside and the butler, grunting and cursing hideously under his breath, fumbled with the locks and bolts.

"Go and wake your master," the horseman instructed the butler when the door opened. The latter, seeing that the horseman was no one he could remember very clearly, weighed the prospect of disobeying an order from a complete stranger against that of awakening his employer at this hour and decided in favor of the former. He was about to shut the door, but the nocturnal visitor's boot prevented him. The butler was just going to apply his shoulder to the door when, displaying far more strength than anyone would give him credit for, the visitor pushed the door open and entered.

The interior of the Baron's mansion was impressive, but the belated guest was never easily impressed. Besides, his being here had nothing to do with collecting impressions. Still, the large original Lebrun on one of the walls drew his attention.

"I want to see your master," the visitor repeated, taking the candelabrum from the flabbergasted butler and giving the painting a long appraising look. After some wavering, the butler went up the stairs tentatively, casting furtive glances over his shoulder. The guest removed his tricorne, threw it on the massive oak table in the middle of the room, approached the Lebrun, and examined it critically. After a while, he smiled, appreciating the casual mastery of the Frenchman's graceful stroke.

Baron McLachlan appeared at the top of the stairs in his night robe, candle in hand. Three servants, armed with muskets and chandeliers, joined him. "Hey!" the Baron shouted hoarsely.

The visitor looked up. "Say," he asked, "is this really a Lebrun? I'm rather fond of good art. The French do seem to be versatile, wouldn't you say?"

"Who are you, sir?" McLachlan demanded sternly.

The guest paused before suggesting, "Kindly send your servants away, my Lord. They can't possibly know enough to appreciate, or to participate in, our discussion; thus, it would be a total waste of time for them to remain. I mean no harm, sir. You are safe."

McLachlan, taking a candelabrum from one of the servants, walked down with a huffy air, deliberately making the steps creak. "I should hope so," he said. "This is my house." He stopped at the foot of the stairs. He studied the visitor. "Strange uniform," he commented. "Are you French?"

"Do I appear French to you?" the visitor raised his eyebrows. "Don't be ridiculous."

"Sit down," the Baron said, indicating a chair with a nod.

The visitor continued standing. After a while, he turned his back on the Baron and resumed his inspection of the painting. McLachlan had no idea what to make of this odd behavior. Suddenly, the visitor spoke again, sounding sincere, "Lebrun is something, after all, wouldn't you say? Just look at those strokes. Such mastery."

The Baron motioned to the servants who, after some hesitation, withdrew.

The visitor, seeing that they were alone now, strode over, placed the candelabrum on the table, removed his wig, rubbed his head with obvious pleasure, and sat. The Baron sat also. The visitor rose again, unbuckled his sword, placed it on the table over his wig, and resumed his seat. This mode of conduct was making the Baron nervous. The visitor reached into his inside pocket and produced a tiny scroll.

"I would like to know, sir," McLachlan insisted, "with whom I have the honor..."

The visitor said promptly, without looking at McLachlan, "General Washington, at your service, My Lord."

"The rebel general!" the Baron exclaimed, taken aback.

Washington winced and looked at the Baron pointedly. "I don't like that word, sir. We are not rebels, but law-abiding citizens who are depressed, I mean oppressed, by the King despite the great number of clauses in our agreement stipulating that he must never treat us like dogs. The King broke the contract. We are merely exercising our rights. Ergo, we can't be rebels."

"What contract?" McLachlan asked, overwhelmed.

"Called the Magna Carta. Ring a bell?"

The General tilted his head slightly backward. There was an unpleasant pause. McLachlan fingered the lapels of his indigo and white nightgown.

The General resumed, "You will, therefore, refrain in the future from using the term rebels in regard to our cause. You will especially take care never to apply it to me personally. Now. You seem to have written to General Howe regarding certain strategic measures we are about to take."

"I did nothing of the..."

"This scroll here – you see, we were able to intercept your messenger. By your leave, sir..." Unrolling the scroll, he began to read from it, "...thus, the rebels are to advance, not on Monday, as was their initial plan, but three days earlier, in order to surprise you at Mappensville..." He looked sternly at the Baron. "Now here's the word rebels again. Granted, I hadn't had the chance to inform you of my opinion of it back when this letter was being written. But I must insist that you never employ the term in the future, sir. It's rather uncouth. Anyway. What I would like to know is how this information about our strategic changes came to your attention; or, to be more precise, who supplied it to you."

McLachlan was silent. Washington rose and approached the Lebrun again. The Roman battle scene depicted in it had every pretentious attribute of stylized antiquity. There was the customary number of very clean cloaks and robes, some very handsome Roman soldiers with seventeenth century French hairdos, some ugly barbarians, some neatly rearing horses with intelligent eyes and teeth. And yet, here and there, very much here and there, was something about a soldier's gesture, posture, eyes, and attitude that was impossibly, ultimately real. A clear case of talent transcending convention. The General nodded, satisfied.

"Why?" McLachlan inquired glumly.

"Why not?" Washington shrugged. "Even generals are entitled to have whims."

"What do I stand to gain by telling you?"

"Oh, you don't know?"

"…I can guess."

"I'm glad."

The General continued studying the painting. There was only one woman in it, and she was, of course, half-naked, her large and smooth ivory breasts illumined by the sun as if it were a spotlight, her lips carefully painted, her cheeks dutifully rouged. She was in the process of recoiling. A gentle foot in a neat leather sandal showed from under her brand new and very clean silken skirt. The General wondered whether the woman was Lebrun's mistress.

"Suppose," McLachlan hazarded, wondering how safe it was to keep contradicting the General, "just suppose His Majesty's soldiers drive you out. Suppose they totally defeat you."

"Impossible," Washington said, a steely note creeping into his voice and further alarming the Baron. "They are well-fed, well-clothed, and completely undisciplined. We are the opposite of all of the above. Actually," he added almost flippantly, "none of this is important."

"I must be going mad," McLachlan said, addressing no one in particular.

The General seemed to be lost in thought for a while. His face with just a touch of aristocratic puffiness was imperturbable. He was tall and thin, which meant, to McLachlan's practiced eye, that he was neither ambitious enough to step on people's faces in his ascent to power, nor indifferent enough to other people's needs to treat his troops cruelly. Throughout history, success belonged to short, chunky generals, while tall and lean usually was a sure sign of self-defeating softness. The tradition had been broken a hundred years ago by Peter the Great of Russia who was successful in the battlefield while being a whole foot taller than his tallest contemporaries. We live in the strangest times, McLachlan thought.

"Look," the General elaborated, "Surprising Howe might be to our advantage as well as not surprising him. But! This particular spy, whoever he is, has been getting on my nerves lately. He's obviously an amateur, an adventurer with no schooling, or he would be dealing, not with you, but with his immediate superiors. In times of peace, we can afford luxury. In times of battle, employing a middleman is a very impractical idea."

The Baron stared into space. Things were going badly. "This is terrible," he complained. "First, those brigands. Now, you."

"Brigands?" Washington asked, intrigued.

"I suppose you're going to pardon them all once you've captured this town."

This puzzled the General. "Why should we, if they're really brigands? Violent crime is punished under any regime; criminal law is not the prerogative of the British."

He returned to the table, sat, looked at the Baron, and grinned.

"Fine," he relented. "You don't have to give him up. Instead, you'll send another courier to General Howe right now; he'll carry a missive, which I'm going to dictate to you right now. "

He rose again, approached the window, and drew the curtain aside. He was constitutionally unable to sit still.

"No," McLachlan said, deciding it was time to take the hard line.

Washington gazed pensively at the night outside, ignoring the Baron's courageous speech. It was snowing lightly. Across the street, slightly to the left, stood an old church. It was mysterious and majestic, illuminated dimly by a lone streetlight. An unknown masterbuilder had erected it for the good citizens of Mappensville half a century earlier. The General's relationship with God was uncertain, but he had a good sense of harmony, divinely inspired harmony in particular.

"You know," he said sadly, "there isn't much decent architecture in this land. We're too young as a nation. Whatever we have ought to be spared. If we were to clash with the Lobsters here, between us we'd level this town to the ground. I want you to write, in your own words, that we are stationed on the outskirts of the Crawford estate. Let the English surprise us out there, since they seem to be in the mood for surprising people. Otherwise, we'd have to surprise them here, under your own window. Which would be unfortunate. For instance, your Lebrun is just opposite the window. It would be riddled with bullets. I would gladly buy it from you right now, except it wouldn't look right. A general like myself has no business buying expensive paintings while half his army is going barefoot. Those stingy bastards in Philadelphia have to make a stink each time they're asked to spend an extra penny on their own army. Worse than the English, parole d'honneur!"

He was not altogether serious, and his French was awful; the Baron, however, was thoroughly intimidated.

An hour later, a courier accepted a fresh scroll from the Baron, mounted, and set off at a gallop. As soon as he was gone, Washington came out on the porch, inhaling the fresh air joyously. He slapped the Baron on the shoulder, smiled, and jumped into the saddle.

"Good night, John," he said. "Maybe I'll drop by when it's all over, we'll talk some more about art. I just hope they don't make me stay in politics. What a childish field, really."

He galloped off.

Baron McLachlan closed and bolted the door himself. He called his servants and, after shouting at them for a while for no particular reason, ordered them to take the Lebrun down and transport it to the basement.

At midnight, it was snowing heavily in Philadelphia. The streets were deserted. The townhouse on Market Street was dark except for the study. Now and then, the man in the study would glance out the window at the brightly lit mansion in the distance, from which music could be heard vaguely.

Thomas Jefferson's dwelling place was a modest colonial affair. The statesman had no use for luxury, although he was rather fond of simple comfort. He was also inquisitive. The miniature telescope on the windowsill was proof enough of that.

A traveler wrapped tightly in a cloak approached the house, regarded the telescope in the window curiously, and knocked on the door. He had to knock again, loudly this time, to alert the butler. The door opened a crack.

"Yes?"

"Is it warm inside?"

"Yeah," the butler said. "Be on your way, fellow."

"Announce me to the star gazer, will you?"

"Who are you?"

"I'm his confessor."

"If you mean…"

"Go and announce me, but let me in first. It's freezing out here."

There was fire in the fireplace. Sprawling in a chair, Jefferson was busy editing a letter, his booted feet resting on the desk. The butler knocked.

"Yes?" Jefferson asked loudly.

"A French priest to see you, sir."

"Show him in."

A strange caller at a strange hour. It might very well be Crawford, but one could never be too certain. Thomas Jefferson picked up the pistol from his desk and inspected the lock. The weapon was in good working condition. The butler opened the door, letting Miles in. Jefferson placed the pistol on the desk again.

"Hello, Crawford," he said. "You're late."

"Hello, Jefferson," Miles said, unconcerned. He unwrapped his cloak, looked at the fireplace. "Sorry," he added nonchalantly. "I've been delayed. Man, it's freezing out."

Jefferson motioned Miles to a seat. Miles declined with a curt movement of his head.

"You don't seem to be in a good mood," Jefferson observed.

"No. You people abandoned me."

Jefferson smiled. "We rescued you, in fact."

"Yeah, when they were transferring me to a different prison with only one guard accompanying. I could have just jumped out and walked away. Your people made a great show of it, dragging the driver off the box and scaring the guard with their beer-ridden breaths. If the authorities had had enough gumption to put two guards in that carriage instead of one…"

"But we knew there would only be one."

"Knew it? How?"

Jefferson opened one of his desk drawers and produces a sheet. He picked up his lorgnette and read aloud, "Crawford will be transferred to a different prison. The King seems to have forgiven him and will assign only one guard in order to make the rescuing easy for us." He looked up at Miles. "That's clear enough, I hope. If that is all you wanted cleared up, then, thank you for your time and good night."

"Whoa, what's that? Wait a minute. I thought…"

"What did you think, Crawford?"

"I thought there was more… uh… work for me to do."

"What kind of work? Do you wish to be a stonemason? Or a farmer, perhaps?"

"I..."

"As a spy you're not worth your keep," Jefferson said dryly. "Divulging state secrets to a mistress. I've never heard of anything so despicably incompetent. Nothing personal, I'm just wondering aloud."

Miles, somewhat embarrassed, picked up a silver statuette depicting Queen Mary of England from the desk. He inspected it carefully.

"Put that down," Jefferson ordered.

Miles obeyed hastily. In the meantime, Jefferson returned to his editing. Introducing phraseological elegance to a rough draft was one of his favorite pastimes. When all is said and done, politicians are sooner remembered for their quotable wit, which almost anyone can appreciate, than for their actual labor, which hardly anyone bothers to understand and almost everyone resents and views as an infringement upon their turf. The quill Jefferson was using faltered. He threw it away and picked up a fresh one. Dipping it in the inkwell, he underscored a word and froze, his eyes scanning the sentence back and forth. He looked blankly at Miles, and then turned his eyes on the paper again.

"Now," he said, "I don't like the way this is phrased. Listen to this, Crawford," he read the beginning of the sentence to him. "We hold these truths to be sacred, that all men are created equal, that they are endowed by their Creator with certain unalienable rights, that among these are... and so on. There's something wrong with the opening, don't you think? Something about the..." he was lost in thought.

Miles disliked grandiloquent speeches of any sort. However, he saw what Jefferson meant and, eager to get on his employer's good side again, decided to help.

"It's nonsense," he said.

Jefferson looked up from the letter and frowned.

"What is?"

"That sentence."

"Why?"

"All truths are sacred. When you say, *These* truths are sacred, you are guilty of redundancy."

"Oh."

Jefferson glanced at the page again. Crawford had a point. This was not really all that important – he was composing a document that, after some editing, was going to be sent to George III of England in order to shut him up, or at least to make him use the word *rebels* less often. It might also serve as evidence that the hostilities against the British military were quite official rather than spontaneous and unsanctioned. The wording was not of any consequence on the large scale, but it was important to Jefferson on a personal level.

"What word would you use?" he asked.

"Let me see," Miles mused. "How about, self-evident? We hold these truths to be self-evident?"

"I don't know," Jefferson rubbed his forehead. "A bit too arrogant, I suppose. Well, never mind. I'll think of something."

He tossed the page and the quill on the desk, rose, and walked over to the window. He looked at the mansion in the distance, chuckled, stuck his hands behind his back and approached Miles. He studied Miles for quite a while. Miles tried not to blink. Finally, Jefferson resumed his seat.

"The question is, then," he said, softening, "what are you going to do with your life from now on?"

There was a long pause. Jefferson expected a reaction. Miles winced, shrugged, and rolled his eyes.

"What makes you tick, Crawford?" the statesman wondered aloud, giving up, knowing from experience that what went on in Miles' head was never quite clear, not even to Miles himself. "Don't you have a dream of some sort, a goal, a purpose, anything? Any ambitions?"

"Yeah."

"Tell me."

"A chair by a fireplace and a robe with tassels," Miles replied promptly, looking Jefferson in the eye.

"With what?"

"Tassels."

"Well, I don't see why this can't be easily arranged. I don't know about the tassels, but a chair and a fireplace..."

Very coldly and matter-of-factly, Miles interrupted the statesman. "Excuse me. The tassels are very important."

"Still..."

"Don't get me wrong, Jefferson."

"I'm trying not to."

"Well.... I'm thirty-four."

"Good. What then?"

He expected Miles to strike a pose before reciting his life's credo, to bend an arm, the elbow close to the solar plexus, the open palm turned upward. He expected him to throw back his head. None of these things happened, from which Jefferson concluded that, for once, Miles was being perfectly serious. His meetings with Crawford were infrequent. Otherwise, he would have known by now that perfectly serious was Miles' general attitude. It was the fellow's delivery, as well as the category of things he treated with perfect seriousness, that usually struck people as flippant and inconsequential.

"I've been doing things ever since I was a child. I remember my very attractive, if somewhat corpulent, young governess…"

"Let's not get too sentimental. Things like what?"

"Huh?"

"Things like what? You said you've been doing things ever since you slept with your governess…"

"I never slept with my governess!" Miles exclaimed, revolted. "The idea! Really, Jefferson, get a grip, will you?"

"I'm sorry. Please continue."

"I might have *wanted* to sleep with her," Miles added upon some reflection. "No matter. You were saying? …"

"Things like what."

"Ah, yes. Things like this stuff on the basis of which you figure you'll no longer require my services. I've been involved in politics since college. I don't like being involved. It just so happens that each time I think it's over, something else turns up. Always."

"Well, there's twenty-four hours in a day…"

"That's just it," Miles snapped, annoyed. "Each time I want to put on a robe with tassels, something turns up, something seemingly insignificant that, in the final analysis, cannot be postponed. Every night, before I fall asleep, I try to analyze my day in retrospect and there's never a single spare moment. I'm at a point now where I don't even *have* a robe with tassels. Thus, getting one would mean traveling, or writing and ordering one…"

"All right. Cut the nonsense."

Jefferson realized Miles needed a rest, a vacation, perhaps. A month or two would probably suffice. He also realized that he might use a vacation himself. He had a vision – Paris… the narrow streets… the taverns… the women. A room on the second floor with the view of something reasonably romantic. Might be fun.

"Just go back to your estate," he told Miles. "Do you have any money?"

"Some savings…. Not much."

"If you need more, just write to me. Here's a hundred – that should be enough to get you there."

He tossed a small leather purse on the desk. Miles picked it up and deposited it in his pocket without looking inside.

"Nothing personal," Jefferson repeated, extending his hand across the desk. They shook.

Half a mile away, the townhouse that Jefferson could see from his window was packed with fashionably dressed guests. The party was in full swing. In the ballroom, a quintet was playing a generic piece – could have been any of the few dozen acclaimed Baroque composers. Wax dropped down from the chandeliers on the guests' wigs and garments now and then. The servants offered fruit and wine periodically.

Two middle-aged gentlemen conversed quietly in a corner, casting ironic glances at the crowd. Suddenly, one of them spotted a familiar face and pointed it out to the other one.

"Look! That's Ruth Crawford."

"Did you hear those rumors about her?" his friend asked, peering.

"One shouldn't believe rumors, my friend. If someone told me your wife were cheating on you, I wouldn't believe them."

"But I'm not married."

"Precisely. When they tell me that the wife of His Majesty the King's close friend and confidant is involved with a pack of brigands, I laugh."

The man gave him a strange look. He was not convinced. Moreover, a new doubt crept into his mind, a terrible suspicion. He remembered something that had happened to him only three months ago. The tiny roadside hut... The woman he had married secretly... Himself, entering, full of tenderness and youthful hope... Finding her in the arms of another man... two weeks after the secret wedding... Her absurd words, "Robert! Please listen to me. It'll never happen again, I promise. It's not what it seems. I was bored, but I should have thought of something else to amuse myself with, I realize that now..." He spotted Hector at one of the windows and hurried over. The latter was studying a scrap of paper.

"Hi, Robert," he said with just a touch of annoyance.

"It's she," Robert said.

"I know."

"Know what? Mr. Eriksson, Lady Crawford *is* Molly Bates!"

"I know," Hector repeated, smiling.

"You do? ..."

Hector shrugged and, taking leave of the Faction's agent, walked out on the terrace. Yes, he owed his fairly good living, his position in society, and many other comfortable things, to his dealings with the odious group. Yes, the Gallic Faction was a powerful political entity. Yes, he had promised to cooperate, and they had agreed to wait until he was done with his current project – the design of the speediest ship ever built. But Hector was his own man. They wanted Molly Bates, but so did he. He had his own agenda. The Faction was going to have to wait.

Jerome, who was on hand, approached Lady Crawford from behind and, leaning towards her, half-whispered, "Madam, shall we dance?"

She turned and regarded him with mild amusement. He was not at all embarrassed. She smiled and nodded.

The clumsy fencer turned out to be a very good dancing partner, graceful and considerate. Lady Crawford was having a good time. She enjoyed parties, fancy garments, and dancing. When she and Miles lived together, he never took her anywhere. He spent most of his time at the fireplace, reading books – history, philosophy, and what have you. He hardly ever read fiction. The one novel he once recommended to her was, in fact, quite good, but when she was done with it, he refused to discuss it with her, calling it *girly literature*. He said the same thing about Sophocles.

"I can't even begin to describe, Madam, how beautiful you are," Jerome said, and this upset her.

"You want my help?" she inquired. "Well, you should start with the eyes, I suppose; most men do. Tell me how radiantly blue they are."

Lady Crawford grinned. Jerome frowned and missed a step. After a brief pause, they resumed dancing. Disconcerted, he waited for inspiration. None came. His next line was lame, "I wish you weren't married."

"Oh? Why, what would you do if I weren't?"

"I'd tell you I fell in love with you at first sight."

Cute, but trite. Lady Crawford laughed. She winked at him. "Surely you've never seen me before, Viscount?"

"Do you suppose I'd be able to forget someone like you? Your smile, your eyes, your lips..."

Lady Crawford shook her head. Her eyes flashed. "My tits, Viscount. You forgot my tits."

He blinked. He was shocked. She was extremely disappointed. The dance was over. Lady Crawford smiled, touched Jerome's shoulder with a gloved hand, and was gone.

The view from the terrace was mysterious and romantic. It had stopped snowing. The sky cleared up. Eighteenth century Philadelphia was a beautiful city, where man and the elements, with God's help, had created a masterpiece of miniature urban planning. The streetlights were lit.

"That's Jupiter," Hector said, pointing. "You can't see too many stars because of the lanterns, but Jupiter is the brightest. You know, Lady Crawford…"

"Please stop talking," she said.

They were silent for a while, looking at the sky.

"I've always loved you, Hector," she said. "Ever since our first encounter.

I vowed to remain faithful to my husband. I've kept my pledge. I'm a strong woman, Hector. I don't cry in public... My husband is dead. Shot by a firing squad. He was exposed as a spy."

Hector looked away, bit his lip, and faced her. "Does anyone else know?"

"Not yet. The message was delivered to me last night, by a close friend."

Hector hung his head. "I'm sorry."

Too vigorous to keep still, Ruth Crawford rushed to the edge of the terrace, looked at the city as if asking its advice (the city was asleep and, therefore, in no position to give her any), and spun around. She wanted to say something – something to provoke him. Something that would make him either stay or go away and never speak to her again.

"Hector!" a voice called from inside.

"Excuse me," Hector said. "I'll be back in a moment."

Almost happily, he went inside. Lady Crawford contemplated the sky for a while.

"A close friend," she muttered.

She walked up and down the terrace, trying to control herself. It was beneath her to go inside and look for him. She was going to wait. If he did not show up in the course of the next ten minutes, she would leave. Forever. She realized she was in love for the first time in her life.

This was disturbing and, in a sense, humiliating. As a child, she had dreamed that the man she fell in love with would be a true knight errant, a handsome hero without fear and without reproach, an international adventurer hobnobbing with kings and prime ministers and playing a pivotal role in deciding the destinies of sovereign territories. She had dreamed bravely and with abandon, and when Miles came along, she suddenly believed he was the man. He sure had the signs – the makings of a true hero. Then, she discovered he was a spy, a womanizer, a rogue, a coward ("What good would challenging him do me, huh? He might cripple me, you know."), and a loafer who had neither ambitions nor aspirations. He had shown her some amazing tricks, improving her fencing and teaching her martial arts she had never heard of, but he would never fight anyone himself. She was sorely disappointed. Now he was dead, and she was once again free to wait for her genuine knight errant, but her timing was off. She was due to fall in love, she was ripe; and so she did, with a ship builder. He carried a sword he never used. He had ambitions, but they were prosaically utilitarian. He had international dealings – with traders and suppliers. And yet, she could not help herself. She wanted him.

Mildred the Baroness came out onto the terrace, distracting Lady Crawford.

"Oh! I apologize, Madam," she said. "It's so dark out here. Did you see Hector just now?"

How very disagreeable.

"Yes. Why?" Lady Crawford inquired sweetly, admiring the girl.

"Ah. I missed him again," Mildred said, frustrated. "He's been running from me all night. I so want him to compliment me on my new gloves."

At the end of the Eighteenth Century, some women wore gloves in order to conceal a defect – shortish fingers, unpleasantly drawn phalanges, unshapely wrists or, in Lady Crawford's case, calluses and broken nails caused by frequent active contact with the hilt of a sword and the butt of a pistol. Others, like the little Baroness, wore gloves only so they could coquettishly remove them in a man's presence or use them as an excuse to get a man's attention – an attitude that irritated Lady Crawford beyond all measure.

"Are you his mistress?" Lady Crawford asked casually.

"No, of course not!" Mildred sounded shocked.

"But don't you wish you were?"

"Well... What strange questions!"

Mildred's freckles were very amusing.

Lady Crawford was not amused. For a moment, she thought what she should do. She had an idea. "Would you like to see something really strange? Come, I'll show you," she said.

Together, they went into the darkest corner of the terrace – Lady Crawford, confident; Mildred, puzzled. Slowly, Lady Crawford turned and faced the Baroness. When Mildred realized she was in trouble, it was already too late. Lady Crawford grabbed her by the throat.

"You'll never be his mistress," she said very quietly, yet matter-of-factly.

The Baroness made an attempt to free herself. Lady Crawford released her throat, slapped her across the face, and grabbed her by the hair. Before the Baroness could utter a cry, Lady Crawford said calmly, "Make a sound, and I'll smash your pearly teeth in. If I ever see you so much as peek at him through a keyhole, never mind look him full in the face, I'll really strangle you. Is that clear?"

The Baroness nodded. Her tormentress smiled sweetly. "Good. From now on, you are to treat him with perfect coldness. Yes? How are you going to treat him from now on?" She paused before adding, "Huh?"

"With... perfect coldness..." Mildred mumbled.

"That's right," Ruth Crawford confirmed. "If you breathe a word of this to anyone, and I mean anyone, you'll be punished. Someone will break your ribs for you, one by one. Or your arms. Are you married? Answer me, beautiful."

"Yes," Mildred shuddered.

"Good. Swear to me that you'll never again think of cheating on your fat, ugly husband."

"He's not..." Mildred started saying and suddenly fell silent again.

"What?"

"He's not ugly."

Lady Crawford pondered.

"But he is fat," she half-asked, pulling a serious face.

"Yes, somewhat."

"Is he handsome?" Lady Crawford demanded fastidiously.

"No... well... not exactly."

"Then he must be ugly. So, swear to me that you'll never so much as think of cheating on him."

"I swear."

"I want to hear the rest."

"I swear that I'll never..."

"So much as think," Lady Crawford prompted.

"So much as think."

"Of cheating."

"Of cheating..."

"On my fat, ugly husband," Lady Crawford concluded, giving Mildred's tresses a final twist.

"On my fat, ugly husband."

"Good. You may go now. Don't forget."

To illustrate the point, Lady Crawford passed the edge of her palm against her own throat and smiled. She winked at the Baroness. The latter walked unsteadily away, turned around once, and ran inside.

In a hall adjacent to the ballroom, Hector and Delacroix - a balding, middle-aged, energetic man – conversed quietly by the fireplace.

"Is it absolutely necessary?" Hector asked.

"Yes."

"There's no other way?"

"Her husband is the King's favorite," Delacroix explained. "We must not offend His Majesty."

"You're a rat, you know," Hector told him.

Delacroix grinned. "Don't do it, then. Walk away from it. Find some other way to finance your stupid projects."

Hector patted the handle of his sword pensively. Seeing this, Delacroix smiled contemptuously.

"Let's not turn this into a balls contest, Eriksson. It must be done, and we do have a contract."

"You know, Delacroix, whenever you mention contracts, you sound exactly like the devil himself."

"I wouldn't know how he sounds; but I'm sure you are an expert in those matters, being one of the fellow's close associates."

"I had no idea she was your wife, Delacroix."

This was a direct insult. Delacroix's eyes flashed. He seethed. Hector bristled at being selfishly misunderstood. When, some months ago, Hector had seduced the lady in question, he had no idea who she was. "Had I known," he said, looking Delacroix in the eye, "I would have enjoyed it more."

Delacroix stared back. Hector turned abruptly on his heel and went out onto the terrace. Delacroix watched him pensively, a tiny ominous smile playing on his lips. A plan formed in his mind, and he began to develop it when, suddenly, the Baroness, pale and agitated, ran up to him.

"Who is that woman?" she asked, tugging on his sleeve and looking over her shoulder.

"What woman?" he asked irritably.

"The one out on the terrace. I couldn't see her face, it's too dark out there."

"I'm sure I don't know," he replied curtly. "Excuse me." He left the room.

Coming out on the terrace, Hector looked around and saw Molly standing at the edge, leaning on the railing, her back to him.

"Ruth?" he called.

She spun around. Her expression was almost savage. "Take me to your place, Hector," she demanded. "Now."

"Are you sure?"

He approached, took her hand, and peered into her eyes.

"Try me, charmer," she replied.

He nodded. Together, they went back inside, crossed the ballroom, descended into the foyer and exited, followed by curious glances and some whispering.

Seeing his master accompanied by a strange lady, Hector's driver jumped off the box and opened the door of the carriage for them. Uncharacteristically vulnerable and nervous, Lady Crawford permitted herself to be assisted by Hector's gallantly proffered hand. She stepped into the carriage. Hector turned to the driver.

"Home, sir?" the driver asked.

"Home?"

"Well, home or to Mappensville."

Hector hesitated. He looked blankly at the driver. The driver stared blankly back. Suddenly, the driver burped. This maddened Hector. Furious, he drew his sword and pounced on his servant. The latter barely managed to avoid the terrible blow. Both started shouting simultaneously, the driver apologizing, Hector scolding. Hector grabbed the driver by the lapel with one hand and stuck the point of his sword to the man's throat.

"Home. Double quick. And mind your manners in the future, you toad." He released him.

Riding in the carriage, Hector and Lady Crawford, he in the back seat, she opposite him, tried not to look at each other. Once, when Hector's expression grew especially somber, Lady Crawford concealed a smile. It took them just under an hour to reach Hector's house.

Hector's dwelling place was a sturdy, large, courageously built colonial affair. He could barely afford it, sinking further and further into debt as bills piled up. Hector jumped out, offering Lady Crawford a hand. She accepted and stepped out, scanning the vicinity.

"Well, here we are," Hector said, nervous.

"I'm impressed," Lady Crawford assured him. She had managed to regain some of her composure. Hesitating, Hector turned away from her. She almost chuckled. She raised her eyebrows. "What's the matter?"

"Tell your escort to go away," he said evenly.

"My escort?"

They glared at each other. Once again, Hector averted his eyes. Lady Crawford nodded and suddenly whistled piercingly. Hector shuddered. A horseman burst out of the woods and rode up to Lady Crawford. He bent down to his horse's mane.

"It's all right, Throaty," she said. "Go home and get some sleep, all of you."

"Are you sure? Molly, do be reasonable."

"I'm sure."

He wavered. Eventually, he nodded, turned around and galloped back into the woods. Lady Crawford faced Hector and said, smiling, "The coast is clear, my valiant knight."

Hector pulled the bell rope. The bell inside chimed melodiously. The door opened.

"Good evening, sir," the butler said.

"Good evening, Emmerich."

Once on his own turf, Hector regained confidence. Lady Crawford was impatient, but, being careful not to offend the man, restrained herself. They sent the butler back to bed. Hector led her to his study.

The study also served as a workshop. There were drafting tables, paper, blueprints, odd-looking maritime devices, and even parts of past and future ships. There were two large maps on one of the walls. Lady Crawford followed Hector's suggestions, inspecting this or that item with an interest that soon became almost genuine. Being practical despite the inherent romantic streak, she found the idea of building the speediest ship ever quite useful. She even asked him to elaborate on some of the finer points of water displacement and the positioning of the cleats along the stern.

He stood behind her and pressed his lips to the side of her neck. The natural smell of her skin was utterly pleasant, very calm and soothing. She only used the bare minimum of perfume.

She felt the tingle caused by the kiss ripple through her body. Her sensuality was slow to awaken, he discovered, realizing that the night was going to be a long one. Some guilt was involved, also – but what he had with Clarisse, he told himself, was purely physical. There was hardly any mystery about Clarisse. Lady Crawford was all mystery. And power. And treason.

They finished the wine and moved to the bedroom – he, leading, she, following. She was no longer nervous. In the bedroom, she was the one to close the door. They kissed – lightly, at first. The brigand chief ran her hand up Hector's thigh. This one gesture revealed to him that his new mistress was a very special woman. Never ordinary in everyday behavior, she was not going to be ordinary in bed either. She was by no means the domineering type, the ghastly horror of all sensual lovers. She was going to succumb to him the way true women do, she was going to let him lead, he realized – but it was going to be on her terms. She was going to obey him when it suited her. He tried to stop her hand, but she grabbed his wrist with her other, letting him know that she was very strong – perhaps stronger than he, certainly quicker and more agile.

All of her body smelled good. She allowed him to undress her, and then waited while he undressed himself, smiling faintly. They embraced and kissed for a while, very tentatively. This was pleasant but not intoxicating. He decided to use a different approach, as painful as it might be at this point. She allowed him to get familiar with the territory. Her feet, when he explored them with his hand, and later with his lips, had no erogenous zones. Her ankles had some. Her thighs responded appreciatively but not sensually. Her stomach was amazingly soft. The area under her ribs was not particularly responsive, but her nipples stood up and caused a deep, gentle sigh to escape her lips when he touched them with his tongue. She pulled him tenderly, urging him to explore her further instead of concentrating on something that he now knew would work. Her shoulders were sensitive. Her neck was vaguely responsive. He turned her over on her stomach and ran his tongue along her spine. She trembled. He explored her arms, and they were, it turned out, almost as sensitive as her back. He returned to her ankles. She turned over.

The scent of her groin was keen; there was something in it reminiscent of the forest and pungent herbs. Hector listened. She would not be teased. She ran her fingers through his hair and, suddenly gripping it, pulled. When he resisted, she released him. He touched her entrance with his tongue. She did not respond. He tried again. She lay motionless and silent. He persisted. Finally, her muscles contracted. She shook. He continued. She moaned. On an impulse, he slid on top of her and slipped inside.

"It will take a while," she said. "I have to get used to you."

He moved inside her, exploring. Suddenly, his arousal was complete. Her body received the message. She relaxed fully and spread her legs wider. His movements became sharper and more precise. But the smile on her lips distracted and distanced him and, after a while, he had to stop.

"It's a long night," she said. "And there are plenty more nights after this one. Wait."

She got out from under him and turned him on his back. It was her turn to explore him. But he was too tense, too full of unfulfilled desires. She knew, and proceeded calmly and confidently to alleviate the tension. Hector, who had never felt quite comfortable with anything that gave his women too much control, knew he could trust *this* woman. She was no expert, but her instinct was a true and excellent guide. After applying her tongue to his aching member for a while, she encircled the tip with her lips. She slid down. He quivered, clenched his fists to prevent himself from peaking, and peaked anyway, responding to her relentlessness. She slowed down and waited until he stopped moving.

"I'm sorry," he said.

"It's all right," she said. "I wanted you to."

Then she started exploring him in earnest. In another five minutes he was aroused again, and this time he was able to relax. She mounted him, and together they climbed – higher and higher; slowly at first, then faster and faster. They moaned. The feeling of detachment was gone, they were finally together. They peaked simultaneously and, panting and sweating, held each other tightly. Some time passed. She rolled over and accepted his caresses, smiling blissfully. Her opalescent skin was so smooth he wanted to cry.

"I have to tell you something," he half-whispered.

"Yes?" she asked in a languid voice.

"A battle is going to take place on your estate tomorrow morning."

"I figured as much."

"Not much of the estate is going to be left untouched, I'm afraid."

"We'll see about that."

He explored her again, this time knowingly. He pleased her, and she was grateful. This time, when he slid inside her, she bit her lips differently, closed her eyes differently. He had her trust. They breathed heavily.

"You think you'll be able to defend the estate?" he asked hoarsely.

"I'll give it a try," her voice was erratic, languid.

"You're a daring woman, Ruth. Would you rather stay with me?"

"No. I can't. My people are going to be there."

"You might get killed."

"I'll take my chances."

She cried out in half-pain, half-pleasure.

In the morning, Hector, who had not been able to fall asleep, listened to Lady Crawford's breathing, watched her in her slumber, smiling. Lifting a corner of the sheet, he wiped the sweat off her temple. Again he wanted to cry. He slipped out of bed and passed into the adjacent room.

Hector re-entered the bedroom wearing boots, trousers, and a shirt. Lady Crawford was still asleep. He lowered himself onto the edge of the bed and stroked her hair. She purred – something unintelligible yet endearing. He lifted the edge of the sheet, admired her back, bent down, and kissed it. He covered her again.

It was very early morning. Hector went out on the porch, rubbing his face and taking deep breaths, still wavering. When the two horsemen appeared, as expected, on the path leading up to his house, he was still undecided. He could still tell them to leave again. But the woman in his bedroom was in great danger, and so was the Great Cause.

The horsemen rode up to the porch. Hector heaved a sigh and nodded to them. They nodded back, dismounted, tethered their horses to the tree next to the entrance, pulled out their pistols, and entered the house. Hector stood still for a moment. Presently, he turned and walked to the stables.

He chose his favorite black horse, patted it on the mane, and saddled it. He bit his lip. He felt like a pig. He was doing the right thing, he knew, but he still felt like a pig.

The two visitors passed directly to the bedroom. They were experts, cold-blooded and emotionless. Before the woman they found in the bedroom was half-awake, her hands were already tied behind her back. They gagged her before she could scream. She wriggled. Calmly, they bound her feet together. Indifferent to her nakedness, they wrapped her in a bed sheet. Then they carried her out – quietly, efficiently, and without exchanging a word.

They threw her across the saddle of one of their two horses. They both mounted. They waited. Presently, Hector galloped over from the stables. He stopped nearby. The woman struggled and eventually was able to turn her profile to him. Her eyes filled with horror when she saw him.

"The Viscount and the Baron say thank you," one of the horsemen said to Hector.

"Always delighted to serve them. My regards, gentlemen."

"Mmmmmmm!" the woman attempted a scream, wriggling.

"Ah, yes," apologetically, Hector inclined his head. "I'm very sorry, Madam."

He spurred his horse and galloped away.

The battle of Mappensville is never mentioned in history textbooks and can hardly be found in any of the chronicles covering the Revolutionary War. It was a disaster for both sides. Washington's earlier incompetence and later brilliance and Howe's impeccable record as a commander played no part in it.

The Royal Army marched into the Crawford estate fully prepared to surprise the rebels. Finding none, some of the senior officers toured the mansion. They found a quantity of wine in the cellar and sampled it for two hours in the living room – good old Bordeaux. It had been a while since they last tasted good wine. They may have gotten carried away a little. It was not their fault.

One of them went down to the cellar again to get more liquor. There were candles in the house, but being in an expansive mood, the officer used a torch instead. Setting it in an empty wine casket – the flame casting just enough light to illumine the place – the intrepid warrior examined bottle after bottle and casket after casket of Miles' cherished wine stock. Eventually, he stumbled upon one casket that contained, not wine, but gunpowder.

The officer was not completely drunk – in fact, his thoughts were crystal-clear. The problem was, in their clarity, they were exceptionally grand, all of them. Thinking on a small scale was beneath him. After examining the casket, he looked further, and discovered another. He pulled the stopper out and satisfied himself that this one, too, was full of gunpowder. This was, no doubt, the enemy's arsenal. The rebels were going to wait until the

Royal Army was asleep, and then they would enter this place, load their guns, and attack suddenly, their courage fortified with excellent French wine. The Frenchies – the eternal enemies of England and everything England held dear – had supplied the wine, of course. Specifically for this purpose. But their cowardly plot was exposed now.

The officer rushed back to rejoin his unsuspecting comrades, to tell them about his discovery. On his way to the stairs, he bumped into a heavy table that had escaped his attention earlier, upsetting it. The table, in falling, knocked down the casket with the lit torch and also one of the caskets containing fire powder. The stopper fell out, and some of the powder spilled onto the floor. The torch rolled towards it. Seeing this, the officer sobered up instantly.

He sprinted up the stairs and into the living room, shouting, "Run! Gunpowder!" He dived out the nearest window.

At that moment, the first explosion rocked the mansion. Coming from the cellar, it shook the ground the great colonial house stood on.

The officers survived. They were in the other half of the mansion, and one casket exploding in the cellar could not seriously harm them. Quick thinkers, they followed their comrade.

The force of the second explosion ripped the mansion in two. Surging upward and outward, it sent the roof into the air, blew out the windows, incinerated the furniture, and surprised both the English, who were waiting for the Americans a hundred yards away, and the Americans, who were at that moment coming to surprise them from the flank.

The battle commenced spontaneously, with neither side adhering to any particular plan. For about five minutes, both armies used the burning house as a shield, sending trial cannon balls over it. Soon they started sending the balls *through* it, which proved more effective. Casualties piled up, with neither side prevailing.

George Washington, who had no use for battles in which he did not have a clear edge and a reasonable chance of winning quickly and decisively. He did not like the way things were developing. He resented the type of senseless slaughter so many other generals were inclined to subject their men to, rather than take it in stride and retreat. The Continental Army, covered by its artillery, began to move laterally towards Mappensville. The maneuver was lost on the British. They did not move in to intercept, and when they finally realized that most of the rebels were actually gone, they did not react quickly enough. General Howe was battling diarrhea and found himself incapable of committing to anything. It soon grew dark, making pursuit impossible. In the morning, the Continental Army was in possession of Mappensville and had prepared many surprises for the Royalists in case they should go mad or remember their honor – whichever came first – and attack the city. After sending a few scouts in to see what was what, Howe re-evaluated the situation and decided to leave Mappensville alone – just as Washington expected.

The few records that do exist of the Battle of Mappensville state flatly that the Continental Army captured the city and leave it at that. This view suited both sides and spared many people a great deal of embarrassment, which was why it was never officially disputed.

FIVE

Treasure Hunting

The night was slightly warmer than the three previous ones. Most of the snow had melted, turning large areas of the great New England forest into a slushy, squeaky quagmire, and upsetting the opossums.

Throaty looked pensively at the moon. Mongoose had some difficulties lighting his pipe.

"Everything's damp," he reported, spitting morosely on the ground.

"I don't want to do it," Throaty announced, addressing no one in particular.

"You and your scruples. Stop annoying me."

"Raiding the treasury was one thing. Now we're talking about Molly's private stash."

Mongoose regarded him strangely.

"It's her own fault," he said didactically. "She shouldn't have slept with that fellow; she wouldn't have been arrested. All women are whores."

Throaty pondered on this, still uncertain.

"I still don't like it." He scratched his neck. "And another ting. Why can't we share it with the others?"

"You can't share everything. Not if you want to get ahead, old man. Where is it?"

Throaty looked around, making some mental calculations involving the moon and the stars. Orion was, for some reason, slightly off to the south, or maybe south was off.

"Here," he said at last, pointing to the ground at his feet. Mongoose came over with a skeptical look.

"How do you know it's here?"

"There's a mark on the tree. Here. Can you feel it?"

Mongoose felt the trunk. There was, in fact, a mark on it. He turned to Throaty.   "I see. So, you knew it was here all along?"

"Yeah," Throaty confirmed.

"So why did you look at the moon and the stars and all that shit?"

"I like looking at the sky. Don't you think it's beautiful?"

Mongoose spat on the ground again. He regarded his partner gloomily. "All right. Where's the shovel?" he asked.

Throaty passed it to him.

For a while, they were engaged in furious digging, taking turns. At last, the shovel hit the lid of a wooden chest reinforced with brass. Throaty threw the shovel away and knelt in front of the hole, urging Mongoose to do the same by tugging on his trousers. Mongoose knelt.

"I need a hand here," Throaty said.

Between them, they extricated the chest. It was not particularly large, but heavy enough to keep their hopes up. Throaty cleaned off the dirt and clay from the lid with his sleeve. He was not aware of it, but the coat-of-arms on the lid was that of his own family. There was an intricately designed lock on it. The key, Throaty knew, was in Molly's bedroom, in the Chinese vase on the mantelpiece. She used to hide it in the harpsichord downstairs before the vase arrived. One was supposed to turn the key twice, counterclockwise, and then once, clockwise.

Mongoose grabbed the shovel again and knocked off the lock. Throaty pulled the lid up. The box was full of jewels and gold coins.

"Nice," Mongoose drawled appreciatively. "Where's my bag?"

"I'm sorry, Molly," Throaty muttered.

No sooner did they transfer the contents of the chest into Mongoose's large leather bag than the clatter of hooves resounded ominously nearby. Mongoose peered into the darkness.

"They have torches," he said disgustedly. "They're looking for us."

"Us?"

"They must have arrested everybody else by now. Let's go."

They ran, Mongoose carrying the bag. Staying away from the path, they advanced deeper and deeper into the forest. The undergrowth was slippery and treacherous. Throaty fell twice, and Mongoose had to help him up both times, cursing hideously under his breath. Once, Mongoose tripped over a reposing opossum. Twice, a very minor predator considered attacking them but was itself attacked by a larger predator. After almost an hour of running, they emerged into a clearing.

There was a camp fire in the middle. A soldier sat beside it, humming a simple melody off key. He took no notice of them. Throaty and Mongoose looked around.

"Think we've lost them?" Mongoose asked, panting.

"It would seem so. Anyway, now that they've got Molly, they won't be going out of their way looking for us. Not around this place."

"That moron by the fire..."

"Just a soldier," Throaty said, peering. "A rebel soldier, of His Excellency General Washington's party. Must have lost his way in the forest, poor soul."

They winked at each other and approached. Noticing them at last, the soldier sprang to his feet.

"Hey! Who you?" he demanded, alarmed.

"Easy, my friend," Mongoose raised a friendly hand. "You know, my mother was of gentle birth. I'm almost a gentleman. Sit."

Relieved, the soldier sat. Reassured by Throaty's phlegmatic appearance and Mongoose's suave attitude, he collected his thoughts slowly and fondly, summing them up thus, "There's going to be no more of your gentlemen kind in this land. We're breaking up with the English swine. Everyone's going to be equal from now on. So none of your snotty stuff. A new world order is just around the corner."

His eyes flashed. He had a vision. He was living in this, like, mansion place, and these, like, former aristocrats and other bloodsucking Loyalists were his servants. And their snotty wives were his, like, concubines. He was a stern but just potentate, treating everybody fairly, and General Washington was a frequent respectful caller.

"Well," Throaty said judiciously, "why don't you ask us to sit down, since we're all equal."

"Uh… Well... Go ahead," the soldier agreed.

Partaking of some bread they suggested the soldier should offer them, Throaty and Mongoose kept casting furtive glances in all directions. After a while, satisfied that no one was pursuing them anymore, both relaxed and started paying attention to what the soldier was saying.

"Just trying to catch up with the others," he reported. He explained further that the General was a great man, while the King was most certainly a filthy pig, in spades.

Mongoose approved of this rather simple yet effective and exciting view of the world by nodding histrionically a few times. His mouth full, he asked, slapping the soldier on the shoulder, whether the latter had any money. The soldier became very evasive and irritable. He complained about the meager wages and horrible conditions, mentioning his bloodsucking officers who had joined the rebels' cause because they had nothing better to do with their miserable lives.

"Say," he suddenly peered into Mongoose's face, "You look familiar, Mister. I knew a fellow who looked just like you. Right after enlisting, he raided the strong box, stole the soldiers' two months' pay, and made off with it; killed two sentinels while he was at it. Jack Something. Some kind of creepy animal. Octopus? Opossum?"

"Mongoose," Mongoose suggested helpfully.

"Mongoose! That's right. Is that you? Oh. Don't worry. I'm not going to report you."

Finishing the bread, Mongoose picked up the Soldier's musket and rose to his feet without any unnecessary haste.

"Hey!" the soldier protested. "Put that down. I said I wasn't going to report you."

"Well, just to make sure that you don't," Mongoose said, aiming the musket and pulling the trigger.

The soldier fell on his back and remained motionless. Mongoose shrugged. Throaty shot to his feet.

"Oh, shit," he said. "What's the matter... with you... oh, no."

Raising his eyebrows, Mongoose proceeded calmly to reload the musket. The soldier's gunpowder had breadcrumbs in it, and his bullets were not the best kind either. The ramrod was bent a little, and this created unnecessary friction inside the muzzle, but all in all, Mongoose managed to complete the task quickly and efficiently. Throaty walked over to the body and touched it with his foot. The soldier was dead. Throaty looked up at the sky. Orion's position did not make any sense. There was a cold feeling in Throaty's stomach. He suddenly saw himself sauntering down a deserted road, walking stick in hand, homeless and alone.

"You really have no pity for anyone, do you?" he asked.

"That's right," Mongoose replied calmly.

"To think that I'm sharing all that dough with you!"

"I don't think so," Mongoose shook his head. He paused before continuing, "That money's just enough to start me on a proper career. I'm thinking of going into politics. Sharing? Not likely. What gave you the idea I was going to share with you?"

"What are you talking about?" Throaty said, already knowing, a lump was in his throat. The stars shined brightly.

Mongoose raised the musket. "Turn around, Throaty."

"I can't believe it!" Throaty shouted. "You're going to shoot me!"

"You're so bright. Turn around, I tell you. I hate shooting people from up front."

Finishing his lunch, Miles settled the bill and inspected his portmanteau. Prices had gone up. Jefferson's bonus was not going to last long. Miles only had one extra suit of clothes. He had not managed to buy anything plausible in Philadelphia. In order to procure a bottle of decent French wine, he had had to pawn his sword and now felt naked without it. What with the political turmoil, the city had fallen behind and was generally oblivious to what went on in the real world – the world of fashion, theatre, philosophy, loose women, and good wine.

Someone fired a musket outside, and then a whole bunch of people answered with a volley.

"Goodness gracious," Miles said to the host. "Is gratuitous shooting a new fashionable sport around here?"

The host did not reply. He was obviously frightened. Miles shrugged and went out on the street. People were running in all directions.

"The rebels are coming!" someone shouted.

"Rebels? What rebels?" Miles wondered aloud. After some pondering, he remembered this was a mostly Loyalist town. He laughed, ever appreciative of historical ironies. He went to the stables behind the tavern where he was in for an unpleasant surprise. His horse lay dead, felled by a stray bullet.

"Oh, no," Miles muttered, distressed, ignoring the continuing gunfire.

There was nothing to it. For a moment he toyed with the idea of buying another horse but decided against it. It was only about nine miles from here to the estate. He had very good horses in his own stables, much better than any silly mare this backwoods town could offer him.

Slinging the portmanteau over his shoulder, he set off.

The road was deserted. It was cold but not very humid – a definite improvement over London. Miles amused himself by singing songs at the top of his lungs and making ribald jokes he would never dream of telling in good company for fear of being misinterpreted. He pictured himself getting into a tub full of warm water once he got home. Fresh linen. New clothes – out of date, but odorless and soft. Last but not least, there was, in his favorite bedroom upstairs, an excellent heavy silk robe with very angry-looking, tacky tassels. A bath first, and then he was going to put on the robe, sit by the fire, and doze off with some boring tome on his knees. Well, it was not that simple.

Miles stopped, shed his coat, vest, and shirt, and opened his portmanteau. The fresh shirt felt good, and the vest was delightful. He stuffed the dirty clothes into the portmanteau. He cheered up.

First, he had to make peace with Ruth. Yes, they were almost strangers, but there was every chance they could get back together now. They had been apart long enough. Miles missed his wife. Her foresty smell, her wonderful soft hair, her somewhat peasant-like powerful hands. Yes, after a good nap by the fire, he would definitely try to make peace with her. She was worth it. She was one in a million. Too bad she was barren. Well, they could adopt a few, now that so many children were orphaned by this thing – the Revolutionary War, they called it. Later, Miles would try to sell the estate.

It was not worth much, the land was so-so, good for mediocre hunting, perhaps. But the mansion was a thing of beauty. The mansion alone could fetch enough money to last a modest couple, like Miles and Ruth, two lifetimes. Maybe they would move to Italy after the sale. Italy was a perfectly decorous, warm country where charitable people of means and no particular occupation were always welcome.

Miles knew something was wrong when he was a mile away from the mansion. There were too many tracks on the ground, for one thing. There was a very familiar odor in the air. Cannon had been used here recently.

Allergic to every manner of organized warfare, Miles winced. He quickened his step. Another minute, and he was around the bend, gazing at his house. Gazing at the spot where his house should have been. There was no house.

"O-la-la," Miles muttered.

They had removed the dead, but cannon balls, tattered military garments, tricornes, and the stench were everywhere. The charred ruins of the Crawford mansion were a sorry sight indeed. Miles wandered around the place for a while, searching for clues. Was Ruth still alive, or had the pathetic clowns killed her?

The place had burned to the ground. Each step raised a cloud of ashes. The only thing that was not charred and deformed past all recognition was, amazingly enough, the very chair from the second floor bedroom into which he had been planning to lower himself. He picked it up, set it on its legs and lowered himself into it. For a good hour he sat, staring at the darkening sky. All hopes of an independent income were dashed. Now he had no choice but to remain in Jefferson's pay. Where was Ruth?

She could be anywhere, including the next world. He did not really believe the latter possibility. She was a survivor and had good instincts. Still, she might be in trouble. He had to go and look for her. It was his duty, in fact. Also, he had to get back to Philadelphia, ask Jefferson for his next assignment, and get an advance. Maybe. Well, nothing personal, but the nasty and mean Gallomaniac yonder would have to recall him anyway sooner or later, so why not now? Might as well be now. But he could not really return to Philadelphia on foot – it would take him days, maybe an entire week, to do so. He needed a horse.

Making up his mind, Miles rose from the chair and set off. The road to Mappensville was to starboard, but he decided to take a shortcut and, after debating for a moment, went straight into the forest.

Soon, it became dark, and then darker. Twice Miles rested, both times very briefly, being afraid of opossums. He had dreaded them ever since he was a little boy. It occurred to him that he might be lost. He had been walking for hours, and still there was no end to this lousy damp forest. Damp! Improvement over London? Not likely. The moon shined sheepishly through the clouds. Fatigued and generally dissatisfied, cursing under his breath, Miles trudged on.

Suddenly, he knew where he was. He almost bumped into an ancient oak and by the feel of its bark could tell that it was the same oak he had climbed often as a child, under his governess' watchful and fond supervision. He should have slept with her. He was nowhere near Mappensville, but there was a village only a mile away. Spend the night, perhaps, and buy a horse in the morning.

He heard a groan and looked around apprehensively, clutching the hilt of his dagger. He listened intently. He heard the groan again. Parting some shrubbery, Miles saw a man lying on the ground and complaining loudly, although not very intelligibly. Miles approached cautiously, squatted, and said without touching the man, "Hey."

The man turned his face to him. It was too dark to make out the features.

"Who are you?" the man asked wearily.

"Just a lonely traveler," Miles replied civilly.

"A lone traveler?"

"No. A lonely one. Not lone; lonely."

"Oh. I can't make out your features."

"Nor I yours."

"Get me out of here, whoever you are," the man demanded feebly, and coughed.

Miles struck a light, set a scrap of paper on fire, and brought it close to the man's face.

"Throaty!" he said, disappointed, upon recognizing his butler of many years.

"Oh. You know me," Throaty said.

After some hesitation, Miles brought the flame up to his own face. Throaty peered.

"Oh," he said hoarsely. "Good evening, My Lord. Welcome back. How was your trip, sir?"

"Tolerably good, thank you."

"And His Majesty's health is all right, I hope?"

"Yes, perfect. How have you been faring in my absence?"

"So-so," Throaty admitted.

"I see."

Miles blew out the flame and, throwing his portmanteau on the ground beside Throaty, sat on it. Throaty's breathing was erratic and noisy, which annoyed Miles. He looked at the sky. Orion's Belt was not where it was supposed to be, and this added to Miles' annoyance.

"Where's my wife?"

"My Lady has disappeared, sir."

"I see. What happened to the house?"

"The stupid toads burned it to the ground, My Lord. I'm very sorry."

"Which toads?"

"Both sides took part. There was a battle right on the estate. Terrible, sir, most terrible."

"What happened to you?"

"Oh, nothing, really. Just a bullet in my guts. Other than that, I'm in the best of health, thank you, sir."

"And the servants? The farmers? Where are they?"

"Some ran away and joined the army."

"Which?"

"You mean, which joined, or which army?"

"Never mind. All right, so, some joined the army. And the rest?"

"Killed. Hanged."

"Hanged!" Miles exclaimed. "Hanged! Goodness gracious. For what?"

"Robbery."

Miles rose, looking at the moon with some loathing. The game was up. It was time to absorb the loss and to move on, to start from scratch. The prospect was tiresome.

"Three made it to Massachusetts," Throaty went on, "hoping to find work on some farm. I doubt they did. The war is in full swing up there."

Miles rubbed his face. He was really in no mood for this now. "Got any tobacco?"

"Uh..."

"Didn't think you would. I'm all out. Been dying for a smoke these past few hours. Damn wretched place this has become. The estate doesn't look right without the house. The view just isn't the same."

"No, sir, it isn't."

"So," Miles reasoned aloud. "Ruth has disappeared. All right. Guess I'd better make it back to Philly. They shot my fucking horse right outside the tavern. Believe it? I was having a bit of a snack, and some drunken rogues started shooting at one another. Hit my horse."

"Scandalous, sir, absolutely scandalous," Throaty agreed.

"*I* don't have enough money on me to buy a new one," Miles explained. "It wouldn't be worth it either, the way they treat horses in these parts. They have no idea what proper breeding is. Kentucky is the nearest place where they know anything about horses. Anyway, there's a village down about this way, I think. I suppose I'd better get going."

He rose and started walking away.

"Hey! My Lord!" Throaty screeched.

Miles turned around. "What?"

"Surely you're not going to... uh... carry me to that village?"

"I'd rather not. I'm tired. It's late. I'll send somebody to pick you up. I'll try not to forget. Here, where's my handkerchief. I'll tie a knot on it, so I can remember."

"I'd rather you carried me there, My Lord. I might die if you don't. I need to see a doctor as soon as possible."

Miles wavered. "Yeah?" he asked uncertainly.

"Please, sir."

"Well... I'd rather not, really... Oh, well, fine." Miles heaved a sigh, returned to Throaty and inspected him. "How do you want me to carry you?"

"Well, in your arms, I'd expect, My Lord."

"Oh, no," Mile shook his head. "No way. People might think all kinds of things. Besides, you smell. What do you say I just drag you there by the leg."

"No, please, sir, I implore you..."

Miles was losing the last of his patience. He wavered. It was either live with Throaty's death on his conscience, or accept the nuisance of carrying the rascal to the village and finding a surgeon for him. It was a wash. "All right," he said. "Shut up."

He lifted Throaty in his arms. The wounded man groaned pitifully and rather loudly.

"Shut up, I said!" Miles snapped, and then, mimicking a fond parent exasperatedly, "I mean, there, there," he added.

"I can't help... it... my Lord."

"Well, just a little bit of will power should do the trick."

He started walking, carrying Throaty in his arms. Throaty screamed.

"Please be careful, sir!"

"No point," Miles told him, frustrated. "My new suit's ruined anyway, you're bleeding all over it."

An opossum waddled across the path. Miles dropped Throaty, whipped out his pistol and fired. He missed.

The village's only inn was closing. The lodgers were asleep, and no more customers were expected that night. The residents of that particular village were neither patriots nor loyalists; simply, they were ready to embrace any government that would leave them to their own devices for an extensive period of time. They had been ready for over a hundred years now.

The door swung open. Miles entered on tottering legs, dragging an unduly sensitive and sporadically noisy Throaty in his wake. He dumped him into a chair. The host contemplated the men glumly. Miles approached him and looked him over, equally glumly.

"You the owner of this glorious establishment, then?" he asked squeamishly.

"Yeah. Are you going to order anything, then?" The host obviously had objections to his place being called glorious and decided some rudeness was in order, assuming the most obnoxious attitude he was capable of. Miles ignored it.

"My friend's had a bit of an accident through his own abominable recklessness. Is there a skillful surgeon in the area?"

The innkeeper scratched his belly and then his armpit. These were not paying customers. The fellow looked like a gentleman from a big city. His sidekick seemed to have been beaten into a pulp. "Doctor Brewster lives around the corner," he answered grimly.

"Good. Send somebody to round him up."

"I have no one to send. My family's out west, hiding."

He was breaking Miles' heart. "I suppose I'll have to go and fetch this Brewster person myself," Miles groaned, clutching his head. "How abominably tiresome. Incidentally, do you know anyone who could sell me a horse?"

Ah, now, that was a different matter altogether. The innkeeper realized he had been mistaken about the fellow. He mellowed out perceptibly, stopped scratching and grunting, and said, with just a touch of servitude and a bit of peasant-type shrewdness in his voice, "That would depend on how much you're prepared to spend, sir."

"Five pounds," Miles offered.

"Don't make me laugh," the innkeeper replied indignantly.

Miles groaned again. He rolled his eyes. His face expressed a mixture of pain and disgust.

"Oh, bother," he said plaintively. "Oh, all right, I suppose I'll just have to teach you some respect... to beat you up a little, I mean. What a wretched day. Come here. Oh, goodness, this is so fatiguing."

With an expression of weary disgust on his face, he rolled up his sleeves. The host backed off, saying threateningly, "Hey, you watch it, Mister." He moved towards the corner behind the bar. With unexpected rapidity, Miles sprang forward and grabbed the shotgun before the host could lay his hairy hand on it.

"Look," Miles admonished. "Five pounds is way above the market."

"Yeah, but the inflation..." the innkeeper intoned, never taking his eyes off the gun.

At that moment, the door opened and a neatly dressed, bespectacled gentleman of about fifty walked in.

"Help! Doctor!" the innkeeper shouted.

"What's going on here?" the doctor inquired calmly and judiciously, as though the matter were purely scientific.

Miles lowered the shotgun. The doctor looked like a reasonable man, and besides, Miles remembered him. He was the nephew of the physician who had treated Miles for a fever when the latter was six. Also, he had once had designs on Miles' cousin, and would have married her had not the entire family complained to the King. His Majesty had made the young medic see reason by sending him to jail for three months.

"My friend the host is absolutely right, Doctor," Miles announced. "We do need your help. This unfortunate acquaintance of mine has been mortally wounded," he indicated Throaty with a nod.

The Doctor looked in Throaty's direction. Throaty smiled apologetically.

"Hi, Doc," he said. "Just a bit of a bullet in my gut, so to speak."

"Sorry to..." Miles began.

"Doc..." the host interrupted in a conspiratorial whisper.

Miles looked hard at the host and rolled his eyes. The host shut up.

"Once again, Doctor," Miles said, "I'm sorry to bother you over such a trifle. I'll pay you whatever you think is fair."

Doctor Brewster went over to Throaty, felt his pulse and nodded. He explained he was going to bring his instruments. There was no time to relocate the patient who was dying fast. The operation was going to take place at the inn. The poor fellow had lost a lot of blood. The good doctor decreed that Miles was going to assist him. When Miles explained that, one, he was very tired and irritable, two, he was not a medical man and, three, stuff of this kind usually put him off his supper, the doctor assured him that no medical knowledge was required. All Miles was going to have to do, really, was hold the patient down and, if and when the patient's screaming and thrashing got in the way of medical progress, Miles would just knock him on the head with something heavy.

"One moment, Doctor," Miles, who was beginning to like the man, said, "I have a question."

"Yes?"

"This is rather important, although, I admit, it won't seem so to you. Do you have a good warm robe at home, the type you put on when you get out of bed?"

"Huh?" the question took Doctor Brewster by surprise. "Well, yes, sure I do..."

"Does it have tassels?"

"Tassels?"

"Like, you know, tassels. Does it have tassels?"

The doctor was genuinely puzzled. He pondered for a while, saying at last, "No, as a matter of fact, I don't think it does."

Miles thanked him resignedly. Shrugging, the doctor left. Miles unloaded the shotgun calmly and tossed it in the corner.

"Hey!" the host protested. "Do you have any idea how much good equipment costs these days?" He picked up the shotgun and rubbed off the barrel with his palm. "People have no respect for anything," he muttered. "Everyone's a thug these days. I thought, now that they'd arrested Molly Bates, we were going to have a few peaceful years around here..."

"What was that?"

"Huh?"

Miles grunted. Approaching the innkeeper, he asked calmly, "Whom did you say they arrested?"

The Host looked at him, beginning to consider the possibility of his rowdy guest being slightly mad.

"Molly Bates. They'll be hanging her tomorrow."

"Tomorrow?"

"Well, yes. There's a rebellion out there, we can't lose any time," the host explained, showing off his expert knowledge of the country's political situation. "Let's face it, if there's to be justice, it had better be passed quickly."

"So she's in jail now," Miles wanted to make sure.

"Yes. Just down the road," the host said helpfully.

Sitting on the floor, her back against the wall, Molly stared into space. Raymond, her ghost from the future, loitered nearby, humming a strange tune. Molly, who was hungry and irritable, had to stop him.

"Since you know so much," she said, "do you have any idea how long they're going to keep me here?"

"I'm not sure," Raymond replied. "But, great things are afoot. As far as I remember, tonight is the night for old George to capture this city."

"George who?"

"George Washington," Raymond explained patiently. "You know. The guy on the dol.... The leader of the rebels. The General."

She pondered. It sounded strange. She had seen the Colonial Army and did not think much of it. Around Mappensville, the Loyalists outnumbered the Patriots three to one. As for taxation without representation, why, the majority of the citizens didn't pay taxes anyway and figured that even if their employers got a break, they would not share the resulting extra cash with their hired labor anyway. "So, the rebels are going to be on top for a while," she theorized.

He threw up his hands in exasperation.

"How many times do I have to tell you. They're winning this war. Yorktown, Burgoyne's unconditional surrender. Remember?"

"I'm sorry, I just find it difficult to believe. Anyway, you're saying they're going to battle on my estate, cannon balls and all?"

"Yes."

"I hope not. I need to get out of here. Surely they're not going to touch the house. They'd better not! It's a beautiful house... I should be there now! I'd show them! ..."

She fell silent. They had issued her prison trousers and a coat and even allowed her to have a blanket. She was still cold. And miserable. And lonely. She tried to keep warm by practicing her martial moves every hour or so, but had no idea how much longer she could keep it up. She was seriously hungry. She blew on her fingers and rubbed her palms together.

"That portrait you told me about. Do I look pretty in it?"

"The likeness is striking," Raymond assured her. "I knew it was you the moment I saw it at the museum. I was twenty back then. You have this impossible blue rose in your hair."

Molly tried to picture herself with a rose in her hair. It did not wash.

"What's the painter's name again?"

"Kenneth Sloan."

"Famous?"

"Not in my time. American artists were never taken seriously until they started doing ugly things... Never mind. Mr. Sloan did very well for himself in the second half of his career. There was another Sloan - John? or Peter? I'm not sure, who was much more talented; lived a hundred years later. They might be related."

The frustrating part about having your own ghost from the future, if one believed anything he said to begin with, was the irritating futility of it. The practical aspect was missing. Raymond was reasonably certain they were not going to hang Molly tomorrow. But what about the next day, and the day after that? And while all the flattering nonsense about the portrait and the monument was intriguing, he had no idea whether she was going to be able to stay ahead of the game or end up in a poor house. What about some of the large-scale events? He assured her that new transportation methods were going to be a hot issue soon. How soon? Oh, in another thirty years. Well, how practical was that? To top it off, she did not for a moment believe the fairy tale about self-propelled wagons hurtling across the country, sending clouds of smoke and steam into the air. When, however, he mentioned that clipper ships were not going to catch on for another fifty years because of the entrepreneur elite's habitual resentment towards all new ideas, Molly felt grim satisfaction. She knew one ship builder who had faith in his clipper projects, and she wanted him dead.

Which was how he was going to end up if only she could get out of this place. For the first time in her life, Molly had opened up completely to a man – and he had shown his gratitude by turning her in. Let him beware, then. She had spent the first two hours of her imprisonment crying unstoppably – two whole hours of tears streaming down her face, with hoarse sobs escaping her throat. Her hopes were dashed, her happiness was not to be. Let him beware.

She would not kill him right away. If she could get out now, she would go home first. Wander about the rooms, read a book, have a glass of wine by the fire, bathe, put on some good clothes. She remembered the last time she dressed properly – a day ago, preparing herself for the great party, changing from her no-nonsense business attire into high society rags. She enjoyed those changes – cozy and comfortable in her favorite bedroom, in front of the mirror, admiring herself. To think that the wretched traitor knew her secret! Let him beware.

Miles rode up to the jailhouse on good Doctor Brewster's ugly horse. The steed refused to break into a gallop and seemed to abhor his rider. Miles alighted, tied the horse to a post, and stuck his tongue out at him. He removed a glove and knocked politely. There was no response. He rolled his eyes, sighed, muttered a curse, and knocked louder. The door screeched open. A very sleepy jailer peeked out.

"What's the problem?" he asked resentfully.

Miles pointed his pistol at him, pushed the poor fellow inside. Covering him with the pistol, he took his bearings.

"Are you alone in here?"

The jailer kept silent. Miles said menacingly, "Let me ask you again. Are you alone here?"

"Yes."

"Good. The keys."

He extended his hand. The jailer unbuckled his belt and handed the keys over to Miles.

"What are the orders regarding the female prisoner?"

The jailer did not reply. Miles figured the fellow found the question boring. He shrugged, shoved the pistol behind his belt, and turned his back to the jailer who promptly drew his own pistol. Spinning rapidly around, Miles knocked him out with a single vicious punch. People just refused to cooperate, and no one could understand why tassels were important. A robe without a tassels is no robe at all. He inspected the jailer's desk. He noticed a sword in a corner and picked it up. There were no papers on, or inside, the desk. Miles wondered how the jailer – or, for that matter, any nocturnal laborer – could spend an entire night without any entertainment. No books, no women, no wine. He was not alone in wondering. A century and a half later, TV was invented and the suffering of many was finally alleviated.

He noticed a dark opening that led, presumably, to the cells, and walked towards it. This brought him into a spooky narrow corridor with a number of heavy doors on either side. A lone torch in a brass holder attached to the wall illuminated the place. Miles approached the first door.

"Ruth?"

No answer. He tried the opposite door.

"Ruth? Hello?"

He squatted and looked through the keyhole. Shrugging, he straightened and inserted a key. The key would not turn. He tried another and was successful. Now he hesitated. He drew the pistol, cutting his finger in the process. He sucked on the finger, cursed, and, going for broke, kicked the door open, storming in angrily. He jumped aside just in time to avoid a collision with an oaken bench flying through the air in his direction. Miles spun around, aiming his pistol at Ruth who, in her underclothes, her face distorted by wild rage, was about to pounce on him.

"How you doing, ugly," he asked with reproachful tenderness. "Don't you even recognize your own husband?"

She could not believe her eyes. She drew back.

"I thought you were dead!"

"I'm sorry to disappoint you. Am I in the way? Shall I leave?"

She took a moment to collect her thoughts. Miles began to smile despite himself, tentatively at first, and soon openly. The way she furrowed her opalescent brow was as endearing as ever, even in this light.

"All right," Ruth conceded. "I'm glad you came."

"Darling!"

"Let me have your pistol and cloak. I need your coat, too. I assume you have hooves outside."

"Aren't you going to kiss me?" he asked without moving, staring at the ceiling.

"No time. He might escape."

"Who might escape?"

"The one who put me in here."

Miles, who was familiar with the situation outside, reflected. Pulling a serious face, he said, "He must have known what he was doing. He practically saved your life."

"What are you talking about?"

"I'm sorry, Ruth. The house was leveled last night."

"You mean?…"

"Yes. Our house. Zip. Pile of ashes. There was a battle, and they chose our estate to conduct it on."

"They burned the house?"

Her eyes widened. She looked exactly like a child who was promised candy and then denied it and spanked viciously for no reason at all.

"I suppose they shelled it first," Miles elaborated. "Took a break, had some tea. Then, they burned it. To the ground. Must have been in the way. Neither company could be sure of taking good aim with the house sitting there between them."

"I loved that house."

He had not expected her to be this distressed over it. She leaned against the wall and pressed her forehead to it. Miles shoved the pistol into his belt, approached, and placed his hand on her shoulder.

"Come on, Ruth. It's not the end of the world. We'll..."

She spun around abruptly, her eyes flashing. Miles jumped back.

"He couldn't have known," she hissed. "No fucking way he knew anything about it. He just betrayed me, the miserable wretch. Give me your pistol, Miles."

She reached for it. Miles grabbed her wrist.

"What's the matter with you, Ruth?"

"He must die."

He twisted her hand sharply. She cried out in pain and surprise.

"Ms. Molly Bates," he said firmly, "I have no intention of setting you loose so that you could indulge in a bit of vengeance. You know full well what my opinion of revenge is. Theoretically, at least. Or do you?"

Taken aback, she looked him full in the face. He raised his eyebrows. She shook her head in frustration.

"Who told you?"

"Who told me what?"

"About Molly Bates."

Miles laughed. She glared at him.

He said, "I knew you were going to like that novel. It's very romantic. No one reads novels anymore except you... Well, I read novels... Now and then. Anyway, imagine – I come home and suddenly I find out that someone by the name of Molly Bates is the third most popular person in the area, ranking immediately behind General Howe and General Washington. I have some of her exploits recited to me – well, I just put two and two together."

"Clever," she said derisively.

"Yes, rather. But, I hate revenge, you see. It is a waste of time and rather poor taste. There's nothing glorious or even exciting about it. And I shall not allow my wife..."

"I'm no longer your wife."

"...not even my estranged and very peevish wife to indulge in it. You may sleep with whomever you like; you may rob His Majesty's loyal subjects all you please and shre the proceeds with a bunch of uncultured cutthroats; you may claim to have your period and your headache and your ennui whenever I ask you for anything; or, you may spend your days and nights doing exactly nothing for the rest of your life – as is your ghastly habit, by the way, when you're not fencing or shooting pigeons with my uncle's rusty pistols which you don't even bother to clean beforehand. But I draw the line at revenge."

She was not listening. She never listened.

"I'm going to do what I like."

"You've done enough of that over the past three years, why don't you take a sabbatical?" he asked.

"Well, look who's talking. How did you manage to escape the firing squad?"

Remembering the events, Miles suddenly abandoned his didactic tone and smiled.

"Connections," he said self-complacently.

"I figured as much. All those broads you sleep with when you're away. You're despicable. I have my own life now."

"You have your own *what* now?"

Outside, there was the sound of ponderous steps. Miles spun around to look at the door which was still open. He turned back to Molly and then to the door again. Two prison guards entered the cell, swords drawn. Miles drew the jailer's sword – it was an inch or two shorter than he liked – and his pistol as well. One of the guards fired a shot at him and missed. Miles fired back and knocked off the fellow's tricorne. The other guard fired and, as Miles ducked, Ruth got hit. Clutching her shoulder, she exchanged a wild look with Miles. The first guard made a thrust at Miles, and the latter countered.

"Oh, Miles," Ruth shouted, clutching her forearm to offset the pain and stop the bleeding. "It hurts like hell. I'm bleeding. Shit!"

Both guards attacked simultaneously. The cowardly loafer and reluctant duelist kept them at bay with surprising skill. Mimicking his wife, he said, "Oh, Miles, it hurts! …"

"Do something!" she bellowed.

"Well, can't you see I'm a little busy here. As soon as I get a breather…"

"Drop your sword, you English swine!" one of the guards shouted.

"Oh, no," Miles said, revolted, countering a flurry of thrusts and retreating. "After all I've done for you people!… How can you be so ungrateful?"

He disarmed one of the guards with a swift stroke. The other continued pressing, less enthusiastically now.

"Besides, I'm an American myself," Miles went on, "by birth if not by upbringing. I was born three hundred yards away from here! And my wife is a native also!"

"What do you mean, a native?" the guard asked obnoxiously in order to show that he was not afraid. "She Injun or something?"

"Not exactly," Miles replied, feigning and managing to scratch his adversary's thigh with the point. "Although, I can't be too sure… Ruth? Do you have any Indian blood?"

"Can we..." she said, biting her lip hard to offset the pain, and then finishing the sentence, "...get this... fucking nonsense... over with? Like, any time soon?"

The swords crossed and re-crossed. Sparks flew. Miles looked away, exposing his chest. The guard's thrust was very powerful. Miles stepped aside, caught the soldier's wrist with his left hand, pulled, and head-butted the fellow in the face. The guard fell and appeared to be oblivious to his surroundings for the time being.

"As you please, dear," Miles said suavely.

The other guard attempted to rise. Miles gave him a preventive kick in the ribs. He offered Ruth his arm. She sniffed contemptuously. Together, they left the cell and found their way out of the jailhouse. Once outside, Miles ripped the shirt on his wife's shoulder and examined the wound. She looked apprehensively at him, but it was just a scratch. It was going to heal in a couple of days. She sighed with relief. Miles took out his Brabant-made handkerchief and wrapped it around Molly's wound. Then, he took off his coat and wrapped her in it.

"The hooves," he said, indicating Doctor Brewster's sarcastic-looking mare with a nod.

Getting most of her composure back, his wife went up to the horse and patted it.

"Pistols," she reminded him. "I need your pistols."

He shook his head.

"You need bandages, a drink and lots of sleep. Look. You won't be able to find him now, and our house is gone. I propose you come with me now. Doctor Brewster might still be awake. We'll have your wound cleaned and dressed properly, spend a few days at some proper inn, then go to Philadelphia. Once I get my finances back on track, we'll think of something else to occupy our time with. Well? What do you say?"

"Give me your pistols, Miles."

He clenched his fists. He stomped his foot desperately and furiously.

"Where do you want to go, huh? The city is captured, there's a curfew, for crying out loud. Can't you understand anything, you stupid cow? Like, hello?"

"That's my business."

Raging, he shouted, "What is your business? Do you know what you're saying? You're not making any sense, woman!"

She jumped into the saddle, wincing from pain. Miles, furious, stared at the sky.

"Could you give me your sword, at least?" she asked. "I'd like to be able to defend myself. I'm a woman, remember?"

"I'm not so sure about that. Women, despite some surface faults, are mostly human. You, on the other hand…"

It was no use. He threw her the jailer's sword, sheath, baldric, and all.

"So long, Miles," she said. "Shit! It still hurts. Thanks for everything. Especially for getting me out."

"Don't mention it," he said ironically. "Any ex-husband as loathed and disdained by his wife as I am would have done as much."

"Don't be sarcastic now. I really appreciate what you've done for me."

She spurred the stubborn horse, forcing it to break into an unenthusiastic trot. Miles shivered and hugged himself, muttering.

"Sarcastic… How am I supposed to get to Philly now?"

Suddenly, it dawned on him. He beat his pockets, panicking. Finding nothing in them, he smiled a queer smile. His purse was gone along with the coat. Miles laughed.

Part Two

Verplaca

SIX

The Titan

The plaza in front of Mappensville's City Hall was crowded. It was a partly cloudy day in this part of the young Republic. The war was over. The nation heaved a great collective sigh of relief. Happiness and optimism were optional, though strongly encouraged. Personal problems were for the moment forgotten by the vast majority of the population, although what the immediate benefits for this same majority were supposed to be was, as yet, unclear.

Some pretty impressive things other than the War had already come and gone. Despite the pressure from certain prominent officers, the Continental Army failed to crown George Washington King of the United States. The French fleet and general infantry that had assisted so well in the Revolution, were thanked cordially and notified they were free to return to their own beautiful and romantic country now. In order to keep them entertained even after they got home, Thomas Jefferson was dispatched to Paris as the country's ambassador – Franklin's charm was already wearing off. Entertain he did, parading his very young mistress in front of the beau monde for some years. In the newly born, free and fair Republic, she was his colored slave; in France, still in the clutches of the monarchy, she became a lady, high society's piquant darling and the heart and soul of every salon in Paris.

If the true measure of society really were what percentage of the population was allowed to have a good time, the Roman Empire at its peak would remain unsurpassed to this day.

The façade of the City Hall was draped in festive colorful banners. The good citizens of Mappensville who were not engaged elsewhere were waiting for the Mayor to come out and make his holiday speech.

Accompanied by a number of local celebrities, including war veterans, traders, revolutionary lawyers, shopkeepers and former Loyalists who could now see the error of their earlier ways, Mayor Dubois, formerly Jack Mongoose, dressed to the nines, mounted the makeshift dais in front of the Hall's sandstone porch.

He was a new man. Gone was the wild curly mane – his hair was neatly trimmed, brushed, tied into a short ponytail with a clean dark-blue ribbon, and powdered to excess. The town's best barber shaved him deferentially every morning.

He had gained some thirty pounds.

Gone also were the cynical expression and cruel grin – he might still be very difficult to deal with, but his attitude was more benevolent now. While his political career lacked style and prominence, locally he was viewed as a great success, as well as a skilled, fair and humane politician, owing this reputation to his intelligence, resourcefulness, quick wit, and boundless energy.

He was, in fact, a passable mayor, a hard negotiator with local and out-of-state traders, a stickler for good form, and a warm advocate of the law-and-order approach (violent crime was all but eliminated within one year of his inauguration). As a result, Mappensville was a different city now. The streets were somehow paved, streetlights illuminated the clean and pleasantly designed houses every evening, and the parks and squares were charming, romantic, and reasonably safe at virtually any hour.

As often happens in politics, Jack's most important accomplishment as an elected official was unknown to the general public. It was this – he had almost single-handedly applied pressure on, and struck a deal with, the group known as the Gallic Faction.

It was Gallic only in name. It was run by predominantly Anglo-Saxon former colonial gentry. It dealt mostly in extortion, and it charged the residents of the area special taxes. Thus, after paying the city, state, Colonial Government, and England, a tradesman was forced to part with some of his remaining profit in favor of the local representative of the Faction or face the grim consequences. When England and Molly Bates had been duly dealt with, the Faction increased the pressure, claiming its share of the resulting surplus. Thus, financially at least, the citizens of Mappensville had gained next to nothing by the Revolution.

Jack Mongoose negotiated patiently, blackmailed skillfully, arrested some, forced others to leave, and eventually agreed to tolerate the group provided it kept its appetites in check. The gain for the city was enormous.

The sound of applause drowned out the hubbub. Mayor Dubois, dressed to the nines, ascended the dais. He waved condescendingly to the crowd. The people greeted him joyously. Mongoose gave them a fatherly smile and raised his hand, assuming a solemn attitude.

"Ladies and gentlemen, permit me, the mayor of this city, to announce the following wonderful news."

The noise from the crowd died down.

"We have just received federal funding for the Molly Bates memorial," Mongoose announced.

There was a dead silence. The crowd was solemnly interested.

"The Republic," Mongoose continued, "our new and free Republic, ladies and gentlemen, shall never be ungrateful. We adore and respect our heroes. Mr. Franklin, Mr. Jefferson, Mr. Adams, and, of course, General Washington – those are the names that will be forever etched in our collective democratic memory. The bearers of those names are the leaders, the visionaries; they are the reason we no longer have to bend under the ugly and unreasonable burden that used to be imposed on us by the King. Poor old George. Boo-hoo!"

King George III was at that time neither old nor particularly poor. Nevertheless, the crowd roared with laughter. The applause was deafening. "Boo-hoo!" several voices shouted joyously. Mongoose raised his hand. The crowed hushed.

"Hear me, hear me!" he continued. "Nearly every town in this country has its own heroes whose deeds may not amount to all that much on a national scale, but whose devotion and loyalty to our cause during the hard times was unquestionable and whose relentless pursuit of justice led them to accomplish great things. Some of them gave their lives for our liberty. Others, luckily, are still living. The name of this town's hero happens to be Molly Bates."

The crowd approved. As if by magic, the clouds parted and the sun drenched the plaza.Shielding his eyes with his palm, Mongoose went on, "Evil tongues, ladies and gentlemen, will speak of Molly Bates' dubious origin, of her alleged marriage to a British nobleman, a political adventurist and a close associate of George III. Nothing could be farther from the truth. Molly Bates was the daughter of a farmer. She never married. When this whole region was on the verge of famine, she took it upon herself to take back from the British-born residents – whose number was considerable, as they treated this hard-working agricultural area as some kind of fashionable exotic resort for themselves – to take back from them and their local side kicks, I say, the funds we the people needed to sustain ourselves and our trades. She did so along with twenty-four brave men. Backed by public opinion, she was successful for a number of years. We..."

Two onlookers, a farmer and a tradesman, exchanged opinions. The farmer leaned to the tradesman's ear and remarked that, according to some people, the Mayor had been Molly's lover. The tradesman concurred and then added that he was not be at all surprised – the Mayor was, in his opinion, a sneaky fox, if ever there was one. The farmer, after some thought, said that, in his present capacity, Jack Dubois was wonderful; Mappensville could not wish for a better Mayor. The fellow really knew his business.

The tradesman observed that knowing one's business in politics was a sure sign of a crook. Both laughed. Someone told them to shut the hell up, and so they did, grinning meaningfully.

"...was arrested and thrown in a dungeon," Mongoose continued pontificating, "immediately after saving this town from utter destruction by the retreating British armed forces. The Brits, who regarded her as one of their most dangerous enemies, hanged her. Now. As I said before, we have received federal funding for the memorial. But we're still a few hundred dollars short. Anyone who wants to make a donation can do so at the front office. My only regret is that Molly Bates cannot be with us today. Thank you, my good people."

The crowd cheered. Mongoose gave a brief bow and stepped down.

Back in his office, Mongoose had his afternoon tea, after which he received a visitor, a middle-aged trader dressed very well but with professional slovenliness. The trader, as some traders tended to be in those days, was excitable, expansive, and impetuous. Mongoose watched him calmly.

"Now do you understand?" the trader exclaimed, pacing back and forth in front of Mongoose's mahogany desk. "I can't afford to build that stupid bridge for you unless you give me my tax exemption."

Mongoose smiled a conqueror's smile.

"Look," he said. "I showed you the calculations based on the figures you supplied. They demonstrate clearly that in five years' time, you'll be making three times as much as you make today if you have that bridge. As it stands now, your hapless suppliers have to travel an extra twenty miles to get their shit to you. Besides, think of how everyone in town will benefit from that bridge. Everyone's income will increase, and so will their purchasing power."

"So why can't they chip in too?"

"They don't have the money right now. You do."

"This is ridiculous, Mr. Mayor."

"I stand by my people, right? You're a newcomer. You have to prove your loyalty before we can start trusting you here. If you like, we'll build that bridge ourselves. All right?"

"Fine," the trader agreed after some hesitation. He figured he was going to make a profit anyway.

Mongoose added, "And then we'll post a dozen guards on it."

"Uh... why?" the trader, taken aback, asked.

"To make sure that your suppliers don't take advantage of anything they haven't paid for."

"But that would be tantamount to giving me up to the competition!" the trader protested.

"So?"

"This city needs me and my business."

Mongoose chuckled. He reached into his desk, produced a cigar, and struck a light.

"Yes," he said, puffing. "But we can always sacrifice a bit of trade where our integrity is at stake. A bit of integrity can go a long way these days. We'll be the winners in the long run."

The trader hesitated. After some more pacing, he produced his wallet.

"All right. Would a thousand dollars be enough? I hear your birthday is just around the corner..."

The gesture and the question made Mongoose glum. For quite some time he remained silent. He put out his cigar. When he spoke, his voice was ominously toneless. "I'll give you a break this time, Mister. Next time you attempt to bribe me, I'll have you arrested and charged. The work on the bridge will commence tomorrow morning. Please be there with the money. I'll visit the site personally to make sure you don't attempt to pull one of your dirty tricks on us."

The trader was taken aback. He would have felt better if Mongoose had shouted at him and pounded his desk with his fist. The Mayor's calm made him feel very uncomfortable.

"Is that clear?" Mongoose inquired suavely.

The trader nodded several times. Mongoose smiled benevolently.

"Wood?" the trader, frightened, asked humbly.

"Wooden bridges don't last very long. Ours is going to be a good, sturdy stone affair, and it will be finished in four months. Good afternoon, sir."

"This is highway robbery!" the trader said.

Mongoose laughed, shaking his head. "No," he said, smiling contemptuously at the thought, exactly like someone who had first-hand knowledge of such things. "No, my dear fellow. It is not."

The trader looked at Mongoose with loathing and fear. He turned on his heel, strode to the door and bumped into the entering secretary, a middle-aged, amiable-looking man.

"Excuse me!" he shouted savagely, marching out.

The secretary approached the desk.

"Yes?" Mongoose asked.

"Memorial donations, Mr. Mayor," he placed the box on the desk.

"Memorial what? Oh, the Molly Bates thing."

He opened the box, poured the gold out, pushed three coins towards the secretary, and pocketed the rest. The secretary, blushing, scooped up his share, smiling bashfully.

"Thank you, Mr. Mayor."

"Thank you, David."

"Brian, sir."

"Yes. Of course. Thank you, Brian."

The person Mayor Dubois had glorified in his patriotic speech now entered the city of Mappensville on foot, looking for affordable lodgings.

After four years of hardship, theft, flight, jail time for the theft, and extensive semi-compulsory travel, mostly on foot, Molly was exhausted, prematurely middle-aged, ill-clothed, and seriously undernourished. Her hair, unattended for considerable periods of time, was in clumps. She was pale and very thin. The veins on her hands stood out like a woman's twice her age. Her legs were covered with bruises and scars. Her toe and fingernails were broken in spots and yellowish.

She had endured and persevered. Where most women would have been dead by now, Molly trudged on, discovering in the process she was amazingly healthy and resilient.

Her Loyalist parents had long since settled down in England. Miles was where he normally was, i.e. at large and impossible to contact. Every member of her former gang was either dead or in jail, she was certain.

She entered the city.

The people she passed in the street never gave her a second thought – the Republic was full of misplaced vagrants. She trudged to the harbor and soon found what she was looking for.

It was a very cheap sort of inn. The crowd was mixed, with crooks, small-time thieves, and seasoned prostitutes prevailing. Upon entering, Molly went directly to the bar and looked nervously for the proprietor. A pleasantly drunken customer of the male gender, fat and perspiring profusely, approached her.

"Hey, babe. How about some fun."

She ignored him.

The proprietor, a twenty-five-year old, muscular, swarthy, rather good-looking man of Mediterranean descent appeared. He cast a glance at Molly and winced. He could simply throw her out, but he had rules he had once promised himself never to break. Bend them a little, maybe. Circumnavigate them now and then to keep it exciting. But never actually break them. At least, not all of them, certainly never all of them at once.

"Yes?" he asked dryly. "How can I help you?"

"I need a room for the night," she said.

"Hey, Luc," the drunken low-life joined in, "I think she's cute."

The proprietor ignored him. She might look like shit, but a woman looking for a room instead of soliciting a donation was still a customer. "All right, there's only one bed in the room, and you'd have to share it."

"Share it?"

"Someone else is staying in that room tonight. Another woman plying her trade."

"Oh."

"That'll be fifteen cents, breakfast included."

The fat low-life decided it was time to make a joke. "You can get me in the package, free of charge," he offered.

He laid his pudgy and sweaty hand on Molly's buttock. Luc was about to interfere when, half-spinning around, Molly buried her elbow in the fellow's face. He roared and pounced on her. She kicked him in the groin, once, twice, and then, grabbing a clay mug from the bar, broke it on his head. Astonished and cursing incoherently, the low-life sat on the floor, clutching his groin with one hand and his head with the other. The proprietor seemed amused.

"Serve you right, Fred," he said. "Okay, Gorgeous, let me take you to your room. Don't worry about the mug, it's on the house."

He picked up a candle, lit it, and led the way. Molly followed. There was a creaky staircase in the back of the inn.

Walking up the steps, the proprietor explained, "I'm trying to turn this place into a high-class establishment. Kinda hard, with all the scum around. But, as my Italian uncle used to say, when you have a definite purpose, perseverance is everything."

He stopped suddenly, turning around and staring dreamily over Molly's head. She nearly bumped into him.

"Imagine," he said, his voice attaining a sobbing edge, like that of a latter-day Italian tenor. "Clean walls, clean floor, a new bar. Curtains. Real glasses instead of clay mugs. Good oil lamps. Maybe a hostess. A new cook – no, not even a cook... What's the word I'm looking for? A chef. High-class people dropping by all the time. Clerks, scribes, navy officers and the like. You know? Some flashy, outrageous upholstery. Clean linen upstairs. Fifty cents a night! Maybe even seventy cents. You know what I mean?"

"I need a job," Molly said quietly.

He ignored her. He told her that he would definitely remove all the crap from the front, all those stupid fucking beer barrels. He would put up a real porch. And the greatest thing of all, he would buy a harpsichord and hire somebody to play it every Friday and maybe every Saturday also. He stood very still, awed and solemn, candle in hand, contemplating all this imaginary splendor in his mind. Presently he turned and continued up the stairs.

"Do you need help around here?" she asked, holding onto the banister.

"What? Uh, no. Not really. Sorry. Here we are."

He pushed a door.

It was a very small and very dirty room with a low ceiling. There was a dingy window with a nondescript view. There was also a bed containing a very vulgar-looking woman of about twenty-five, snoring sonorously. Molly suppressed a scream – a rat darted across the room and out the door.

"Well, here we are," Luc repeated. "That's the bed, so to speak. That's the nightpot. Keep it clean. That's our local whore, Patty. That's the window. There's no lock. If you need anything, just wait till morning. What's your name, by the way?"

"Ruth," Molly said.

"I'm Luc. Pleased to make your acquaintance, Ruth."

He further explained, as some wax from the candle melted and dripped onto the floor, that he made it his business to be exquisitely polite with everyone ("...even with low-class vermin like you.") He figured it must be that noble streak in him that his grandmother used to talk about all the time. He was supposed to be related to some Italian gentry, nothing grand, some small-time Neapolitan landowners.

"No offense, but your odor is abominable," he said. "You have a good night. Oh, and it was great, the way you got old Freddy in the balls. Don't do it again, though. He's a paying regular. I'll talk him out of getting back at you for kicking him; so don't let me down afterwards, all right?"

"Suppose he should attack me again?"

"Just don't do any more kicking. Just use a lot of words, all right? Don't let me down."

She asked if he could leave her the candle. He declined, explaining that candles were expensive, said good night, and left.

With the candle gone, the room was now pitch dark. Molly had seen worse. She shed some of her rags, removed her horrible tattered Sioux footwear, and climbed into bed without any further ado. The bed was not exactly narrow; still, the other party had to be moved a little for Molly to settle properly in it. She pushed her new roommate not very gently. The latter immediately complained.

"Oh. Excuse me," Molly said.

"Hey. Who the fuck are you?" the roommate demanded hoarsely.

"I'm Ruth. I won't bother you."

"Oh yeah? Shit! I thought I'd get me a nice fucking nap for once. Fucking Luc, the way he always saddles me with an extra body in here! I don't know what I'm paying him good money for. He thinks, because I'm a whore, I'm not entitled to a few hours of peaceful sleep."

"I'm sorry."

The roommate continued grumbling, "Sorry. She's sorry. Shit."

In a moment, Molly was fast asleep. The other woman grumbled some more but, seeing that it produced no effect, turned over on her side and soon was asleep also.

Some hours passed. Molly saw strange, inexplicable dreams. She could not quite tell what the things she saw were all about. In one of the sequences, she danced with George III, her former husband's best friend. They danced and danced an ancient minuet, and Miles accompanied them on his Spanish guitar. Then, she saw the young Sioux girl by the name of Winona, which means firstborn, with whom she had once spent three months in the mountains. Later still, she dreamed she arrived in Raymond's future and managed to save his life by mowing down two assassins with a magic weapon – all one had to do was press the trigger and hold it down, and the bullets just kept raining on one's targets. Still asleep, but vaguely aware of her surroundings, she realized she was getting seriously ill.

Opening her eyes in the morning, she saw Patty standing by the window, adjusting her very vulgar, very cheap clothes. The woman's features were irregular but not unpleasant. She had flaming red hair. There were freckles on her nose and cheeks. Her eyes were the color of North Carolina meadows.

"Good morning, sleepy head," the woman said. "How's tricks?"

"Where am I?" Molly asked quietly.

"Well, dearie, if it ain't hell, it's damn close by. Hungry?"

"Yes."

The harlot turned out to be a kind, understanding person. "Guess you and I will have to do a morning chore before breakfast. I'm flat broke, and you don't seem to have a penny on you either. What's your line?"

"Line?"

"The way I see it, unwed females of our age and position are only good for two things. So, which is it? The front door or the back door?"

Frowning, Molly sat up in bed. She found herself almost fully dressed in her last night's clothes.

"What?"

"You sell your body at the backdoor," the harlot elaborated. "You beg at the front door. Either way, they won't let you come inside, and that's the bottom line. Personally I prefer the back door. Pays better. I figure, there's always going to be time enough to enjoy the front door, like when they don't want your ass at the back door anymore because you're too old and ugly. I'm a whore and proud of it. What's your line?"

Molly was too weak to be amused by the harlot's cocky attitude.

"Why do you call yourself a whore?"

"Because," the harlot said, "that's what I am. I like being honest about it."

"Well, yes, but whore is the wrong word for it." Molly tried to get out of bed, but felt dizzy and had to wait for the world to stop spinning erratically in front of her eyes. "A whore," she said in order to keep her grasp on reality, "is a woman who sleeps with men exclusively for her own pleasure plus whatever else turns her on; stuff like boats, clothes, nightlife, theatre, etc. People engaging in prostitution, which is the act of selling yourself for ready money, are called harlots or prostitutes. Not all prostitutes are whores; certainly not too many whores are prostitutes as well."

The harlot was so impressed, she came over and sat on the edge of the bed.

"Wow! I never thought of it that way. You're real smart, you know? So how come all that scum keep calling me a whore? They're just ignorant, that's what."

The world blurred. Molly put out a hand to keep her balance. She mumbled something unintelligible and fell on her back.

There were sounds and vague images and then a door slammed a few times. A drunken male voice said, "Get that bitch out of here! I paid to get laid, not to be watched! Think I'm a pervert?" and the harlot's, replying, "No way, buster. She's my friend. Buzz off!" There was a flurry of memories – Miles, Hector, the brigands, the little Baroness, the travels. She was delirious.

When Molly opened her eyes, she had no idea how much time had passed – twenty minutes? Twenty hours? The harlot's face was close to hers. She smiled sympathetically.

"Feeling better, honey?" and immediately, a different voice, a voice from the past, blended into the cacophony of other sounds, "Draw the line... revenge..." and another one, "Sorry, Madam."

"No. No," Molly said and blacked out again.

She was delirious. Sweating. Feverish. Quivering.

Then, there was silence and Doctor Brewster's cold hand on her wrist, feeling the pulse.

He was sitting on the edge of the bed. His clothes smelled of whiskey and cheap tobacco. Patty the harlot, agitated, stared at the good doctor, her eyes full of frightened hope.

"So, what do you say, Doc?" she asked.

"Just a fever. She'll be fine."

"You hear that, hon?" the harlot shouted joyously. "You're going to be fine again."

"She could use a bath, though," the good doctor said, wrinkling his nose.

Molly fell asleep.

She dreamed that she was pregnant.

Morning came. Molly found herself sitting up in bed, with the harlot spoon-feeding her hot porridge.

"You're very pale, hon. That's right. Just one more spoon. You do look better, pumpkin. You know, if I were as cute as you, I'd marry someone wealthy."

Molly thought of her aged body, her puffy cheeks, her bad teeth, her veiny hands, her ruddy complexion.

"I've tried that," she said. "Men are pigs."

"Not all of them, hon. The important thing is, you've got to find the right one. Wealthy, you know."

"I was married to a wealthy guy for four years."

The harlot almost dropped the spoon. "You're shitting me."

"He only thought of himself. He was a rogue. And then there was another one. He betrayed me."

Patty nodded sagely. "They were both wrong for you. People like you and me, we need a steady, staid, home-loving man. The genuinely wealthy type who doesn't have to do anything all day and is proud of his fortune. Who won't squander his money on silly projects... Were you very rich?"

"Yeah, I guess."

"Well, you know how it is. The old up-and-down, up-and-down thing. You shouldn't despair. Maybe you'll be wealthy again one day. All right, let me run down and see if there's any business. If you need to pee, just let me know."

Another night, another morning. Molly could walk again.

She thought of herself as Ruth. Sauntering around the city in which her name was legendary and never once being recognized, Molly wondered what her next move should be.

In the young, energetic, hopeful and healthy Republic – as well as in the rest of the world – an aging woman's opportunities were severely limited. She could perhaps do what Patty the harlot did – in fact, she had some experience in the field herself – but that should be left for last – the last resort. Her sexuality was dormant, not dead, and instinctively, she intended to keep it that way. No need to kill it yet. She could not become a governess in her present condition and anyway, while her French was good and her German fluent, she disliked other people's kids, especially the rich and spoiled ones who had made her suffer more than once in the past four years, driving her out of towns and villages with insults, rocks, attempts to set her on fire when she was asleep, and other innocent pranks – even while their parents were inclined to leave her alone. She could not join a gang of brigands – in her travels, she had lost the aura of command; no one would follow her. As for becoming an ordinary brigand, why, no gang would take her – she was a woman.

She was not very good at sewing, and besides, seamstresses were a dime a dozen. All chambermaid positions required verifiable references. She was not temperamentally suited to become a nun.

Considering that prostitution was a punishable offense, Molly was worse off than a freed slave who, when the going got tough, could always sell himself back into slavery, thus obtaining shelter and two meals a day. Molly could not even do that – in 1781, slavery was already firmly and irrevocably color-codified. She could pretend to have African blood – indeed, for all she knew, she might have some – but she could not imitate the peculiar brand of English that was customary among the slaves.

And holding people up in dark lanes late at night was beneath her.

She left the inn and Patty's company, and for two days wandered around town looking for a chance job.

It was early afternoon. A typical weekday: the people in the streets were either unemployed or well-provided for. Except one.

She noticed him when she leaned against a wall to give her feet and thighs some rest. He was a strange-looking fellow indeed.

His appearance would not attract too many glances in Philadelphia or New York, let alone Paris, London, or Amsterdam. Here in Mappensville, however, his long mauve doublet, canvas boots and crude cotton robe seemed decidedly out of place. So was his russet shoulder-length loose-hanging hair. He was pushing a wheeled rack fastened to which were a number of oil paintings on stretchers, unframed.

Kenneth was returning from his appointment with the Mayor's secretary who had declined all of Kenneth's offers and refused to let him speak to the big man himself. Needless to say, Kenneth's mood matched his current prospects.

For an eighteenth century American artist of no particular school, life was a sorry affair. In Europe, the competition was fierce, even among the locals, with all available contracts snapped up five years in advance, while back at home there were neither competitors nor clients. The middle and low income customers could not pay Kenneth enough to support him, let alone grasp why an oil painting, no matter how good, was worth a week's rent at a cheap inn. Not even when the painting was their own portrait. The rich, on the other hand, did not trust native talent enough to encourage it with purchases, preferring instead to collect and brag about currently fashionable European masters.

Kenneth Sloan had studied painting in Boston as a youth. His teacher was an old Dutchman who, to make ends meet, gave watercolor lessons to the rosy-cheeked daughters of His Majesty's wealthier American subjects. The Dutchman was a mediocre painter but a brilliant teacher. He quickly discovered that Kenneth was no ordinary farmer's son. He taught the bright-eyed Yankee the laws of perspective and how to make a layer of paint seem transparent. His best advise was, "Never practice without a plan, son. Even a bad plan is better than none. You can always change or break a bad plan. When you're sketching without one, the only thing you can break is yourself."

Getting a job as a sailor on a seal hunter's ship, Kenneth reached Europe, where he settled for some years, working as an apprentice at various painters' workshops in Milan, Paris, and London. This helped develop his skills but still left him in obscurity. Instinctively, his teachers knew they were dealing with someone far more talented and imaginative than themselves and quite intentionally sabotaged his career. Returning to Mappensville on another hunter's ship, Kenneth rented a cheap house on the outskirts with the last of his savings. Just before he began seriously to starve, he ran into a client.

Baron McLachlan's one-time nocturnal visitor was preparing his troops for battle when he noticed an easel set up in the middle of what was projected to be the battlefield, and a strange man who seemed unhappy about the untimely arrival of the Continental Army, laying strokes on the canvas. Kenneth had discovered the *plain aire* technique long before the Impressionists.

The General approached and contemplated the work in progress for quite a while and then asked, very politely, whether he could see the painter's other pieces. The battle was subsequently called off – fortunately, since the English regiments arriving on the field two hours later would have outnumbered the Americans five to one. The General visited Kenneth at his ramshackle dwellings and was so impressed by the fellow's production that he bought three landscapes on the spot, at three hundred pounds each. To Kenneth, the sum was enormous. The money lasted him four years and would have lasted him ten but for his passion (imported from Europe) for good Bordeaux. He purchased at least one bottle every month.

Let us not blame poor Kenneth. The jury is still out on whether an artist's work is any less important or less strenuous than a statesman's. Like statesmen, artists should be allowed to have weaknesses. When he finished his second term as President, Miles Crawford's employer's wine bill topped ten thousand dollars. Let us cut Kenneth some slack.

For four years, painting at his leisure which in his case meant three to six hours every day, Sundays included, he made considerable progress and now, at thirty-two, was a complete master. The only problem was – money was running short again. The General seemed to have forgotten him. Kenneth sent letters to Mt. Vernon, but the secretary sorting out the future President's fan mail disposed of all missives whose authors were unfamiliar to him in an invariably disrespectful manner – in the fireplace. The General himself was too busy keeping the Army together after the Revolution to give much thought to the future of American art.

Kenneth decided he would sell out. To that end, after studying the Mayor's face at a number of outdoor public functions, he painted two likenesses of Jack Dubois and, loading them on the wheeled rack along with a few other portraits and landscapes, journeyed to the City Hall, where he discovered that there was no interest whatsoever in his product.

Casting a glance at a large portrait, Molly blinked. She could hardly believe her eyes. Mongoose's face smiled compassionately at her from the canvas. Molly ran after the artist.

"Excuse me! Sir!" she shouted.

Without stopping, he told her, "I don't have anything. I'm sorry."

Puzzled, Molly pondered hard. It took her some time to realize what the answer meant. She clenched her teeth. She ran after him again.

"Keep your money," she said, walking alongside the rack. "I just want to know a few things."

"Read the Bible, then," was his advice. "It's all in there."

"I mean, I want to know something about your paintings."

Amused, Kenneth stopped. He figured he might as well use a little rest. As he rolled the rack closer to the wall, he ran it over a bump in the road, causing one of the paintings to fall off and land, face down, on the poorly paved road.

"Shit!" he said.

Molly rushed to assist him. Putting a hand out, he said curtly, "No. Don't touch my work."

He picked up the Mongoose portrait, blew on it wildly and scraped off the little piece of pigeon droppings stuck to it. He leaned the painting against the wall, produced a pipe, and proceeded to light it. Molly stared at the portrait.

"So, what would you like to know?" he asked, grinning, blowing a cloud of smoke savoring of honey and springtime.

"Well, first of all," Molly said through her teeth, "one must not judge a book by its cover."

"Oh," he said, taken aback a little. "You being the book, presumably."

"What school do you follow?" she asked bluntly.

This was not what he expected. Was she pulling his leg? Perhaps not. Any low-life knows that artists belong to schools.

"I'm mostly a portrait painter," he informed her. "Which would naturally suggest a Rembrandt man. Does the name mean anything to you, beautiful?"

"Well," she said, examining a landscape critically, "to tell you the truth, I don't see much of his influence in your... uh... stuff. You seem to admire the Italians more."

Kenneth dropped his pipe and stooped to pick it up.

"Shit! Which Italians?" he asked irritably.

"Well, look at that lass over there," she suggested, pointing to a picture. "That's almost an exact copy of a Rafael. And this one," she pointed at a group portrait, "has Titian written all over it."

He was revolted.

"Not Titian! I hate Titian. I totally, totally hate and despise him. He's just no good. Titian? Impossible."

"Hate and love are close cousins, I believe? Or, look at this one."

She pointed calmly at the Mongoose portrait.

"Yes. What about it?" he demanded.

"I'm not sure. Boticelli, I think, in not being truthful with the subject matter."

"How am I not being truthful?"

"The man depicted in the picture is obviously a crook, a thief, and a rapist. Yet, you gave him an air of total respectability."

He smiled triumphantly. "Aha!" he said. "Wrong. The man in the picture is the Mayor of this city, one of the most respected people in the area."

"The Mayor?" Molly squinted at him. "Are you sure?"

"Mr. Jack Dubois, in person. I was just trying to sell it to him. He said he would have to think about it," he lied.

A sudden thought occurred to him. No way was this woman a mere tramp. Dutch school, Italian school. What next? No artist is entitled to pass up on a chance, no matter how long the odds. You never know how much this or that person is prepared to spend before he or she is done dealing with you. You never know where your canvases are going to end up and how many prospective clients will look at them, in whose living room or ballroom. He regarded Molly suspiciously. "Say, how would you like me to paint your portrait?"

"Uh... Why?" she asked absentmindedly, her eyes still glued to Mongoose's likeness.

"You have some interesting features."

That was nonsense. There is a difference between someone who, on a whim, dresses as a tramp; and someone who has been tramping for some time. But struggling artists believe what they want to believe most and, unlike prostitutes, who nearly always know whether they have a client, will strike a deal with and start working for a hobo who asked them for a nickel an hour ago. The mind conveniently edits out all evidence suggesting the project might be less profitable than one would like.

Turning away from Kenneth, Molly gave the matter some thought, a wry smile playing on her lips.

"How much would you charge me?" she asked without looking at him.

"Nothing. It's the challenge of it." Something kept bothering him. Ah, yes. The bad teeth and the broken fingernails. Maybe she was a real tramp, after all. Well, if that was the case, he would just paint her and keep the portrait. She had some very interesting features. "Look, I live at the end of this road, the last house. Drop by sometime next week. I'm always home after nine. I must paint you."

After a long pause, Molly said, "I might."

Pipe in mouth, Kenneth picked up the Mongoose portrait and fastened it to the rack.

"Just do me a favor," he added. "Put on some decent clothes before you come over."

"Suppose I don't have any decent clothes."

"Oh, come on. You can't fool me. I'm an artist. You're a rich lady in disguise, and you have a mansion down at the south shore. Well? Am I right?" Now I'm being plain silly, he thought.

Remembering her ghost's story about the portrait, Molly, ever practical, tried to recall the name her so-called descendent had mentioned. Was it all true?

"Kenneth Sloan," she said. "Right?"

"Hey, yeah!" he was astounded. "That's my name. How did you know?"

"Never mind," she said quietly. She looked at him almost fondly, smiled, turned, and set off for the City Hall.

The reason Mongoose could not see the painter was that he and Hector Eriksson were in the middle of a conference. Hector's largely self-serving, though on the whole fairly valid and reasonable theory was that in order to grow and prosper, Mappensville needed more trade, and in order to attract more trade, the city had to feature a modern harbor where trans-Atlantic ships could dock without delays or misadventures. In order to bring the harbor up to date, new docks had to be built. The ugly, embarrassing incident of two months ago, when a large cargo vessel from Liverpool, carrying, among other things, expensive Chinese tea, had damaged its keel in Mappensville's shallow waters, was as good a signal as any.

Jack Dubois agreed with Hector on all points except the timeframe. He argued that many streets had to be repaved, new inns built, and highways improved connecting Mappensville with Philadelphia and New York. The market place had to be modernized. More bridges needed to be constructed, and the existing ones repaired. All these works required workmen.

"But the docks, man!"

"You're right, Eriksson, and I agree with you whole-heartedly, " Mongoose assured him. "We must have those new docks finished in a year."

"Couldn't we shorten that?"

"There's a shortage of hands everywhere. In any case, you have my full support. I advise you to speak to Jerome. It's funny how he's discovered he has a good business sense – being a Briton as well as an aristocrat. He's been investing in new ventures like mad, and he's mostly successful."

"I'll talk to him," Hector said without much enthusiasm.

"You do that," Mongoose rose.

He hardly remembered he once had had Hector Eriksson in the sights of his musket. Different life, different people. Supposedly. The woman chief, getting out of the carriage in front of the ship builder's house; the ship builder himself; the woman's old butler, now deceased, hiding, like Mongoose, behind the trees. "You will only shoot when I tell you," the butler had told Mongoose before riding out into the open to exchange words with the woman. No, Mongoose hardly ever recalled that particular scene these days. Still, no man can help feeling a little differently towards someone he once took good aim at. Mongoose grunted.

Hector rose. The two shook hands across the desk. Hector picked up his tricorne and turned to go.

"By the way," Mongoose stopped him. "What's the Gallic Faction been doing lately?"

Hector's smile vanished. "How would I know? I'm not affiliated with them."

"No, but surely you still have lots of friends in that circle?"

Hector attempted a tight smile and failed. The matter was not funny.

"Most of them have lived in this country for so long, they've lost all (touch with France. The new arrivals are largely disoriented. There are disturbances in Paris; Versailles has no time for American affairs."

In fact, after nearly a hundred years, the Faction still took orders from France – when it suited the Faction's own purposes.

Mongoose did not for a moment believe Hector. "And Delacroix?" he asked.

"Delacroix? He's up to his ears in business. The only thing French about him is his surname. Your own surname is French also."

"Ah, yes, but mine is assumed."

Feigning interest, Hector asked, "It is?"

Feigning sincerity, Mongoose proclaimed histrionically, "No one else knows this. I know I can trust *you*, Eriksson. I, Jack Dubois, have a shady past. Yes. That's a fact. But, serving the Republic to the best of my ability, I redeemed myself. The past is forgotten. Please don't tell anyone."

"No, of course not," Hector said somberly. "Well, good afternoon, Mr. Mayor."

He left. Mongoose looked over the pile of papers on the desk, peered, picked up a sheet and inspected it closely, frowning. What the hell, every single figure was off. He sat, armed himself with a quill, dipped it in ink, and started making corrections when was interrupted by someone knocking at the door.

"Yes?" Mongoose shouted.

Entering, the secretary said, "A woman to see you, Mr. Mayor, sir."

Mongoose made another correction, threw away the quill, and looked up.

"Show her in."

The Secretary bowed and left. Mongoose, ready for his bi-weekly adventure, straightened his clothes, smoothed out his hair with his palms, and smiled radiantly. The door opened and the visitor entered. The Mayor's smile disappeared gradually. It was not the person he had expected.

"Yes? What do you want?" he asked.

The tramp looked sideways and then, almost pleadingly, at him. He was about to call his secretary or maybe throw her out himself but something about her appearance stopped him.

"Don't I know you?"

The tramp nodded slowly. He stared at her. Suddenly it all came back to him. He could hardly believe his eyes. He closed them, inhaled, and counted to three. He looked again. There was no mistake. Satisfied, he resumed his aloof manner. He had the makings of a great statesman. His self-control was on par, and his ability to reason soberly in any situation was as good as any politician's. The only thing he lacked, really, was the unmistakable gloss of a well-bred, well-educated person that back then was already necessary in large-scale politics at the end of the Eighteenth Century.

"What brings you here?" he inquired dryly.

"I see you recognize me," she said very quietly.

"Thought you were dead."

"I thought so too for a while."

"What can I do for you?" he asked bluntly.

"Never fear. I'd love to blackmail you if I had the strength and the resources, but I don't."

"Ah, yes," he said. "You would, wouldn't you?"

"I'm destitute. I haven't eaten in two days."

A pang of guilt. He was a little moved. He softened perceptibly. He was about to say something rash and sentimental when the door opened again and Mildred, the miniature Baroness, entered, followed by the secretary. The latter began to speak before noticing Molly.

"This is the lady, Mr. Mayor, she insisted... Hey! How did you get in here?"

He glared at Molly.

"It's all right," Mongoose told him. "Thank you." Then, addressing the Baroness, "My dear, please wait in the anteroom," he said.

Mildred was revolted. "You're kidding me, Jack! I've been..."

Coldly and peremptorily, he repeated, "I said, In the anteroom."

The Baroness hesitated. She had quite a reputation and spent most of her free time denying ugly hypocritical rumors. Being, like nearly all shallow people, excessively touchy, she resented any affront, no matter how slight. Now she wanted to shout, to pick up something heavy with a jagged edge and throw it at Mongoose's ugly head. She controlled herself. She shrugged, turned haughtily on her heel, and swept out, accompanied by the reluctant secretary who on his way to the door cast a surprised glance over his shoulder.

Evidently, the Baroness had not kept her promise to be always faithful to her fat, ugly husband. Lady Crawford, however, was in no position to call her to account for it. She was happy the Baroness hadn't recognized her.

"What happened to all the money?" Mongoose asked when, once again, he and Molly were alone.

"Someone raided the treasury."

"The boys did. As soon as they smelled gunpowder, they forced the lock. I took part in the festivities, naturally, it would be silly of me to deny it. But, I was sure you had a good portion of it stashed away someplace for your own private use."

"I did. That was stolen too."

He clicked his tongue sympathetically. "Really! That's just too bad, isn't it? Anyway, your husband never came back?"

"Haven't seen him in years."

There was a painful pause. Molly looked down. Mongoose fidgeted.

"Well, I don't know what to tell you."

"I'm hungry, Mongoose."

"Yeah. I suppose you should be. Yes. You haven't eaten in two days. You just told me so yourself."

"Could you get me something to eat?"

This had honestly never occurred to him. He was suddenly embarrassed. He blushed. Even politicians can be human at lunchtime.

"Uh... yeah, sure."

He reached for the bell and rang. The secretary re-entered. Mongoose inquired sternly whether there were any breakfast leftovers in the den. There were some rolls, the secretary was certain, as well as a pot of tea. Maybe some butter, also. Mongoose ordered the secretary to bring it all up.

"In here, Mr. Mayor?"

Mongoose raised his eyebrows in mock surprise. The secretary bowed.

On his way through the anteroom, the secretary glanced at the Baroness sitting on the couch and looking very displeased, freckles and all.

"Hey!" she demanded peevishly. "What's going on in there?"

He hesitated before replying, "I'm not sure."

"Who is that heap of rotten wood shavings, his cousin from sunny Louisiana?"

"I have no idea, Madam."

In the meantime, Mongoose and Molly lightened up somewhat. Molly sat on the edge of her seat, her elbows on her knees, looking up at Mongoose who perched on the edge of the desk.

"Remember the Southy house?" he asked.

Both giggled.

"Wasn't he something?" she recalled. "Remember how he yelled, James, get these ugly-looking vagabond players out of my house!"

"Yeah. And then his wife came out. Said," Mongoose mimicked a fastidious woman of gentle birth stammering in a high-pitched voice, "Dear, are these your guests?"

Molly laughed. They reminisced some more. When the secretary entered carrying a tray, they fell silent. Mongoose motioned the secretary to place the tray on the desk.

"Thank you, Russell."

"It's Brian, sir."

"Yes, yes. Brian, of course."

When the secretary left, Mongoose invited Molly to partake. She rose, moved rapidly to the desk, and grabbed a roll. She wolfed into it. Mongoose placed his palm over her wrist.

"Slow down. You want to be able to hold it in."

She gave him a blurry look. He poured her a cup of cold tea. She thanked him twice, her mouth full. After about five minutes of ravenous feeding – he had to stop her from time to time, telling her to slow down and holding her hand – she managed to relax a little.

"Would I be out of line if I told you I'm looking for work?"

She resumed eating, casting hopeful glances at him.

"Work? Work... Ah, yes. I know someone who needs a chambermaid. You wouldn't mind being one, would you?"

"I'm not in a position to be picky, I'm afraid."

"Great!" he said, sincerely pleased. "Let me write a letter of recommendation for you."

He jumped off the desk, sat in his chair, opened a drawer, and produced a clean sheet of paper. Molly resumed eating.

"Actually," he said. "he's an old acquaintance of yours. I hope you don't mind."

"Well, no. Who is he?"

"Jerome."

"Jerome who?"

"The handsome fair-haired lad we met at the Viscount's place one night. You two used the occasion to indulge in some bad-ass fencing, if I remember correctly."

Molly thought hard about this. For a moment, she stopped eating.

"Oh!" she said at last. "The blond fellow with the thin lips?"

"The same."

"He saw me at a party in Philadelphia. We danced, I think."

"His eyesight has been extremely poor lately. And he's too inhibited to wear glasses when there are people around."

They exchanged glances. Both were suddenly embarrassed again. Grunting bashfully, Mongoose started writing. Molly, ill at ease, hung her head and experimented with not breathing for a while.

"He's a fairly agreeable person," Mongoose promised. "Does a lot of business in this city. Here."

Molly wiped off a tear. Mongoose signed, folded and sealed the letter. With some surprise, Molly observed his very efficient, matter-of-fact working habits. He handed the letter to her.

"But..." she began.

He rose, reached into his pocket, and produced some golden coins.

"Oh, no. No, no, no..." she mumbled.

"Listen. We're old friends, right? You have to pull yourself together. Hire a room at a decent inn, wash up, buy some clothes. Get some proper dinner; get a lot of sleep. Tomorrow morning, go see Jerome. He won't refuse you. What name do you trade under these days?"

"Uh... Ruth, I guess."

"Well, good luck, Ruth. Thanks for dropping by."

Molly accepted the gold reluctantly and shook Mongoose's hand. He beamed at her with professional courtesy. She wept.

"Thank you, Jack."

He flirted for a moment with the idea of giving her a hug, but she was just too dirty and smelly. He waved at her instead.

When she was gone, he returned to his desk, opened the third drawer from the top and sighed, looking at the diamond necklace. In a few moments, he was able to suppress the pangs of guilt and the tremors of nostalgia. He shut the drawer and locked it.

SEVEN

Pursuit Of Happiness

Kenneth Sloan's studio, which also served as his living room, dining room, study, library, and so on, was a mess. The furniture made of blocks and planks of unpainted, unpolished wood, was chaotically arranged. There were paint smears everywhere. The air was permeated with turpentine fumes. A large easel with a blank canvas towered majestically in the middle.

There was a tiny bedroom, not much larger than a closet. Kenneth, in a shabby canvas robe, was inspecting some ink sketches and casting tentative glances at an unfinished canvas when he heard a knock at the door. He went to open it while still inspecting a drawing. At the door, he paused as some compositional detail arrested his attention. He turned and, without giving the door any further thought, went back to the easel. The knocking repeated. Once again conscious of the noise, Kenneth set the sketches down on the table, strode to the door and flung it open. Molly – bathed, brushed, wearing a new dress and looking younger – smiled at him. She had a basket in her hand.

"Hello," she said brightly.

"Oh. Yes?"

Evidently, he failed to recognize her. Besides, he had no use for company at the moment. He was eager to transfer some of the sketch onto canvas and maybe put in the first layer of paint.

"We met yesterday. Remember?"

"No. Where? When?"

"In the afternoon. You were lugging some of your doodling from the City Hall."

"Ah, yes. Oh! So it's you." He still had no idea who she was or what to expect from her.

"Aren't you going to ask me to come inside?"

He gave it some confused thought. He stepped aside. Molly entered, looked around, placed the basket on the table, removed the cloth, produced a bottle of wine, and showed it to Kenneth.

"Bordeaux. Napkins. I thought you wanted to do my portrait."

He looked at her blankly. Suddenly, he brightened up.

"Of course! The rich lady in disguise," he said.

He closed the door. He hesitated, knit his eyebrows, looked over his shoulder furtively, hesitated some more; at last, he threw on the latch, nodding to himself. Artists, when they nod to themselves, do not look particularly intelligent.

In addition to the wine, the basket contained some vegetables, ham, cheese and fresh bread. After a bit of random searching, a reasonably clean knife was found and used on the bread and ham. Kenneth's table manners were abominable, but his conversation was amiable enough. They discussed the current political setup. The artist's views were childishly naïve and sincere. Molly's were more or less non-existent. His knowledge of human nature, on the other hand, was far more elaborate, rooted as it was in personal experience. His opinion of himself was high and poetic. He took his talent for granted, but expatiated eloquently and at great length on his inner world, his feelings, his great generous spirit, his affairs with women, his smashing success in Europe. According to him, he had exhibited many times at prestigious art events in Rome, Milan, and Berlin (a magnificent city located in Northern Poland), and had sold many paintings to rich and sophisticated Europeans. They had practically begged him to sell, all the time. Most of them were terrible snobs who only spoke French and disdained Americans, but they knew genuine value when they saw it. Alas, life in Europe was very expensive, which was why hapless Kenneth had spent all his money before coming home to Mappensville. Now he was waiting for a certain rich military man from Mt. Vernon to offer him a contract for three dozen large paintings. He had sold to him before, so the imposing old geezer knew what Kenneth could do. Unfortunately, he was a little busy right now, which was why Kenneth was broke.

Molly listened to all Kenneth's nonsense without interrupting.

They finished lunch. Kenneth, wine glass in hand, set up a fresh canvas and made Molly sit astride a wooden bench. He picked up a piece of charcoal and started sketching her.

"I don't know anyone in this city. Would you mind awfully if I spent the night?" she asked.

"Of course not..." he said. "But..." he added, sketching and trying to sound casual, "I have only one bedroom."

"Really," Molly said. "How many beds?"

"Uh... Just one, I'm afraid."

"Poor dear. Life of a struggling artist. Well, we'll just see if we can make the best of it, right?"

She sipped from her glass and smiled.

She was patient. Kenneth lost track of time, as artists tend to do when they work. Molly did not complain. The sketch was finished in five minutes flat, but instantly Kenneth, saying "I'll only put in a few strokes, it won't take a minute," dug up a palette, some brushes, paints, and a wine bottle containing turpentine, and started mixing pigments and laying strokes over the sketch. Two hours later, he was dead tired. Molly was even more tired than he – the pose she had had to hold was an uncomfortable one. They passed into the bedroom.

He was surprisingly shy. She was not at all interested in him as a lover. She bid him to turn around, undressed and slipped under the sheets. These were not particularly fresh, but Molly had been through enough in this life not to mind the little things. She covered herself up to the chin and told Kenneth to cut the crap and undress. He removed his robe and stood blinking beside the bed in his long undershirt. He stared at her from a respectful distance.

"Are you sure you wouldn't be more comfortable if I slept on the floor?" he asked.

"Get in here," she ordered. "I'm exhausted. Let's end this discussion and get some sleep, shall we?"

He slipped in tentatively. Molly was dead to the world in an instant. Kenneth lay beside her, staring at the ceiling and uncertain as to what his next move should be. He raised himself on an elbow, extended his hand towards Molly's neck. He listened to her breathing. He withdrew his hand. He turned over and lay motionless, face down, for a long time. He felt stupid. He realized he was seriously aroused. He sprang to his feet. He stood beside the bed looking at the woman in it – the first woman in his bed in many months. He shrugged, flirted with the idea of lying down beside Molly again, changed his mind and looked for his pipe instead. Lighting it, he went back to the easel, examined the first layer of the portrait and found it promising. He examined it again and it was still promising. He decided not to touch it until tomorrow. He finished his pipe and fixed some of the coloring. He examined the results. Still promising. He went back to the bedroom, slipped under the sheets next to Molly, turned on his back, found himself aroused again, and fell asleep. He dreamed that all of the walls at the Painting Salon in Paris (an imaginary place back then) were painted white, and that the Archbishop of Notre Dame came and said to him, "Kenneth, here are walls!" Kenneth toiled for a whole year, covering the walls with splendid frescos, but then a bunch of East Coast blue-bloods showed up and had the walls whitened again because they could not stand the idea of an American defiling them.

Jerome's house was the best house in Mappensville. Built by a Dutchman a century earlier, it had been renovated many times by contractors of various schools and now was as capriciously eclectic as any colonial residence. A French roof had been added some years ago, complete with a mansard; and the upstairs/downstairs concept had been introduced, after the British fashion, by the current owner. Architecturally, the house was a very happy accident, and no one with a flair for good design could pass it by without his eye lingering on it for some time.

An aging English butler opened the door for Molly, took the Mayor's letter from her, and went to announce to his master that a woman had arrived seeking the position of chambermaid. After a while, Molly was invited to the master's study.

Jerome had changed a great deal since their last encounter. He was no longer slender; he had lost most of his youthful impetuousness. It would not occur to Margaret the Viscountess today to dub him Goldie Locks. His receding hairline, puffy cheeks, and extreme nearsightedness were terrible handicaps. At twenty-six, Jerome looked at least ten years older.

When Molly entered, Jerome turned his back to her and pretended to inspect the miniature model of Westminster Abbey on his mantelpiece. Stealthily, he removed his eyeglasses. He tried not to squint when he faced Molly again.

"The Mayor seems to have a very favorable opinion of you."

"Yes, sir."

"I do need a chambermaid. Are you married?"

"No, sir."

"How old are you?"

"Twenty-nine."

"Ever been a chambermaid before?"

"Yes, sir."

Jerome assumed an important air. He paused for emphasis before saying, "All right. No stealing. No meddling with my papers. Are you, perchance, literate?"

"Yes, sir."

He was taken aback.

"You are?"

"Yes, sir."

"Fine," he said. "I'll introduce you to the housekeeper and the cook."

He picked up the bell and rang.

EIGHT

The Dagger

There was enough iodine in the air to disinfect the wounds of the entire Royal Army after the Battle of Trenton. It was a busy day at the shipyard. A bare ship structure was being dressed. A German inventor and pistol maker, fat, sweaty, debonair, oddly attired and carrying a small portmanteau, watched the proceedings curiously. He had asked permission to be here from the shipyard's supervisor – a tall, dark-haired man with a touch of artistic madness in his dark blue eyes. Hector Eriksson had not changed much over the past five years.

After giving the workers enough assignments to keep them busy for the next half hour, Hector, blueprint in hand, joined the foreigner, asking him how he liked it so far. The German assured him that, like most of his compatriots, he was but a middling seaman; however, what he had witnessed today was absolutely fantastic, even in a layman's eyes. Hector, the German believed, was not a typical American himself? Hector assured him that he would, perhaps, look more typical in New York.

"We Germans are keen on heritage. What's your background?"

"My mother was born in Jutland."

"Jutland? Oh, that's just over the border, then. Danish countryside."

"Precisely. Some forty miles out of Aarhus."

"And your dear father?"

"My dear father was a Castilian pirate."

The German laughed incredulously.

"Pirate? A real pirate? The mustache, red kerchief, dagger type?"

"Yes."

"You don't say!" the fellow exclaimed joyously. "Well, that's why your hair is dark, I suppose. A real pirate! But, yes, of course; the Vikings on one side, the Spaniards on the other. It was your destiny to become a seaman."

Hector shrugged. "I'm not a seaman. I just build the bastards."

"Funny thing, I'm not much of a marksman, yet I make pistols. The delicious irony of life and fate, so to speak!"

He was truly pleased with himself. One of the workmen dropped his hammer and sucked his finger furiously. Seeing this, Hector excused himself, approached the worker and picked up the hammer.

"That's what comes of not being able to handle your own tools."

"Sir …ah, shit! …" the workman exclaimed apologetically. "I'm usually good at this."

"Shut up," Hector ordered. "How many times do you need to hit that stupid nail!"

"Well…"

"Watch," Hector suggested. "It's two and a half, genius. The half is to nudge it in. One full blow to get it going; and one more to finish the task."

Suiting his words to action, he picked up a nail and after illustrating his point, returned the hammer to the workman. He rejoined the German.

"My goodness," the latter said. "*Donnerwetter*! What a lesson for the poor bungler! Listen. I'd like you to have something from me as a souvenir."

He opened his portmanteau and produced a leather-bound flat box. He opened it. Inside was a well-made pistol of an unusual design.

"I'm not the first one to make little chums of this kind," the German explained. "People have been trying for two centuries. I believe, however, that my improvements will finally convince some affluent manufacturers to take up the idea once again. See this drum? It can rotate, like this, see? Which allows you to fire four shots in succession."

He rotated the drum some more, admiring his work. Hector was politely interested.

"Some of the power is lost, and you need to carry a supply of cartridges... They're difficult to make... But the end result is worth it. If we are to have pistols, the least we can do is make them efficient. It's yours, now. Please. Take it."

Smiling, Hector accepted the gift. Politely, he tried spinning the drum with his finger. He stuck the weapon in his pocket and shook the German's hand. He was about to invite him to lunch when he heard a familiar voice call his name.

"Eriksson!"

Spinning around, Hector saw Miles Crawford. The latter was dressed for a journey, well-armed, and mounted. Hector approached. He could not believe his eyes. He had known Miles slightly in the past, but when Miles' wife told him her husband had been shot, he believed her – and, blushing now, he remembered that he had wanted to believe her all along. Now, it was evident she had lied to him. Or, taking her straightforwardness into consideration, one could assume she had been honestly mistaken. Or... This was embarrassing. He had not seen Lady Crawford since... He had tried... She was gone when...

"Hello, Crawford," he said.

Miles alighted, patted the horse's mane, and hesitated. Seeing that Hector was not about to offer him his hand, he pursed his lips, rolled his eyes, and grinned.

"Building ships, as usual," he remarked.

"Yeah. Why are you here?"

"I'm just passing through. A business trip."

"Business? You mean, they've pardoned you?"

What a stupid question. What a lame way to get one's bearings.

"That depends on whom you mean when you say *they*," Miles said absentmindedly. Then he added, pulling a serious face, "In my branch of diplomacy, there's always a shortage of competent hands. The idiots had no choice but to hire me again."

Hector had no idea what any of that meant. He was not sure whether he should mention Miles' wife. He had no clue how much Miles knew about the matter, or whether he was aware of the role Hector had played in Lady Crawford's disappearance. He did not wish to talk to Miles right now. He suddenly wanted to be alone.

"You've changed," he said at last.

"So have you. Are you married yet?"

"No. You?"

Miles chuckled. "I'm not sure. Haven't seen the... uh... my beloved wife in four years."

Once again, the pause stretched and became embarrassing.

"Been in touch with the Gallic Faction?" Miles asked point-blank.

Hector's eyes flashed, to Miles' amusement.

Hector's affiliation with the group kept resurfacing, to his chagrin, no matter how hard he tried to keep it in the past, to let bygones be bygones, to disassociate himself from the grim clique.

"Look," Hector said with loathing, "I have nothing, repeat, nothing to do with them. All right? Tongues may wag, but I've never really been affiliated with that gang. Got it?"

They should have shot the impudent fellow for spying when they had their chance. Hector spun around huffily and walked away.

"Hey!" Miles called after him, "I was just making conversation? Hello?"

Without turning, Hector replied, "Go make it someplace else."

Miles laughed, turned his horse around and galloped off.

Two months later, while dusting and scrubbing Jerome's cozy library, Molly kept the door leading to the adjacent living room ajar. She was not quite certain why she wanted to find out more about the master of the house, except that it seemed like the correct thing to do. She was a survivor; to survivors, no information is superfluous. She might be able to learn some facts with which she could blackmail him. Whatever. She was good at keeping a house clean, she knew. But she could not imagine doing it for the rest of her life.

There were voices in the next room. She drew closer to the door. One of the voices belonged to Jerome; the other was painfully familiar to Molly. She had to bite her lip to keep from screaming.

"No, my dear fellow," Jerome was saying, "I'm not interested in any new docks. But your idea for a new type of ship is curious. Now, that's something I wouldn't mind looking into."

"Why?" Hector asked glumly.

"Why would I want to look into it? I have my reasons. If it works, I'll get money and recognition as its first supporter, is one."

"I see. How much would you be willing to invest?"

"Nothing at this point. Get the prototype ready, put it to the test, and if it turns out the way you say it will, I'll finance five more. From that point on, we'll just play it by ear."

Molly stepped away from the door. She closed her eyes. She had wanted to see Hector – she had come back to Mappensville to see him – but now she found herself completely unprepared.

On her lunch break, she went back to Kenneth's studio. Her first portrait was already finished, and her second was coming along just fine. Without any preliminary ado, Kenneth stuck a rose in her hair, seated her on the bench and went behind the easel. In the portrait, the rose was bright blue rather than red. For a while, they were silent.

"If only I could get a model who wouldn't mind posing in the nude," Kenneth said thoughtfully. "This country is so full of puritans, even harlots refuse to sit for me. It's the very height of perversion to sell your body to a drunken sailor while utterly refusing the mere sight of it to an honest and handsome artist."

Molly smiled wryly. Kenneth looked up and raised his eyebrows.

"Something funny?"

"I might know someone who wouldn't mind sitting for you. Lots of curves."

It took Kenneth some time to process this information. At last, he smiled and threw away the brushes and palette.

"Let me wash up," he said.

Molly knit her eyebrows and, when the meaning sank in, laughed almost happily and in a touchingly feminine manner. He blushed.

"No," she said. "No, you bungling moron. Someone else. You'd have to pay her, though."

Testily, he said, "Oh. I see. Someone from the house you've been scrubbing to earn your keep, I presume?"

"No."

Kenneth picked up his pipe. Filling it, he kept throwing furtive glances at the half-finished portrait. There was something intangibly universal about this new work of his, something ineffably alluring about its general quality. It was going to be a masterpiece, Kenneth knew.

"How much would she charge me?" he asked.

"You'll have to discuss that with her."

"How soon can you bring her here?"

"Tonight, if you like."

It was a sunny day. The walk back was invigorating. Molly inhaled the fresh air feeling that she was, once again, full of life and energy. Her youth and beauty were gone – a little earlier than expected, perhaps; but her vitality was back. She could once again organize people, channel their efforts, make them feel alive, force them into decision-making mode. A touch of the old radiance reappeared in her smile.

Back at Jerome's house, she went to the master's study directly and, to get his attention, cleared her throat sarcastically. He tore off his eyeglasses and threw the book he had been reading on the desk.

"What do you want?"

Broom in hand, she struck a pose. She told him. He was revolted.

"What do you mean you need the night off? The guestroom is a mess. I'm expecting someone tonight. You've only been working here two months, and you're already taking liberties!"

She waited for him to stop raving.

"You could fuck her in the master bedroom," she suggested.

Livid, he shouted, "Hold your tongue, wench!"

"Look," she said firmly. "I've been keeping this pigsty of yours clean all this time. Aren't you satisfied with my performance? Don't I also, upon your request, go through your deeds once in a while to give them some semblance of order?"

"Shut up, I said."

He calmed down somewhat – a typical choleric, he could not keep angry for any meaningful period of time.

"Yes," he admitted. "You're diligent, industrious, occasionally resourceful, and completely tactless – which I like, as a matter of fact. But, you see, I can't fuck her, as you put it, in the master bedroom because the lady is awfully fond of her strong-smelling perfume that tends to linger afterwards, on account of which my permanent mistress will castrate me the moment she sniffs it."

Molly considered this possibility and suppressed a laugh when she pictured Jerome being castrated by his mistress.

"Let's cut a deal," she said. "You get your cook and your housekeeper to clean up in the guest room as best they can; and I won't call you names for two whole weeks."

"You're a witch," he assured her. "That's what you are: a witch. This is the proverbial democracy all those idiots are screaming about. In the old days, I'd have you whipped."

"In the old days, I would be married and drinking champagne in Philadelphia or London instead of scrubbing your stupid floors for you.

Incidentally, I think you should have agreed to finance, at least in part, Eriksson's current project. The new docks, and all. The rest would have been paid by the City Hall."

Interested, he reflected, and eventually asked, "You think so? Why?"

"This is a coastal city. If Eriksson's idea of faster ships is valid, then before you know it, we'll have more traffic than ever in this harbor. We'll need new docks to accommodate greater and greater numbers every year."

Jerome tried to find some fault with this gibberish, and failed.

"All right," he said. "Take the night off."

"Thank you, Master. Shall I kiss your buttock now or afterwards? Oh, you want it now? All right, off with your pants."

"Just mount that broom of yours and off with you through the chimney."

Predictably, Patty the harlot had her doubts. Molly had to muster all her powers of persuasion and even relate to the feisty puritan the highlights of a cultured person's outlook on Western art and nudity, in order to alleviate Patty's fears.

All their worries were in vain. The moment Patty laid eyes on Kenneth, she was ready to do anything – strip, belly dance, give all her money to charity, compose intricate trochaic verse, work on a farm. She was smitten. Molly, after some pondering, realized that the artist's mixture of impudence, confidence, and panache was indeed unusual and, to a woman of Patty's station who had never seen a live artist before, extremely attractive. At the same time, his manners and attitude were just vulgar enough not to intimidate the good-natured commoner. They had a drink. Molly excused herself and went out for a stroll. Shyly, Patty asked Kenneth whether he wanted her to strip in the bedroom or in front of the easel.

Kenneth was judicious and calm. He made some suggestions in an important voice and soon Patty was standing on the bench in a graceful pose, her luxuriant, if poorly washed, red hair streaming down her bare back. It did not take her long to realize that modeling was, in fact, hard physical work. She managed to hold the pose for about five minutes. Kenneth was polite, amiable, and considerate. He explained she could take as many breaks as she wished.

"And, if you would like anything to eat, Ms... uh..."

"Patty. Just Patty."

"All right. Patty. Some tea?"

When Molly came back, Patty and Kenneth were telling each other ridiculous stories and laughing.

"So! How was the session?" Molly asked conversationally.

Patty looked down, hiding a tiny half-smile. Kenneth, pipe in hand, tasted his tea, nodding approvingly.

"Miss Patty," he informed Molly in a solemn voice, "has been absolutely charming. You were right, Ruth. She is, indeed, very beautiful. And her form is a happy blend of classical and Rubenesque."

Patty, wearing one of Kenneth's canvas robes, choked on her tea, covered her mouth with her hand, and looked terribly embarrassed. Molly suppressed a burst of giggles. There was loud knocking at the front door. Kenneth excused himself and went to open it.

"How was it?" Molly asked quickly and quietly.

Patty's eyes widened conspiratorially. "It felt a bit strange at first," she whispered. "Especially as he didn't... doesn't seem to... He doesn't treat me as... as a woman. I might as well be a lamppost. You know?"

"That's just on the surface," Molly shrugged.

"Think so? Anyway, he paid me. He's a real gentleman. You wouldn't be able to tell from the way this place looks that he's rich."

"He isn't. Whatever gave you that idea?"

"Of course he is, Ruth! He says I'm to come here every night for five weeks, and each time he'll pay me. The money's good. Just under my usual daily take. Sure beats whoring, this. I mean, not whoring, but... what was the word you used?"

"Prostitution."

"That's it. Sure beats that. Is this how he amuses himself?"

"No. I believe he's a professional."

"Oh. Meaning what?"

"He does this for a living."

She picked up her tea. Looking at Patty, she set the cup down again, sprang to her feet and hugged her friend impulsively. She stepped back.

"What was that for?" Patty asked, puzzled.

"No reason."

Molly sat, looking dejectedly out the window. She turned to Patty again.

"What's that word he used? About my body? Ruben something?" Patty asked.

"Rubenesque. Pleasantly rounded."

"Oh? And the other one?"

"Classical?"

"Yeah. What's that mean?"

"Finely drawn."

Patty was not sure she was quite grasping it, except that it sounded highbrow and very flattering.

"I have to learn some big words," she said with quiet, determined enthusiasm. "He sure is a gentleman. Listen, thanks! You're a real friend, you know. I owe you."

Molly studied the charcoal sketch on the canvas, with patches of paint here and there. It was different from the European nudes she was familiar with. It might be the air, or the East Coast flora, but American painters differ from their far better known European colleagues in one aspect – the immediacy and liveliness of the subject matter. This does not take away from their sense of continuum.

Kenneth returned, accompanied by Hector. The two were too absorbed in their conversation to look at the two women. Hector, in his perpetual military tricorne, his long indigo overcoat, his snobbish silken gloves, was the same Hector Molly remembered. Patty blabbed some nonsense, but Molly was not listening.

"...sounds interesting," Kenneth, intrigued, said.

"Whatever. I just need it done as soon as..." Hector's words stuck in his throat when he saw Molly. He grew very pale.

"What's the matter?" Kenneth inquired. "Hey, Eriksson? What's the problem? Sit down, have some tea. Girls, this is Hector Eriksson, an old friend of mine. Eriksson – I want you to meet Ruth and Patty."

"Nice to meet you, sir," Patty said brightly. "Are you a painter also?"

"No, madam," Hector said, cleared his throat and said, "No, madam," again. This time they could hear him.

"Hello, Hector," Molly said, her features calm. A radiant smile played on her lips.

There was suddenly so much awkwardness in the atmosphere that even Kenneth, who was usually oblivious to such matters, became perceptibly nervous. Molly rose and wished everyone a pleasant evening. Hector explained that he had to leave also and then offered Molly a ride home. She regarded him mockingly and then, surprising herself, said, "Ah, yes, of course, Mr. Eriksson."

He dropped his gloves and then his tricorne. He offered her his arm. He re-offered it after adjusting his coat hastily. Shouldering the driver aside, he opened the carriage door for her and then asked whether she would mind taking a stroll with him along the shore. She chuckled dryly and agreed. They rode in silence, thinking very different thoughts. At last, the carriage stopped. Hector jumped out and offered his arm again.

Still in silence, they walked along the shoreline. The breeze from the sea played with Molly's hair. She realized he expected her to speak first.

"I meant to take revenge on you," she said.

"I don't blame you," he replied quickly. "When I arrived at the city jail to get you out, your cell was empty. I..."

She shook her head and laid a hand on his shoulder.

"Please don't lie now. The war was in full swing, and you betrayed me. There is no city jail in Mappensville. They put me in the one in Brownville, ten miles away."

"Brownville, of course."

"You didn't even know."

"Of course I knew!" he protested, realizing it was hopeless. He had no proof. She would never believe him. "I was there, I tell you! I had an agreement with them, they were going to put you in jail for two days. You would have gotten yourself killed otherwise."

"You just said you came for me the next day."

"Yes, I did! You would have jumped right into the fray; the battle was on your estate; the house was leveled..."

"You don't have to do this," she said in a maddeningly dismissive tone. "Please. It's pathetic. I don't like blatant lies. You're not a natural liar, Mr. Eriksson, and it doesn't become you."

He sighed. In helpless rage, he bit his lip. Blood came. He could cry. He covered his face.

"I really did go there to set you free!"

He was getting on her nerves with this nonsense.

"You could have just kept me at your place until it was over," she said coldly.

"I had to go away for a few hours."

"Please stop. You might end up telling me you turned me over to them because you loved me."

"That's exactly why... Look, I know it's hard to believe..."

She stopped abruptly and, raising a hand and turning away from him, said, "Please. I don't want to hear it. Have some respect for me and for yourself. Stuff of that sort just happens. There are moments when we have no choice but to betray others."

They stood motionless for a while, and then resumed walking. Hector was grimly silent.

Molly felt almost happy. She was free, no longer homeless, and her best years were still ahead of her. She felt strong and healthy. And womanly, in a way she had never felt before. Even at twenty-three, when she first met Hector, she was still a little too young. She had been sexually dormant all these years. Now, she was fully developed – she wanted a man, sex, the scent and movement of sex, the exchange of life forces and fluids, the screams and roars. She figured she deserved it. The man she had once loved was beside her, as handsome as ever. Suddenly Molly stopped and faced him.

"Have I changed much?"

"Yes."

"Do I look much older?"

"No. There's something new about your mannerisms. Unfamiliar, slightly vulgar, and very enticing."

He made his reply without thinking, reckoning that, since things could not get any worse, there was no point in not telling the truth.

The planks of the pier were damp and creaky. He turned away from her, sat on a cleat, stared at the water. Molly approached him from behind, squatted at his side, looked up at him, half-rose, took his head between her palms, and kissed him on the lips. Once the initial shock was over, he returned the kiss. He rose, lifting her to her feet. The second kiss was longer and more aggressive. Molly made an unostentatious movement. A dagger, glittering in the moonlight, flew throw the air and fell into the water.

NINE

A Year Later

Kenneth Sloan made two impulsive trips to New York and came back with some money both times, managing to sell a number of pieces to a number of young, unscrupulous and needlessly aggressive art dealers. Also, he wrote and sent another letter to Mt. Vernon, and this time there was a reply from the landowner himself. The gist of the missive was that an artist of such prodigious ability as Mr. Sloan should be able to make his name known without anyone's help. It was suggested to Mr. Sloan that he should work hard, never give up, and believe in himself. The author of the letter informed the addressee that he was too busy to continue corresponding with the artist. The messenger who delivered the letter presented Kenneth with a neat leather purse containing three hundred newly coined dollars.

Patty was so smitten, she moved in with the artist and became his principle model, cook, chambermaid, mistress, active assistant and secretary, not necessarily in that order.

Reclining on the bench half-naked, which was her new and gratifying habit – he had explained to her that there was nothing quite as beautiful as a woman's body – a book in her hand, Patty shook her mane of red tresses and looked up at Kenneth.

"Great stuff, this. Lots of words I don't understand, but it's fascinating anyway."

"What?"

"The book I'm reading." She looked at the cover. "Who's this... Shakespeare fellow, anyway?"

"A playwright, I guess. I don't know much about literature. Reading takes away from my inspiration."

"So how come you've got all these books?"

"Friends. I have lots of literary friends, and they all want to educate me. They keep giving me books."

Kenneth's private library consisted of twenty three volumes – translations from Greek and Latin, one King James Bible, one two-hundred-year old Spanish satire, one British spoof on naval exploits, some British plays, some poorly adapted French plays, and three neatly bound copies of Thomas Paine's *Common Sense*. He never opened any of them.

"I had no idea reading could be so much fun," Patty told him. "It's like a different world. I used to think rich people read books in order to make everyone else look stupid."

"Nah," Kenneth said. "I think people *write* books to do that."

In more ways than one, Patty was very much a child. Still, being street-smart, she knew instinctively that only a person of Kenneth's stamp would agree to live with her. For hundreds of miles – indeed, for thousands and thousands of miles – no man, no matter how low his station, would share his life with a harlot – even a former harlot – on equal terms. It was not a matter of individual taste. It was public opinion, stubbornly concerned with the currently popular set of rules and notions of propriety, that would not allow an ordinary man to live in peace if his wife's past included prostitution. Across the world, the rule for women was, get the best man you can, stick to him like glue, live off him – and abuse anyone who does not subscribe to your philosophy. The question no one ever thought of asking was, how different is prostitution from this kind of acceptable behavior? Shortly after Miles married Molly, he mentioned to her that "In any epoch, people stick to what they know, and while what they normally know is hardly worth knowing, they are too lazy or too intimidated to consider other possibilities, which is why they always fall back on jejune hypocrisy." Molly never attached much significance to what her light-hearted, roguish husband said. Patty might have listened.

Kenneth finished priming a canvas, set it aside, and began to stretch the next one. The stretcher cracked. Kenneth cursed under his breath, found a suitable plank in the wastebasket, fished a pair of nails out of the pile of hardware on the table, and started repairing the stretcher.

"How's our friend Ruth doing?" he asked.

"She's married now."

"You're kidding me. Who's the luckiest fellow alive?"

"Your client. Hector Eriksson."

Kenneth dropped the hammer.

"Eriksson! She must be out of her mind."

"Why?"

"He's the most notorious ladies' man in town."

"He's rich, isn't he?"

"He's in debt."

"You're kidding! Why?"

Kenneth drove the first nail into the plank. The stretcher's side split. He swore and threw the hammer away.

"He keeps investing all his money in his ship projects," he said. "It would help if he got a big contract. That's what I'm doing for him, by the way – a picture of one of his future ships, the way he sees it, so he can show it off to someone who's promised to finance his next venture."

"Oh."

Kenneth went into a corner, rummaged in the batch of canvases stacked there, extracted one, brought it over and showed it to Patty. They called them *clipper* ships, he explained. According to Hector, the best clipper ever was being designed right now. It was going to be the fastest and most durable one yet. Hector had brought Kenneth the first draft, explaining what was what, so it could be painted. Hector expected to make a lot of money on it.

"You're so talented! ..." she said admiringly.

She studied the picture. The ocean looked a lot like weak tea with lumps of sugar floating despondently in it, but the ship itself was a beauty – slender, slick, the masts stretching elegantly towards the mauve sky, the canvas sails fluttering in the morning breeze. Patty shook her head in awe. Kenneth was as easy to please as any gifted artist. His face reddened with pleasure.

"Oh, and another thing..." Patty said, leaning the canvas cautiously against the bench, "She's pregnant."

"Who, Ruth? Wow! She is? ..." He considered this. The idea appealed to his sense of humor. He was not a particularly bright man, but his talent enabled him to glimpse more future possibilities than most others could envision. He could not explain how he saw what he saw. "You know, Hector used to have a mansion in these parts," he said thoughtfully.

"They now live in a two-story house just off the business district. They have a maid."

The windows of the two-story house just off the business district looked out on a square. In order to finance the prototype clipper so that Jerome could assess it and give him money to build five more, Hector had sold his house on the outskirts.

Molly, hugely and happily pregnant, in a slovenly-looking yet clean dress, sat at the window, her eyes half-closed, her lips forming a half-happy, half-mischievous smile. For a moment, she stopped smiling, and suddenly the Molly Bates of yesteryear was gone. The face was that of a woman of almost thirty who was confident and authoritative in a hard, relentless, punishing way. She gazed across the square. Standing at the opposite side of it was a man in light-colored clothes, his left hand resting casually on the hilt of his sword. The posture suggested Miles. Molly did not bat an eye. The past no longer bothered her. Miles was part of the past. He was an adventurer, a rogue, and a spy. His illegitimate offspring were scattered all over the globe, yet in the course of their marriage he never managed to give her a child, prompting a doctor to diagnose her as barren. Go away, Miles. We'll never meet again. We have no use for each other.

A voice behind her said, "Told you."

Molly turned. Raymond, in jeans, hands in pockets, gazed at her mockingly. Her own loquacious ghost from the future.

"You were right about a lot of things."

Indicating her belly with a nod, he observed, "My ancestor, I presume."

"I guess so."

"And the portrait?"

She chuckled happily.

"Oh! You're vain, too!" he drawled mockingly.

"It was a big hit in Paris, or so they tell me. Unfortunately, there's a lot of civil unrest in France. Poor Kenneth had to go back home again. He now lives with a friend of mine. They're considering marriage. I don't think they're going to erect a monument for me, though, so you were wrong there."

There was the sound of steps. Molly glanced at the door. She looked back at Raymond and realized he was gone. The door opened. Hector stormed in and ran to her. She rose with some difficulty to meet him. They embraced.

"Darling," he whispered.

She stroked his hair. She kissed him passionately.

"Listen," he said excitedly. "I got a short-term contract in Boston; they want me to design a battleship. Should take me about two weeks."

"You're going away?" she asked, darkening.

Part Three

Praxidice

TEN

Ten Years Later: Jefferson's Man In Paris

A breathtakingly graceful and fantastically speedy ship traveled across the roaring Atlantic, carrying a simple-looking, wax-sealed letter. The missive was delivered to the addressee twenty days after the vessel's departure from Boston. The letter said, "*October 9, 1791. Dear Crawford. I can hardly express my gratitude. Your kind and selfless support has worked miracles for me. Mr. Hamilton and Mr. Jefferson are now both keenly interested in my projects. If everything goes according to plan, I shall get an order from the Government for a large number of ships. They seem to want a few for their coast guard. My competitors are bursting with envy. Ruth doesn't know anything yet. Of my two children are coming along nicely. The older one is now ten and is a beauty. My son has just turned four. You exaggerated when you said that I saved your life. Anyone in my place would have given you a warning. Speaking of gratitude. The ship by which this letter arrives is yours. Jerome, in his atrocious greed, overestimated the demand, and we built one too many. No one seems to be able to afford her; the company had to take a loss. I have no use for ships once they're out in open sea. My place is the shipyard, not the fishpond. If you think you could maintain her properly, she will be kind to you. False modesty aside, she's one of the fastest movers on this planet. My estimate is that she can cover the distance between Boston and Dover in a mere fifteen days. See if you can top that. Ruth sends her regards.*
Sincerely Yours, Hector Eriksson.
P.S. They tell me the King has gone bananas. I'm curious. Has he, really?"

It was the age of light, darkness, and what not, and the ancient city of Paris was in turmoil. The third year of the Revolution was almost over, the King was dead, the Queen was in prison and had no power, the National Assembly did have power but could not decide how it might, or should, use it, the *sharp maiden, newly born and called La Guillotine* had been recently adopted as the tool of choice for chopping people's heads off to amuse the rabble. When the rabble got tired of watching the maiden's melancholy act, they provided their own entertainment, hanging suspected aristocrats, immigrants, and their alleged sympathizers, from lampposts which made the said offenders look like human pendulums. A number of European monarchies threatened to invade, and food ran short. Street muggings were common but half-hearted since few people had anything in which the muggers might be interested. And, of course, there were rumors.

For instance, some people maintained that either Marat or Robespierre was soon going to be crowned at Notre Dame and, after pardoning Marie Antoinette, would marry her. Others whispered conspiratorially that England would soon annex most of the Isle-de-France, put an end to the anarchy, and feed everybody English mutton and beer. Still others had it from most reputable sources that America, currently known as *L'Etats Unis*, was about to give Robespierre twenty million in platinum American francs to feed and clothe the Republican Army that would subsequently invade England and bring back English mutton, clothes, horses, gold and what not, after which the people of Paris would be guaranteed easy living for the next ten years.

On the second floor of a large, sturdy house on the Rue des Escoufes in Marais, there were two apartments. The one on the right-hand side was occupied by a revolutionary lawyer from the provinces (all other lawyer types ran the risk of being hanged from a lamppost). The apartment to the left of the stairs had been hired out to an American some years ago who used to have other, more respectable, lodgings in the city and used the place exclusively to conduct an illicit love affair with a very good-looking, enchantingly young woman of partly African origin.

The American had left three years ago but, shortly before his departure, he had turned the place over to a friend of his who was a foreign nobleman of sorts. The new lodger's presence in the house soon resulted in some very drastic changes. Thus, the third-floor tenant, a common thief, after being thrown down the stairs twice in the course of only ten minutes, ceased urinating on the landing and even did some necessary cleaning in the foyer now and then. The landlord, who occupied the rooms on the first floor, purchased some rat poison and used it well and also, after a closed-door chat with the new lodger, limited his wife-beating sessions to one per week, always making sure first that the lodger was not at home.

Miles Crawford's sojourn in Paris was pleasant enough at first. No city can offer a true epicurean so many exquisite opportunities as Paris – in times of peace. But with the advent of pendulum justice, Miles could no longer enjoy himself properly.

Some days previously, a line of coaches transporting priests to a prison was attacked by a furious mob consisting mostly of career criminals, petty pranksters, and uneducated youngsters who figured they could now get away with pretty much anything. The revolutionaries escorting the priests joined the mob in hacking the nineteen prelates into little pieces using knives, sabers, and axes. Later on that evening, a convent that was being used as a prison for one hundred and fifty priests was raided and most of the inmates were murdered.

The blood-frenzy prevailed throughout the city. Proclamations were / distributed everywhere, spreading the message that some very egregious people sitting in a prison were plotting a breakout and would help the Prussians take Paris. Why the Prussians in particular, or which prison, was unknown and, in the final analysis, completely unimportant. In order to ruin this royalist plot, the publishers of the proclamations demanded the murder of the priests and former Swiss Guards in all prisons. A court was set up most of whose officers were paid thugs. They were authorized to execute the court's orders. Most of the prisoners murdered had little to do with politics; they were petty criminals. In one of the women's prisons, the mob killed thirty prostitutes.

Princess de Lamballe, after deciding naively to be brave and noble in the face of adversity, refused to condemn the monarchy and was locked up. When the rage reached her prison, she was dragged out of her cell, raped, beaten, raped again, sexually mutilated with knives, and then beheaded.

Miles breakfasted at the café adjacent to the general shop across the street from his apartment house. A benevolent-looking elderly Jew by the name of Abraham, who was fond of his customer enough to be willing to give him his only daughter in marriage, owned both establishments. The daughter, Sarah, who was far more conservative than her father (and, let us mention it in passing, far more intelligent), would not mind marrying Miles, perhaps (who, at fifty, was still very much a quintessential knight errant, sans fear and sans reproach), but for the fact that his levity in such matters promised no future to which she could comfortably resign herself. She had a suitor – a thin, boisterous Hebrew youth from the Notre Dame vicinity whom she was determined to marry when the political situation in the country stabilized itself. Jumping the gun, let us mention right now before we forget, that she did marry him eventually and that their great-granddaughter went on to become the most famous stage actress in French history.

It was a mild September morning. Miles was peacefully having breakfast at the café, savoring the delicate omelet, frowning at the coffee that was a little too weak, and generally minding his own business when something occurred that would have put a less squeamish man than Miles off his food. A well-dressed woman burst into the place, her eyes round with fear, her face deathly pale, her hands trembling. Miles wished he had brought a book in which he could now hide his face. The woman was Louise, also known as Madame de Coligny, of the family's southern branch. Only a month ago, she and Miles had been lovers.

"Monsieurs!" she cried, "please help me! They're after me! They're going to kill me!"

Sarah and one of the waiters rushed to assist her. She was about to faint. Abraham came out, attracted by the noise.

"What's going on?" he demanded.

At that moment, four men came stomping in – neither young nor old, but sweaty, unwashed, and with unhealthy fire in their eyes.

"Hey!" one of them shouted, "that bitch is an aristocrat who refuses to condemn the monarchy! Let her go, we're going to do to her what we did to the Lamballe whore – get out of the way, people!"

They pushed Sarah and the waiter aside, knocked a table over, and grabbed Madame De Coligny. She screamed. In another moment, they threw her on the floor and tore off the top of her dress.

"You will get out of here," Abraham shouted, shaking with rage, fear, and loathing, "and before you go, you will give me your names. I will report you to the police."

"Our names?" one of the men raised his head and, without releasing the poor woman's arm and throat, seethed eerily. "My name is Justice. His name," he nodded, indicating one of his comrades who was in the meantime fumbling with Madame De Coligny's skirt, "is Vengeance. And their names," he indicated the other two, who were in the meantime tearing apart the woman's bodice, "are People's Glory and People's Blood."

"And my name," a voice behind them said, "is Miles Crawford. And I'll give you toads five seconds to make yourselves scarce. And if you don't, I'll have no choice but to cut off your balls, one at a time, with a very blunt and very rusty kitchen knife."

They were astonished. They were insulted. One of them continued holding Louise down while the others scrambled to their feet and pounced on Miles. They were vigorous, determined, and vicious, but the lack of room in the café hindered them. They could not surround Miles at once. One of them pulled out a knife. Miles had no time to draw his sword. He kicked the knife bearer in the groin and grabbed his wrist, simultaneously elbowing the second thug in the face. The wrist cracked and the knife fell to the floor. Absorbing a blow to the head from the third attacker, Miles flew into a rage.

No combat specialist can get the better of more than three attackers at a time out in the open. But in an enclosed space, contests become a matter of angles, distances, and timing. The power of the first blow Miles managed to land would have been sufficient to make a hole in the thick limestone wall of the café. The third attacker's jaw shattered. Miles chopped the second thug's neck. The fourth man, releasing Louise, produced a pistol. Miles, having disposed of the other three, kicked the pistol away, grabbed the fellow's collar, and punched him squarely in the face seven or eight times in quick succession.

The fellow who had gotten it in the neck was coughing up blood.

One by one, Miles lifted his prostrate adversaries to their feet and shoved them out.

He approached the bar. The waiter poured him a glass of wine silently and reverentially. Miles downed it.

"Monsieur," Abraham said.

"Abraham," Miles interrupted him. "I'm sorry, but I believe it would be better for everyone if you left town for a few months. Shut up shop, take your daughter, and vanish. You've done nothing wrong, but they will be back, and there will be more of them. They'll be angry and they'll thrash the place. You have about an hour."

Abraham immediately saw the wisdom of Miles' advice. "Monsieur," he said, "would you mind not leaving in the next ten minutes?"

"No problem."

Abraham disappeared into the living quarters. Sarah stared at Miles. Madame De Coligny groped for the parts of her clothes on the floor. Miles pulled his coat from the chair and, walking over, wrapped her in it. She rose to her feet, fumbling with the sleeves.

"You're coming with me," Miles said.

"Craw-FORE," she stammered, gallicizing his name.

"It's all right, Louise. Have a drink."

Ten minutes later, Abraham came out, carrying a small portmanteau. Sarah ran to him and pressed her head to his shoulder.

"Good luck, Abraham," Miles said.

"Thank you, Monsieur. This is very unfortunate."

"Yes, I know. I'm terribly sorry."

"Good luck to you too."

Sarah ran up to Miles and kissed him impulsively on the cheek. Unexpectedly, he blushed.

Leading Louise out of the café, he dragged her through the Place de Vosges, and further. After expressing her gratitude humbly, she confessed she had no idea what to do now. They would certainly come for her if she went home. She had to leave the city.

"I should have left with the Jew," she said.

Miles winced. "Abraham has a lot of problems of his own, and he has a daughter to take care of."

"I'd pay him."

"He'd decline. Anyway, I thought you were well-protected. What happened?"

"We quarreled."

"Goodness gracious, when?"

"Yesterday."

"Why?"

"I called him a murderer."

"What about your husband?"

"He's dead."

"And the children?"

"In England, with their uncle."

Miles stopped and looked at her. Love and pity are cousins. She was just over thirty, and still very pretty, in a fragrantly vague Parisian way. She was almost as tall as he, dark, with enormous eyes and touching tiny freckles on her nose.

She was well-educated, not particularly bright, bubbly and a drifter, and had an annoying habit of calling everyone My Little Friend. It sounded a little less absurd in French; but it was still pretty stupid and embarrassing, especially in good company. She also, Miles had to admit, knew how to be absolutely happy most of the time. She enjoyed life unconditionally. Among the things that made her happy were a sunny day, a rainy day, the Big Dipper, Orion's Belt, falling leaves, cigar smoke, fresh air, good wine, bad wine, handsome men, ugly women, German music, picnics, balls, dancing, goofing around, morning dew, fine food, simple food, English novels in French translation, diamonds, Russia, sweets, honey, ill-paved streets, medieval architecture, Italy, rough sex, tender and sensual sex, elegant clothes, peasant clothes, Africa, elephants, Marie-Antoinette, General Washington, bathing, Greek mythology, *Figaro's Marriage*, and, until very recently, the Revolution. She was also fond of church bells.

"You'd better take care of yourself, you know. You only have a day," she said sadly.

"Meaning?"

"They're going to arrest every Englishman in Paris tomorrow."

"Whence this news?"

"He told me."

"I'm not an Englishman. I'm a Yankee."

"You look like an Englishman, my little friend. You dress like an

Englishman."

"Thanks for telling me. Now I know what to do."

They turned a corner. They walked quickly down the street, passing the square with the fountain and reaching a tiny side lane where the people they encountered looked strange and hostile. Miles knocked on a door. He knocked again. The door opened a crack, a suspicious eye scanning the visitors.

"Yes?"

"I need to see Vasquez."

"Your name?"

"Jacquot."

Apparently, Miles had a number of different identities in Paris.

The door closed. A minute later, it opened again, wider this time. Miles led Louise into the house.

On the second floor, in a shabby room full of very shady characters and foul odors, he introduced Louise to Vasquez, a middle-aged, wiry fellow with an eye patch.

"Listen," Miles said. "This is Louise. I'll be back sometime in the late afternoon. I want you to take care of her."

"Yeah?" Vasquez smiled ominously.

Louise trembled.

"Tell your cutthroats to leave the room for a few moments," Miles suggested.

Vasquez considered this. The longer the pause stretched, the more important he looked in everyone's eyes. Eventually, he motioned to the others. They exchanged derisive looks and filed out.

"Listen," Miles said. "She loves to talk, and so do you, but neither of you like to admit it. Here's your chance. Talk your silly heads off. I just want you two to be inseparable until I come back."

"That'll cost you," Vasquez said.

"I know. It doesn't matter. But I mean it. If you need to pee, take her with you. If she needs to pee, follow her and watch her. Hope you're into that kind of thing, cause, personally, I'm not. If anyone, and I mean *anyone*, lays a hand on her or even speaks to her kindly about the weather, I'll hold you personally responsible. You will die an ugly death, Vasquez."

"No need to threaten me," Vasquez said angrily. "If you're paying, I don't see a problem."

Miles threw a leather purse to Vasquez. The latter caught it deftly.

"That's the advance. You'll get the rest when I come back. Louise, don't be afraid of anything. He's very reliable. He has a noble heart." Vasquez reddened suddenly with pleasure. "Tell him about your trip to Africa as a child, he loves innocent adventures."

She had no choice. Besides, she liked Vasquez. The eye patch made him look like a pirate from a fairy tale, which instantly made her unreasonably happy.

Miles returned to the Place de Vosges, and from there continued to the Rue de Rivoli. He crossed the river and found himself on the Isle of St. Louis. During his sojourn in Paris, he spent at least an hour here every day. The tiny island, with its formidable buildings and narrow lanes, appealed to Miles' sense of coziness. He wondered what it would take to put up some bad-ass fortifications around it, blow up the bridges, and declare an independent state. The north side of the island could be cleared of buildings and transformed into a farm large enough to sustain the population. The south side, with its magnificent view of Notre Dame across the river, had wonderful possibilities as a fashionable embankment. And in the middle of this paradise on earth, Miles would select a roomy apartment with a good fireplace and finally don his robe with tassels. Thunder and lightning.

The robe was definitely a problem. In Paris, there were shortages of everything now. The robes that were available were either tassel-less, much too tight, or much too heavy to relax inside of. Generally, the kind of robe Miles favored was made in only two places on the planet. Essex, England was one. Tuxedo, New York, was the other. Thomas Jefferson, his employer, never took his passion for robes seriously and, despite promising Miles before departing for the States that he would absolutely, definitely, assuredly order one upon arrival and send it over promptly, had never lived up to his promise. The traditional fickleness of a politician. Now that he was Secretary of State, all he sent Miles was orders. Using his own contacts, Miles had twice shipped money to England and once his dream robe was on its way across the Channel when, unexpectedly, the schooner was boarded by self-complacent revolutionary pirates who, after grappling her, talked the crew into joining them. The schooner was abandoned in the middle of the Channel. She drifted back towards England, where she was sunk by a cannon volley from one of His Majesty's frigates whose captain mistook it for a Dutch reconnaissance vessel.

Today, Miles walked through the isle without stopping and crossed over to another one, the heart of Paris called the Cite. Passing Notre Dame and the market, he strolled one block down the Embankment and crossed the water again using the Pont St. Michel. He normally spent some time in each of the three bookstores there. Not today.

At fifty, Miles was pretty much the same man he had been at thirty-four, at the beginning of our story. Yes, there were streaks of gray in his long jet-black hair, and his hairline was receding at the temples. He now wore a short, neat beard and mustache – and there was some gray in those as well. But the erect posture, intelligent hazel eyes, wiry strength, superhuman agility, and unstoppable energy that came and went in great bursts were still his, as was the perpetual snobbish fastidiousness of his everyday facial expression. The rabble that thought nothing of hanging a passing aristocrat from the nearest lamppost invariably found themselves wondering collectively whether picking on Miles was worth the trouble he might give them. About once a month, a crowd got too confident, too sure of its overwhelming numbers and too incensed by Miles' obviously beau monde, albeit foreign, clothes, to consider the consequences, and attacked him. A dozen times, he was able to keep them at bay with his sword and pistol. Twice, he was able to talk his way out of trouble. Once, he admitted he was an American official – and was let go. America was an ally.

Today, none of that had any significance. Miles knew that his sojourn in Paris was over. A good thing, too. He had no idea how much longer he would be able to contemplate lamppost justice, all those surreal pendulums swinging in the wind and, in the streets, all those begging children, unwashed and unfed men and women in rags – it was bad for one's morale, it threatened to skew one's sense of aesthetics. And while *Figaro's Marriage* was a fine play, it was not the only play in the world, no matter what the Parisian theatre entrepreneurs thought. A long-forgotten playwright from the Elizabethan era was being re-discovered in England and in the States, called Shakespeare, and Miles, a bibliophile in his own right, was eager to see a live performance of *Hamlet*. Listening to Danton and Marat in public places was fun at first, what with the mob's amusing reactions of "Hear, hear!" and "That's the stuff, yeah!" But the novelty soon wore off, especially after Miles realized that each time the mob listened to one of those temperamental orators, it would then run around en masse in quest of fresh defenseless victims it could beat up and hang from lampposts. Simply walking down the street had become a chore. The rabble, as the rabble will when impunity is guaranteed, defied every well-dressed man and woman with sickening obnoxiousness, blocking people's way, asking them rudely to move over, bumping everybody and proceeding without an apology. They behaved as though they owned the city which, to an extent, they did. They were somewhat more cautious around Miles, feeling instinctively that the man was neither particularly patient nor meek. Still, an atmosphere of fear and loathing hung over the city at all times and was depressing.

Well, a letter from Philly had arrived last week, and he had to deliver

Jefferson's answer to the National Assembly before leaving. Jefferson wrote, simply, that the President of the United States, wielding his power of veto like an expert politician, refused unequivocally to side with France and insisted that regardless of what happened between this other newly born Republic and the surrounding monarchies, America was going to maintain strict neutrality. Jefferson, very partial to France, resented the President's stance but was powerless, or so he claimed, to help. It now fell to Miles ("*I'm awfully sorry, Crawford*") to inform the revolutionary government of the situation.

This was *so* unfair that for a moment Miles considered retiring permanently to South Africa or some other naturally exotic place. Irresponsible nonsense, that, since he had no other employer or income, and had just saddled himself with another responsibility – that of getting his former mistress out of the city, and perhaps out of the country as well. He had not asked for it, but there it was.

As for the present task, it was merely a matter of choosing, from a reasonably large field, a National Assembly member and delivering the joyous news to him. That was a no-brainer. Marat was a hothead who did not think much of American support to begin with. He might not take Miles and his message seriously. There was Danton, who believed in clothing and feeding the army and, perhaps, the civilians also, soon – or else, now that they knew how, the liberated citizens of the Republic would soon give the Assembly a fresh armed revolt to deal with. Danton counted on the Americans and would be sorely disappointed. Besides, Miles did not like him personally. The fact that Danton was Louise's lover did not help at all. Miles had no special feelings for Louise, but her choice of successor struck him as absurd and, to some degree, tactless.

This left a number of lesser patriots, plus the short, swarthy fellow called Maximillian Robespierre.

Miles had the private addresses of all the principle big shots. Robespierre resided on the Rue de Vaugirard, a block away from the Luxemburg Gardens. Perhaps the fact that, of all the members of the Assembly, his house was closest to Miles' daily itinerary was the deciding factor in the latter's choice. The Medici Fountain, in which two centuries earlier the proud Queen-mother had her lovers drowned when she grew tired of them, had a bad aura about it. Casual walkers and lovers, of whom in the Gardens there was never a shortage, avoided it like a plague. Miles bravely approached the fountain and, squatting at the edge, loaded both his pistols, measuring the powder exactly, using the ramrod carefully. He drew his sword and examined the edges and the point meticulously. He opened his portmanteau, satisfying himself that his spurs were inside, next to Jefferson's scribbling and the money, as well as the *Kastoweh* (a feathered hat, in the Mohawk language) that he meant to present to Robespierre as a peace offering, and some other things. At last he was ready. He looked at the Fountain with some disgust.

"Fucking bitch," he muttered.

Two revolutionary guards stopped him at the entrance of Robespierre's house.

"State your business, Monsieur."

Miles produced a scroll with a seal depicting an airborne bald eagle.

"I'm here on behalf of the Secretary of State of the United States of America."

"Oh, really?" one of the guards drawled doubtfully. "Your French is too good, Monsieur. Are you sure you aren't French?"

"Oh, geez," Miles said frustratedly. "You should have been a professional phonetician, man. You should quit your job and join some, I don't know, some linguistic society, or something. Go and announce me, you mangy frog."

The guards laughed. One of them stayed with Miles while the other went upstairs.

"The weather's been very bad lately," the guard who remained said.

"So it would seem."

"Hey, did you hear those rumors about improving the Guillotine?"

"No."

"Hey, it's, like, state-of-the-art now. It's very efficient."

Miles winced.

"The Republic has too many enemies," the guard announced didactically. "We're short of executioners."

"Maybe you should volunteer."

"Maybe. They don't pay much, though. Most executioners work for free. Hey, Monsieur, you're an American, right? What language do you folks speak in America?"

"Polish."

"Really? Wow. My brother speaks some Dutch and Spanish. So, what's the difference between an American and a Pole?"

The other guard returned.

"You may proceed, Monsieur."

"Thank you."

"*Vive la République!*"

Miles straightened his coat. "But of course," he said, stepping over the threshold.

In his youth, Robespierre had been a mild, debonair type, cringing at the sight of dead animals and practicing partial vegetarianism. His ascent to power had been marked by a drastic change of attitude. There were rumors about an unhappy love affair. Be that as it may, the man Miles had to deal with now was a cynical and cruel hypocrite. And yet, there was something appealing about him. No man, no matter how ruthless, can expect to attain a high position in society without someone liking him.

"Good afternoon, Milord," Robespierre said with mild sarcasm. "What news?"

"The weather's been very bad lately," Miles reported. "There are lots of provincials in Paris these days. Because a great deal of native Parisians are, for one reason or another, gone, there's a sort of vacuum out there that attracts others. You can rent an apartment now anywhere in the city at half the usual price."

"Indeed," Robespierre said gravely. "Pray sit down, Monsieur."

"Yes, thank you," Miles continued, seating himself and crossing his legs. "Also, the food, where it's still available, is extremely pricey. Another thing is, no one cleans the streets anymore, which is why the city is full of queer odors. New epidemics may be around the corner."

Unsmiling, Robespierre raised his hand, bidding Miles to be quiet for a moment.

"I'm not interested in any of that," he said.

"I didn't think you were. Things would be different if you took a little interest in everyday matters."

"I'm mostly curious about the Americans' position," Robespierre reminded him. "Your people promised us money and soldiers. We are besieged by every monarchy in Europe."

"Who made this promise, Monsieur?"

"Why, Monsieur Jefferson did."

Robespierre became concerned. From Miles' attitude, he could deduce that there might be a delay. At least. The Americans were being cautious. Neither gold nor soldiers could be expected soon.

"Monsieur Jefferson is a very kind man," Miles said. "He's also my immediate superior. However, in his capacity as ambassador, he had no right to make any such promises, I'll have you know."

"I hear he has a different job now."

Miles laughed. Robespierre was taken aback.

"Yes," Miles said, "That is your own fault."

Robespierre was not fully accustomed to Miles' diplomatic methods. He fell into Jefferson's man's trap by asking, "What do you mean, Monsieur?"

"If you hadn't started this circus with human pendulums hanging from lampposts, Monsieur Jefferson would still be in Paris. He's very fond of this city. Of course, it would have delayed the writing of the Constitution and presidential election, but, hey, there are two sides to every coin, unless it's counterfeit."

Robespierre studied Miles. The two men knew each other from previous encounters. Jefferson's man in Paris, with his graying black hair, his mocking hazel eyes, his haughty posture, did not fit the Frenchman's notions of a foreign representative. Robespierre, who regarded himself as an expert, had a hard time figuring Miles out. An American with the attitude of an English lord who spoke French better than most Frenchmen, a rogue adored by women and feared by men (as Robespierre's spies assured him), a diplomat who shunned public functions and frequented Left Bank cafes, was an enigma.

"The measure of society, Monsieur," Robespierre said sternly, "is how it treats the average person. The Republic cannot cease punishing its enemies simply because a foreign diplomat finds the view from his window a little disturbing. Monsieur Jefferson made certain promises…"

"The measure of society," Miles interrupted him, "is how it treats the simple pleasures of a man like myself. I have seen many societies, Monsieur, and so far, I have found them all oddly inadequate in that aspect."

"I don't want to argue with you, Monsieur."

"Nor I with you, Monsieur."

"Do you have any news for me?"

"Yes."

"Let's have it."

This was it. No more verbal fencing. Miles had to tell him. He had no choice. He was cornered. Jefferson had set him up. A politician's gratitude for many years of service. For the sterling track record. For the French Army and Navy assisting in America's cause. For the scandals hushed up in Prussia. For Sweden's neutrality. For Russia's silent approval and gold. For Spain's grudging approval and non-interference. For History's indifference – the chronicles were going to ascribe everything to Franklin's efforts. For all that, Miles now had to deliver the bad news. Thank you, Jefferson. Thank you.

"Monsieur," he said. "I understand there are two things you wish to know. One, will America send her sons to die for this country's independence? Two, will America give you funds so that you can hire other professional soldiers to defend your independence? The answer to both questions is in the negative. As an official representative of the United States, I hereby inform you that America will maintain strict neutrality in regard to your conflicts with foreign powers."

Robespierre grew very pale.

"Do you realize what you're saying, Monsieur?" he asked ominously. "We were counting on your support! We have repeatedly told the people of France that they were safe from foreign invasions because the Americans would never let us down! There will be panic in the city! Panic in the Republic! There will be armed revolts!"

Miles stroked the pommel of his sword thoughtfully.

"I suppose you're right," he said. "You've made too many promises to your people. I'm terribly sorry."

"*I* made promises!"

"Yes."

"Monsieur, I'm here to ensure that the interests of all Frenchmen are properly safeguarded. I…"

"The best way to ensure that, Monsieur," Miles said seriously, "is to put all Frenchmen in jail and triple the number of guards."

Miles rose. Robespierre rose also, glaring. Miles bowed politely, turned on his heel, and left the room, deciding that, what with his belligerent attitude, the Frenchman did not deserve the *Kastoveh*. Robespierre rang. A guard entered.

"Quick," Robespierre said. "Don't let him leave the quarter. Stab him, shoot him! The population must never find out that the Americans are abandoning us to the whim of fate!"

He was a passionate man. He was also a rash man, which eventually led him to the Guillotine.

Miles knew. He left Robespierre's house as quickly as he dared. Reaching the corner, he ran. Reaching the Luxemburg Gardens, he made for the gate, but it was locked.

"Fucking frogs!" Miles muttered, cursing the nation's disgusting habit of locking gates at any time under the flimsiest pretexts. He ran further, through the Latin Quarter, and onto the Embankment. He looked around. There were no signs of pursuit. He breathed easier. He crossed over to Marais. He saw two guards at the end of the street and turned immediately, walking briskly along the Rue St. Antoine. He noticed a carriage parked at the ancient church. The anti-clerical movement was in full swing. The church was empty. Miles jumped onto the box, causing the driver to cry out in surprise. Pressing the muzzle of his pistol to the fellow's solar plexus, Miles said, "Towards the Bastille, and I'll tell you where to turn once we get there. Quick."

"Hey," the driver protested.

"In the name of the Republic," Miles added meaningfully. "Unless you wish to end your miserable days on the Guillotine."

The argument worked. The driver lashed the horses. They were young, vigorous animals. They set off at a trot. On an impulse, Miles started singing *La Marseillaise*, a new and popular revolutionary ditty whose opening bars were lifted directly from Mozart's *Piano Concerto No. 25*.

"Allons enfants de la Patrie! Le jour de gloire est arrivé!"

He discovered he was in voice. This pleased him immensely. When he started the second verse, the driver joined in, singing an octave higher.

"Que veut cette horde d'esclaves, De traîtres, de rois conjurés?"

They had to slow down at the place where the Bastille used to stand. Upon Miles' instructions, the driver, patriotic fire in his eyes, turned left. There was some traffic. Suddenly, a number of pedestrians began to sing along. Soon, the entire street was shaking with the mighty chorus. Miles felt a wave of patriotism surge through him. He tore off his hat and brandished it. The entire street followed his example. The carriage crossed the Rue des Archives and the song ended.

They stopped at the familiar door. Miles gave the driver ten francs and a warm hug. There were tears in the driver's eyes.

"Thank you, Monsieur," he said. *"Vive La République!"*

"Absolutely," Miles agreed.

Louise and Vasquez were playing chess.

Miles asked for some ink and paper and quickly composed a letter to a certain Englishman he knew who, in turn, knew all other Englishmen in the city. He sealed the letter, made Vasquez summon one of his errand boys, and instructed him to deliver the missive immediately. After paying Vasquez, who in the three hours of Miles' absence seemed to have grown extraordinarily fond of his pretty charge (who was already calling him her little friend and laughing melodiously), Miles and Louise traveled further away from Marais. They reached the outskirts, where a large, sturdy, crudely built house stood at the foot of a great hill. Miles peered through the gate and noticed the servant in the courtyard. He motioned him to approach.

"We're here to see Benjamin Carlyle," he said in English.

"And who may you be, sir?"

"Lord Crawford."

"One moment, My Lord. I'm going to announce you right now. I apologize for not letting you in right away. One cannot be too cautious in this city."

He went inside. Soon, a youngish, burly man came out and looked at Miles cheerfully.

"Hey, look who's here!" Carlyle's son Hugo said.

"Where's your father?"

"Inside."

"Would you please let us in?" Miles demanded.

"Who's the lady?"

"My wife."

"She speak any English?"

"No."

Hugo Carlyle unlocked the gate. His grin was ambiguous. Two marble wenches in suggestive poses, barely dressed, pretended to prop up the pediment over the entrance. Louise trembled, hanging on Miles' arm. He gave her a soothing look.

Benjamin's other son, Charles, was also present. The living room was neither clean nor cozily furnished. Benjamin Carlyle was a provincial baronet who had made his fortune in London some thirty years ago by revitalizing one of the Secret Service's branches, Miles was not sure which, and arresting many high society conspirators. He was a frequent guest of high society functions. And yet, he somehow managed to keep his slovenly west country habits. His two sons, big, powerful men, accompanied their father everywhere.

"Now look who's here," Benjamin smiled with malicious joy, rising. "Gustave's buttocks! It's Lord Crawford, in person. Who's the beautiful lady?"

"My wife," Miles said.

"Small wonder," the baronet chuckled. The crude ambiguity amused him. "What news, my dear fellow?"

Miles noticed that Hugo had in the meantime positioned himself between him and the door. Louise was about to faint again. The fact that the conversation was being conducted in a language with which she was not familiar added to her anxiety.

"I do have some news," Miles said. "That's why I'm here."

"You wouldn't mind passing your sword to me?" Benjamin asked sweetly, extending his hand. Out of the corner of his eye, Miles saw Charles leveling a musket at him.

"Yes, I would mind, for the moment," Miles said. "Not to worry, though. I will surrender it to you when the time comes."

"The order says, dead or alive, I believe?" Benjamin raised his bushy eyebrows.

"Yes," Miles confirmed. "But I'm sure they would pay you less for a corpse."

"That's true," Benjamin agreed. "Which is why I don't want any nonsense here. Give me your sword, Crawford. You have to understand, it's nothing personal. Gustave's buttocks, I could even put in a word for you, so that they just hang you without breaking you on the wheel first."

"Hear me out."

Benjamin regarded him arrogantly for a while.

"All right," he said. "Speak."

"My wife and I came here…"

Louise said, "What's going on?"

"Excuse me, gentlemen," Miles said and switched to French. "Everything's going according to plan. We'll be in England in less than a week, whereupon I will hand you over to your brother-in-law. Now, to ensure that nothing goes wrong, I need to speak to these creeps."

"Watch whom you're calling creeps," Hugo said maliciously in heavily accented but perfectly intelligible French.

"Sorry," Miles shrugged. "Didn't know you knew French."

"That's no excuse."

"All right, I apologize. What do you want me to do, drink castor oil? Anyway," he switched to English again, "We're here so that you, who are not creeps but respectable and trustworthy English gentlemen, can arrest me and transport me to England. After…" he emphasized the word, "*after* we drop my wife off at her relative's place, you will conduct me to London, receive your reward, and be reasonably happy for a while."

Benjamin considered the offer. Hugo and Charles looked at him expectantly.

"What's to prevent us," Benjamin said, "from throwing this… wife of yours, or whoever she is… from throwing her out and taking you directly to London?"

"A number of things," Miles assured him.

"Such as?"

"If you take me up on my offer, I will cooperate all the way. If not, the journey might become rather trying for you."

"He's threatening us," Hugo said incredulously.

"Another thing is, getting from here to Calais or even to Dieppe might be a chore, and you never know when an extra pair of hands capable of handling a sword might come to be useful. Yet another thing is, we have to set out now, I mean right now, because tomorrow every Englishman in Paris will be arrested and very possibly cut to little pieces."

Charles whistled, lowering the musket. Hugo frowned. Benjamin blinked.
"You can't be serious," he said.

"In order to survive, we have to stay ahead of the decree, gentlemen," Miles explained.

"Is this official?" Hugo demanded quickly.

"Quite."

"How did you find out?"

"From a person close to Danton."

"Shit!" Hugo said.

Benjamin was lost in thought for some time. There was something fishy about the whole business, although ugly rumors had circulated for a while and all prudent Englishmen and Englishwomen had already crossed the Channel.

"Why did you come to us?" Benjamin asked at last. "Why couldn't you just take your... ahem... wife and just, sort of like, go to England?"

"There's civil unrest everywhere," Miles elaborated. "I wouldn't feel safe with a woman at my side. Alone, I can defend myself against an army. A woman, who can be injured, raped, held hostage, or in front of whom they can humiliate you, becomes a liability. I'm sure you know the feeling."

They thought about this. They would not normally think about such outlandish psychological subtleties, but extreme situations tend to sharpen one's wits.

"He's right," Charles, normally taciturn, volunteered.

"He is," Benjamin agreed. "But how can we be sure there's no treachery involved? I've known this ingrate for thirty years. Always something up his sleeve. Gustave's buttocks! What about the rest of us? Our brothers and sisters? Huh?"

Miles explained about the warning letter he had sent. He noticed that Hugo's and Charles' attitude changed in his favor almost instantly. There was now some respect even in Benjamin's eyes. Although American-born, Miles was still an English duke whom these three sportsmen were preparing to carry to his death; and yet they were concerned about the fate of other Englishmen who were, so far, merely in danger of being arrested. Moreover, Miles knew that they had enemies among their compatriots in Paris, while on his part, he had done nothing that might classify him as an enemy in the Carlyles' eyes, except that it was Benjamin to whom fifteen years ago the news of Miles' dealings with Jefferson had been delivered by a woman whose name Miles no longer even remembered.

"What do you stand to lose?" Miles asked.

Benjamin spread his massive arms, looking from one of his sons to the other. They nodded.

Once all particulars were agreed upon, the Carlyles treated Louise and
Miles to a frugal dinner. Louise began to relax and to get accustomed to the
Englishmen, and even spoke to Hugo in French. They waited until it was
dark outside.

The post – perhaps the quickest way to travel through France in that
epoch, with relays of fresh horses awaiting one at every station – was out
of service due to the Revolution. Louise, like all aristocratic Frenchwomen,
knew a thing or two about riding. Nevertheless, she could not be expected
to make the four-day journey on horseback. Thus, the Carlyles' carriage
was selected, from which the coat-of-arms was prudently knocked off by
Benjamin himself. The Fabourg de Montmartre was chosen. Charles and
Miles mounted the box; Benjamin, Hugo, Louise and the butler got inside.
They set out.

Hugo held the reins. Miles had two loaded pistols in his boots, a musket
at his feet. Inside, five loaded muskets were at hand. Hugo and Louise
conversed quietly about this and that – hunting, history, art, war, and
eventually discovered that both were extremely fond of Greek mythology.

A block away from the Fabourg, Miles opened his portmanteau and, to
Charles's great surprise, donned the Mohawk *Kastoweh*. About time, as
the guards at the Fabourg aimed their muskets at them.

"Who goes there?"

The brigadier stepped forward, holding up a lantern. Miles' headwear
shocked him.

"Hey!"

"We're American representatives," Miles told him, adding a little German
accent to his Blois-pure French.

"What's that on your head, my good man?"

"Traditional American headwear. If you're ever in America, I suggest
you get one. They're very comfortable and beautiful. Anyway, Monsieur,
we're rather in a hurry. We have to warn the American regiments in Bretagne
that the English are preparing to land in Calais."

"What!"

"You heard me."

"Why aren't you on horseback, then? It would be quicker if..."

"We'll be transporting American gold back to Paris."

"Oh," the brigadier said, still staring at the feathers. "Well, thanks and
good luck. The Americans are experts at kicking British ass, or so I hear.
We could use your people's help. Hey, is it true that you scalp your

prisoners?"

"Only if they're British," Miles assured him.

"All right, then," the brigadier exclaimed enthusiastically, now truly admiring the feathers. "Boys, let them pass. *Vive L'Amerique!*"

Miles pressed his right hand to his heart and bowed politely. The carriage rolled on. Suddenly, Charles and Miles heard Hugo's uproarious laughter from inside the carriage, counterpointed by Louise's melodious mirth.

"What did you tell him?" Charles asked.

Miles translated, and, apparently, so did Hugo. Charles had no sense of humor, but Benjamin laughed heartily, and the butler soon joined in. Both sons had participated in the American campaign under General Burgoyne.

They made excellent progress during the night. In the morning, in a small town called Blanche, Hugo and Miles were able to strike a deal with a local horse breeder, replacing their horses with fresh and excellent ones. Benjamin and Hugo relieved Miles and Charles on the box. The carriage set off again, at a gallop.

Louise, who had peed in the bushes under Miles' watchful eye, was able to fall asleep. Charles dozed off. The butler was soon dead to the world as well, muttering obsenities. Miles drew the curtain aside to let in some fresh air.

Hugo and Louise became great friends. He was promoted from *Monsieur* to *Mon Petit Ami* on the second day of the journey. He started teaching her English words. Her accent was so impossibly charming that Charles suddenly became quite jealous.

They managed to get to Dieppe almost without incident. Twice Miles and Charles exchanged shots with local brigands, and once a squad of Prussian scouts pursued the carriage. Upon learning that the travelers were English, the Prussians left them alone.

The schooner the Carlyles hired in Dieppe was called the *Lightning* and was the slowest, ugliest, most uncomfortable vessel Miles had ever encountered. The captain, a bearded, burly middle-aged Dutchman with a weathered face, agreed to take the five travelers across, no problem, provided they were not fugitives from French justice but respectable and honest business travelers, which, they assured him, they were. Gustave's buttocks, wasn't it bloody obvious? The news from Paris about the arrest of all English citizens had not reached Dieppe yet.

The Channel was unusually calm, yet the voyage took the rest of the day, all night, and all of the hazy, chilly morning. The shoreline finally came into view. Louise stood on the main deck, looking with melancholy at the English seagulls flapping their silly wings to starboard, expecting food. Except for the helmsman and the lone sailor squatting at the railing and suffering acutely from hangover, the deck was deserted. Louise looked over her shoulder. France was gone, perhaps forever, for her.

Her mind was blank. Her two children, with whom she was going to reunite in England, were born very early – before she turned twenty. Various nurses, nannies, and tutors, had been taking care of them all these years. Louise had never had the chance to develop any maternal feelings. Her husband was dead, and her lover, Danton, had turned out to be one of the lowest dogs she had ever met. She was thirty-two. She wondered what her life was going to be like from now on.

There was something strangely attractive about this Hugo fellow, who spoke bad French but had an excellent sense of humor – or so it seemed to her. His manners were those of a peasant; he was very powerfully built, his chest was like a barrel. She found the combination intriguing. After the Duc de Coligny, an aristocratic degenerate with a passion for board games; after two or three depraved and decadent lovers; after Miles with his wiry strength, appalling laziness and tendency to lay back and expect to be served, Hugo seemed a breath of fresh air.

The Dutch captain scrambled out onto the deck and, without taking notice of Louise, proceeded towards the bow. On tottering legs, he managed to move to starboard and steady himself. He fumbled with his trousers for a while and then pissed peacefully into the sea, whistling a silly popular tune off key. Once done, he fumbled with his trousers again, and eventually fell overboard. Sobering up somewhat in the cold water, he screamed for help. Some time later, the helmsman noticed a head sticking out of the water in the schooner's wake and went to look for the captain to report that there was a man overboard. Not finding the captain, he returned and rang the ship's bell. Some sailors scrambled out onto the deck and immediately began to shout at one another. It occurred to someone to reduce sail, and when they did, it turned out that they were now headed back to France. The captain was still missing. Eventually they discovered him floating on the surface about a mile away. He was, in fact, much closer than looking through the wrong end of an outdated telescope led them to believe. The helmsman turned the ship towards the captain and would have certainly split the hapless fellow's head with the keel if it hadn't been for an unexpected gust of wind hitting the mainsail flat and jerking the schooner to port. Someone threw a rope, and the captain, shaking, wet, and semi-paralyzed, climbed on board and punched the helmsman in the ear before retiring to his cabin to warm up.

ELEVEN

Traveling Through England: Tourism In The Eighteenth Century

Landing at Portsmouth was a happy accident, considering that the Dutchman's navigation was very approximate, the idea being that, barring galactic miracles and other highly unusual events, one would sooner or later hit England if only one continued traveling north. Louise's brother-in-law's house was only a few miles away. Hiring a carriage, however, turned out to be a problem. Most of the afternoon was thus wasted.

There was a huge feeling of relief – and, after a very hearty meal at Louise's relatives with lots of excellent French wine of which there was such a great shortage in Paris, after her teary reunion with her children who, it turned out, had hardly missed her, and, in fact, barely remembered her, everyone felt sleepy, including Miles and the Carlyles. Louise's brother-in-law showed the guests their rooms. Benjamin and Charles insisted they had to spend the night in the same room as Miles.

"You're a great fellow, Crawford," Charles, whom wine had made loquacious, announced, his arm around Miles' shoulders.

Benjamin, following them down the hallway, grunted approval. In the room, Benjamin and Charles argued who was going to watch Miles first while the other slept. They finally agreed that Benjamin would sleep a little bit in a chair, and then wake up, while Charles took the bed. Both were pleased, for some reason, with this arrangement. When they looked around, they discovered that Miles was missing. This puzzled them. They searched the room, figuring he was playing hide-and-seek. They even shouted a couple of times, "Olly-olly-ox-in-free!" Then, it occurred to Benjamin to look out the window. Gustave's buttocks, but it was pitch-dark outside! He invited Charles to take a peek. Both were now satisfied that there was nothing out there to be seen. They decided to search for Louise but, going to the door, discovered that it was locked. Neither of them had the key.

Three months later, Hugo married Louise. They bought a tiny house some miles out of Dorchester. In addition to Louise's two existing children, they had another three, and this time around, Louise was adamant about performing all maternal duties herself. Louise and her little friend Hugo were mad about each other until the end of their days – and they died ancient.

King George III, in a long nightshirt and slippers, walked slowly along the wall with enormous windows through which sunlight streamed, bouncing off the walls and drenching the great hall. Suddenly, at one of the windows, the King nearly bumped into Miles. His Majesty pleased to giggle. Miles pressed his finger to his lips and smiled.

Both men had aged since their last encounter, but while Miles still looked fresh and upbeat, George was now fat and slovenly, with a slightly mad look in his eyes.

"Good morning, Your Majesty," Miles said quietly and kindly.

"Hello, Miles. You're here again," the King replied, beaming.

"Yes, your Majesty."

"The Frog Prince is dead," the King informed him right away. "Did they tell you? They chopped the bungler's head off. Poor moron. I never liked him much; still, I think I shall miss him. When's the last time we spoke?"

Miles made some mental calculations and was impressed.

"Fifteen years ago, Your Majesty."

"Ah, yes," George was not at all surprised. He recalled that last encounter, saying, "You were handcuffed. Aren't you supposed to be handcuffed now?"

"No, your Majesty."

"Why not?"

"I don't know," Miles said, shrugging. "Too kinky, I guess."

"Good for you," George paused. His pauses were not at all embarrassing. True thinkers need time in which to think. "Any news from the Colonies?"

"I haven't been there in three years. Going there now."

George looked around with a conspiratorial air. His eyes sparkled. His smile was that of a mischievous schoolboy.

"Listen," he said, "if you ever run across any of those vivacious fellows... those gentlemen on the make... you know, Jefferson, Washington, any of those gallows birds... Just tell them it's all right," he nodded meaningfully a few times. "Just tell them old George will pardon them if they mend their ways and rejoin the Empire," he reflected for a moment, then laughed. "I wouldn't pardon all of them, mind you. Just some," he furrowed his brow. "One has to teach the insolent bastards a lesson, you understand. All the same, just tell them I'll pardon them all, just mention it to them."

"Very well, Your Majesty," Miles said, bowing slightly. "I'll tell them."

George sat on the floor and hugged his knees. Miles remained standing. Pity had no place here. In a way, the King was better off than a lot of people. As an epicurean, Miles could appreciate another epicurean's decision to observe without participating.

"Remember I fed you pudding once?" George asked. He pouted. "No one will ever feed me pudding when I fall down. They hate me here."

He got on all fours and crossed over to the opposite wall. He spoke without looking at Miles.

"They showed me that... little scrap of paper... Proclamation of something or other... about how they want to be by themselves now, and how I'm supposed to be the scum of the earth, and all. Scribble, scribble, scribble... We never get what we really want. Partly because we don't know what we really want, or how badly. You know? For instance. Some people are born with an inny; others have an outy. I think outies are funnier. Only the other day, I stood naked in front of the mirror and I looked at my navel. Just to see whether I had an inny or an outy. Do you have any idea what I discovered?"

"I'm sure I don't know, Sire."

"I discovered... this is strictly between you and me, you understand... don't let it get around... I discovered that I don't have a belly button at all. Maybe I should have searched some more... 'Cause, you must realize, the only other person I've heard of who didn't have one was Adam. Maybe I am Adam. Except I have no taste whatsoever for apples. I prefer cherries."

Miles looked out the window. The garden was a mixture of warm yellow and pale green, sprinkled with reddish-brown here and there. Late September in England. Perhaps he could go to a theatre in the evening. See if any Shakespeare was on. If he stayed a couple of days longer, he might investigate further. A French play in English – now that was something he had not seen in ages. It was a little early in the season for opera, but who knew what émigré companies found refuge in London these days and what their schedules were. He had heard so much about Mozart's operas, it was a shame he had never seen a live performance of one. He especially liked the idea of *Don Giovanni*, Molieresque in style and Italian in execution, set to music.

George rose, walked over, and joined Miles. Together, they contemplated the courtyard for a while.

"Things have changed, Miles," George said in a confidential undertone. "There used to be more fun around this place, know what I mean? Now, it's just cold-blooded egotism and hypocrisy. Take this silly plot to assassinate Jefferson, for instance. In the old days, they would have at least come to me for confirmation. Today, the blackguards merely inform me after the fact. Not two hours ago, they had the insolence to drop by to tell me that the murderer is already on his way to the Colonies. Samuel Doome,

I think his name is. Doome. Imagine. Now, I'm not particularly fond of Jefferson myself. But this just goes to show how much respect I get these days."

The meaning finally registered. Thoughts raced back and forth through Miles' mind. The Gallic Faction knew that Jefferson's attempts to convince the President were in vain. The reason was unclear. It would be silly to suppose, as most people did, that Washington still bore the French a grudge for the humiliating defeat they had made him suffer at Fort Necessity almost forty years ago. After all, he and Rochambeau, a quintessential Frenchman, had fought shoulder-to-shoulder at Yorktown. Miles' own take on the President's obstinacy was more rational and less romantic than the popular theory. He reasoned that, because both Rochambeau and Lafayette had assisted the Continental Army on King Louis' orders, Washington did not feel obligated to offer any kind of aid to his ally's murderers. The Faction, however, figured it would be safer still if the Secretary of State was not pro-French. The Faction's alliance with England had grown stronger since the Revolution.

Not two hours ago, eh? There was another worry for Miles. He had to overtake the mercenary, or he could forget London theatre life for a while.

"Samuel Doome?" he asked.

"Ugly name, isn't it? You know, the dark-haired fellow I almost hanged last year."

The name was familiar to Miles. The plot to assassinate Prince Potyomkin in St. Petersburg fell apart when, shivering and squinting in the frosty wind laced with snowflakes, Miles put the hitman out of action for three weeks under the windows of the Winter Palace. The one-eyed Prince, the omnipotent minister of voluptuous Catherine II of Russia, was just preparing to issue orders concerning the shipment of German weapons and Siberian gold to Boston.

"With the scar over his left eyebrow?" Miles wanted to make sure.

George looked at Miles with admiration. He slapped him on the shoulder. "You know, Miles, you and I are the only observant men left in England. I remember that scar also. I wonder how he got it. Do you know?"

Suddenly, he was perfectly sane. He looked at Miles steadily with a mixture of irony and insight.

"Well?"

Miles winked at him. "He pricked himself on the point of my sword ten years ago."

"Really! Good for you, Miles. This same sword?" he pointed at the sword Miles carried.

Miles nodded. The King touched the pommel respectfully. Suddenly, he became concerned.

"Say," he inquired, "how did they let you carry your sword in here? I mean, on my part, I'd trust you to the end of the world, but, you know, I don't remember it being customary for people to carry arms in their sovereign's presence unless they're my personal bleeding guards or..."

He stopped speaking. Miles smiled. "Is it customary for me to be in your presence at all, Your Majesty?"

George had to think about this. He nodded knowingly.

"I see. You sneaked in." He added in a weepy voice, "Just to see me. You're a true friend, Miles."

"When did you say Mr. Doome departed for the Colonies, Your Majesty?"

"Oh," the King pondered. "I'm sure I can't remember. About a week ago, I think."

"A week ago!" Miles exclaimed, growing more and more alarmed.

"Yes. Why? You look concerned."

Miles chuckled mirthlessly. "You too would be concerned, Sire, if you were told that someone with the idea of murdering your sole source of income had a week's start on you."

"Oh!" the King's eyes opened wide. "You're in Jefferson's pay, then?"

"More or less."

The King clicked his tongue sympathetically.

"I'm sorry. You'll have to find someone else, I'm afraid. Samuel Doome has a sure hand and is as sneaky as a fox. He's murdered scores of prominent scoundrels, and he's never been caught."

A sudden commotion at the far end of the hall attracted their attention. Five guards ran towards them, swords drawn.

"Uh-oh. That's for sneaking in, I guess," the King said apologetically.

"Yes," Miles confirmed. "Unfortunately. I wish we could chat some more. I must take leave of you, Sire."

He drew his sword and stepped up onto the windowsill. The guards were close. Their sergeant, brandishing his weapon, shouted very loudly, "Hold it right there!"

"Your Majesty," Miles said from the windowsill. "One more thing."

"Yes?" the King said and then, turning to the guards, bellowed, "Stop and shut your filthy traps, you swine. There aren't too many clever people in this country. It might do you good to listen to one. You might learn something." Turning to Miles again, he said politely and almost affectionately, "Please continue."

"Sire, most of my business has been in France and Austria these past three years. For a while, I was trying to rationalize what I was doing in England at all. Surprisingly, I must now conclude that my sole reason for coming here was to see you, Sire. Oddly enough, we appear to have been friends all these years."

The King was touched. "You don't say!" he shouted. "What a splendid fellow you are, Miles. Coming over to England just to see me!" he bellowed at the guards, "See, you ugly morons? And you wanted to kill him just now! You should be ashamed of your selves. How old are you now, Miles? Forty-seven? Forty eight?"

"Fifty-one next month, Sire. Anyway, as a friend, permit me to give you a piece of advice."

"By all means, my dear fellow."

"Going mad is just one way to retire from politics, Sire. It is by far not the best way. In fact, it's pathetic. If I were you, I'd think of something else."

George laughed heartily. "Can't," he said. "I'm too far gone."

"Oh. I see. I apologize."

"It's all right," the King assured him. "Has its up side too. Some aspects are rather convenient. You can insult anyone you like. You can pee in public. Thank you, Miles. Now, please continue making your escape. I'll just stand here and watch. I love it when things are done competently."

"Very well, Sire."

He bowed to the King and faced the guards. They hesitated. Miles pushed the window open with his back and fell clean out. The guards rushed to the window and stuck out their heads. They were flabbergasted. The courtyard was deserted; there were no signs of Miles anywhere. George III laughed uproariously.

"Bungling idiots! Can't even catch anyone!" he continued laughing.

The horses at the King's stables were splendid as usual. There was only one guard on duty. Miles got rid of him by shouting, "The Americans are coming! Run and tell your officer, quick!"

"Where are they coming from?" the guard shouted back, stunned.

"They landed at Westminster fifteen minutes ago!"

The guard ran, not necessarily to inform his officer. He had no interest in finding out what Miles' sources were, or, for that matter, what the Star-Spangled Banner was doing fluttering in the wind over Windsor Castle.

Miles selected a horse at random, saddled it, and covered the sixty miles separating London from Dover in just under four hours. He sold the horse to a breeder for pennies. After galloping the entire distance, the animal was not the same, and never would be again.

In the harbor, Miles assessed the ships. Since turning over all of his business in England to a barrister by the name of Sommers, he had no idea whether he could still claim the ship Hector Eriksson had so graciously given him a year ago.

Hector's ships were ahead of their time. Only a major government could afford their maintenance, the idea of transporting small quantities of very expensive, time-dependent cargo being as yet unappreciated by the traditionally slow and overly conservative merchant class.

No ordinary ship suited Miles' purposes. He had to be in the States ahead of Doome, who had a week's start on him. Which was why Miles figured he was in luck when he spotted one of Hector Eriksson's creations. A clipper is unmistakable. It might be the same clipper Eriksson had given Miles as a present, although it mattered little whether it belonged to Miles or not. He had to get on board and set out immediately.

Opening his portmanteau, he produced a portable telescope and scanned the ship, which was anchored some fifty yards from shore. He did not like what he saw.

The sailors sauntered around the main deck, looking dejected and casting furtive glances at the company of British guards amusing themselves with a game on a makeshift card table. Two more guards stood at the portside, close to the bow. There were some others.

Suddenly, one of them tensed up perceptibly.

"To port. A row boat," he said loudly.

The players abandoned their game, some unwillingly, and rushed dutifully to take a glance.

"There's no one in it," one of them commented.

The guards exchanged puzzled looks. In the meantime, Miles surfaced on the other side of the ship and climbed up the anchor chain, carrying his tricorne in his teeth. In another instant, he was on board. Dropping his wet portmanteau, he made directly for the bridge. The ship's captain, looking over his shoulder, rushed to meet him.

"You must be Mr. Sommers," he said.

"Yes, my dear fellow," Miles said. "I am Mr. Sommers, and all my folks are called Sommers as well. How soon can we sail?"

"As soon as those fellows check your papers, sir. No American ship has left this place in a week without all the passengers' papers being checked. The Lobsters are looking for some spy."

A guard materialized to the left of them, prepared to accost the newcomer. Miles pushed him overboard without interrupting the conversation.

"How many of them here?" Miles asked.

"Uh…" the captain hesitated. "About six, sir, not counting the Lieutenant."

"Good. Throw the lines, up with the sails. We're getting out of here."

Two other guards, swords drawn, appeared and rushed at Miles. He raised a hand.

"Gentlemen!"

"Are you Miles Crawford?"

The Carlyles, Miles thought. They just had to get back at me. I spend an extra day in London taking in the sights, and they use the interval to inform the right people. They're probably looking for me at every port, those ungrateful swine.

"Gentlemen," he said, "I protest. This is my ship. I don't remember inviting you here."

Taken aback by his icy tone more than by the meaning of his words, the guards nevertheless made an attempt to approach.

"The King's orders, sir," one of them said.

"The King's?" Miles' attitude changed. "Oh," he said. "I'm sorry. I surrender, of course."

The two guards relaxed and exchanged triumphant glances. Miles walked towards them, subdued, and stood between them.

"Should we take him to…" one of them managed to say before Miles sent him flying overboard.

"Hey!" the other guard protested. "Why did you push him overboard?"

"Because he wouldn't jump of his own accord," Miles explained. "Some people need a little push to motivate them. Do you?"

"Uh… Lieutenant! Lieu…"

He made a thrust in Miles' direction with his sword. Miles stepped aside and called to the captain, "I don't hear you issuing orders."

"Uh…" the captain hesitated. "Yes, of course… sir… Hey! Raise the anchor, somebody! All hands on deck!"

The guard stared at the Captain in astonishment. Using this brief moment of distraction, Miles got hold of the fellow's coat and sent him flying overboard.

On the other side of the ship, the guards scattered around the deck, looking for the source of the confusion. The Lieutenant, alarmed, drew his sword.

"What was that?" he shouted. "What anchor? Somebody here wants to be hanged from the main mast, I gather!"

One of his troops, looking overboard, pointed with his finger, "Look! There's Bill. Hey, Bill, what's the big idea? Taking a swim in the middle of October?"

Miles appeared behind his back and was about to push him. He lay a hand on the guard's shoulder. He changed his mind. He turned the guard around and extracted the pistol from behind the guard's belt.

"I'll take that, thank you."

Now he turned the stupefied guard around again and propelled him over the side. The Lieutenant appeared on the mast barrel, aiming his pistol at Miles.

"Freeze!" he shouted.

Miles, pistol in hand, turned to the Lieutenant. "Are you in charge here?"

"You're damn right I'm in charge here! Why, do you wish to tell me something?"

"Not really."

"Then why do you ask?"

"I was just curious, that's all."

Another guard materialized to Miles' left. He extended his hand to grab him. Without taking his eyes off the Lieutenant, Miles beat the guard to the punch by extending his own hand, catching the guard by the wrist, and, with a sharp twist, forcing the fellow overboard.

"You people have no respect for private property, that's what," Miles told the Lieutenant. "One would think we were in France."

The Lieutenant fired. The bullet knocked off Miles' tricorne. Miles spun around. The tricorne fell into the water. Incensed, Miles shouted, "That was my best hat! I bought it in Paris, you brainless Lobster! How do you expect me to take it off in ladies' presence now! Huh?" He roared, "Did you think of that, you mannerless skunk!"

He fired his own pistol, knocking off the Lieutenant's tricorne.

"There!" he said, satisfied.

Suddenly, the slick vessel tilted. The wind filled the sails. The captain appeared on the bridge.

"Where to, sir?" he asked.

"Philadelphia please, and do be quick, there's a good fellow. I seem to be running late."

Two more guards appeared, aiming their muskets at Miles. Two American sailors pounced on them from behind, disarmed them, and tossed them overboard.

"About time," Miles grumbled. He addressed the Lieutenant, "You can use my row boat, you and your cutthroats. The oars are included."

The lieutenant looked past the bow. The lone rowboat rocked gently on the waves. The defeated guards were swimming towards it. Not one of them wished to risk climbing the anchor chain. The Lieutenant drew his sword, jumped off the barrel, and walked very slowly towards Miles, who waited, arms akimbo. The Lieutenant very obviously knew who Miles was and had been instructed anent his reputation. Suddenly, the Lieutenant sheathed his sword.

"All right. An officer must never abandon his troops. Sorry about that hat."

He jumped.

TWELVE

An Old Friend Returns

In Mappensville, the two-story house whose windows gave on the square had gained two new tenants over the past ten years. Approaching forty, Molly was still vital-looking. Yes, there were some wrinkles around the eyes, and some gray streaks in her hair. Her breasts sagged. She had varicose veins.

However, wrinkles, depending on one's attitude, can speak of experience far more than the imminence of old age; blondes go gray smoothly and, in some cases, attractively; more than three fourths of all sexually active women on the planet have sagging breasts; and pearly teeth are overrated. Molly's smile had lost none of its radiance, her energy had hardly diminished over the years, her gait was as light as ever, her skin silky, and her posture haughty. Men still regarded her with awe and admiration; women, with envy and loathing.

The only two persons who were never truly impressed by Molly's outstanding qualities were her children. Just now, she was in the process of reprimanding her son, four years of age, russet-haired, thin, and defiant. He was never defiant except in his mother's presence. He was not paying much attention to the lecture.

"Either you stop throwing cake at the maid or else," Molly concluded. "Do you understand? I'm talking to you! If you want to share it with her, just offer her some. You always share. We both know you're a good boy. Are you a good boy? ... Well, go play now."

Relieved, the boy vanished. The maid, humbly but very attractively dressed, twenty-five years of age and ravishing in a naïve manner, the way country girls sometimes are, entered. Molly did not like her, suspecting her of foul play with Hector behind her back.

"Someone to see you, Madam."

"Yes? And the name is?" Molly asked arrogantly.

"It's a man. Looks like a hobo."

"So do you. What does he want?"

"He won't say."

"Tell him to go away."

"I did."

"And?"

"He insists he's an old friend of yours."

Molly looked contemptuously at the maid. "You're so helpless, Jennifer. Show him in."

She turned away. The maid hesitated. Then, with poorly concealed malice, she informed Molly that her husband had sent a message earlier. He was going to be late for dinner again. He had important business to attend to at the shipyard.

"Get out."

The maid obeyed. Molly approached the window. Lifting her skirt and scratching nosily the inner side of her thigh, she looked out. The square was all yellow in these last days of September. Throaty entered.

She did not turn around right away, and when she did, she had no idea who he was. He had aged monstrously and ungracefully. He was bent. He had lost most of his hair and teeth. His skin hung in folds, and his clothes were in tatters. He cleared his throat.

Molly winced, asking him with some distaste who the hell he was.

"Your humble and obedient, as always, Molly," he said.

Struck, she shut her eyes and opened them again, exclaiming involuntarily, "Ah, goodness! Throaty!"

She was not the type of person who leaves her friends in need. Ten minutes later, Throaty was sitting at the kitchen table, devouring soup, steak, bread, and chasing it all down with excellent Boston beer brewed by one of the Revolution's original heroes.

His mouth full, he finished his story, "That was my last sortie. If only I could lay my hands on that scum. Someone else might have done that by now. Anyway, even if he were alive, I don't think I'd be able to find him. It's a big world out there."

Molly, who knew a thing or two about the matter, said, "Not as big as you think."

He did not care one way or the other. He growled appreciatively over the food, as an old dog might.

"He's been mayor of this city for the past twelve years," Molly informed him. "He's seeking re-election as we speak."

Throaty's eyes flashed. He rose impetuously, upsetting the chair. Immediately, he doubled over from pain. His back failed him. Molly made him sit down again, picking up the chair and moving it towards him. His face distorted, he sat, looking at her like a cornered rat. She went over to her seat, and, leaning towards him and looking him in the eye, asked whether he really wanted to take revenge on his nemesis, or was he only trying to make conversation. He shook his head. He was obviously in no position to take revenge on anyone. He whimpered and complained like a whiny child. Molly was very patient. She listened to his soliloquy, waited for him to cease pitying himself for a moment, and posed the question again. Would he or would he not? He explained he was in no position... and so on.

"Would you do it, though, if you had the chance?" she insisted.

At last he nodded. "The creep ruined me, ruined my life, took everything I had, including you, my mistress."

"Be careful how you use that word, Throaty. It has a second meaning."

"Sorry, Ma'am."

"Revenge, then."

"If only there was one chance, one chance out of a million..."

"Nonsense," Molly straightened, poured some wine, and sipped. "A couple of weeks of sound rest. Lots of sleep, lots of food, some exercise. You'll be as fit as an elephant."

He grunted doubtfully. She frowned. Looking at her, he was beginning to believe again. It was not for nothing she had once been the leader of two dozen cutthroats. The brigands were a rough lot, completely unscrupulous, but they had always listened to her. She moved away from the table, sipping her wine calmly. Then, spinning around, she swooped on him.

"You will do it, and you will do it right. Which means you must listen to me and follow my instructions to the letter. Killing Mongoose is a simple enough matter. Killing him and not getting caught and hanged is less simple."

"I don't care whether I'm caught or not. It'll be my last mission in this life, I guess."

"Shut up and stop overdramatizing. I'll help you. You'll do it. Now. You can't stay here. Let's find you some lodgings."

He finished his meal. She led him to the washroom and ordered him to undress. He was horrified.

"Don't argue with me, Throaty," she told him sternly. "I was a nurse for six months once. I saved more wounded than there are hairs left on your body, and I washed people whose body odor was far worse than yours."

That was perfectly true. Molly had served, had been on hand at the Battle of Trenton, and the Continental Army owed her for cleansing, washing, bandaging and soothing over a hundred souls.

"Undress, I tell you."

She warmed some water.

An hour later, he was clean and dressed in fresh linen and clothes that the maid, on Molly's orders, had purchased at a second-hand garment shop. Throaty's expression, each time he looked at Molly, was positively canine. Assessing his appearance, Molly found him somewhat more presentable than earlier, and ordered him to come along. They crossed the city diagonally and stopped in front of the inn at which Molly had spent the night ten years ago.

The place was much cleaner now, and so was the clientele. Luc, the feisty proprietor, older but still a dreamer, towered over the bar. He was sincerely glad to see Molly whom he knew as Ruth. He came out to meet her, shook hands with her, invited her to sit with him at the bar, and offered her a drink. She introduced Throaty as an old friend of hers. Luc appeared to be skeptical. She asked him whether he could put him up for a few nights. Luc nodded. There was more. She gave Luc some money and asked him to buy Throaty some decent clothes. A healthy diet was in order. Three meals a day. Molly promised she was going to pick up the tab.

"Just don't serve him any liquor."

"What? No liquor?" Throaty, who only a moment ago could hardly believe his good fortune, was unpleasantly surprised.

"None."

"Must be a duke in disguise," the proprietor said, pulling a serious face.

"Something like that," Molly pulled a serious face also. She turned to Throaty, "Now. I'll drop by in a couple of weeks and we'll discuss the matter further. Take care of yourself."

Luc led Throaty to the room Patty once occupied. When Throaty asked to leave him the candle, Luc refused, citing that over the past ten years, candles had not gotten any cheaper.

Tripling the number of streetlights in Mappensville's residential district was the next item on the Mayor's agenda. There was an obvious shortage of them, imparting to the city, with its mostly colonial ensemble studded with European niceties – archways and courtyards here and there – a touch of unnecessary spookiness in the night hours. Preposterous as it may seem today, the idea was strongly opposed by the local blue-bloods. Aware of the recent events in France, the aristocrats reckoned that the shortage might save many of their kind should the idea of hanging them from lampposts occur to the disgruntled population during the next crisis. As it was, there were only so many lampposts one could reasonably expect to be hanged from.

Molly the former brigand and Patty the former harlot strolled down the deserted street. Molly was preoccupied with Throaty's return and the resulting options and paid little attention to what Patty was saying. She figured she might be able to use Throaty without endangering him. She decided she was going to think it through when she was alone. She turned to her friend and, by listening to her chatter, soon deduced that the redhead was talking about Kenneth. She asked Patty whether he had been painting a lot lately.

"On and off. He keeps talking about Italy. Says he's well known there. Says if only he could exhibit there once, we'd be on easy street for the rest of our lives."

"Is this true, you think?"

"I don't know anymore. I mean, we've been living together for ten years now... I know him... He's always nursing an insane project or two. I was going to leave him once."

"Why didn't you?"

"Where would I go?"

"Stands to reason."

They walked in silence for a while. The one streetlight that was meant to illuminate the street was out – had run out of oil, or maybe the attendant was drunk that night.

"Besides," Patty suddenly went on, "I don't really want to leave him. He's so helpless at times, it's ridiculous. He keeps forgetting things. If I weren't there, I think he'd forget to get out of bed one day. I suppose I do love him after all. If I could scrape enough money together, I guess we'd be in Italy now. You think I'm crazy?"

Molly shrugged, smiling wanly.

Patty's devotion was commendable, although not, strictly speaking, extraordinary. Living with an artist, though trying at times for some women, is not as excruciating an experience as most people imagine. One's duties are few, and the demands are usually minimal. The rewards are oftentimes colossal when one considers the entertainment value. Artists are magnificent entertainers when they are in the mood – which is, admittedly, a rare occasion. The rest of the time, the spouse's task consists mostly of being able to entertain herself and to stay out of the way as much as humanly possible. Being more intelligent than Kenneth, Patty occupied her time with reading, chores, and strolls with Molly and some other friends.

Suddenly, the two were confronted by three low-ranking navy officers who seemed to have had a drink or two earlier – the proverbial Tom, Dick and Harry of the maritime variety.

"Hello, ladies," Tom said.

"Oh, no," Patty whispered.

"You are beautiful, both of you," Dick, who had a mustache, observed. "What are you two doing out here so late? Don't you think it's dangerous for a pair of gorgeous women like yourselves to be wandering through the dark streets without an escort?"

"What with all kinds of bad-ass wicked people roaming all over the place," Harry, a big, muscle-bound fellow, added.

They surrounded the two women. There was no one else in the street.

"How about you two let us be your escort for the rest of the night," Tom suggested.

"Yeah," the third one said. "We'll protect you against whatever bad people you might encounter."

Dick laid his hand on Molly's shoulder. Molly looked at the hand and then turned her eyes on the officer. Was she being paranoid, or was there someone in the city intent on thwarting her plans? Were these three freelancing amateur rapists, or paid thugs?

"Look, boys," Patty pleaded, "there's no reason to get obnoxious..."

"No, no, please, don't misunderstand," Tom assured her. "We want to be kind to you ladies. This is going to be a very memorable night for you two. There, do you see that archway?"

"Just don't scream too loud now," Dick cautioned.

"Yeah, that's right," Harry said. "Screaming makes me edgy."

"I attest to that," Tom confirmed. "And when he's edgy, he's liable to slit someone's throat by accident."

Putting up any meaningful resistance would have been unwise. The group moved towards the archway, the men pushing the women, not too kindly. Patty feared for her friend Ruth more than she did for herself. In her view, Ruth was a very delicate being, and might soon get seriously hurt, both physically and mentally. Patty could not stand the idea of Ruth being humiliated. She glanced at her companion. It was too dark to make out anything. Was her friend in shock?

The archway was dark. A lone barrel stood at the wall.

"Listen, boys," Patty said reasonably. "Just don't touch her, all right? You can do anything you like with me, I don't care. Just don't touch my friend. She's a real lady."

"You're selfish," Tom disagreed, stroking his mustache. "You want everything for yourself. Why should she be denied her share of pleasure? Even real ladies can appreciate a good fuck."

"Watch your language, fellow," Harry said sternly.

"Please, boys," Patty pleaded.

Muscle-bound Dick started undressing Patty. Muscle-bound Harry stood Molly against the wall and began, somewhat impatiently, to untie her bodice. Patty attempted a scream and was slapped preventively across the face. Tom was, for now, more or less on the lookout; but there could be no doubt that he too intended to get his full share.

Untying a string, Harry said to Molly, "You're a good girl, aren't you. You're not going to put up any resistance, like your friend tried to do just then. You'll enjoy it more this way."

Undressing Patty, Dick commented, "No, she's come to her senses, I think. She realizes it'll be better for everyone if she just lets us do what we want to do."

Harry, unable to untie and unhook Molly's dress quickly enough, became impatient and started tearing it open furiously.

"No!" Patty shouted.

"Sorry, gorgeous," Harry muttered. "Too many strings."

Dick slapped Patty again and brought his index finger to her nose as a warning. Molly's dress fell to her feet. She now stood in her white corset and long white lace underpants ending in ruffles under the knee. She stepped out of the dress, revealing a pair of neat leather shoes, and looked calmly at her rapist.

"Wow," he said. "You are good-looking."

He stepped back to take a better look. Molly continued standing in front of him with perfect calm.

"Well," he went on with severe authority in his voice, "Aren't you going to thank me, you dirty slut, for removing your dress for you? You now have all the freedom of movement for the little game you're going to play with me, and then with the other two."

"Thank you."

"Thank me some more. Now!"

"Thank you kindly for giving me my freedom of movement. You can't imagine what a great service you've just rendered me."

"Lovely, isn't she?" the fellow addressed the others. "A bit aged, but it's dark in here anyway. I like it when they're submissive."

"On your knees, wench," Dick told Patty.

Harry stepped forward, placed his hand on Molly's breast and moved his profile close to her face.

"I like her, I swear. She's so soft and submissive. Her husband must be a no-good moron. Hey, babe, when's the last time he did this to you?"

He turned his face to her. Molly's hand passed to the hilt of his sword. Gripping it, she head-butted him in the face, putting all of her weight into it. As he fell backwards, his sword, whose hilt Molly still clutched, slipped out of the sheath. He rolled on the ground, cursing and hollering. Dick abandoned Patty and sprang at Molly. She jumped aside and, catching him by the wrist, tripped him. Tom jumped back and drew his sword.

Harry shouted, "Bitch! I'm going to kill her."

He rose to one knee and drew his pistol. Molly slammed the entire sole of her foot into his face and, as he fell again, stepped on the hand gripping the pistol. He roared in pain. Tom made a thrust. Molly countered.

They fenced furiously. Molly was out of practice, which made her angry. Dick rose with difficulty, gathered his strength, and attacked Molly from behind. She leaped aside, and then backwards onto the barrel, managing in the process to land a blow to his head with the hilt of the sword. He fell.

Tom was reluctant to continue. He was still on his guard, but his blade pointed downward. Molly looked down on him from the barrel.

Taunting him, she called, "Come on, charmer. Show me what you've got. I know I turn you on."

"Dumb slut," he said through his teeth.

Molly laughed the way she used to laugh fifteen years ago.

"Watch your tongue, handsome. I may be a dumb slut, but just now I happen to be the hottest fucking thing around. Come on, fight, man, fight!"

He made a thrust. She countered. He made another one. Again, she countered. He lunged forward, this time with more determination. Molly jumped off the barrel and backed away. Encouraged, Tom charged at her and stumbled, making an awkward thrust. Molly, turning sideways, disarmed him with a kick and drove her blade rapidly into his thigh, removing it just as quickly. He fell, clutching his leg.

With her foot, Molly rolled Dick rudely onto his back. She placed the point of the sword against his throat.

"Get up," she said. "Up, up, on your feet, fellow."

He rose unsteadily. Molly went around him and, applying the point to his back, forced him to walk over to Patty. The latter, her chest bare, her dress in tatters, rose from her knees.

"Slap him," Molly ordered. "Slap him as hard as you can and as many times as you can. Now!"

"No..." Patty protested. "No..."

"Do it myself, then."

She threw away the sword and turned Dick around. He appeared to be in a daze. She slapped him viciously several times across the face. He did not make a sound. Blood gushed from his nose. When she was done, he fell slowly on one side. Molly grinned contemptuously, heaved a sigh, and attended to her toilette. The strap under the knee was undone. She tied it. She picked up her dress and inspected it. Patty was beginning to come around.

"Wow," she said. "I can't believe it. It's a dream. You're a regular Molly Bates, Ruth."

Molly froze for a moment, and laughed.

"Just do me a favor," she said. "Don't tell anyone about what happened here."

"Why not? Awwww, I'm so proud of you, Ruth. You're so courageous, and so skillful, too! I just can't get over it."

She limped over to Dick and kicked him in the ribs. He groaned.

"Serve you right, you filthy punk!"

"Please," Molly insisted. "Did you hear what I said? Look, it's really important that you don't..."

"Oh. All right. Boom! The way you got that jerk! Boom! Whisk!"

She imitated a sword thrust. Molly continued attending to her toilette, waiting for Patty's excitement to subside.

"Can you teach me?" the artist's companion asked.

Losing her patience, Molly said tartly, "Listen. Please." She shouted, "Shut up and listen!" Then, quietly, firmly, "It's very important... do you understand? ... important! ... that you don't breathe a word of what you saw here to anyone. It's a matter of life and death. Mine and, to some extent, yours as well."

"Oh. All right," Patty agreed. "I mean, if you don't want me to tell anyone... If it's so important to you that I don't... I don't mind not telling... I mean, I do mind, but I won't..."

At home, still keenly excited, Patty paced in front of Kenneth who, reclining in a chair and wearing a simple night robe without tassels, sketched absentmindedly on a piece of scrap paper.

"And then she went, boom! Whisk!"

She demonstrated, imitating a sword thrust. Kenneth threw away the pencil and rose. He looked at her morosely.

"Are you all right?"

"I'll live."

"Are you hurt?"

"No. Well, listen, she asked me not to tell anyone, so don't let me down."

"What about the money? Can she lend us some?"

"No."

"Thought not."

"She explained it all to me. She'd be happy to help us if she could. She doesn't have much cash right now."

"Yeah."

"Surely you don't think she's lying?"

"No, not exactly. No. You're right. Ruth doesn't lie. Anyhow, look, I don't know what to do anymore. No one seems to want their portraits painted. I must get to Italy somehow."

"I'll find the money," she said casually. "Don't worry about it."

"How, may I ask?"

Vaguely, she replied, "Well... I have lots of friends... Just don't worry about anything, sweetheart. I just want you to be happy. I'd do anything for you."

She embraced him and ruffled his hair. He was apathetic.

"Oooo, you look so serious," she jeered. "Silly! Kenny darling, put it out of your mind at once. You'll have your money in two weeks. Three weeks, tops. All right?"

He did not ask how she was going to get the money. He looked at her doubtfully. She ruffled his hair again.

THIRTEEN

The Doome Conspiracy

Jerome resided at the same house as before. Today, he was one of the Faction's principle leaders. Like all useless yet influential organizations, the Faction favored men who had no sense of humor.

He asked his guest to sit down.

Samuel Doome, forty years old and innocuous-looking, thanked the host and seated himself in an elegant chair. His demeanor was that of a well-to-do shopkeeper – one of his favorite disguises. His coat was very flashy and colorful, his boots shiny. He was neatly shaved. He carried a gold watch made by Zurich enthusiasts; the buttons of his coat were Limoge porcelain. His tiny brown eyes fixed on Jerome. Uncharacteristically, the latter had his glasses on. The occasion was too important to worry about appearances.

Their conversation was slow, polite, and dangerous.

"So," Jerome said, "those were the orders."

"Yes, My Lord."

"And they specifically told you that I was to give you further instructions?"

"Yes."

"As well as provide you with the necessary tools."

"Yes."

Jerome removed his glasses for a moment and rubbed his eyes with the back of his hand. He relaxed. All strain was gone from his voice. The experienced middle-aged diplomat glanced, somewhat ironically, at Samuel Doome who, sensing that the tension was, in fact, escalating rapidly, made an attempt to collect his nerve – and failed. He was suddenly ill at ease – he who had traversed half the globe, seen most of its major capitals, and killed prominent people in some of them. He was not really a man of the world; he could play the role now and then, but staying in character for any meaningful period of time was a problem, his exotic profession notwithstanding.

Jerome pondered aloud, "That's what's wrong with the powers-that-be today. They insist on sending in their own people. They have no faith in local talent. Which will be their ruin one of these days."

He moved away from the mantelpiece, put on his glasses again, sat in a chair opposite Doome's and crossed his legs. He asked suavely whether Doome was at all familiar with the area's geography. Doome was not. Jerome grinned. The English were hopeless. All they should have done, really, was send a coded message. The Faction would have obliged them. He thought of how he might convey his extreme displeasure to them. How? Through this clown in the bright-colored tacky coat, of course. Whatever he was told here, he was going to relate to his superiors yonder.

"You know," Jerome said, "my original idea of making Washington king was the only reasonable option at the time. It had plenty of support even among those who are currently at the head of the administration this side of the pond. Even Hamilton, their financial wonder boy, seemed to be in favor of it. The army was certainly on our side. But the sages in Philly and the sages in London said no. Their pride would have been hurt, if you please, by such a turn of events."

Doome was looking at the fire. This was really none of his business; he did not want to hear it. The less you know, the better. Jerome, aware of the lad's attitude, pressed his point.

"With Washington on the throne, this whole place would have remained, as it had been for so many years, a vassal to the British crown. But they wouldn't listen to me. The result is, now they have to engage in all kinds of plots to send mercenaries in to assassinate perfectly decent people. Jefferson is a clever, well-meaning man, a man of scruples. What better diplomat can you think of, as far as the Empire is concerned? Now they want him dead. Really, they should trust the locals more."

He rose and moved back to the mantelpiece. This was the last service the Faction was rendering England. Once the Faction's plans of the State's secession from the Union came through, England, after paying her share in ships and military help, would have to fend for herself. His heartburn was really something. What had he eaten last night? Well, anyway.

"All right, anyway," he said, "I'll give you a carriage, two horses, and a pair of pistols. Some sort of per diem is in order. Jefferson is in the habit of taking a stroll before bed. Wait for him at his house, follow him, and, just as he's about to turn back, shoot him. Make absolutely sure there are no witnesses. If you see any nocturnal sightseers other than the man himself, go away, come back another night. I'll give you a map of Philly..."

"Philly, My Lord?"

The fellow was really listening. Good.

"Philadelphia. Local lingo. I'll give you a map with the man's house marked. Make sure it doesn't fall into the wrong hands."

Still he did not have a good feeling about this. He wished he could send someone else. He downed a glass of water and poured another one.

They were distracted by two pirate ships and had to bear south. The clipper reached the East Coast twelve days after its departure from Dover. They were seventy miles southeast of Philadelphia. Miles ran down the gangplank, jumped, landed, sprained his foot slightly, winced, looked around, and trudged limping towards one of the harbor's inns. He had no idea what town it was. Nothing looked familiar.

Inside, some regulars conversed noisily – a commoner's means of self-assertion. Miles burst in limping and shouted as if this were a market place in Sicily, "Somebody! I need hooves!"

The talking stopped abruptly. All heads turned. He insisted, explaining that he did not have the whole day. They were neither impressed nor moved. They studied him with their eyes, exchanged looks, and grinned. Miles waited.

"He's English," one of the regulars theorized.

"Yeah, that's what he sounds like, all right," another one agreed.

"Sorry, My Lord," a third one said. "All horses are engaged, and all parties and balls in Philadelphia and Boston are canceled till further notice."

They laughed obnoxiously. Miles, ignoring their mirth, made an impatient gesture.

"I must have a horse," he explained. "I'd be perfectly happy even if I had to buy one. Well? One horse for the price of two!"

"That's not bad. Hey, Mister, I'd be happy to sell you mine, seeing that you're generous; unfortunately, my uncle is using it right now."

Wearily, hopelessly, Miles complained, "I've been so out of luck lately. Anyone else have a horse?"

The regulars chuckled derisively and turned to their drinks.

Miles stood in the middle of the inn and was beginning to feel stupid. He said, "I can't believe there are no horses available in a mostly agricultural country."

Like the previous ones, this fresh argument failed to produce any meaningful effect. Suddenly, Miles heard a horse neighing outside. Spinning around, he stormed out.

Outside, another regular rode up to the door. His horse was neither pretty nor young. However, in view of the fact that, for the moment at least, the demand for horses exceeded the supply, Miles pounced on the unfortunate rider. He dragged him out of the saddle and left him kicking and panting on the ground. He mounted and, producing a leather purse from his weather-beaten portmanteau, threw it to the miserable drunkard.

"Fifty," he said.

"Hey! What's the big idea?" the fellow demanded.

Fair enough – Miles figured he owed the fellow an explanation. Turning the horse around, he said, "Democracy and my wages. Mostly my wages."

He spurred the horse. The lucky owner of the fifty gold pieces, happy and optimistic, clutching the purse, rose and moved unsteadily towards the inn, crooning a popular tune of which Miles' words reminded him,

"I searched the woods,
I searched the fields,
High, low, and all around,
I searched the sea;
Democracy
Was nowhere to be found.

I missed her so
Two days ago
Sipping my whiskey neat
From my clay cup
Till I threw up,
Democracy, my sweet."

Reaching the door of the inn, he pushed it open, fell, and was greeted by a burst of laughter from inside.

After an hour and a half of trotting through the woods, Miles reined in his steed, dismounted, eyed the forest around him suspiciously for a while, and finally had to admit he was thoroughly lost. This was not part of the original plan. Arms akimbo, he looked at the sky, and then at his boots. He regarded the horse testily.

"Look, Hooves," he said. "You're supposed to be an intelligent animal. I thought I could depend on you. We have to get to Philly. Which is a large city, right? It should be easy to find. Don't tell me we're lost."

The horse neighed noncommittally.

"Dickhead," Miles said.

Turning around, he looked at the sky again. He mused aloud, "Supposed to be due west. Which is... what time is it?" He had ruined his watch during his swim at Dover. "Say it's noon. I mean, it can be two or three or four o'clock for all I know. Or maybe eleven. Whatever. Let's just assume, for argument's sake, that it's noon. Which means that the sun... is all the way up. Which means due west can be... absolutely anywhere. We could wait for the sun to come down a bit and just follow it. Which would be going due west, more or less. Which will bring us to Philadelphia, which is on the other side of the Delaware river, provided we haven't already missed it. I can't imagine how one can miss the Delaware, but I'm sure I've done stranger things in this life without noticing."

The horse began to partake of the roadside grass. Miles reflected some more. Presently, he saw how the horse was occupying himself and was instantly annoyed.

"Stop," he said peremptorily. "Do you hear? Stop it, I tell you. I hate when I'm trying to think and people just keep on eating right in my face. Ruth used to do it a lot. You two are a pair."

Some hours later, it grew dark. Miles rode down the path leisurely. He had followed the setting sun, but it had set too quickly for him to be able to get his bearings properly, and afterwards, thick clouds covered up the sky, and the three forks in the road he passed had disoriented the rider completely.

"Yeah, well," he said to himself. "Getting old, I guess." It seemed to him that not ten years ago, he would have selected the right path on an impulse, would have been in Philadelphia by now. "You hear that, moron?" he asked the horse. "I said I must be getting old."

He entered a clearing and the fact that there was yet another fork in the road was nearly lost on him. He noticed it at the last moment, reined in the horse, and dismounted.

"A fork in the road," he said thoughtfully. "Now, do you think... it matters much at this point? Not likely. We should have hit the Delaware centuries ago. We should have found a ferry and crossed over by now. I could have built a whole fucking ferry from scratch in all the time we've lost because of you. Aren't American horses supposed to know where their capital is?"

He looked up. At that moment, there occurred an oval-shaped opening in the clouds. A row of three bright stars shone through it.

"Orion," Miles said blankly. "Orion!" he shouted.

He calmed down. Jumping into the saddle, he turned left at the fork and set off at a gallop.

Market Street was deserted. Thomas Jefferson walked leisurely, his hands behind his back, in the direction of the Pennsylvania State House, humming quietly the aria from the First Act of *Figaro's Marriage*, Mozart's famous variation on Salieri's tune.

Robert Smith was the fellow's name. Robert Smith was still in the process of leaving his mark on the city. The steeple of St. Peter's Church, Old Pine Street Church, Carpenter's Hall. The jewels of colonial simplicity. In Jefferson's opinion, however, Smith was not fastidious enough. A church builder should not build prisons as well, no matter how fat the contract. Still, the steeple was magnificent.

Philadelphia was a promising city, favored by the aristocracy and recently marked by a number of historical events whose impact on the world's destiny was impossible to overestimate. And yet, having seen a number of cities in his life and having studied the topography and history of countless others, Jefferson could not envision the area as being the true center of gravity in the future. It did not have the aura of the Holy City, where the architecture was of secondary importance; it did not have the down-to-earth partiality, the seamless unity with the natural surroundings, of the Eternal City where the actual layout mattered little in the shadow of the noble ruins. It lacked the odd mixture of intimacy, depravity, flippancy, and majesty of the Jolly City. No, Philadelphia had had its moment of glory. The Republic's center had become unstable and was going to shift north any day now. Not too far north either – Boston, another historical outpost and major port, was neither ready nor indeed willing to take the brunt of cultural clashes characteristic of any metropolis. Jefferson was fairly certain that whatever hopes his country had as a cultural heavyweight lay in the delta of the Hudson River.

Jefferson sat on a bench in the square behind the Pennsylvania State House, looking dreamily at the sky. An amateur astronomer, he had his favorite constellation – Orion – as well as his favorite planet – Jupiter. A very young couple crossed the square, laughing and singing out of tune.

"I missed her so..." Jefferson heard. "Two days ago... Democracy, my sweet!"

The couple laughed uproariously. They attempted to sing the chorus together,

"Oh, Democracy,

Oh, don't you cry for me,

We've been fucked by the aristocracy..."

They giggled melodiously, could not go on, laughed loudly, and resumed, "'Cause we turn them on, you see..."

Still laughing, they disappeared from sight. Jefferson shrugged, chuckled, and rose. He had no idea that someone not too far away was watching him carefully. Jefferson passed through the archway and walked down the street. There were pedestrians everywhere. He reached his house without incident. The butler let him in. Jefferson went directly to his study. He picked up a clean sheet, chewed on the quill for a while, thinking of Sally, and started writing. "*Cheri...*"

The ferryman's hut was easy to locate. It was a ramshackle, ugly log cabin that clashed with the perfect harmony of the forest and river. Miles forced his steed to a stop in front of the door. The ferryman was bearded, dirty, and fat. They haggled about the price. The man did not like the idea of transporting the horse.

"Maybe we should just put him in tow behind us," he suggested.

"I'd sooner put *you* in tow behind us," Miles told him.

The ferry, which was barely larger than a lifeboat, threatened to capsize twice, but eventually drifted to the other side.

Miles paid the owner and got off onto the riverbank leading his horse by the reins.

"Hey, Mister," the owner called after him. "This ain't enough."

"That's my last money," Miles snapped. "Take it or leave it."

"We had an agreement."

"Bah! Agreements!"

"You English swine! Give me my dough right now!"

"Yeah, yeah. Go on, shout some more."

English. They all thought he was English. He had to do something about his Oxford pronunciation. The riverbank was slippery.

"I'll show you," the owner promised.

He jumped onto the bank, musket in hand, and ran after Miles. The latter, who was just about to mount his horse, turned around and faced his adversary. There was neither astonishment nor disgust in his hazel eyes now, just good ancient loathing for the greedy, unscrupulous, obnoxious ways of the uneducated. He reached into his inside pocket and produced a purse.

"All right," he said trying to sound like Ruth's uncle, born and raised in Maine. "Here."

With the arrogance of a conqueror, the ferry owner extended his hand. Miles sprang forward and grabbed the musket. He head-butted the stubborn fellow, who fell on his back, leaving the musket in Miles' possession.

Miles dropped the purse back in his pocket and, towering over the poor ignorant bungler, said, "Let me tell you something, you miserable river rat... you repulsive turtle..."

"Ouch."

"This..." he produced the purse again, and spoke very calmly, "...is really my last money. The great are oftentimes forgetful, the amount of services you render them over the years notwithstanding. Regardless of the outcome of tonight's venture, I must have good lodgings, a soft bed, and a big fat beautiful breakfast tomorrow. A non-conservative girl would be nice too, although that's optional in view of their limited availability these days." He paused before shouting savagely, "You understand that?" In his ordinary voice, he asked, "Do you understand that there are people in this world to whom not having breakfast is tantamount to being spat upon by a drunken whore? Huh? Imagine me tomorrow - drowsy, angry, unrefreshed, unbathed; there's just no way I can go without breakfast! The entire world would be in danger! You may insult me, imprison me, deny me my robe with tassels, steal my women, defile my family name. I am not easily insulted, believe you me. I'm seasoned. I'm callous. I'm hardly sensitive. But don't ever think of depriving me of breakfast. Not having breakfast..." he paused again; he bellowed, aiming the musket at the prostrate ferry owner's head, "...makes me extremely nervous!!! Do you hear, you sack of last year's manure? Extremely!! FUCKING!! NERVOUS!!!"

He spun around, mounted his horse, and galloped away, carrying the musket.

The ferryman crawled back to his ferry, crossed the river, ran into his hut, opened a cabinet, grabbed the whiskey bottle, pulled the cork out with his teeth, and gulped down more than half of the bottle's contents.

Thomas Jefferson walked down Market Street slowly, his expression tense. Reaching an intersection, he turned the corner, stopped and listened. His hand clutched the handle of the pistol behind his belt.

At the sound of cautious steps, Jefferson clenched his teeth. A very drunk young man passed by who did not appear to notice Jefferson. The statesman heaved a muffled but powerful sigh of relief. Slowly, he released his weapon and stepped out into the open. His eyes widened. The muzzle of a pistol, not three paces away, was aimed at him.

Suddenly, the person holding the pistol cried out. His hand was forced upward. Miles, clutching Doome's wrist, head-butted him from the side. Doome, struggling to free the hand holding the pistol, refused to lose his balance. Miles head-butted him again. Doome was still standing. Exasperated, Miles drove his knee into the other man's groin. Doome grunted and bent his knees slightly. Miles head-butted him again. This time, Doome fell, releasing the pistol. Miles grabbed it before it hit the ground.

"Stubborn bastard," Miles said angrily, kicking Doome in the ribs.

"Hello, Miles," Jefferson said, sticking his own pistol behind his belt again.

"Oh, hi, Thomas. You should tell your friend Mr. Hamilton to put up some road signs. Milestones would be nice as well. And this must be Mr. Doome. Hello? Doome?"

Doome mumbled something.

"By the way, Thomas," Mile said, squatting by his victim, turning him over on his stomach, and getting out a length of rope. "King George says hello and wants you to know that he'll pardon some of you hot-headed gallows birds if only you mend your ways."

"Does he?" Jefferson said, also squatting, studying Doome curiously.

Doome roared. Miles tied his hands together, straightened, and, with one vicious jerk lifted the man to his feet.

"The King's too kind," Miles said. "Personally, I'd have you hanged, Thomas. From a lamppost."

"I'll bear that in mind," Jefferson said. "Miles, I'm indebted to you for life."

"It's nothing," Miles said. "Don't even mention it. I need a drink and some money. And a little rest before I go adventuring again."

FOURTEEN

Former Lovers

The two revolutions that put an end to Feudalism and gave the world yet another interesting economic structure were, in the long run, a boon to many and a nuisance to few. A number of curious side effects occurred. Most historians were so fascinated by the sheer novelty of the bombastic slogans, mottoes, and truisms on the protesters' banners; by the new meaning of the word *liberty*; by the new and intriguing connotation the word *equality* had suddenly attained through Franklin's and Jefferson's efforts; and by the general hopefulness of the new order, that they conveniently overlooked everything that was, in fact, essential. Thus, for instance, no one seemed to have noticed that in the eight-year period between the two Revolutions, there was a proliferation, on both sides of the Atlantic, of women approaching forty and looking ten years younger; that the greatest composer of the era died; that the greatest English-language poet of the era was born; that the wig was going rapidly out of fashion; and that all development in architecture stopped dead, waiting for the next world-class dictator to jump-start it. That, of course, was never going to happen. No one in his right might would willingly give up liberty, equality and, in certain countries, fraternity, whatever *that* meant, for a bit of architectural splendor. Who needed good architecture, anyway? Well, apparently, some people did, for, only a few years later, Napoleon was crowned at Notre Dame.

Washington's and Jefferson's policy prevented a great deal of ugliness that is known to follow political upheavals. Thus, although every Loyalist and every Englishman had long since left Mappensville, their property was neither confiscated nor leased to anyone else. Now, gradually, some of them were beginning to come back. Their housekeepers, butlers, and barristers preceded them. Assessing decay levels, they hired contractors, who, in turn, hired bricklayers, blacksmiths, carpenters, and masterbuilders, who in turn needed lodgings, clothes, food, medicine, and entertainment.

Jack Dubois, the insightful, pragmatic mayor, doubled the town's police force to ensure safety for the, ahem, *traitors*. The proliferation of new projects quickly led the city out of the financial crisis it had been languishing in for over a year.

A certain medium-sized townhouse on King's Pleasures Drive, now called Liberty Street, received a new façade. The rooms were repaired, repainted, reupholstered, and refurnished. A new fireplace was installed in every room. Because of the limited availability of paintings in the vicinity, Kenneth Sloan was able to sell a few patriotic landscapes to replace the portraits of the current British dynasty; three of his paintings landed in Liberty Street's townhouse.

Clarisse, aging gracefully, sat in a graceful pose on a gracefully shaped seat in her gracefully furnished and tastefully decorated living room. Hector, in his customary indigo coat, was filling his pipe by the fireplace.

"So he died in England and you came back," he said uncertainly.

"Yes. I'm now officially a rich widow, something I always wanted to be."

"Are you happy, then?"

"It's been disappointing so far. How about you? Are you happy, being married to... what's her name again? ... Rachel? Esther?"

"Ruth."

"That's right. Are you happy with her?"

"Yes."

"I see."

She kicked off a shoe and stretched her leg gracefully, admiring it. Hector placed his pipe on the mantelpiece.

"I still have beautiful legs," she suggested, turning her foot this way and that. "Don't you think?"

"Yes, you do."

"Like what you see?"

"What is this, a come on?"

"Why not?"

"You come back after ten years and just drop me a note. Just like that."

"You were quick enough to respond to that note, dear."

She admired him. He was tall (well... she was taller...), lean, and somewhat more angular than before. His hair was partly gray. The odd blend of Mediterranean sharpness and Scandinavian puffiness of his features produced, now that he was fifty, an almost regal countenance. And, of course, he was more than just a handsome lover. In an era when the populations of entire countries found themselves uncertain as to what their purpose was, he was a man on a mission. Democratic republics needed ships as much as monarchies did. His vocation transcended epochs and economic structures, which was why he could afford to regard the great global changes with the incredulity of a child and the condescending smile of a genius at the same time. Clarisse reddened perceptibly.

He came over and squatted beside her, taking her foot in his hand.

"Clarisse. I just want to make one thing perfectly clear. I love my wife. I would not leave her for the whole world."

"Not even if you had to choose between her and the shipyard?"

"She doesn't interfere with my business activities."

Clarisse looked at him ironically. He avoided her eyes.

"Well, maybe she does, but not too much," he said, not very confidently

She giggled. He blushed. Still a child, at fifty. Somehow men of no particular occupation, including some bankers, tend to mature quicker.

"I'd never stand between you and your ships," she announced. "I know that's what you do. She doesn't. She thinks..."

"If you think you're going to achieve anything by disparaging Ruth, you're wrong."

"Then tell me what I should do to achieve it."

"Achieve what?"

"I don't know. You're the one who used the word just now." She made an impatient gesture. "Oh, Hector, I missed you so much all these years. Why couldn't the silly bitch stay married to Crawford? He was never home; his money was always at her disposal. If she was lonely, she should have just taken a lover. Your wife is an extremely selfish woman, Hector."

Hector released her foot and straightened.

"You don't know her," he said coldly.

"I used to. She has a value system that she thinks is universal. Others must either adjust or face her noble wrath."

"Everyone on earth is more or less guilty of that."

"Not to the degree she is. Her hypocrisy is very subtle. It would never occur to anyone to call her a bad person no matter what she said or did. But subtlety doesn't change the essence; she's still a hypocrite."

"How can you say that! You know nothing about her!" he snapped, angry despite himself.

"Don't be naive, Hector."

"I insist you tell me."

"How about a drink first?"

"No. Tell me."

"No?"

"...Yes, all right."

Clarisse sprang to her feet with the agility of a teenager. Though very tall, she was extremely feminine and light-footed. She flew to the oaken cabinet from which she produced a bottle and two glasses.

"French brandy from the province of Cognac. Distilled twice. Aged to perfection in oaken barrels, hence the color. Have you heard from Crawford lately?"

"He just came back from England."

"Is he in town?"

"Yes. Renting a townhouse, I believe. Funny thing, I never liked him much, but of all the people I know, Crawford seems to be the most decent. Amazing."

"But of course. Just recently, he saved a very prominent person's life."

"How so?"

She filled the glasses, handed him one, and told him a story.

Once upon a time, a great-minded man lived in a very large country whose wealthier citizens paid tribute to a smaller state and were forced to make up for the loss, at least in part, by paying their employees less and their slaves nothing. The great man studied people and life. Both interested him immensely. He could not help noticing that people oftentimes lived like dogs, or worse. Many were poorly clothed, ill-fed, exposed to all kinds of peril, and largely benighted.

The man decided to help his people live better. To that end, he set out to accomplish two things – the smaller country had to be shown the door; and a new order of things had to be devised.

The former was achieved in the traditional manner – with the bayonet. It took a little longer than expected, but eventually, after many people died in the battlefield, the task was completed.

The latter required some thinking.

The problem with all new ideologies that are meant to raise the living standards of a nation is that they are all based on an erroneous premise, namely, that people, when left to their own devices, are generally good, considerate, responsible, and kind, as opposed to vindictive, obnoxious, greedy, envious, and indifferent towards their neighbor's problems. The reason for the misconception is that every new ideology is, in a nutshell, just another attempt on man's part to live without God. The Creator's order, as anyone who has read the Bible knows, is based on love and mercy. Man's order is based on fear and mistrust, as evidenced by the penal code present in every set of laws humanity has ever devised. To summarize, if you try to be a good person on God's territory, the chances are you'll gain entrance to the Kingdom of Heaven. If you abide by every human law (and there are usually volumes upon volumes of those), the chances are, the authorities might actually leave you alone. Maybe.

The great man authored one document and influenced the author of another; these two documents were the ones in which the new nation placed its trust.

The man saw the fundamental error of his concept early enough. He realized that alliances had to be formed, and reforms instituted constantly in order to keep the new system working. Which, unfortunately, was not enough. He admitted as much in a letter to a friend, saying, "What country can preserve its liberties, if its rulers are not warned from time to time that the people preserve the spirit of resistance? Let them take arms... The tree of liberty must be refreshed from time to time, with the blood of patriots and tyrants."

At one point, he wanted to make friends with a different country whose culture, architecture, and nightlife appealed to him most. Unfortunately, a powerful group of people who had a great deal of influence in the new nation wished to make friends with yet another country. The great man was in the way; they decided to eliminate him.

A mercenary was hired by the group. They gave him the great man's address, issued an advance and promised more money once the task was completed.

Fortunately, the great man and his country were saved by a lucky accident. This was not the first time it happened to him, which would have led a less obstinate philosopher to the conclusion that Divine Providence, and not mere chance, interfered with the enemy's plans. A person who laughed at politics, disdained the military, resented organized combat, and scoffed at the idea of affiliation with any party, group, or gang, a knight errant of the first and purest order, came to the rescue and disarmed the mercenary before the latter could strike the fatal blow.

Clarisse told the story in a jocose manner, sort of. Hector was stunned. The matter concerned him personally. After a while he became very angry and had to excuse himself. He left Clarisse's house quickly. She was very disappointed.

Jerome never married. As a young idealist, he was not very popular with women. Growing older and somewhat wiser, he came to disdain them, which was perfectly childish and yet, in his case, understandable. To Mildred the Baroness, however, he was still the golden-haired youth who had once, sword in hand, challenged an entire company of brigands. Sixteen years later, after Jerome quarreled with a mistress, Mildred took the opportunity to supplant her, for old times' sake.

For Jerome, she was a quintessence of convenience. She had no demands; she visited twice or three times a week; she never asked for gifts or to go out; she did not have any unpleasant body odors.

They were kissing passionately in his study – she, sitting on the desk, he, standing in front of her – when the disturbance occurred.

"Jerome! Jerome, damn it!" Hector's voice called from the anteroom.

"Hold it," Jerome told Mildred.

He let go of her. The diminutive Baroness slid off the desk. The door flung open before Jerome could touch the knob.

"Well!" Hector shouted, entering.

"Yes, Eriksson. What is it?" Jerome asked testily.

"Was it you who sanctioned Jefferson's murder?"

"No. Any more questions like that?"

"Look, I'm not meddling in your affairs. Don't you meddle in mine. Our relationship is just business, do you understand? Jefferson and Hamilton are offering me a contract. This is my chance to build a dozen ships for the Government. It's not official yet. So just don't spoil it all with your political nonsense! Understand?"

"You're poorly informed, Eriksson. I don't deal in politics anymore. Just business."

"Just business my ass. Good morning, Baroness, you're more charming than ever. Like I said, cut the crap, Jerome. You Gallic Faction people have been getting on everyone's nerves lately. We're living in a new era, Jerome. The Republic is for good, just get that through your paranoid mind. And stop lying. Crawford has just returned from Philadelphia. A man called Samuel Doome has been arrested and is awaiting trial. You expect me to believe this is the first time you've heard that name?"

Jerome's features contorted. He drew back from Hector.

"Ah, shit," he said.

"Besides, what's the big idea, anyway? Jefferson is a wonderful person, I think. I can't imagine how he could get in the way of anyone in this country. If your sole purpose is to arrange for a reign of terror, maybe you should become a pirate, or a music teacher. Terrorizing an entire country is absurd. It will only make everyone miserable, including yourself."

He made for the door. Jerome – pale, stunned, sat in a chair at his desk. Hector stopped in the doorway. Having vented his anger, he regained his calm quickly, saying over his shoulder, "Just let me build those ships,

Jerome. Just lay off politics until they're built and put out to sea. You may kill off half the Government after that, for all I care. Just give me enough time to get established."

He slammed the door. Jerome stood still for a moment, thinking frantically. Mildred stared at him, frightened.

"Looks like the end of the rope, eh?" he asked, addressing no one in particular.

And so it was. The leader of the Faction had to have an impeccable track record. Jerome had been successful for years. This was his first major failure, and it was going to cost him his reputation, his future, and, if they chose to make him the scapegoat, his life. It was time to act.

He picked up the bell and rang.

"Are you leaving?" Mildred asked.

"I'm afraid so."

"What time do you expect to be back?"

"Oh, I don't know. Around noon, I suppose."

"Oh. Could you make it a little later?"

"No problem."

Jerome's servant entered.

"Because, you see, I have to do something tomorrow," Mildred explained apologetically.

"Tomorrow? Yes, of course," Jerome said absentmindedly.

"I mean, a little bit past noon tomorrow, right?"

"No. Around noon, ten or fifteen years from now. Xavier, my carriage, please, and fill a trunk with everything necessary for a long journey."

"Ten years?" Mildred exclaimed incredulously. 'What are you talking about?"

"I have to stay out of the country long enough for the morons to forget my name."

She was stunned. "Tell me you're joking," she said.

"I don't have a sense of humor. You know that."

"Take me with you."

"Xavier," Jerome shouted savagely, "what are you waiting for?"

"Are you going to dismiss me, sir?"

"Three months' wages. That's the best I can do right now. Also, for a little extra, kindly load my pistols and sharpen my sword. Get me my best suit, too. I have to pay someone a visit before I go."

When he was gone, Mildred, her mind blank, spent some time in the study. She had always known she meant nothing to Jerome. Their frequent trysts, however, had softened the effect and once or twice, in his bedroom, she had been able to forget everything and simply treat him as her husband, helping him into his robe, brushing his hair for him, cuddling up to him before dozing off, having a cup of tea while sitting naked on his lap.

Leaving his house for the last time, she walked to the harbor, kicked off her shoes and strolled on the cold and damp sand. She could not yet grasp what had just happened. She was numb. She felt some vague resentment towards Hector who was, she thought, the principle cause of Jerome's precipitated departure; she further theorized that whoever it was who had failed to assassinate, what was his name, Jeffers? Geoffrey? was disgustingly incompetent; and not a good person either: he had interfered with Jerome's plans and, lo, Jerome was gone.

Jerome was gone! That was it. Gone. Forever. She would never see him again.

She discovered she was crying softly. Was it possible she had loved him all these years? She had slept with many, but wasn't it Jerome she had always loved — at a distance at first, and then up-close? Had she not dreamed of the proverbial uninhabited isle where she and Jerome might live one day, under the palm trees, sipping champagne, eating olives and oysters at the tavern by the surf — for even an uninhabited island must have at least one tavern?

Good old Mildred.

Clarisse, relaxing in her fluffy soft bed, unfolded Hector's note and held it up to the light pouring from the window.

The letter read, "*Dear Clarisse. Please don't send me any more letters if you don't wish to compromise me. My wife will be spending the night at her friend's place. Please come by at ten. Hopefully, the children will be asleep by then. I have many things to tell you, none of them pleasant. I would call on you myself, except I seem to have a bad cold. Yours Truly, Hector.*"

Clarisse threw the cover off and raised one leg, admiring it. She smiled mischievously.

FIFTEEN

Mappensville's Own Big-Time Murder Mystery

Molly, in a man's suit, dropped by Kenneth and Patty's place for some tea. Kenneth devoured her with his eyes. He thought she looked ravishing. He said so.

Patty tugged at his sleeve. "Kenneth."

No, he insisted, there was just no getting around it. He went on staring. He said they had to do it. What did they have to do? He had to paint her in that costume. Oh.

Molly smiled. "Not tonight."

"I thought you were going to spend the night," he reminded her.

"Yes. Still, I'm not in the mood. Some other time. I'm sorry."

Kenneth pouted. Patty was pleased and looked gratefully at Molly. The latter nodded and rose. She explained she felt like taking a stroll. Patty looked at her with deep admiration. So understanding! So true! Kenneth was still pouting.

"Sure," he said. "One of your ever-so-pleasant evening strolls. All alone, walking down the street. Selfish people..."

Patty interrupted him. "She can take care of herself, dear."

Molly, realizing she had been betrayed, yet having expected it all along, sort of, shook her head and smiled sadly. Patty blushed.

Kenneth, oblivious as usual, continued grumbling about selfish people who enjoyed solitude after getting their fill of others' company for the day. They never wanted to give anything back.

"Now, dear," Patty said.

"Kennie," Molly beamed, "I know how you feel, dear. But I'm human too. Don't pout like that, you look ridiculous."

With joyous indignation, Patty exclaimed, "He does not!"

"All right," Molly agreed. "He doesn't."

She picked up her gloves and walked out, as graceful and vital as ever. The front door screeched closed. For a while, Kenneth and Patty sat in silence. Kenneth was soon distracted by Patty's favorite Cherokee doll that had been in the house for ten years, and when Patty, her eyes shining, demanded that he tell her the truth, he ignored her. She insisted. Irritably, he turned to her.

"The truth? The truth. What truth?"

"Promise you'll be honest."

"Yeah, all right," he said indifferently. His mind was obviously elsewhere. Instinctively, his eyes searched for something he could draw with.

"Was she ever your mistress?"

He sprang to his feet and dashed across the room. In the corner, he picked up a blank crumpled sheet and a piece of charcoal. He rushed back to the table. He spread and straightened the sheet as best he could. He managed an overall draft of Molly in a man's suit before the question finally sank in.

"No," he said incredulously. "What? My mistress? No," he sounded guilty this time. He reddened. "No, of course not. Uh... Why's this important?"

"Because I have news for you."

"What?" He abandoned the sketch. There was a long pause. He stammered, "Are you.... darling! I hope... I dare not hope..."

He moved towards her, his expression a quintessence of tenderness.

"Tomorrow's our anniversary," she told him.

"Oh."

He was disappointed. He sat down and started seriously to sulk.

"I'm sorry," she said ruefully. "I know what you must have imagined. I'm sorry, Kenny. I'm afraid I just can't do that."

On an impulse, he threw the charcoal away, took her hand in his, and planted a gentle kiss on her wrist.

Molly walked briskly down the street towards a nervous-looking carriage parked tentatively at the sidewalk. Throaty was on the box. He looked over his shoulder. He scrambled down. Molly acknowledged his presence by inkling her head just slightly. She opened the door of the carriage and lifted the back seat, pulling out a pistol. Throaty took it from her, examining it closely. It was the same pistol Hector had once received from the German inventor as a present: a four-shot revolver. It struck Throaty as weird.

"The drum turns every time you fire a shot," Molly instructed him. "Four shots in quick succession. It's important that you don't fire more than three times, though. Yes? How many time are you going to fire?"

He assured her that one was going to be enough. She nodded. He was a good marksman. Did he remember the plan? Yes, he did, but was she sure the lad was going to be there? Well, if not, they would try again another night. But yes, she was pretty sure.

"He's always there at this hour. He goes through his papers every night. Some shady dealings, or something. Anyway, don't forget which window. The necklace is in the third right-hand drawer from the top. Most important, don't hesitate."

"Don't worry about it," he said, grinning.

"Good luck."

Throaty shoved the pistol behind his belt. Molly climbed onto the box and pulled off. He filled his pipe, thinking of what he was going to say to Mongoose before pulling the trigger. It had to be big. It had to be meaningful. It had to be gratifying.

In the meantime, Jerome, dressed for a journey, and Mongoose were engaged in a quiet, intense conversation at the Mayor's office. Jack DuBois was trying to convince the Faction's leader that jumping ship without naming a successor was not a good move.

"Delacroix will do in the interim," Jerome disagreed. "Later, we'll think of someone else."

"His name is too French."

"So what. After all, I'd hate people to think that we're called the Gallic Faction for nothing."

"Delacroix doesn't have your ability. He can't control everything. The farms, the textiles, the arms factory – we're talking about one hell of an establishment here."

Jerome was annoyed. He never gave the Mayor's cerebral powers much credit, but it should have been obvious to any idiot that when a man like himself had to leave town on such a short notice, it was never for a pleasure trip. Well. There was no reason to conceal anything anymore.

"Look, stupid," he said. "I thought I was making myself perfectly clear when I told you I couldn't stay. An important affair was botched, our fellow is in their hands. If I stay, they'll arrest me, since the jerk must have mentioned my name by now. Once I'm arrested, they'll have their leads. The Gallic Faction as we know it will cease to exist, and the diplomatic relations between England and this Republic thing here will be severed. If I leave, I'll have my life and my freedom; and you and Delacroix will have the power. Get it? All right. Let me put it in a way even you will understand. Do you want to run for governor come the next election? Huh, moron?"

"Well, since you put it this way..."

"Now. I need something to sell to the Parliament gentlemen so that they get off my back for a while. Some compromising correspondence. Can you arrange that?"

"I have some letters."

"Good. Here?"

"In the safe box downstairs. One from Hamilton in which he's trying to bribe someone; one from Jefferson, in which he reveals too much of the

Government's policy to a German diplomat."

"Bring them here."

"Now?"

Jerome smote the desk exasperatedly with his fist.

"All right, fine," Mongoose said hastily. "Just don't get angry, please. Gees, I feel like such an idiot when you get angry."

He shook his head, lingered for a moment, and left the room. Jerome sprawled in the Mayor's chair, turning his back to the door.

Throaty crossed the plaza and tried the front door. It opened easily. He entered, scanning the surroundings. Not seeing anyone, he very confidently and without any unnecessary haste crossed the vestibule and walked up the stairs.

He turned the knob slowly, pushed the door and peeked in. The office was semi-dark. The Mayor sat in his chair behind the desk, his back to the door.

Quietly and evenly, Throaty said, "Don't move. Don't say anything. I have a loaded pistol in my hand."

His prey made a minuscule movement. Throaty raised his voice a notch.

"I said, don't move."

The prey froze. Throaty aimed the pistol at his nemesis' head.

"The time for reckoning has come," he announced. "This is more than personal, my friend. At first, I thought I'd make it personal. Revenge, pure and simple. But, no. It wouldn't be fair to the dozens of your other victims. I'm not the only one whose life you've screwed up; not the only one you've betrayed or killed. In fact, there must have been so many you can't even remember their names now. You have sunk so deeply in vice, you've been living in iniquity for so long, it's a routine matter for you to take a human life. I'm not merely a vindictive nut come to settle a score with you. All of your victims are speaking through me now; all can see you through my eyes. Dozens of hearts are beating in my chest, dozens of hands are clutching pistols. What goes around comes around. I'm the instrument of fate and justice. I will not give you the satisfaction of dying a martyr's death. I will not torture you. I will not show you my face. I will not name myself. You will die painlessly, easily, and quickly, and you will go straight to hell. Your presence on this earth is equally abhorrent to man and God. So long."

He fired a single shot. The figure in the chair went limp. Throaty crossed to the window and threw the curtain aside. Moonlight flooded the room. At that moment, the hat fell off his prey's head, and, turning, Throaty saw Jerome's blond locks.

In a toneless voice, Throaty said, "Ah, shit."

He rushed to Jerome and looked at his face.

"Fuck," he whispered. "Fuck! Big-time fuck!"

He wiped the sweat off his forehead. He shoved the pistol behind his belt. He remembered the necklace. Which drawer? The third one. The third one from the top, on the right. It was locked. There was no time for fancy burglar tricks. He put the muzzle of the revolver to the keyhole and pulled the trigger. The bullet shattered the lock. He tore open the drawer, and there it was. Hastily, he shoved the necklace in his pocket. He slammed the drawer closed. A superstitious tremor ripping gently through him, Throaty picked up Jerome's hat and stuck it on the corpse's head.

He thought he knew the man. Holding his breath, Throaty studied Jerome's features.

A handsome man. Powerful. Intelligent. Slightly idealistic. Not much success with women, for whatever reason. Goodness gracious, Throaty thought, what have I done. There were obviously people out there to whom in one way or another, Jerome was important. Throaty, old and experienced, could read people's faces well. In his turbulent life, he had comforted no one but himself. Jerome must have comforted many. That much was obvious to Throaty.

There were steps out in the hallway. People. Guards. Throaty dashed to the window and opened it. He stepped onto the sill. He saw a carriage rolling up the street. It was about to pass under the window. Casting one last glance over his shoulder at Jerome's corpse, Throaty leaped and landed on the carriage's roof. For a moment, the world stood still.

The door opened. Mongoose came in, carrying two letters.

"Here they are. You owe me one. I thought I heard a pistol shot. I must be getting paranoid."

He threw the letters on the table. He went to the window and looked out.

"Look at that moon. What a moronic grin. I must be getting old, or something. In the old days, I'd look at the ground first. Now, it's the sky. We get terribly sentimental as we get older."

He turned around and, at last, he saw. He got out his watch and marked the time. He was in shock, but his thoughts were clear and rational. Something about his desk struck him as odd. He was not sure what it was. Yes, of course. The drawer. It was not closed properly. He pulled it out. The necklace, a memento he kept to remind him of the old days, was missing. He picked up his hat and dashed out of the room.

They galloped a few blocks and turned twice. Molly reined in the horses. After checking the pistol in her belt, she jumped off the box, leaving Throaty alone on it. She circumvented the house quickly. Throaty heard the back door opening slowly. He stared in front of himself. Molly came back running, leaped onto the box, grabbed the reins from him and started off.

When Mongoose and McLachlan, who was officially the Police Commissioner of Mappensville, came into the Mayor's office, armed with lit candles, Jerome's body was still in the chair; the pose was the same also.

"There," Mongoose said. He sounded frustrated. "Take a look at that, if you please."

"Yes, sir," McLachlan said impassively.

He went over to take a look. He whistled softly. Placing the chandelier on the desk, he studied the murdered man's pose. He removed the hat off and examined the wound. He looked at the window. He nodded.

"Like what you see?" Mongoose asked testily.

"No, sir."

"I want to know the son of a bitch who did it."

He calmed down somewhat, walked over to the window and looked out.

"The window was open when I came in," he added pensively. "You can't very well jump from here to the ground without breaking a leg. They must have used a ladder."

"Or the roof of a carriage."

He continued inspecting Jerome's wound. Then he cast a brief glance at the drawer with the shot-through lock. He said nothing.

"Look, Baron," Mongoose said. McLachlan shuddered. "I kept you on after we drove out the English because you're an expert. I want you to find the murderer; and I want you to do it quickly."

John McLachlan closed his eyes, counted to ten, and was just able to control himself.

"Well, Mr. Mayor," he said, "as an expert, I'm beginning to have doubts."

"What are you talking about?"

"I'm not sure, nor do I know what makes *you* so certain, about the perpetrator's motives. For instance, what gave you the idea it was this… uh… mountebank here, and not yourself, whom the murderer targeted originally?"

Mongoose's eyes widened. He was as disgusted with this theory as McLachlan was pleased with it.

"You're saying this might have been a mistake?" he inquired, squinting at McLachlan. "They thought it was me in that chair? We don't look alike, man."

"It was dark in here. Also, there's no guarantee the assassin knew what his target was supposed to look like. Contract murders of this sort are by no means uncommon. He was told where he could find you at this hour. He was told you would most likely be alone. Now, what do we do?"

"I don't know. I guess we need a little more time to think."

"That's not what I asked. Where do we go from this point? Do we proceed with the investigation, or do we close it for lack of evidence?"

"What lack of evidence!"

"Oh, there's plenty of evidence, all right, but if you knew who the assassin was, perhaps you wouldn't be so eager to go on?"

"You mean the Gallic Faction."

"I don't mean, or anyway I'm not suggesting anything at all at this point. The evidence might show us some very nasty angles here. If it were, as you put it, the Gallic Faction, then what reasons would they have for murdering him, or you, for that matter? He was their leader, and you are still, I believe, on excellent terms with them."

"I have no dealings with them," Mongoose snapped.

McLachlan frowned. "I'm an expert, sir. I make it my affair to know as much about the people in this city as possible. What you choose to say in court is your business, but don't insult my intelligence by telling me Cherokee bedtime stories."

The Commissioner was a knowledgeable man, a man of insight. Like most intelligent people, however, he had a very vague idea of what was happening in his own backyard – or so Mongoose thought. The Mayor shrugged.

"Yes," McLachlan said quietly, "I understand your skepticism. It's ironic, but, you see, I do know about my wife also."

Mongoose looked at him sharply.

"Has nothing to do with the official business, sir," McLachlan said coldly. "Technically, we are both on duty, and you are my superior. My next official question is, do you think anyone might bear you a grudge?"

Mongoose sat in a chair and scratched his head. He was taken aback somewhat. McLachlan, after giving him another hard stare, resumed his inspection of the wound.

"Very interesting," he commented. "Look at this. A musket ball would have made a huge hole in the fellow's head at this range. We must assume, then, that it was a pistol. But pistols don't make neat wounds like this either. The skull isn't broken; it's cut through. So, it might not have been a pistol, or, at least, not the type of pistol you habitually use to shoot members of the Gallic Faction with. Again, at this range – and, judging from the small amount of blood spilled, the shot was fired from close range... If so, the bullet should have drilled the lad's head right through. It didn't. As a matter of fact, it's lodged very close to the opening. Does anyone in this city own weak pistols?"

"Weak? ... I don't know."

"I do," McLachlan said, reflecting. "Some ten years ago, a German gentleman visited us and distributed some presents, among which there were two pistols, or devices that looked and functioned like pistols. You could fire four shots in quick succession with them. The bullets, I remember, were peculiarly shaped. Miles Crawford has one."

"Miles Crawford!"

"Yes. But Miles Crawford has been away for years. Which leaves us with only one unexplored possibility. I received a note this morning."

He reached into his inside pocket, produced the note, and handed it over the desk to Mongoose. The latter, rising, took it, and, after staring at the Baron for a good five seconds, unfolded it.

"*Bad trouble tonight,*" the note said blandly. "*Look at the wound. No standard weapon could have done that.*"

Mongoose had a cold feeling in his stomach. McLachlan's professional attitude was beginning to frighten him. Someone was after him, good Mayor DuBois, he had no idea who it was. It was someone with whom it was impossible to communicate, someone resourceful, secretive, and intelligent. What good are locks when there are such enormous windows in every room? What good are bodyguards when a good marksman can blow your brains out at three hundred paces? What good are your good deeds if there are people in the world who will bear you a grudge for decades? What good is your seemingly great popularity among thousands if it takes just one person to send you to the Ultimate Evaluator of Merits?

"The bad trouble is, in all likelihood, this," McLachlan observed calmly, indicating the body in the chair. "I'm not familiar with the handwriting, and besides, it looks forged. The only other weapon belongs to Mr. Eriksson the shipbuilder, whom we always suspected of being closely affiliated with you know who. He may have owed them. Well?"

"Well?"

"The Gallic Faction?"

"I don't know anymore," Mongoose said dully.

"Fine. So. Do we arrest him? Should I send for my intrepid lads? Or do we let him get away with it?"

Impossible! Hector Eriksson? The fellow would not hurt a fly. His wife?

Oh. Yes, Mongoose knew her very well, but they had been on excellent terms lately. Someone else in the household? The maid? The *kids*? It did not make sense. Someone must have come and borrowed or stolen the weapon – if the Commissioner was right about the weapon. Who was this someone?

Somewhere in the past, he must have left a loose end. Someone must have survived the stab, the musket shot, the fatal push off a cliff's edge – he had a dozen names to choose from. Who? And why would anyone wait so many years?

Kenneth was busy touching up a landscape. Patty, agitated, paced in front of him.

"I don't know, there must be something wrong."

"Yeah," he said glumly.

"I mean, she takes a stroll, then she comes back for a second, and suddenly she's off again. Oh, I hope she's all right."

Kenneth hurled the brush across the studio. It smacked into the wall, leaving a large mauve and yellow smear. He spun around.

"She'll be fine," he said quietly and unpleasantly. "Nothing ever happens to her."

"Hey! What's the matter with you?"

"It'll never occur to anyone to say anything half-bad about her. She's kind, considerate, industrious, and loyal. She always puts herself in a position where she can't be blamed for anything. It's her specialty."

"Are you mad at her?"

"Me?" he shouted. "No! Of course not! Whatever gave you that idea! Good old Ruth. She's a model human being. She's beyond reproach!"

"Is this because she didn't give you the money?"

He laughed, clutching his head, and had to sit down.

"Don't be silly!" he said, waving her off. "When Ruth says she has no money to give, I believe her. I have no reason to doubt her, do I? Everyone knows she's a saint. It's not her fault that she's never made anyone happy. That is a saint's job, isn't it? Making people happy? She's never had the chance, that's all. In the ten years I've known her, she hasn't been blessed with a single opportunity to make someone unbearably happy. She hurts people sometimes, but that's because she's very frank and open with everybody. She's very sincere. She says what she thinks. Besides, what's ten years compared to eternity? It took Washington less than that to drive the English out, but that's because in politics everyone's always running around like a mad monkey. Ruth is in no rush! She takes things as they come; slow and steady..."

"You're being stupid. Ruth's a wonderful person."

"Of course she is. Wonderful? Wonderful doesn't even begin to describe it. She's a saint, I tell you! It's the others who are rats and creeps. You know, when she was here tonight, I thought I saw a halo over her head. I'm serious. I wanted to perpetuate it immediately on canvas, except I discovered I didn't have the right fucking paint!"

Patty sat astride the bench and looked down. She was deeply hurt. Still, Kenneth's anger had struck a note she could not immediately identify. It was going to bother her vaguely for a while.

Wrapped up in his robe, Hector rested in a chair. He was obviously sick. His eyes were bloodshot, his face puffy. He wiped his nose with a handkerchief. He sipped wine from a crystal glass. He set the glass down and suddenly sneezed, loudly and painfully. Ruth entered in her men's costume, unbuckled her sword and thew it on the table, sheath, baldric, and all. Hector was surprised and slightly frightened.

"Ruth? Hello... darling."

"Hi. Look, I'm sorry. I might... Well, I shouldn't have gone. It was selfish of me to leave knowing you were sick. Are the kids in bed?"

"Yes, they..."

"Let's just spend the night by the fire place, shall we? Just you and I, darling. Just like the old days."

"Look, Ruth..."

"Here, that fire needs more wood."

She went to the fireplace and threw a fresh log in it. Hector cast a furtive glance at the clock on the wall.

This was monstrously embarrassing. And frightening. Wives and mistresses do not like one another, although there must be some satisfaction in jealousy – it would not be so astonishingly popular otherwise. There is tragedy in being cheated on, and every true tragedy contains a grain of beauty.

Was she beginning to suspect something? How much did she know? How much did the mother of his children, his wife of the past ten years, was aware of? He was not guilty of anything – not yet, certainly not where Clarisse, with whom he had had an affair long before he married Ruth, was concerned. Was he ready and willing to renew the relationship? He was not certain. There had been, to be sure, some detachment in Ruth's recent attitude. Now, Clarisse was coming, Clarisse expected to find him alone, Clarisse was going to barge in wearing her sexiest dress., Clarisse in her stocking feet, shoes in one hand — she was fond of taking her shoes off and tiptoeing her way through life. The maid was spending the night at her aunt's place, and Ruth was going to open the door.

Sick and anxious, he cast another glance at the clock. Molly rose from her chair. She walked over to the mahogany table and fingered the pommel of the sword. Suddenly, Hector rose and, trying to appear casual, stretched.

"Let me get a breath of fresh air."

"Excuse me?" she asked coldly.

"Some air. I need air. I'll be right back."

"I wouldn't recommend it, Hector. It's very cold out."

"I think the cold will do me good. I'll only be a moment."

"No. Don't go. Another hour."

"I'll go. I'll be right back."

He moved towards the door. Molly picked up the sword, ran across the room and blocked his way.

"Back in your chair, Hector."

"What are you doing, Ruth?"

"I'm ordering you to get back in your chair."

Attempting to preserve his dignity, he said in a formal voice, "Pardon me. Let me pass please."

"I wouldn't if I were you."

He stepped forward. Molly pushed him in the chest with her left hand. He stumbled back, bristled, summoned all of his strength and made a crazy attempt to force his way out. A brief struggle followed. Molly struck him in the face with the hilt of her sword. He spun around, staggered and fell to his knees, pressing his palm to his cheekbone. He looked at his hand. There was blood on it.

Coldly, deliberately, she repeated, "Back in the chair, Hector."

"You're mad, Ruth."

She drew her sword and threw away the sheath.

"Come on. Move."

He rose, wiping the blood off with his sleeve.

"If this has anything to do with..."

"In that chair, Hector."

He trudged back to the chair, weak, humiliated, and uncertain. What was the crazy bitch going to do? This was definitely about Clarisse. Ruth had plans. Was she going to, upon Clarisse's arrival, beat them both up? He wouldn't put it past her. She had never tried to abuse him physically before. But she was who she was, and her previous husband had taught her some positively atrocious ways of hurting people.

He sat. Molly walked over to the table and poured some water from the pitcher on her handkerchief. Turning around, she saw Hector flirting with the idea of dashing for the door again. She handed him her handkerchief.

"Here, dab your gash with this."

He accepted the monogrammed piece of silk. "R.E.," for Ruth Eriksson. Molly went to the door and threw on the latch.

Assisted by her maid, Clarisse dressed. The maid tightened the corset for her.

"Not too tight, please," Clarisse said with a chuckle. "I'm a widow. I'm entitled to a bit of negligence here and there, it's my prerogative."

She sprinkled perfume on her neck and chest. The maid tied the lace strings under Clarisse's knees. Clarisse stepped into a pair of very graceful English shoes. She looked in the mirror critically.

"What do you think? Am I still attractive, even a little bit?"

"You are positively ravishing, Madam. No man could resist you."

"Rubbish. Ordinary men will always follow the vogue. Just now, little round-faced creatures of sixteen are in fashion. An older woman stands no chance in today's society. Worthless cretins! But then, unless I'm terribly mistaken, Hector is not an ordinary man."

She ran her palm along her thigh. She held her breasts up with her hands and inclined her head.

"What can a sixteen year old give a man, besides the grate?"

"Nothing, Madam," the maid agreed obsequiously.

"I'm scared. I'm so scared."

The maid looked at her tenderly. They embraced.

"Don't be scared, Madam," this time, the maid's voice was quite sincere.

"He's a married man."

"Yes, Madam."

"He loves his wife. They have children."

The maid sighed.

What was she hoping to achieve? Clarisse was not sure. She might be able to become his mistress. That would be something. Secrecy and adventure, spiced-up lovemaking in the weirdest places. She could not make him divorce his wife – he was a loyal man, and there were children. The *classical woman*, as Margaret the Viscountess had once referred to her, was there to stay. What else? They would not be able to go out together, or travel around the world. He was away on business a great deal. She would meet him – in Boston, in Philly, in Dover; still, there were going to be no public outings. Ship builders had colleagues in every port, and their colleagues had tongues.

About her own reputation Clarisse did not give a flying fuck, but Hector needed his contracts and peace at home. The most reasonable thing to do was to tell the driver to turn around. Go home, change, and board the next ship for Holland. Fall in love with an impoverished artist there and support him. There were plenty of artists in Europe. There were none in America. Rent an apartment in Milan or Paris. Rubbish.

The carriage stopped a hundred paces from the entrance. The young driver jumped off the box and opened the door. Clarisse hopped out, as light and merry as a swallow, without waiting for the Driver to assist her.

"Should I wait here, Madam?"

"Let me see."

She studied the façade of Hector's house. There was a touch of acute tragedy in her reckless mirth. Her eyes flashed.

"No. Go. I won't be coming back tonight."

"Very well, Madam."

He climbed back on the box. She waited for the carriage to leave.

Hector sat in his chair, hunched, pitiful, hugging his knees. Ten paces away, Molly occupied a chair by the table, her feet up on the mahogany, her sword across her knees.

"What are we waiting for, exactly?" he asked hopelessly.

"You really want to know, don't you."

"Well, yes."

"Remember what happened fifteen years ago?"

"No."

"Are you sure?"

The vestibule was dark. The front door, which Molly had left unlocked, opened slowly and soundlessly. Clarisse walked in stealthily, took her shoes off, and carrying them in one hand, crossed the vestibule in her stocking feet, on tiptoe. Approaching the living room door, she heard voices inside. She froze. Her first impulse was to beat an uncouth retreat, to clear out and run like the wind, and never look back. She clenched her teeth and forced herself to draw closer and squat at the keyhole. She looked in, her heart beating frantically. She could not see much other than the seascape, in which the water looked like weak tea with lumps of sugar floating on the surface, over the fireplace. She put her ear to the keyhole.

"...And that's what you did," Molly concluded.

"I did not turn you over to them, Ruth. Not in any direct sense of the word. I thought I had explained the whole matter to you. Sticking you in jail for the night was the only way to keep you out of trouble. I came for you the next day, but your cell was empty."

"You expect me to believe that?"

"Yes, damn it! And even if it weren't true, don't you see how absurd it is to go back to it now, after ten years of marriage, two kids, and all the crap we've had to go through?"

"I didn't ask to go through any crap. You're a jerk, Hector."

"I may be a jerk, but I still love you."

He might just as well have named the winner of the elections in South Carolina, for all the effect his words produced.

"I didn't shoot you back then, fifteen years ago," Molly explained coldly, "because I figured you might not even care. I didn't kill you like a mad dog ten years ago, when I had my chance, because I thought that would be letting you off too easy. I suppose I did love you once, Hector... Anyway, now's the perfect time. And you're going to get what you deserve."

"You're going to kill me?"

The question amused her. She laughed – a brief, dry laugh. She had never shown him this side of her character. This was not the aggressively romantic high society lass whose opalescent neck he had kissed out on the frosty terrace of a Philadelphia mansion. Nor was it the alluring and mysterious brigand chief, the horror of the wealthy Loyalists and Patriots alike. Nor the prematurely wise survivor type keeping an aristocrat's mansion clean for a living. Nor yet the considerate, understanding housewife married to a shipbuilder she adored and rearing their two children. In front of him was a woman who disdained people – and who found the question, "Are you going to kill me?" mildly amusing, while knowing full well that she could, in fact, kill him very easily if she wished.

"Are you frightened? Good. No. I'm not going to kill you. An hour from now at the latest, the police are going to be here. I'll turn you over to them."

"The police! Why?"

"You're wanted for murder," she said evenly.

"Goodness gracious, Ruth. Whom did you kill?"

"I? No one. But the Mayor is dead, the weapon is in this house, and you'll be hanged before the week is over."

He swallowed hard. His throat hurt.

"I believe you're actually serious."

"Perfectly serious."

"What about the children?"

"What about them? They'll forget you in a month. Every time you go away, they miss you the first three or four days, maybe, and then they stop mentioning you."

"You do realize you're crazy, I hope?."

"Perhaps. I don't love you anymore, Hector. I'm sorry if this upsets you."

On the other side of the door, Clarisse straightened, drew away from the keyhole, and crossed the vestibule on tip-toe. Halfway across she stopped to massage her thigh – her right leg was asleep. She got out soundlessly, put on her shoes, and looked frantically around. This was neither London, Paris, nor Philadelphia. This was Mappensville, where carriages never cruised at night looking for fares. Clarisse ran down the street.

Miles kicked the door open. He shed his cloak and, unbuckling the sword, threw it on table. He took off his tricorne and let it drop to the floor. He stretched. He gazed absentmindedly around and suddenly froze. He was in shock. His eyes fixed on a chair spread across which was a luxurious mauve robe with heavy, angry, ridiculously tacky, most excellent silken tassels. For a good minute, Miles was unable to move. Advancing tentatively, he extended his hand. There was a symbolic knock at the door. His butler entered.

"My Lord..." he said.

His eyes still on the robe, Miles snapped, "Get out."

"There's a lady downstairs; she wants to see you."

"Penny?"

"Her intimate friends might call her that, my Lord," the servant suggested.

"So, it's not Penny. You know Penny. A lady, huh?" he continued eyeing the robe. "Did I ever sleep with her?"

"I'm sure I don't know, sir."

"Tell her to be very patient for my sake for about half an hour. Now, get out."

"Very well, my Lord."

The butler withdrew. Miles shed his coat, throwing it carelessly on the floor. He was beginning to go slightly insane. He picked up the robe and pressed it tenderly to his chest.

"Shit! Here we are, Milesey, old chum. Here we are," he said in awe.

He could not believe it. It might be a dream. He was not certain he was even entitled to believe it. Slowly, fondly, he made sure the sleeves were long enough. They were. He fingered the tassels. A mindless smile played on his lips. The butler reentered.

"I'm sorry to disturb you again, my Lord..."

"You're going to die a horrible death right now, James," Miles promised.

"There's yet another uh... woman... downstairs. She says she must see you instantly. She..."

Clarisse burst into the room, shouting, "Lord Crawford! You must come with me immediately. Take your carriage."

"Not now, my dear lady, not now," Miles said slowly. However, part of his maniacal confidence was already gone, dispelled by the urgency in her voice. Something was up. "Can't you see, I'm a little busy here."

"Hector Eriksson is in trouble, and he needs your help."

"He'll have to wait, poor fellow."

"He can't wait. His wife is holding him prisoner. She's waiting for the police to come and arrest him for murder."

"What kind of fresh nonsense is... What? How do you know all this?"

"I was there just now. She didn't see me. She's perfectly insane; perfectly."

"What were you doing there?"

"I'm Hector's mistress."

"Never a dull moment," Miles shook his head.

She had no reason to lie to him. Hector was a good fellow, and Miles' ex was, well, she was who she was. Hector had once rendered Miles a great service. One can laugh all one likes at justice and chivalry, but gratitude is another matter. Miles turned to Clarisse again. He looked at her glumly. "You are unnaturally tall. Did you know that?"

He sighed. Slowly and carefully, he placed the robe across the chair. Hastily, he picked up his sword and coat. As he and Clarisse hurried to the door, Miles shouted to the butler, "You take care of Penny when she comes again; give her some tea or something. Sleep with her if that's what she insists on... So long..."

Rushing to the door, the butler shouted, "When can I expect you to back, my Lord?"

Miles, already at the front door, shouted back, "Sometime this century, I hope. Good night, James."

Hector, fidgety, sick, and miserable, sat in his chair, hugging his knees. Molly opened the cupboard, inspecting its contents the way a housewife does – critically and with some distaste. Yes, it was still her house.

"Would you care for some wine?" she asked calmly, in an everyday manner.

"No."

"Just asking. No reason to get glum. It's excellent vintage. Are you sure you wouldn't like some?"

She poured a glassful and sipped. The wine was, in fact, quite good. She

had ordered it through her friends in Philadelphia. Molly was so sociable
and compassionate, people enjoyed rendering her little services of this kind.
She never had to pay for her silverware or linen, had unlimited credit with
the greengrocer, butcher, baker, and blacksmith, and one audacious New
York businessman insisted she use his stationary for free, sending her a
new batch of colorful supplies every month.

She heard the sound she expected to hear – a carriage rolling up to the
front door.

"Here they are," she said. "We don't have to wait much longer."

"What are you going to live on?" he asked hopelessly.

"I'll sell some of the property."

"What about the kids?"

"We'll manage. I'll think of something. One thing at a time."

Someone knocked at the door, rudely and authoritatively. Hector cringed
and grew paler. Strangers were in his house.

"How did they get in?"

"I left the front door open."

She went to the door and, looking over her shoulder at Hector, undid
the latch. She turned the knob and flung the door open. When she turned
to greet the visitors, her mind went blank for a moment.

Miles entered, scanning the room in a propriatorial manner. Unbuckling
his cloak, he threw it casually on the floor.

"Damn it!" she exclaimed.

Miles went to the table, picked up Molly's glass, inspected it, and looked
at Hector morosely.

"Crawford," Hector muttered. "You, of all people. I can't believe it; you
– working for the police!"

Ignoring Hector's remark, as he tended to ignore all absurd statements
unless they struck him as funny, Miles addressed Molly, "So, the adventures
just keep rolling on. After us the deluge... One would think you'd come to
your senses and settle down after all these years. Apparently not.
Apparently, there weren't any senses to come to, to begin with. No senses
as such."

"What are..." she began to say when he interrupted her.

"There's an original question. What am I doing here? Don't know yet.
Give me a minute, I'll figure it out."

"Why are you..."

"Aw, shut up. Eriksson, you look sick. She beat you up?"

Hector remained silent. He realized at last that Miles was not the person
Molly had expected to see, but that hardly helped the situation.

"Get out," Molly said, pulling herself together.

"I'll get out when it suits me," Miles told her absentmindedly, still looking at Hector.

He walked over to him and examined his face critically. There was the gash, and there was a fresh bruise. Hector turned away.

"Vindictive bitch," Miles said through his teeth.

He went to the door. Molly, guessing his intentions, ran to prevent him. She was too late. He kicked the door shut and bolted it. She froze, hesitating. He inclined his head and winked at her. She composed herself.

"All right, buster," she said, tossing her head back proudly, "You asked for it."

She ran to the table and grabbed her sword. Miles, glass in hand, watched her ironically. He sipped. He nodded approvingly, finding the wine quite good. He promised himself to ask her where she ordered the stuff when this was all over.

"Can't help but admire her, Eriksson," he said pensively, holding up the glass and studying the color. "She'd kill me and have you hanged. That's a hell of a way to deal with one's past; unfortunately for the two of us, it's the one method our brave lass here seems to favor."

He turned to Molly. Yes, she was beautiful now, sword in hand, eyes flashing. She was a natural. He did not for a moment regret teaching her the tricks.

"You're meddling in my affairs, Miles," she said ominously.

She marched towards him. At four paces, she stopped.

"Will you leave my house of your own accord; or do you prefer to be carried out feet first?"

"Manners, Ruth, manners," he admonished, still admiring her.

She raised her sword. Miles raised his drink.

"May I at least put this down someplace? I hate wasting good liquor."

She hesitated, sniffing contemptuously; and finally indicated the table with a nod. She had to turn slightly in order to do so. As she turned back to him, he threw the contents of the glass in her face.

"Son of a bitch!" she shouted.

Stepping back, Miles drew his sword.

"There isn't a worthy thought in your mind, Ruth, that he didn't deposit there," he said, suddenly and quite unexpectedly acknowledging Hector's contribution to Molly's intellectual development. "There isn't a trick in your fencing and brawling technique that I didn't teach you. You have nothing – nothing decent, anyway – that you could call your own in this life."

She was not listening. She never listened to him. She made a thrust and he countered. They crossed and locked swords. Molly attempted a head-butt. Miles moved his head, making her butt his shoulder instead. She tried again, and the result was the same.

"Amateur stuff, that," Miles said, grinning. "Doesn't work against professionals. Are you ready for your fencing lesson, *ma petite amie?*"

She pushed. He drew back. She feigned and leaped forward. He sidestepped her. For a moment, they were engaged in some skillful fencing.

"A bit rusty, aren't we? Both of us?" Miles commented.

"Crawford... Please..." Hector said from his chair.

"Leave me alone, Eriksson," Miles said sternly. "Can't you see we're busy. You're a ship builder. This isn't your area of expertise."

Molly blundered, lunging forward and committing herself too early. Miles let her weight and momentum carry her forward. He countered, stepped aside, and, as she staggered past him, kicked her viciously. Molly grunted in pain, frustration, and anger, rubbing her buttock.

"You can't commit yourself immediately after a feign," Miles lectured. "How many times do I have to tell you?"

"All right, charmer. All right," she snapped. "Just make sure you take care of your own end."

They resumed fencing. This time, Molly was less hotheaded and more precise. There was now poise in her carriage and purpose in her strokes and thrusts. She actually began to press Miles. He retreated to the table, waited, feigned, and jumped onto the tabletop.

Hector was fascinated. For the moment, he seemed to have forgotten his own problems, watching the action with the curiosity and enthusiasm of a child listening to a fast-paced fairy tale.

Molly attacked. Miles drew back, looking down on her from the table.

"It's very difficult," he said, using his best pedantic voice, "to get at a person who's positioned three feet higher than you. Lure me off the table, stupid."

She made a thrust, and he managed to force her blade down with his. She slipped; her blade hit the table flat, and Miles stepped onto it.

"Crunch!" he said mockingly. "What are you going to do now? Sit down, think about it?"

She was furious. She tried to extricate the sword. She pulled, she twisted, she punched Miles in the leg.

"Hey!" he yelled, revolted. "Do that again, and I'll kick you in the face, woman!"

"You're an empty spot, Miles! You're nothing!"

Miles stepped off the blade. Molly could no longer control herself. She was livid and trembling with rage.

"How fucking noble of you, Miles!" she bellowed. "Preventing your former wife from taking revenge on someone! You're a saint, Miles. I thought I saw a halo just now. You've fought a thousand duels without killing anyone! You always wanted to instill Christian values in me! Huh! You know what I'm going to do now, Miles? Guess! No? I'll tell you. I'm going to kill him myself! I'm going to wring his neck now! You wanna see? You're going to like this! You're going to like it a lot!"

Suddenly, Miles made an abrupt movement. The point of his sword touched Molly's forearm. She screamed and dropped her weapon. Miles jumped down from the table.

"I'm sorry. Did I hurt you? Just a scratch, I hope."

Enraged, she pounced on him. He slapped her across the face. This sobered her up. She stopped. He sheathed his sword. He picked up hers and broke it on his knee, wincing disgustedly and throwing the two halves on the floor.

Calmly, he said, "Stupid unreasonable bitch. Eriksson, get up. We'd better get moving. Come on, man, move!"

Clutching her arm, Molly said quietly, "Too late. They'll be here any second now."

"Oh, really?" Miles peered at her, trying to read her thoughts.

"There will be at least four of them, and they'll have pistols. Here they are! Did you hear that?"

In fact, the sound of another carriage rolling up to the house was distinctly audible. Miles' blood rushed to his temples, his sight blurred. He had been *married* to this woman once. And the lanky fellow in the chair was *still* married to her. Neither of them was a complete moron. Why, then? She was somewhat pretty, she had very cute toes, and she had one special smile that was breathtaking. She could also be rational, and she could flatter you when you were down and your self-esteem went to the dogs. And that was it. There was nothing else. One looked for more good qualities than that in choosing one's greengrocer. Goodness gracious.

"Why," Miles asked listlessly. "Why are you doing this, Ruth?"

"You'll never understand," she said contemptuously. "I owe it to myself to finish him off!"

"He's your husband. He's the father of your children."

"I don't love him anymore."

"So fucking what!"

"So, what do you suggest, that I should spare him? Stay with him out of pity?"

Miles cringed. Molly, still clutching her arm, went to the door.

"You know, pity and love are cousins, Ruth."

"Crawford, please," Hector said suddenly. "It's all right. They can't prove anything. I know I didn't do it. You know it too."

"That's where you're wrong, Hector," Molly said evenly. "I thought I mentioned to you earlier that the murder weapon is in this house, and it's a very special one, at that. You're the only person in the city who owns a weapon of that sort."

"I don't own any weapons," Hector said, perplexed. "Except my sword, which I never use."

Unbolting the door, Molly chuckled maliciously, "Wrong, Hector. Remember the German inventor?"

The German inventor, Miles thought. The German... But of course! The two revolvers. Almost ten years ago. Long live German engineering. So, that was how she was going to frame Eriksson. Interesting.

Miles cleared his throat. "Then who's to say you didn't do it yourself? Murder weapon and all?" he asked.

"I have an alibi," she said simply. "I was at the Sloans' two hours ago."

"Really? Good for you," Miles said pensively. "Oh!" he cried suddenly. "Of course. The weapon in this house is not the only one in the area. Here's another one."

He pulled the pistol from his belt and showed it to her. During the ten years of carrying it, he had forgotten who had given it to him initially and come to assume that it had been with him all along, possibly since birth.

Molly stared at it. Hector rose from his chair.

"Crawford..." he said.

"Yes, I went after the inventor because I thought he might be a spy. I hate spies, they annoy me, I just shoot the buggers on sight. He turned out to be all right. We became instant friends. He gave me this pistol because he thought I was an expert. Which I am."

"What are you doing, Miles?" Molly asked unpleasantly.

"I'm the murderer," he admitted with austere manly sorrow. He struck a pose. "I did it." He frowned. "I believe the idiots are actually laying siege to this place. What's taking them so long? I don't intend to put up any resistance."

"Crawford, don't be absurd!" Hector shouted. "This might be serious."

Miles cast him a huffy look. "Yeah, I know. Except, you see, I've been denied my robe with tassels again. I'm thoroughly pissed at the world right now. Really, I am. Imagine – I was just putting on the robe... I actually managed to get one sleeve on! – suddenly, boom, bang, whisk, smash, the tall bitch enters running! Says…" he imitated a high-pitched female voice, although Clarisse's was a low, velvety mezzo, "…you must come with me right now!" He sighed. "It's useless, don't you see. Why don't I just die at the hands of the authorities; everyone will benefit, I assure you. You'll have your miserable life, such as it is; the authorities and the public will have their entertainment. And maybe this slut here will get it through her deranged head that getting back at someone is neither a chivalrous nor, indeed, a controllable act! If there's one thing I really loathe, other than not having a big breakfast, it's revenge. I loathe and disdain it with every fiber of my immortal soul. It's poor taste; I find it uncouth."

Four men in uniform entered the room. McLachlan, the Police Commissioner, came in last.

He said, "I'm very sorry to disturb you at this hour, folks. There is a weapon in this house…"

"Here it is, Baron," Miles said promptly, "No need to display the search warrant. Let's get it over with."

"No!" Molly shouted. "Don't listen to him. That man here," she pointed at Hector, "is the one you want."

"Baron," Miles called.

Taking the pistol from him, McLachlan said dryly, "Commissioner, if you don't mind. We'll just search for the other one, with your permission."

"No need, Baron," Miles assured him. "Look, this fellow is sick as a dog; he's obviously in no shape to have harmed anyone two hours ago. The woman has an alibi; she was visiting a friend of hers. The friend is a whore, I believe, which has no bearing on the case… There's a history of whores testifying in court. Juries love them. They find them congenial. Anyway, I'm the one who killed the Mayor. I confess."

"The Mayor?" McLachlan asked nonchalantly.

"Yes. The Mayor. He got on my nerves, and I shot him. Let that be a lesson to everybody."

"I'm sorry, sir," McLachlan said coldly, his face imperturbable. "I left the Mayor not ten minutes ago. He's in the best of health."

The guards accompanying the Police Commissioner were trying to look detached. Miles blinked.

Revolted, Molly shouted, "What do you mean he's in the best of health? He hasn't been shot?"

"No, madam. The leader of the criminal group known as the Gallic Faction was shot and killed in the Mayor's office two hours ago. Someone rendered the community a great service, but the law is the law."

"Fine, then," Miles said impatiently, "let's not utter any more platitudes. It's him I killed, so why don't you arrest me for that. Anyone else been shot lately? Whoever it might be, I did it. Please. Here's my sword."

He unbuckled his sword and offered it to McLachlan, baldric and all.

"What was your motive, sir?" the latter demanded without accepting the sword.

"Huh?"

"Did you have any reason to shoot Jerome?"

"I'd had a lousy day, thought, maybe if I shot somebody I'd feel better."

"Why the Mayor's office, then? Aren't there less exotic places to kill people?"

He was beginning to get on Miles' nerves. Miles regretted giving up the pistol so soon.

"Well?" McLachlan insisted.

Miles was just able to control himself.

"Oh, I don't know. Memories, I guess. The Mayor's office, the plush chairs and all." He realized there was a quicker way to ensure McLachlan's cooperation. He grinned. "That's where I fucked your wife last month. The Mayor is a very charitable person. He'll let anyone use his office for that. Half the city has fucked your wife in that office, Baron."

"All right, arrest him," McLachlan said, turning pale.

Miles drew his sword and threw away the sheath.

"How about a bit of fun before we start? Only a few thrusts, for the road."

He made a move. The four men backed off. One of them drew his pistol.

"Just kidding," Miles said.

"Commissioner," Molly interrupted at last, "you're an idiot. Can't you see he's laughing at you?"

"Crawford," Hector added, "I don't know what you're doing, but..."

Miles regarded Hector with sincere pity. "Did you know what you were doing when you married her? Did you? Do we ever know what we're doing, especially when we're around Ruth? Guess not. Except some of us have to pay for the mistakes of others as well as for our own. And some people seem to get away with anything, including murder."

In the meantime, one of the policemen got hold of Miles' sword. The other two stood on either side of Miles and took him by the arms.

"Onward, gentlemen," he commanded.

Molly shook her head and covered her face.

SIXTEEN

The Arrival Of Jefferson's Brigade

It was late afternoon in the middle of October. Kenneth, contrary to his habits, was trying to read *Common Sense*, shielding his eyes from the sun with the back of his hand. Patty came in, threw off her hat and cloak, and sat. She had good news. She was radiant. She was full of love and affection. He turned his eyes on her.

"What's up."

"I have the money."

"Money? What money?" he frowned.

"For our trip to Italy."

"Oh," he nodded. "All right."

"Aren't you happy?" she asked, taken aback.

"Sure."

"You don't sound happy."

"Look, I'm not in a good mood right now."

Testily, she said, "I see."

She sat and watched him for a while as he read. After about three minutes, she rose and stormed out, slamming the door. Kenneth grunted, reckoning he must have said or done something terribly wrong. He tried to determine what that might be. He failed. Shrugging, he made himself some tea and picked up *Common Sense* again. The book puzzled him. He was not sure why so many self-evident things had to be written down and thousands of copies (as his friends assured him) published. He wondered whether all literature was like that.

Throaty, in shabby clothes, a canvas bag slung over his shoulder, a Biblical-looking staff in his hand, sauntered down the road. There was a distinct nip in the air. The warm season was over. Mappensville was far behind. Future was ahead. What kind of future? Some future. He would see what turned up.

A group of twenty horsemen dressed in identical light-blue coats rode in the opposite direction. All of them were young and handsome and had a superior air about them. Their Captain, a dangerously attractive blond man of twenty-five, motioned for the others to stop and rode up to Throaty.

"Hey, Gramps," he said, bending to his horse's mane. "Is this the way to

Mappensville?"

"No," Throaty said, stopping and looking into the rider's honest blue eyes.

"How close are we?"

"Three weeks," Throaty said apologetically. "Bear right at the fork."

"Are you from Mappensville?"

"No."

"Any commotions there?"

"No, it's been quiet for ages."

"I see. How many people were involved?"

"None."

The Leader considered Throaty's information for a moment. He removed his left-hand glove and inspected his fingernails. Throaty waited politely. He had no pressing business anywhere, no emergency appointments scheduled.

"Ever heard of the Gallic Faction?" the horseman asked at last.

"No," Throaty replied promptly.

"Huh?" the Captain demanded threateningly.

"No, sir!"

"Good," the Captain approved. "Are they conspiring to take over soon?"

"Not that I know of."

The Captain turned around and rejoined the group. He pondered a little, saying eventually, "Sounds pretty bad, boys. The fellow's from Mappensville, which is an hour's ride from here. The whole city is astir; the syndicate is going to grab the power any moment now. Do we send for backups, or are we skilled and determined enough to control the situation by ourselves, as Mr. Jefferson is certain we are?"

"We'll control it," one of his comrades said.

"Yeah," another one concurred.

The rest mumbled affirmatively. The Captain nodded, rode back to Throaty who was contemplating the cavalcade at a respectful distance, and threw him a coin. Throaty caught it deftly.

"Thanks, old man," the Captain said. "What's your name?"

"Molly Bates," Throaty replied politely.

"Nice meeting you, Ms. Bates. You have a good day now."

He spurred his horse and galloped on, the rest following. Throaty dropped the coin in his pocket and resumed his journey.

At the harbor inn, Luc the proprietor, pencil in hand, haggled with Patty at the bar. The place was empty. The harbor was deserted. It had been a slow couple of days.

"Let's just total it up again," he calculated the total on a scrap of paper.

"You know, Luc... I never really liked you," Patty said pensively.

"I'm aware of that," he told her, verifying his figures. "I'll live. All right, the total comes out to seventeen and change. I'll give you a break. Fifteen even and let's forget about the broken china."

"I didn't break it."

"One of your clients did. I thought we had agreed that all damages were your responsibility."

"You were afraid of that guy, which is why you didn't put it on his bill. You're a coward, Luc."

"He was paying well. Besides, he's a regular."

"All right. Let's just get it over with."

She got out her purse and tossed some coins on the bar. Luc picked up the coins and inspected them.

"When's the next time?" he asked.

"There's going to be no next time for me, thank you very much, charmer."

He lit a cigar. It stank abominably. He looked critically at Patty.

"Let's be realistic here," he proposed. "You claim you stayed out of the business for ten years. Fine. But, just the same, you came back. Once a whore, always a whore."

She laughed contemptuously. She had no respect for ignorant people.

"Let me explain something to you, handsome. A whore is a woman who sleeps with men exclusively for physical pleasure plus whatever else turns her on; stuff like boats, clothes, nightlife, theatre, and so forth. People dealing in prostitution, which is the act of selling yourself for ready money, are called harlots or prostitutes. Not all prostitutes are whores. The Baron's wife is a whore."

"Shhhh!" he said, his eyes widening. "You'll get me in trouble one of these days. Anyway, words are words. They don't change anything."

"My point is, you're as much of a prostitute as I am, perhaps more; no reason to call me names."

"I don't sell myself for ready money."

She waved him off. He was hopeless. At that moment, the door opened and five men from the group of horsemen Throaty had encountered earlier barged in. The Captain approached Luc and gave him a dazzling smile.

"Innkeeper! We need lodgings. There are twenty of us, and we'll double your usual price. We'll need ten rooms for three weeks."

"I don't have ten rooms available, I'm afraid."

"How many do you have?"

"Six are unoccupied at the moment, but I'm expecting a few people the day after tomorrow."

"Splendid. Just make the other four available in an hour; and you'll tell your few people, when they come, to go away again. Federal business, my friend. We have no time to stand on ceremony with every vagrant who wants a room here. In the meantime, we want some food and wine, and oats for our horses. Here's a little advance for you. Spend it wisely."

He threw several gold coins on the bar.

Cowed, Luc said obsequiously, "Yes, sir. I'll see what I can do, sir."

Patty grinned. "You don't, huh?"

Luc made a face and motioned her to clear out. She stuck her tongue out at him. One of Jefferson's men motioned to her, but she only shrugged and walked out decorously, holding her head high.

SEVENTEEN

A Bit Of Girly Gossip

Mappensville's traffic was getting heavier by the year, what with the new bridges and tax breaks for carriage makers and horse breeders. Two carriages, one moving faster than the other, collided in the middle of an intersection. The drivers jumped off their respective boxes.

"You son of a bitch!" the first driver shouted. "Don't you even watch where the fuck you're going!"

"I do," the second driver shouted back, "but I can't read every asshole's mind! How the hell was I supposed to know you'd start turning around like a whore in heat!"

"What did you just say?"

"You heard me!"

"You're dead meat, sucker."

"Oh, yeah? Show me what you got, dickhead!"

They tore off their jackets. The two lady passengers came out of their respective carriages. Margaret the Viscountess was one. Clarisse was the other.

"Stop it at once!" Margaret commanded. "Do you hear? I have to get to Philadelphia before dark!"

"Cut the nonsense, you imbeciles!" Clarisse shouted almost simultaneously.

The two women froze and goggled at each other.

"I'll show you!" the first driver continued less loudly.

"What can you show me besides your fat ass!" the second driver snapped back.

Margaret kicked her driver in the seat of his pants. He jumped and stared at her, intimidated.

"Margaret!" Clarisse cried.

"Clarisse!" Margaret dropped her fan.

They fell into each other's arms. The Viscountess, aging less gracefully than Clarisse, had nevertheless managed to keep most of her worldly air.

"Where have you been all these years?" Clarisse wanted to know.

"Oh, here and there. In Italy, mostly. Do you live here now?"

"Yes. Come, you'll stay with me for a few days!"

"Certainly. Where?"

"Avenue of the New Republic. Formerly Empire Street."

"Excellent." She turned to her driver. "You. Go back to the inn. I'll send for you in a few days. Here."

She tossed him a gold coin.

They rode together, eyeing each other greedily, assessing, and smiling. The assessment and the smiles were sincere. They had never been close in the past, which was why, perhaps, they now had no scores to settle with each other. Instead, they had memories and news to share.

"Imagine," Margaret said, "Italy is so full of wonderful people. There are almost no peasants. A lot of artists, though, and street singers, too. They're very poor, but they laugh a lot; most are very friendly."

"You haven't changed at all," Clarisse said at last.

"Well, you have, my dear – for the better, I think. When's the last time we saw each other?"

"Five years ago, in London."

"Precisely. My husband is an awful bore. You know that. Ever since we moved to London, he's been talking politics. I told him I needed a vacation."

"Did you enjoy it?"

"What?"

"Your vacation."

"Oh, I'm still enjoying it. It's been three years so far. I'll stay in this country for a while, then maybe I'll visit India. I always wanted to go to India, to see all those olive-colored people, and the elephants. You know, they make piano keys out of their tusks. I cringe now every time I hear piano music."

Ten minutes later, they were in Clarisse's garden. The sun beamed down kindly; the walls kept in the warm air. The garden was utterly luxurious, deliberately overcrowded with odd-looking trees and flowers; an exotic forest with paths just wide enough for two persons to stroll together. Clarisse and Margaret walked down one of them. The Viscountess was frankly enchanted.

"My dear Clarisse. This is so wonderful! Did you arrange it all yourself?"

"I had to hire a few people. My late husband was a hopeless urbanite. Some of his attitude must have rubbed off on me. I can't live too far away from the city. But I missed the countryside so much, I just had to move it here into my backyard."

"Some backyard. What are those?"

"Wild orchids."

"Wow. And what happened to... what was his name? The feisty and silly one... tiny creature... freckles... the Baron's wife?"

"They're still married and live together." Smiling, Clarisse added, "Some marriages are more durable than one would expect."

"Oh yes. And the poor Baron?"

"The new mayor kept him on as the Police Commissioner."

"You don't say!"

Both laughed. To Clarisse's mock horror, Margaret lit a cigar and puffed joyfully. A cat stepped out on the path and regarded the two women with some apprehension. Margaret inclined her head and imitated the cat's cautious, alert pose. Clarisse giggled. The cat ran away.

"And what about that..." Margaret paused, "The classical woman, I used to call her... shaped like an early version of a Greek statue, a lot of smoothness and no curves? Er... Lady Crawford, I believe?"

"I don't know," Clarisse said coldly.

"Oh. You don't know."

"They say she disappeared for a number of years; later, she came back and married again."

"I see. Lord Crawford must be dead, then."

"No. It's all very vague. I believe they got a divorce; or else they were never legally married."

Margaret knew Clarisse was lying, which was fine with her. She was a very patient woman and did not mind waiting a little. Others would fill her in later.

"Life in the Colonies," she said. "I didn't realize I missed it so much."

They walked in silence for a while.

"And – what's his name?" the Viscountess pursued, "you know, the dark, strikingly handsome fellow, the ship builder? Danish or Spanish or some such?"

Now, *this*, she needed to know right away. She had her reasons.

"Both Danish and Spanish," Clarisse said matter-of-factly.

"Yes, precisely. What's become of him?"

"Margaret."

"Yes, dear."

"Can you keep a secret?"

"No, but tell me anyway."

"I'm very happy to see you. You're a breath of fresh air."

They embraced. Clarisse seemed to be on the verge of tears.

EIGHTEEN

The Memorial

Hector leaned on the mantelpiece, casting a furtive glance at Molly, who turned her profile to him. He filled his pipe. In less than a month, she had revealed more of herself to him than in the preceding decade of their marriage. To his horror, he began to discover numerous and hitherto unknown traits in her. She was, it turned out, disagreeably stubborn, levelheaded, grudge-bearing, and appallingly shameless, which was perfectly fine with him; but she was also petty, needlessly arrogant, cruel, and tactless – which was not.

Reclining in her chair, Molly looked absentmindedly out the window.

"Please don't smoke, Hector," she said without looking at him. "You know I can't stand it."

He turned pale. He put out the pipe and shoved it into his pocket.

"I've decided to turn myself in."

She did not change her pose. She did not bat an eye.

"What do you mean? Turn yourself in?"

"I'll just go there and surrender. I'll tell them I did it. I'll prove it to them."

"Oh, please. You can't prove anything. Not even to me. You're a phony and you know it."

Another recently revealed and very unpleasant detail was his wife's true opinion of him. He was in her eyes, it turned out, a weakling, a selfish brat without a backbone, a mediocre ship builder, a very inadequate father, a scoundrel, and now a phony.

"How am I a phony?"

"Skip it. You're not turning yourself in, and that's that."

"Crawford's been sitting in that cell for a month now."

"It'll do him good. He's too restless. This is his chance to calm down a bit."

"They'll hang him."

"They can't do that without a trial. There hasn't been any trial, as far as I know."

"I'm going there. I'll hire a lawyer to prove that I'm guilty."

"You're living in a fantasy world. Besides, you don't know any good lawyers."

"Hamilton is a lawyer..." Hector pictured the Secretary of Finance coming over to Mappensville in order to prove, upon Hector's own request, that the latter was a murderer, and almost laughed. "Listen... Just a month ago, you wanted me dead. All of a sudden..."

"I can't support the children by myself."

"You weren't worried about that a month ago."

"Well, I am now."

"You're very consistent."

She did not like the sarcasm.

"I think you'd better go now," she said.

Hector looked at her with a mixture of surprise and disgust. He walked out. The front door slammed.

The political equilibrium in Mappensville was in jeopardy now that Jerome was gone. The new leader of the Gallic Faction, whoever he was going to be, was likely to demand changes and create waves.

Mongoose sat at his desk, looking gloomily at McLachlan who, arms akimbo, was busy pacing.

"Which is why," the Police Commissioner developed his thought, "I would love to lay my hands on whoever killed Jerome. Everything is out of control. No one reports to work anymore. Before you know it, we're going to have an armed revolt on our hands. I'm fed up. I resign."

In fact, Jerome's assassination triggered many discoveries in sociology and economy in the Mappensville area. The farmers discovered that the taxes were unreasonably high while the wholesale prices depressingly low.

Most tenants suddenly found that their landlords were bloodsuckers. Crime was up again, for which the Mayor was being blamed. The townspeople thought he was incompetent. They had not thought so before. Carriage owners discovered that the roads were very poorly and inexpertly paved. Some people already felt nostalgic and whispered that the King was not such a bad fellow after all. Some questioned their congressman's knowledge of local affairs – naturally, since the said gentleman had not set foot in Mappensville in years, preferring to conduct his business out of his New York and Philadelphia offices, paid for by the taxpayers. And so on.

"You will not resign," Mongoose said firmly.

"You will kindly accept my resignation, sir, immediately after which I'll have the honor of sending you my challenge."

"Your wife..."

"Don't talk to me about my wife, you vermin!" McLachlan exploded.

The door flew open. In came the blond Captain followed by five of his horsemen. Jefferson's Own Brigade, even this small portion of it, made the Mayor's office look tiny.

"Hello, gentlemen," the Captain said brightly. "Mr. Mayor, I presume. And you, sir, must be the Police Commissioner. My word, it's stuffy in here."

He strode to the window, opened it, and looked out cheerily. His smile was positively luminous.

"I beg your pardon," McLachlan, ever civil, said. "May I have the honor?.."

"My name is of no importance to you, sir," the Captain said peremptorily. "In my line of business, we don't bandy names about. Suffice it to say that I represent the Government in general and Mr. Jefferson, Mr. Hamilton, and President Washington in particular. First thing's first. Commissioner, you were, I believe, the acting mayor of this city at some point?"

McLachlan looked hard at the Captain who smiled at him radiantly.

"So I was," the Baron said. "May I see some identification?"

"Authorization, you mean," the Captain corrected him. "Here."

He produced a sheet of paper adorned with a picturesque constellation of seals and signatures. McLachlan scanned it. Mongoose looked inquiringly at the Commissioner; the latter nodded resignedly, confirming the document's authenticity. The Mayor turned pale and looked sideways.

"Mr. President," the Captain explained, "has authorized me to inquire about a certain painting you seem to own, among other things. A Lebrun, I believe. He wishes to buy it from you. No written contract is necessary. Your word and your price will do. You don't have to answer now. I'll be here the next three weeks. Now. A certain person named Samuel Doome..."

Mongoose blinked. An experienced politician, always in control of his feelings and mimicry, he suddenly found himself lacking in many respects compared to this hot shot from Philly. There was, after all, a difference between the metropolis and the provinces. The Captain chuckled.

"Yes. That's no longer a state secret. Mr. Doome has been arrested; in exchange for a few years knocked off his sentence, he was kind enough to supply us the names, addresses, and current status of all members of the criminal syndicate known as the Gallic Faction. We'll be apprehending the entire group shortly. Some of them will have to be deported, others jailed. What I would like to know is the degree of Mr. Mayor's personal involvement in the syndicate's past dealings. Commissioner, please leave the room. You may go home, uh, for now."

McLachlan hesitated. The captain approached him and placed his hand on the other man's shoulder.

"I couldn't help overhearing you, Commissioner. You were shouting louder than a thousand drunken elephants. Never fear. The population is under control. The police have their orders."

"Who gave them these orders?" McLachlan demanded.

"I did. There's going to be no revolt, no talk of secession. Law and order, sir. Tomorrow, the good and charitable people of Mappensville will return to work as innocuous and quiet as lambs. Go home and get some rest, Mr. McLachlan. Incidentally, do you happen to know a certain Miles Crawford?"

"Crawford? ... Yes, of course..."

"Do you know his address?"

"Uh... He's in jail now."

This was embarrassing. If these upbeat fellows chose to conduct an investigation, they would soon discover that Mappensville's Police Commissioner had used the newly constructed city prison unlawfully by locking up an innocent man on account of a personal grudge.

"In jail!" Jefferson's man exclaimed. "What in the world for?"

"Uh... for murder, sir."

"Can you prove it? Is there enough evidence?"

"There seems to be no one else who... uh... could have done it... sir."

"Well, that sounds conclusive," the Captain approved. "There's no way he can escape hanging now." He turned to his troops. "You and you. Go there now, release the poor fellow, and tell him to drop by the inn tonight."

Two of the horsemen rushed out. The Captain stared at McLachlan. The latter hesitated a moment longer, turned on his heel and, muttering profanities, left quickly.

"Sir..." Mongoose began.

"I know you weren't seriously involved in anything," the captain waved him off magnanimously. "They didn't trust you enough, you lucky son of a gun, you. However…" he suddenly swooped on Mongoose, "Corruption is a fact of life, Mr. Mayor. It's the degree of it that's important. An honest statesman knows how to keep corruption in check. Show me your budget books."

"Uh…"

"Now, Mr. Mayor."

Miles disliked intensely the middle-aged barber the authorities had assigned to him. He would much prefer shaving himself, but that was not allowed. After the barber wiped Miles' face with a towel, "How is it outside?" Miles asked.

"Oh, it's getting warmer, sir. Indian Summer."

He collected his tools and knocked on the door. A guard opened it from the outside and let the barber out. He shut and locked the door immediately.

"Sunny," Miles muttered. "All right, I've had enough."

He leaped to the door and kicked it loudly several times. The guard unlocked it and opened it an inch. He fully intended to open it further, but Miles kept him from doing so by kicking it hard. The guard screamed. Now Miles opened the door himself and found the guard nursing a broken finger. Miles instantly reached for the fellow's pistol and sword. The guard made a movement.

"I'm going to head-butt you. Would you like me to head-butt you?" Miles warned him.

The poor lad, no older than eighteen, shook his head. His eyes were round with fear, pain and surprise. Miles drew the sword and attempted to shove the guard's pistol behind his belt. He realized he had no belt. Suddenly, it turned out that the youngster had a sense of humor. Seeing Miles' difficulty, he giggled, despite the pain. Miles giggled also. They were beginning to like each other.

Suddenly turning savage, Miles shouted, "I don't think it's funny!"

He was about to leave when one of the blue-coated horsemen entered.

"Mr. Crawford?"

Miles aimed the pistol at him.

"Lord Crawford," he corrected.

"But of course. A message for you from Mr. Jefferson. Here. Please come with me."

"Oh? And where are you going?" Miles inquired suspiciously.

"Lord Crawford!" Jefferson's man threw up his arms. "I apologize. You are free, of course. Do you imagine that, if Mr. Jefferson wished to arrest you, he would send in just one agent?"

Now, this was true, but also flattering, coming as it was from a professional who thus acknowledged Miles' superiority. Miles grinned.

"Where's the message?" he asked.

"Right here, sir."

He handed Miles a scroll. Miles handed the pistol to the young guard. "Hold this."

Stupefied, the guard took the pistol with his good hand. Miles broke the seal. The letter read, "*My dear Crawford. Thank you for the great amount of splendid work you have performed overseas. Do get some rest now; you deserve it. A certain sum of money...*"

In the meantime, the captain of Jefferson's Own Brigade sat in the Mayor's chair, leafing through a log. Mongoose stood silently at the window, his hands behind his back, his expression defiant. He felt a little silly.

"Excellent," the Captain observed. "I haven't seen such wonderful books in a long time. Mr. Hamilton will be overjoyed. Just one thing. Please step over here, Mr. Mayor."

Mongoose did, and looked over the Captain's shoulder. The latter pointed at a spot in the book.

"This item here, marked M, B, M. A nice, round sum of money. What is it?"

"Uh..."

"Yes?"

"The Molly Bates Memorial."

"Now, this is the second time in one day I hear that name. Tell me, Mr. Mayor, who is, or was, this Molly Bates person?"

There was no simple answer to this, and had there been one, Mongoose would not have been eager to supply it. He wondered how much he could reveal without incriminating himself. The great flaw of the Fifth Amendment was suddenly obvious to him. The Constitution protected you only after you were charged, when it was clearly too late. You had no right to conceal anything before that. Mongoose feared that the Federal slicker's next question might be, Did you know her personally?

"She's... She's the city's heroine. She... fought bravely against the Lobsters... they captured and hanged her."

"Splendid," the Captain sounded positively ecstatic. "We'll take a little walk, just you and I, and you'll show me the memorial. I love memorials."

"Uh... there is no memorial."

"I'm sorry. The mark here goes back ten years. Surely ten years is time enough to build a pedestal and stick a statue on it?"

"Uh..."

The Captain's mock debonair air was gone. He looked coldly at Mongoose, asking sternly, "Where's the money?"

"The money's still in the treasury."

"It had better be. Now," he said, softening again, "the memorial fund is the only fault I've been able to find with your books." Mongoose felt enormous relief. "Be reasonable, Mr. Mayor. Must we disappoint Mr. Hamilton, who would otherwise give you an award for your splendid management?"

Mongoose, shamefaced, shrugged.

"Don't shrug at me, young man." Mongoose's eyes flashed at this new pleasantry from a man who was at least twenty years his junior. "I'll give you a break. The memorial will go up in two weeks. I realize, what with the inflation rates, that the amount documented here is no longer sufficient. Well, you'll have to add your own money. Should you refuse, then, regrettably, I'd have to make a report. You'll be impeached, and Mr. Hamilton will make sure you never enter politics again."

Had Mongoose been ten years younger, he would have laughed. Ten years ago, starting from scratch, perhaps in Canada or England (he was not quite certain whether people spoke English anywhere else), would have been fun. The satisfaction of making a new fortune, in a place where one was in charge of his own reputation and did not have to dread people from the past resurfacing and getting in the way all the time – he would have enjoyed the challenge.

Today, a content and well-respected member of the community, a trusted public officer, a wealthy landlord who hobnobbed with leading figures at various soirees, Mongoose was getting good at golf and growing pleasantly round about the waist. He looked on the past with a mixture of resentment and incredulity. There were times when he seriously doubted whether he and the ruthless brigand with the cruel smile, curly mane of greasy hair and trigger-happy finger were really the same person. Even his former *nom-de-guerre* struck him as odd and dangerous. If someone similarly nicknamed asked him for an appointment, he would probably refuse to see him. Yes, he dealt with the Gallic Faction a lot, but the exchanges were invariably civil. He had not used a weapon of any sort in ages.

"Two weeks!" he said, shaking his head.

"You must know some artists around here," the Captain said. "One of them, I'm sure, will be very happy to design it for you. Then, you'll get some stone masons, as well as some specialists in bronze."

He shut the book and rose.

"Two weeks, Mr. Mayor. Good afternoon."

Kenneth threw the brush down and wiped his forehead with the back of his hand. This left a brown, blue, yellow, green, red, white, and orange stain on his face, as it invariably did. Patty relaxed and took a chair. Her Antoinette dress was not conducive to sitting. She rose again and took it off.

The painting was one of Kenneth's bi-monthly claims to fame. It was hardly marketable. No one in his right mind would ever dream of purchasing Kenneth's original and highly inaccurate vision of the ill-fated Queen's arrest – in the street, dressed to the nines – by exotically and stylishly attired Assembly guards, with some very interesting and mostly Italian architecture in the background, recalled from the darker recesses of Kenneth's memory to serve as a backdrop depicting Versailles. However, people who are in their right minds never seem to help artists' careers anyway.

"And then he crossed the sea," Kenneth continued telling Patty's favorite story, "and found that there was a huge mountain range on the other side of the island and, standing on one of the peaks, he made out the silhouette of another mountain range, way across the ocean. So, he reckoned..."

Someone knocked very loudly at the door.

"I'll get it," Patty said.

She threw on Kenneth's robe – it was rather comfortable even though it lacked tassels. The knocking repeated before she could reach the door. She unlocked it. Mongoose stormed in, pale and agitated.

"Hey, uh... Hello," he said. "I'm the Mayor of this city. You must be..." He consulted a scrap of paper, "Kenneth Saloon...

"Sloan," the artist corrected him.

They locked eyes. Full of mistrust, suspicion, and occasional loathing, the relations between artist and statesman had not changed much since the first impractical dreamer with a pair of talented hands was ordered to adorn the walls of the tribal chief's cave with hunting scenes. The pay must have been abominably small. The women were warned not to make eyes at the doodler, or else. The two men, in loin wraps, must have maintained eye contact less than three seconds before they began to loathe each other even while recognizing they could not do without each other's support, which only intensified the loathing.

"That's right. Sloan," Mongoose said. "Listen, Sloan, do you want to make an easy couple of bucks real quick?"

Kenneth pricked up his ears. Patty was so awed to have the Mayor visit their humble abode, she just stood silently at the still open door.

"I need a statue built for the Molly Bates memorial," Mongoose announced. "The likeness is unimportant. I need it to look more or less like a woman, sword in hand."

"Built? … Uh…" Kenneth furrowed his brow. "But I'm not a sculptor."

"You're not? Oh. Well, sorry. Do you know any sculptors I could talk to about this?"

"No."

"Shit. Listen, you have a good day, Sloan."

"But I could give it a try."

Mongoose wavered. "Surely there are professional sculptors in this city?" he asked.

"None. But I might, uh, prove... uh... equal to the task. You mentioned money, I believe?"

"Yeah, well..."

Kenneth rose and, fixing Mongoose with a slightly mad look, spoke with confidence. "New challenges always inspire me. Bronze or marble?"

"We don't have any marble, I'm afraid," Mongoose knew the area well. "Anyway, the statue has to be finished in a week."

"A week!"

Kenneth laughed incredulously. He invited Patty to share his incredulity, but she was still in a trance.

"Don't tell me now it can't be done!" the Mayor urged. "You artists are such abominable loafers. Certain major countries were captured in less than a week!"

"That's because war and politics are for juveniles!" Kenneth retorted. "We're talking about serious work here!"

Mongoose bristled. He stuck his hands in his pockets and looked Kenneth straight in the face.

"Yes or no? I want an answer. I'll give you a thousand dollars, and I'm prepared to pay half of it in advance; right now, that is."

Patty gasped.

"Two thousand," Kenneth said.

"Fifteen hundred."

"It's a deal."

Mongoose tossed a leather purse on the table.

"I'll drop by in a couple of days; the statue had better be well under way by then. Do you know any stone masons?"

Kenneth thought about this.

"There's one living in the green house with the slanting roof, just up the road."

"Thank you," Mongoose said. "See you later."

He stormed out. Kenneth picked up the purse and weighed it in his hand. Patty looked at him expectantly.

"Do you know anything about sculpting?" she asked.

"Next to nothing. I know enough to realize it cannot be done in a week."

"So, what are you going to do?"

"I'm going to sculpt it. In one week."

"But you just said it can't be done."

He threw the money on the table and looked around the room, at his canvases, finished and half-finished, on the floor, on the walls.

"Look at all this, Patty. No human being could have painted any of those; not in two weeks; not in two centuries; and yet, there they are. Each time an artist picks up a brush, he sets out to do something that cannot be done."

She gazed at him proudly. He was all business now.

"All right. We seem to be short on time. Put on one of my suits, find something that looks like a sword, and stand on the table. In the meantime, I'll go out and dig up some workable clay."

He threw on a coat and left. She sat at the table, propping her chin with the back of her hand. She giggled incredulously and happily. What an incredible man Kenneth was! What a baby! How much vaster and deeper was his baby vision than the supposedly enlightened, practical, insightful, politically and economically sound wisdom of most grownups!

She believed in him. He was going to finish that statue in a week. He was going to use her as the model. Imagine – Patty, posing as Molly Bates! Woman of legend! The mysterious, intrepid, magnanimous and fair Molly Bates, who had, like our own Robin Hood, robbed the rich and given the money to the poor; who had fought fearlessly against the British dogs and their sidekick Loyalist oppressors; who had died a virgin, like Joan of Arc, and to whose ingenuity both Washington and Lafayette owed their lives! Molly Bates – who could, when she was alive, single-handedly defeat a dozen well-armed ferocious men with unheard-of combat methods! Yes! She was going to be perpetuated in bronze by dear, tender, gifted, irresistible Kenneth – and later generations were going to study her features – Patty's own features – and think, in awe, "Ah, so that's what Molly Bates looked like!"

She remembered that, according to the legend, Molly Bates had always dressed as a man. Ah! So that's why Kenneth had mentioned she should put on one of his suits! She couldn't believe it – how Kenneth always thought of everything when it came to art. She opened a closet, and then the other one, going through Kenneth's wardrobe hastily. She tried on a pair of trousers, and then a shirt, discovering that both made her look very attractive and feminine, accentuating the fullness of her breasts and the exquisite slenderness of her neck. The boots were much too large for her. Of the three swords Kenneth owned and often used as props for his historical paintings, she selected the one whose hilt struck her as the most phallic. She girded it and, looking in the mirror and adjusting the baldric, found that something was lacking. What? She reflected. She closed her eyes. She opened them again. Yes! A tricorne. She grabbed the largest one from the rack and donned it. Except for the boots, the image was complete.

"Here I am, Posterity," she said proudly, addressing an invisible audience. "Name's Molly Bates! Greetings!"

NINETEEN

The Fall Of The Gallic Faction

It was quite possibly the last warm afternoon in Mappensville that year. The plaza in front of the City Hall was crowded. Hundreds of people were going about their business. Delacroix, accompanied by a dozen friends, appeared and jumped onto a makeshift podium.

"Ladies and gentlemen!" he shouted cheerily. "May I have your attention, please!"

The hubbub died down, heads turned.

"Ladies and gentlemen, once again, as always, we've been fooled by the Federal Government. The taxes are heavier today than they were under the English rule. There are shortages of everything. We, the true friends of the people, the most revered citizens of the city, are here to propose a plan. Were this state to secede from the Union, we would...."

He was interrupted by the deep booming baritone of the blue-coated Captain of the Horsemen who, materializing in front of the podium, bellowed, "Is your name Delacroix, sir?"

Delacroix turned to his friends and asked disgustedly, "Who is this?"

The Captain jumped onto the podium beside Delacroix, grabbed the orator's sleeve, and addressed the crowd.

"Ladies and gentlemen. This city has seen enough hardship. We, agents of the Federal Government, have been sent here to investigate a problem. Some members of the Administration, and especially Mr. Hamilton and Mr. Jefferson, are concerned that, while this state, and this county, and especially this city, are among the greatest producers of everything, the population has virtually no money on their hands. We have solved the riddle. A certain group known as the Gallic Faction has usurped the power here. Acting illegally and posing as Government agents, these people have been collecting twice the taxes they were supposed to collect; and, while sending one half of the revenue to Philadelphia, they simply kept the other half for themselves."

"I protest," Delacroix shouted, trying desperately to free himself. "This is monstrously untrue."

"Ladies and gentlemen," the Captain went on, tightening his grip on Delacroix's arm until the latter was ready to shriek pitifully, "This city of yours has been robbed long enough. To compensate for your losses the Government has decided to take extreme measures. In order to enable you all to get back on track; to feed your children; to clothe your wives; to clean your homes; to get new tools; to give you people a boost, it has been decreed – pardon my terminology, but I'm using the word we are all familiar with – that this city will not pay any Federal taxes for the next six months."

The crowd was frankly awed. After a brief pause, shouts of joy flew over the plaza.

Turning to Delacroix, the Captain said quietly, "You're under arrest. So are you friends."

Ten horsemen in light-blue suits appeared and lay their hands on Delacroix's friends' shoulders.

Delacroix shouted in the Captain's face, "This is an outrage! It's illegal, sir! There's no longer any law in this country!"

"Oh yes there is," the Captain assured him. "Here's one law that you'll follow religiously from now on unless you wish to be beaten into a pulp." He paused for emphasis. He bellowed, "There's going to be no more shouting in my face!" Calmly, he added, "Let's go."

"What are the charges, sir?"

"I thought that was perfectly clear."

"Oh, yeah? What? Treason? Subversive activities?"

"Tax evasion."

Let us note in passing that permanently removing an integral component from any political body, whether legal or illegal – and the Gallic Faction had been playing a major role in Mappensville's politics for two hundred years – can lead to a great deal of instability. The city's economy, once every member of the Faction was arrested, took an abrupt turn for the worse. It was only thanks to Federal aid, the Mayor's valiant efforts to stabilize the situation, and the completion of the new docks Hector Eriksson had so desperately sought, that the area was saved from utter ruin. Three years later, it prospered again – as much as any city could prosper in those days.

It continued prospering. Presidents came and went, Mr. Madison's War raged in the vicinity for two weeks but somehow the city was spared. The Gallic Faction, once its principal members returned from federal prison, made a number of subtle attempts to regain lobbying powers. Most of the members had grownup children, some of whom agreed to take over. The Faction was never the same, though.

After the Civil War, various heritages blended into the city's population. Many citizens participated in the Spanish-American War, and then in World War I. The Great Depression hit the city hard, depopulating it almost entirely. The New Deal revived it somewhat, and World War II gave it yet another boost, what with major auto manufacturers building a number of plants on the outskirts. The various movements of the 'Sixties almost ruined Mappensville again, but the area's hippies grew up quickly, donning business suits and investing heavily in tourism. As the Twentieth Century drew to a close, only the City Hall, the old church once admired by Washington, and some of the monuments remained to remind the citizens of the glory days – all other architecture was from later epochs. The old City Hall was now a museum.

Summer was late that year. On the Sixth of July, the sky cleared up and suddenly it was beastly hot – the asphalt softened, the air conditioners buzzed, the people spoke slowly and incoherently.

Waking up with a start, his hair damp, his limbs sweating, Raymond Ericson cast a brief glance at the window of his motel room. The blinding morning light caused him instantly to forget his dream – a strange one, in which he seemed to have visited a female ancestor of his in various stages of her life. Only a vague impression remained. He believed he had seen some pretty fascinating things, some of which might have been... educational? Important? He wasn't certain. He had no time for reconstructing dreams. Not now.

He threw away the damp sheet and, springing to his feet, discovered he was seriously thirsty. He poured a glass of water. He turned on his portable espresso machine. He showered, shaved, and had a cup of very strong coffee by the window, contemplating the industrial landscape outside. It was a Sunday, which was why, perhaps, there was no smog.

Raymond inspected his wardrobe, selecting his favorite silk pants and canvas jacket. Remembering appreciatively that in the summer one had some leeway in the way of clothes, he dismissed the idea of wearing soft leather shoes and picked up a pair of British sandals instead – a gift from a shoemaker he had met in Glasgow.

This is not Raymond's story. We will return to Molly and Miles once we have covered the facts necessary for the reader to get a complete picture of the events.

It took Raymond twenty minutes to reach the nearest metro station and another twenty to get to the very heart of the city called Jefferson Square, formerly Her Majesty's Plaza. In his time, Jefferson resented Mappensville, but three decades after his death, the good citizenry decided they liked the man anyway. They went ahead and named the square after him, letting bygones be bygones. Now, a possibility existed that, in view of some recently discovered facts, the population might soon cease to like Jefferson; the square might have to be renamed again, perhaps after the famous tennis player who had lived in Mappensville once and, not unlike Jefferson, resented it.

The old City Hall towered majestically over the square. Brave Patty, in bronze, still posed coquettishly as Molly Bates on her limestone pedestal in the middle, but all the other structures around the perimeter were new, and the one campaign to spare the cobblestone pavement had failed fifty years ago.

A manhole thirty feet southeast from the statue was open and two men fussed around it, giving unsound advice to a third one, fussing inside. All three wore yellow plastic helmets meant to prevent head injuries caused by heavy objects falling vertically on the wearer's head.

"There's Ray," one of the workers said, pointing and inadvertently spilling hot coffee from his paper cup down his colleague's back. The colleague objected loudly and energetically.

"Hi, guys," Raymond said, waving.

"Hey, Ray! Wow, look at them clothes! What is this, interviewing for an office job?"

"Not really."

He crossed the square, heading for one of the side streets.

The luxury apartment building he entered had been erected in the middle of the Nineteenth Century, replacing an old tavern with stables in the back. Raymond approached the doorman, handing him a hundred-dollar bill and receiving a key. No words were exchanged. The doorman's understanding was, this was the last time he was doing the strange visitor a favor.

Raymond took the elevator to the fourth floor and entered one of the apartments, using the key.

It was a charming duplex with very high ceilings and a living room an average New Yorker might risk being called a racist for – with a large functional fireplace opposite the pair of enormous French windows. The logs Raymond had brought earlier were piled up in the fireplace. He lit them with his lighter now.

After consulting his wrist watch, he ran upstairs, entered one of the three bedrooms, opened a closet and squatted at the massive safe that was partly concealed by various garments on hangers. He dialed the combination, opened the safe, and extracted the batch of papers it contained. He locked the safe again. He was about to leave the room when he remembered something. Re-entering the closet, he reached up and from just above the doorframe removed the tiny camera. He dropped it into his pocket.

In the adjacent bedroom, he opened the dresser and extracted from under the silk underwear and some sex toys it contained a large, impressive-looking hand gun.

Running downstairs again, he satisfied himself that the fire now crackled merrily. He threw the papers on the oak table, grabbed a chair, placed it between the table and the fireplace, sat, took the gun out, snapped off the safety and chambered the first round. He did not have to wait long. Four minutes later, someone opened the front door.

There were two voices – a high but not unpleasant soprano and a squeaky baritone with the occasional unnaturally high note. Raymond crossed his legs. The woman laughed, the man said something about a new sound system, and the woman laughed again. Suddenly, the six speakers positioned strategically around the perimeter of the living room came alive and light music poured softly through them. Raymond frowned. The couple entered the living room laughing.

The man was swarthy, rather tall, and corpulent. The woman was graceful and light, her face still retaining some of her adolescence although, as Raymond knew, she was going to turn thirty next month. The music confused them for a moment, but eventually they did notice Raymond and froze.

"Please sit down," Raymond said, "and don't utter any platitudes, like, what are you doing here? And all that. I'm going to explain what I'm doing here presently. I just want to make one thing clear before we start. This is your gun, Leonard. Like most hand-held firearms, it has the right end and the wrong end. Just now, you're facing the wrong end. I haven't the slightest intention of killing you, but if I even begin to suspect that you might be interfering with my plans here, I'll see if I can hit a man in the leg from where I'm sitting. Sit down, folks."

"You're such a creep, Ray," the woman said.

"Ah, yes, Annie, and how are you today?" Raymond re-crossed his legs. "I might be a creep, darling, but just now I happen to be the hottest fucking thing around here, so, you'll sit and listen like a good girl, okay?"

Once both Leonard and Annie were seated and began to exchange desperate looks, Raymond took a deep breath, collected his thoughts, ignored a déjà vu of sorts, and said, "Once upon a time there were a man and a woman who were so happy together that everyone who knew them could not help weeping for joy all the time."

"Could you..." Leonard began and stopped.

"Yes?"

"Could you... uh... not point that gun at... uh... us... like that?"

"Sorry," Raymond said. "This won't take long, I promise. Anyway, where was I? Talking about a man and a woman...Ah, yes. Oh, by the way, the woman would be Annie. There she is. In that chair. What a coincidence. So! The woman decided she could be happier still with a different man. Now, wait a minute! He's here also. That's him," Raymond indicated Leonard with the gun – the latter cringed. "How considerate of you to drop by today, Leonard."

Annie, running a graceful hand through her jet-black hair, grinned contemptuously from habit. She followed the gun with her eyes.

"Anyway," Raymond went on, "Stuff like that happens all the time, and nobody really minds, except the woman decided she could increase the amount of her personal happiness further still by making her former husband thoroughly miserable. He was kind of wealthy, you see. She figured she'd take away most of his income. Well, her former husband asked, don't you have enough money between you and your, uh, something or other? She did not reply. She only raised her eyebrows mysteriously, which in her language meant that no matter how much you have, a little extra can't hurt, even if, in order to get it, you make others suffer... only it's too unlady-like to say so. Now, the judge might have ruled in favor of the injured party, as judges will, except it was up to the lawyers to decide which of the two parties was the injured one. Thus, the former husband, figuring he couldn't take any chances, turned all his assets into cash and gave it to a bunch of Bohemian screw balls in New York. Whaddya know, the money was all gone in a week. There still remained the former husband's considerable salary, of course. Well, he quit his job and got another one in the sewer. This brought down the amount of monthly alimony he might have been forced to pay to about three hundred and seventy-seven dollars, twenty-eight cents. In the meantime, Annie's lover's parents went bankrupt." He turned to Leonard. "Accept my sympathy, uh, Leonard. Just when you were done with your graduate program – liberal arts, isn't it? – and figured you'd never have to do anything you didn't want to do. Ooops. The old clowns lost their fortune and had to cut your daily allowance."

He paused solemnly, pretending to be lost in thought. A song came on the speakers whose opening bars caught his attention. He listened to the deep mezzo with a slight Hispanic accent singing the lyrics passionately –

The anguished elms are reeling in the storm.

And, as the wild Noreaster groans and stutters,

Woman, you have a duty to perform –

A sacred rite behind the oaken shutters.

Come forth to him and shed the needless clothes.

Stir his despondency with gentle toes.

Raymond nodded approvingly. There was an orchestral intermezzo. He was going to listen to it when Annie spoke cautiously, "What are you doing, Ray? What are you trying to achieve here?"

"We'll come to that, don't worry." Raymond winked at her. "The happy couple figured they had yet another asset. The great fat lover remembered there were, uh, some papers he had inherited from his uncle, and that some of those papers were as good as gold, or nearly so, as they gave him shares in various profitable enterprises all over the globe. Neither the uncle nor the nephew had thought of claiming their rights earlier – never really got around to doing so. Now, things were different. It was time to call some lawyers, historians, and other kinds of specialists. The nephew took the papers of out their safe deposit box and brought them home. Which was a mistake."

Leonard made a movement. Raymond's ominous smile made him sit back in the chair again. He was genuinely frightened now. The smile had all the qualities of the one that used to frighten his ancestor's enemies out of their wits. Annie went very pale, her hands trembling slightly. The second verse of the song came on –

Drown his despair in a ferocious rush

Of burning kisses and prolonged caresses,
So that again his hand could hold the brush.
Shield him from nagging grief with auburn tresses.
She's taken his beloved child away.
You are his respite. Darling, make him stay.

For a moment, Raymond's mind went blank. A note rang out in his memory he could not easily dismiss. A vision came to him – a shipyard with large, elegant-looking vessels... a champagne bottle broken against the stern... A thin, dark-haired man issuing orders...

"Okay," Leonard said.

"Shut up," Raymond snapped. He was pointing the gun directly at Leonard's face. His features contorted. Annie screamed. Leonard shut his eyes. Raymond bit his lip and lowered the gun. The third verse came on.

The stakes are high. The essence of his art
You must preserve by joining in his grieving –
Not civilly, but with your legs apart,
Your nipples hard, your bosom wildly heaving,
Your thighs out of control, your feet at rest,
Their outer edges to his ankles pressed.

The thin, dark-haired man was in bed with a very good-looking woman. She stroked his chest with amazingly long fingers, and smiled so cozily and lovingly at him that Raymond, who was anything but sentimental, suddenly wanted to cry. An echo from the past – this was his *other* ancestor... He could not make any sense of it. He shook his head. For a moment, he felt guilty. Was it really his business – meddling in other people's affairs, shattering their lives? What right did he have to be here, in their house... He clenched his teeth. He took a deep breath. His once again focused on Leonard MacLachlan and his spouse.

"Okay," Leonard said, trying to sound reasonable. "How much do you want? Fifty percent?"

Raymond laughed.

"Your mistake, Leonard, is that you always approach others with your own measure. You shouldn't. Granted, people like you constitute the majority of the human race today. But there are exceptions."

"You want all of it?"

Raymond laughed again, very sincerely.

"No," he said, " you incredibly obtuse non-entity, I don't want any of it. Can you get that through your head? I'm neither avaricious nor silly. I want you two to suffer a little. That's my goal."

He picked up the top sheet from the pile on the table and glanced over it briefly.

"Some kind of archeological research," he said pensively. "In Italy. Well, someone else will own all those vases and night pots," he threw the sheet in the fireplace.

"Stop," John said.

"Make me."

"You son of a bitch," Annie shouted.

"Tut, tut. Watch your tongue, young lady. I want you guys to suffer. This place," he indicated the surroundings with his eyes, "will have to go. The one in New York will have to go as well. Also, the one in Florida. And the tiny hut... by the beach... the Rivera... good-bye! Next!"

He picked up another sheet.

"Don't do it," Leonard said. "Stop. Please!"

"What's this? GF," Raymond inspected the letter head. The sheet was yellow – ancient. "Something very old. Names... places... the historical value of this one might actually be greater than its business value... or not. I don't know. Anyway, all those swanky parties, elegant soirees – bye-bye!"

He deposited it into the fireplace.

"Symbolic, isn't it? There's something about fireplaces that no incinerator can match. Next! Ah! This – from... I don't know... Russian aristocracy. Wow. Now that they're back in Russia claiming their natural rights, this must be worth something. Some mines in Siberia, I would imagine. Okay, skiing in the Alps, snowboarding in Colorado – bye-bye! Oh, what's this? Here are those strange letters again, GF. General Financing. Get Fucked. Whatever. Spending time on the links with former Presidents – away with it! And this? Very yellow. Must be two hundred years old. All those clubs in Palm Beach, where Donald Trump is not allowed... bye-bye!"

So it went. Sheet by sheet, the stack vanished into the fireplace.

"It's splitsville for the happy couple," Raymond said sympathetically. "You might as well do it now, while you're still on good terms with each other."

"Why should we?" Leonard asked – frightened, angry – and sincerely curious. Annie remained silent. She knew.

"Why should you?" Raymond shrugged.

"Yes. That's what I asked. Why should we?"

"Oh, well. Well... You see, Leonard... I wouldn't want to overtax your imagination, but think about it – farmers toiling from dawn to dusk, planes taking off and landing, sweatshops in Asia burning the midnight oil... Wall Street playing its cautious and incompetent hand, with the Federal Reserve watching it like a hawk to keep us all out of trouble... the Marines making sure America's interests are taken into account in every corner of the world... and so on."

"Is he insane?" Leonard asked, addressing Annie but looking at Raymond.

The latter winked at him, continuing his thought without verbally acknowledging Leonard's remark, "So that Leonard and Annie could go on with their honeymoon. A month. Six months. A year. Two years. When it was hot, Leonard and Annie went mountain climbing in the Himalayas. When it was too cold, they sunbathed in Rio. When they were in the mood for a medieval background, they went to Scotland. When nightlife was their fancy, they jetted over to Paris. Italian Renaissance in Florence. Russian opera in St. Petersburg. German opera in Bayreuth. Sushi in Japan. Pizza in New York. Scuba diving in French Polinesia. Meditation in Tibet. Bull fights in Madrid. Elephant hunting – perfectly illegal, by the way – in Africa. Back to New York when New Jersey tomatoes are back in season. Now, that's what I call romance. You see, you've been able, up to this point, to avoid the two things that are the surest romance killers – employment and boredom. What I'm doing right now is introducing both to your marriage, just to see if it holds. Call it a social experiment."

The next pause was long and painful. Raymond smiled, unloaded the gun, and threw it on the table casually. Before Annie could stop him, Leonard was out of his chair and all over Raymond. At least, he thought he was. Raymond was out of his chair as well, slipping under Leonard's elbow and, with a single blow to the back of the head, felling his nemesis. It took Leonard a few seconds to realize what had happened. He sat up on the floor.

"I hope you're satisfied now," Annie said to Raymond. She rose, walked over, and kneeled beside Leonard. She pressed her cheek to his forehead. We'll be fine."

"No," Raymond said. "I'm not satisfied – not yet. I expect to be satisfied two or three years from now, when the two of you are flipping burgers at the greasy spoon just down the road. I'll be completely satisfied when I drop by and tip you a dollar each."

The MacLachlan family archive smoldered in the fireplace. It had contained, among other things, all remaining documented evidence that the Gallic Fraction, an organization that had once wielded more power than an average European country, ever existed. From now on, no one could conclusively prove anything – the Faction was a thing of legend only. Professional historians never really believed it existed anyway. There was never a shortage of plausible explanations for the three thousand and one mysterious events that took place in the Seventeenth, Eighteenth, and Nineteenth Century – from the notorious Salem witch hunt to Lincoln's assassination.

The Gallic Fraction now joined the Camelot, Leif Eriksson's settlement in Newfoundland, and Aeneas' miraculous and fateful escape from burning Troj in the realm of speculative history.

TWENTY

The Reunion

Leaning on the banister separating the terrace from the garden, Hector stood gazing at the exotic trees in Clarisse's garden. Some unruly birds chirped peevishly. Tears ran down Hector's cheeks.

He had come here because he couldn't think of any other place to be for a while. He had spent the morning and part of the afternoon in the garden, popping out just once to check on the progress at the shipyard. He wished to be alone with Clarisse. He did not want to speak to her, or even be in the same room with her – he just wanted her presence in the house. He was in no mood for anyone else's presence.

Too bad.

Miles Crawford visited and entertained Clarisse with the highlights of *Figaro's Marriage*, a play whose copies circulated throughout Europe and the East Coast and which Clarisse had somehow managed to miss altogether. Crawford's Blois-pure French was getting on Hector's nerves.

Later, Margaret the Viscountess dropped by for some coffee with brandy in it. She and Miles had a big argument about a British playwright, rediscovered recently, called Shakespeare. Miles, who was an ardent fan, insisted that Shakespeare was the greatest playwright ever; the Viscountess laughed and maintained that time and the public were the only true judges, and when a dramatist was forgotten, it was always because of the essential weakness of his works, and no efforts on the historian's part were going to make any difference. The current interest in Shakespeare ("Is that what you said his name was? Shakespeare?") was merely a passing craze, a momentary fad that was going to fade soon. She challenged Miles to quote something. He performed a monologue rather well. The Viscountess laughed again and said the piece was amateurish and flat – much too simple; not enough flare; not enough poetry.

She was still in the house someplace – taking her tea and olives with Clarisse, or something.

Suddenly, she appeared behind Hector. She observed him silently from the back for a while. She crossed the terrace and placed her hand on his shoulder. He dabbed his forehead with his handkerchief and turned around.

"Is it... the children?" she asked.

He closed his eyes. He applied the handkerchief again.

"I see them once or twice a week," he said. "What business is it of yours? But yes, it is the children, mostly. What are you doing here?"

"I'm quite the ghost from the past, am I not? Sit down."

He sat in one of the wicker chairs. She remained standing.

"Awww, poor dear Hector. What are you going to do?"

"I don't know."

"You finally got that Government contract, right? For a dozen ships?"

"Yes."

"Money is no longer an issue, then. Your wife has a maid, I believe?"

"Yes."

"Has she expressed any desire to travel yet?"

Frightened, he replied quickly, "No."

"She will. Be prepared."

"And..."

"With the children. You'll have to get used to the idea of not seeing them for months. And each time you see them, you'll have to pay."

Her words did not hurt him. They were not very soothing either. It was not words he wanted now. He was weak and vulnerable; any woman could, with a little affection rather than lust, console him temporarily. He could not even get drunk – the mere smell of alcohol made him nauseous now. The sight of food upset his stomach.

"Poor dear Hector. I'll be gone in a moment. I wanted to leave last night, but I just couldn't, not without seeing you first. You've changed. Clarisse adores you..."

He was ill at ease. He looked sideways.

"Oh, you puritans!" she exclaimed. "Listen, I must tell you something." She smiled kindly, actually reminding him of his wife, the way the latter had looked ten years ago. Slightly warn, yet undaunted. "I love you, you see. I have loved you all these years. I fell in love with you at a party, at my husband's mansion on the outskirts of this city, which you may or may not remember. They used to call it, Our Answer to Versailles. You and

Clarisse went upstairs to fornicate. I had known you prior to that, but it was at that party when I realized you were special. You brought me a new composition, written by Gluck. I've treasured it ever since. And then there were the brigands, and I had to give up my necklace. Yesterday, Clarisse and I were taking a stroll, and we met your wife. She was wearing that necklace. I have no idea how she ever got to own it. I love you still, Hector. I think I'll always love you."

He looked up at her and bit his lip in a child-like manner.

"You could have told me."

She laughed. He was incredible. Any other man would have just kept silent.

"I couldn't. You see, all these years, I've been faithful to my husband. A pledge is a pledge. Good bye, Hector. Please don't follow me."

She went back into the house quickly. In another moment, he heard Shakespeare's critic's carriage roll slowly away.

He went back inside.

Some time passed. He fidgeted in a chair and tried to read, but could not concentrate. He stood by the window. It was dark. Clarisse spoke to him, but he never replied. She had dinner by herself, after which she read a little. It was the very novel Miles had once recommended to his then-spouse; the adventures of a dashing lass named Molly Bates. It began with the words, "It was the first truly cold night of the year, reminding everyone that the season was nearly over." Contrary to Miles' opinion, it was not a girly novel.

Clarisse finished her toilette, sprinkled some perfume on her wrists and neck, and re-entered the living room. She found Hector in the same pose as before, by the window. She shed her dress and, in only her underwear, went up to him. He did not stir. She pressed herself to his back and smelled his hair. Being taller than he, she was able easily to kiss his neck. He became tense but made no movement. She ran her hands around him and started untying his shirt. She continued kissing him.

He allowed her to lead him to the bedroom where with languid caresses she was able to bring him back to life somewhat. He embraced her very gently. The words, "At last!" flashed through her mind. The last time they had made love was on board his newly built ship. Fifteen years is a long time. He was not himself yet, but he was getting there.

Outside, a thunderstorm raged. The shutters complained, the wind wailed and stuttered. Inside, it was warm and cozy. And getting warmer still. Soon, Clarisse saw a different Hector – part-savage, part-temperate. He was almost raping her – and sparing her at the same time.

"I love you, Hector," she said into his ear and immediately cried out.

The smell of their lovemaking became monstrously alluring. She could no longer contain herself and peaked wildly, thrashing, writhing, wriggling. Hector allowed her passion to subside and continued relentlessly to push her back to the giddy brink. Almost immediately, she peaked again. And again. And again. The smell became pungent. Now they attacked each other furiously, kissing, licking, biting, slipping scratching. She screamed and he roared, and they peaked. He lay on top of her, drained, and, for the moment, happy – his mind was blank. She touched the back of her hand to her eyes – they were damp. So were the sheets. The fire crackled merrily in the fireplace. There was lightning, and a burst of thunder – like the final chord of a symphony's first movement.

They rested. Hector rolled off her and turned onto his back, staring at the ceiling. Clarisse, propping herself on an elbow, stroked his chest. Ten minutes went by. His respiration was back to normal. She smiled kindly. He squinted.

"What are you thinking of?"

"The Viscountess," he replied.

"Margaret? Oh."

"She told me the strangest thing before she left."

"What, that she was in love with you but she had to be faithful to her husband?"

"No, about a necklace... What?"

"She told you that she loved you. What necklace?"

"How did you know?"

"No one wants to suffer alone. Now that she's shared it with you, you're going to feel guilty, and maybe you'll suffer just a little bit. Makes her feel better. As for being faithful to her husband, well, perhaps she has been. I don't know. I think she's frigid."

Hector knit his brows and turned to her.

"How would you know that?"

"I'm not sure. She might have told me. I don't remember. What was that about a necklace?"

Hector turned away from her, trying to control himself. He failed. He started laughing hysterically.

"What's the matter?" she demanded, concerned. "Something funny?"

"Women!" he shouted.

He sprang out of bed and, still laughing, ran to the mantelpiece.

"Where's my pipe?" he asked angrily.

TWENTY-ONE

Three Months Later

The statue, a fine piece of sculpting depicting Patty, stood on its sandstone pedestal. The legend stated unequivocally that this was, in fact, Molly Bates (1751-1776), and that the citizens of Mappensville were grateful. The stonemason had neglected to make clear whether the two facts were in any way related.

Molly sat on the painted wooden bench in front of the statue. An ironic smile played on her lips. Mongoose approached, went around the bench, and sat beside her. It was a sunny afternoon. The square was deserted.

"Like it?" he asked.

"Hello, Jack," she said, turning to him. She grinned. "Love it."

Endowed, like all talented artists, with a superlative sense of continuum, Kenneth had been able to convey his mistress's past and future in his rendition of her person. The angle at which her right arm was bent suggested a woman whose attitude towards sex had changed drastically when she was middle-aged – a trait characteristic of former governesses, mature feminists, and reformed prostitutes changing their lifestyles early enough. The left hand, resting coquettishly on the pommel of the sword, was the hand of someone who had never in her life handled weapons of any kind. The posture was more vulnerable than aggressive. Patty's face, youthened sufficiently to fit the character she impersonated, was nevertheless very much Patty's. Most intriguing of all, the woman on the pedestal had breasts twice Molly's size – a detail that amused Molly immensely. The tricorne (Molly, proud of her luscious blond locks, never wore one), completed the image. The mask was missing.

"Listen, uh..." Mongoose said. "Mrs. Eriksson... I'm really sorry about... what I did that night. What I attempted to do that night. What you prevented me from doing that night."

The calm blue of her eyes resembled that of the winter sky over the mountains in Maine.

"What night?"

"The night we met."

"That's a very long time ago, Jack," she said, wrinkling her nose.

He suddenly noticed the necklace. He was shocked, but, recovering quickly, figured he had nothing to lose anymore. He decided to go for broke.

"Here's what I have to say. I'm now a totally different man, a well-respected statesman... Respected, at any rate, to the degree that any politician can be respected... I have money and some connections. A clout, to put it bluntly. The only thing I don't have is a family of my own. I'm tired of politics; tired of adventures; tired of pretty much everything except the one thing I never had. A home."

She was perfectly calm, listening to his flurry of clichés. Home. He wanted a home. Home and little kiddies. And a wifey-poo. Poor dear Mongoose, who thought he could make a woman feel the way she never felt before. The intrepid pioneer of female feelings. The principle phallus of Mappensville.

He was suddenly embarrassed. He rose, stuck his hands in his pockets, and looked at the sky.

"Nice weather..." he said importantly. "You just think about what I told you. Don't say anything now, just think about it."

He walked slowly away. Molly turned her eyes back on the monument.

At that moment, a group of four appeared at the far end of the square. Clarisse, Hector, and Miles were old friends. Penny was a newcomer.

She was a charming blond creature of twenty, very slender. She had boyish manners and was in love with life.

"Look!" she cried excitedly. Her voice had a shrill adolescent note in the upper registers, but it was not at all annoying. "All those birds!"

She started chasing the pigeons. The three others smiled. The men looked in the direction of the statue and saw Molly. Both stopped smiling immediately.

"Don't worry," Miles said quietly. "She won't see us. Her eyes are not what they used to be. Besides, she doesn't appear to be armed..."

He peered, trying to discern a sword at Molly's hip.

"No, she's not armed," he confirmed. "Chose the right place, didn't she? If you ask her now, it was mere chance that brought her here and dumped her on that silly-looking painted bench in front of her own memorial."

"Stop talking nonsense, men," Clarisse said.

"I wasn't talking at all," Hector pointed out.

"You're a boor," she told him. "If you weren't such a boor, you'd be talking too now, saying all kinds of nasty things about her. You two must have hurt her as much as she hurt you. And she's all alone now."

Miles was skeptically silent. Hector grew pale. Alone? His ex had his children. Clarisse realized she was being tactless. Miles cleared his throat.

"Something I always wanted to ask you, Clarisse," he said. "I hear that, when a man has two mistresses, their periods begin to coincide at some point. I just want to hear your opinion on..."

"Shut up, Crawford... What a charming creature."

She obviously meant Penny, who was still skipping around the square, chasing birds and laughing. Miles smiled.

"Cute, isn't she?" he asked.

His masculine shallowness annoyed Clarisse.

"I can't imagine what she finds in you that's so wonderful, Crawford. She's so young..."

"That's exactly what her dear old mother said," he told her. He imitated a high-pitched female voice, "What does she find in you?"

"You met her mother?"

"Sure. Her Dad, too. He wasn't as polite and far less kind. Used perfectly awful language."

"Of course," Clarisse seemed to approve of Penny's parents' behavior. "You're old enough to..."

"Yes," he said, "I'm old enough. In fact, I am two or three years her father's senior. Which is not the point, because men old enough to be their brides' grandfathers still go through with it and nobody minds. It's mostly the class differences that Penny's family seems to be concerned with."

"Class differences?" Hector was not sure he heard Miles right.

"I'm a duke, you know," Miles said, shrugging. "These wealthy Yankees are as snobbish as the most conservative of the aristocrats. Nothing will do but she must marry some awful patriotic commoner, provided, of course, that his Mom and Dad have a great deal of real estate and a bit of cash. Or maybe shares in the East India Tea Company. Or a plantation full of slaves."

He was lying. The Roosevelts were a respectable, if not particularly rich, family; Penny's parents had a sense of humor. Miles had managed to charm them both. The fact that he was an aristocrat was in his favor. Miles would have been very amused to learn that an island in the East River and an avenue in Thomas Jefferson's favorite foreign city would bear the name of one of his descendants a century and a half later.

Clarisse suggested, "If you're just playing with the girl's feelings, then you must be a very cruel person, Miles. I, for my part..."

"Playing, sure," Miles scoffed. "I'm pretty much trapped, you know. Playing! Choose your words with a little more tact, will you."

"What do you mean? Trapped?" she asked.

"Oh, leave me alone... What. Stop staring at me. You know, Clarisse, the main thing about you is that you're just too tall to ignore... What? I knocked her up. Didn't mean to. It just happened. Looks like I'm going to be a father soon."

She stared at him. He smiled apologetically.

Hector said suddenly, "I'd like to see Africa. I always wanted to find out what elephant hunting is like. You know? Imagine, there's this huge sweaty animal, and it's running and going booooo! with its trunk, and you take quiet aim..."

Clarisse pursed her lips and made eyes at him. Penny, laughing, rejoined the group and threw herself on Miles' neck.

"Oh, darling," she screamed, "I love you so."

She was light and shapely, and very well groomed. There is beauty created through consistent breeding, where more quality is purchased by each succeeding generation; and there is spontaneous, natural beauty that springs to life for no apparent reason, when two ordinary-looking parents suddenly produce extraordinary-looking offspring. Because in the latter's case the milieu is usually unworthy of the miracle, the beauty is wasted on the lucky fellow who comes with beer-ridden breath and unwashed hair to claim the prize.

Now, Miles was no such fellow. Miles, despite some surface faults and past errors, was a connoisseur and, when he wished to be, a loyal and considerate companion.

Clarisse nodded resignedly and turned her eyes on Hector. The latter was looking in the direction of the bench. Molly was gone.

It was a busy day at the harbor, but the beach was all but deserted. Half a mile from the docks, Molly, in a man's suit, and Patty walked along the surf in their stocking feet, carrying their shoes in their hands.

"...and after all that," Molly said disgustedly, "he says I've betrayed him."

"You never really told me what happened," Patty said.

"He backstabbed me the day I became his mistress. Later, he was never really a husband; his children never had a father. He never really talked to them. He never really played with them. They'd be playing beside him, and he'd be reading, or sketching his stupid ships. Lately, he's been talking about visiting Africa, imagine. He stopped talking to me centuries ago. And yet, I'm supposed to be the bad guy."

"He must have hurt you a lot."

"He did. After all I did for him, he hurt me."

"What did you do for him?"

"Everything."

Patty had no reason to doubt her friend's words. Molly had done a great deal for her, as well as for Kenneth. It would only be reasonable to assume that she had done much more for her own husband. In Patty's view, Molly was the most generous person on earth.

They saw a couple locked in an embrace. Molly recognized them, grinned, turned and walked in the opposite direction, dragging Patty along.

The Baroness sobbed, pressing her face against her husband's chest. McLachlan stroked her hair tenderly, gazing at the horizon. They were going to go home soon, to their little daughter Juliana.

"Still, I'd be lying if I told you I felt great about things," Molly said, looking over her shoulder. "Life can get pretty scary sometimes. But there are always consolations. You know what I'd like to do?"

"What?" Patty asked, interested.

"Get really drunk someplace. Let's just go to some sleazy hole and get plastered."

Patty laughed. "You're looking for trouble, Ruth."

"Yes, sort of. I wouldn't mind picking a fight with somebody and beating the shit out of them. Come on. What's the matter? Scared?"

"I'm game. Anything you say. I'll watch."

"There's this new joint on the outskirts, real seedy and squalid. I remember seeing some sailors go there."

"Aren't we stopping by your place? You'll need a sword."

It was Molly's turn to laugh. "The bastards will lend me one of their own."

In the three months Miles had been in Mappensville, minus the jail time, his butler, under his master's abusive and pedantic supervision, turned the townhouse into the coziest place in the hemisphere.

Miles and Penny entered laughing, jostling each other playfully. Miles tore off his coat and vest. He was about to undo the lace strings of his shirt when his eyes suddenly fixed on something. He gasped. A luxurious robe with tassels was thrown over the back of a chair. Miles released Penny. Slowly, cautiously, he walked over and picked up the robe.

He had forgotten all about it. When he was in jail, the butler put it away. Miles had been so busy lately, what with helping Hector find a good lawyer, corresponding and bickering with Jefferson, reading and taking apart Voltaire's humanitarian scribbling ("Masses, he says, should be, not educated, but guided... *By me*, he forgets to add, *by me*! Ha, ha, ha!"), giving manners lessons to people who insisted they had a right to annoy him, telling scary stories to Hector's kids, and entertaining Penny day and night, that he had neglected completely to inquire after the robe's whereabouts. Today, the butler had remembered it himself and taken it out of the closet.

"Penny," Miles half-whispered mysteriously. "Do me a favor. Just... Just don't say anything for a couple of minutes. Just... sit in a chair."

"Why?" she asked, pouting.

"Please," he insisted.

"All right," she said, pouting harder, stroking her large belly absentmindedly.

She sat. Miles lay the robe tenderly on the chair again. He leaped to the table, grabbed the bell, and rang frantically. The butler rushed in.

"James," Miles said gravely. "Run downstairs and make me some tea. While you're at it, look in the library, see if you can find me a good book. Nothing captivating, mind you. No adventures, no science, nothing that could unduly excite a reasonably advanced mind. Something very dull, philosophy, medical history, anything. Something that would make a right-thinking man doze off in five minutes flat."

"Yes, my Lord."

"Also," Miles added quickly, nervously, "don't bring the whole tea pot up here. Just pour one cup, place it on the tray, and just... you know. Got it?"

"Lemon or milk, then, sir?"

"Uh... lemon. No, well, I'd like one with... Tell you what; pour two cups. Two. All right? Put a slice of lemon in one; splash some milk in the other; and bring them both up. And please see that no one – do you hear? *no one* – disturbs me during the next few hours."

"Pardon me, sir. There's a message for you. A gentleman in light-blue clothes left it this morning. Said it was extremely urgent."

"Yeah? ..." Miles asked, trembling, thinking of something else.

"Yes, my Lord. Here it is."

He produced a scroll and handed it over to Miles. He left the room. Miles broke the seal and groaned.

The letter, composed in Jefferson's casual handwriting, said, "*My dear Crawford. I believe you speak fluent German. It has become necessary for us to send someone to Austria. I realize you need more rest, but the matter is very pressing. You must set off for Philadelphia immediately upon receipt of this letter in order to get detailed instructions. Affectionately Yours, Thomas Jefferson.*"

Miles dropped the letter and stared into space. Penny watched him, afraid to speak. Miles spun around, scanned the floor, and eventually located his coat. He picked it up slowly. He went to the fireplace to get his sword. He sighed.

"Are you leaving?" Penny asked.

He nodded. He attached the sword and threw on the coat. He cast a final glance at the robe. He motioned for Penny to follow him.

Outside, Miles told Penny to wait, ran to the stables behind the house, saddled his horse quickly and led it by the reins to the front porch. He kissed Penny tenderly on the neck. She was silent.

The butler ran out, carrying a tray.

"Your tea, My Lord."

"Tea... Well..." Miles pondered. It was a difficult choice. "I'll have some in Vienna," he said at last.

He jumped into the saddle.

Introducing Richard V. Hamilton's next EFP novel, planned for release in Spring 2003

The Kept Women Of New Orleans

Excerpts From The Prologue.

It was a sunny morning. The good people of New Orleans had no idea what they really wanted from this life on that particular morning. They were fairly certain, however, that what they did have was not it. This is a common problem. Extremely unpleasant consequences are known to have resulted from considering it seriously or even lightly, which is why it is seldom considered at all.

The streets looked especially festive that morning. The houses were newly decorated with colorful flags of all sorts. The fruit stands under the Arcade near the St. Charles Wharf touted their very best wares. Wine barrels were everywhere. No duels were scheduled under the Duelling Oaks. The taverns were freshly swept, cleaned and dusted. The people in the streets wore their Sunday best, although it was only Thursday. The city held its breath in anticipation.

Even the new Mayor, notorious for never bothering to find out what was going on in his city, was alert. He looked out the window of his City Hall office twice with genuine concern. After contemplating the festivities for a while, he decided it must be another one of those barbaric Creole carnivals. He went back to his correspondence.

Only the Irish immigrants continued toiling morosely in the harbor, being reasonably certain that no matter what happened, it was not going to change their lot for the better any time soon.

A great man was expected anxiously to arrive – or *the* great man, in fact. The one and only, the incomparable, the generous – the King of Louisiana, as some of the local reporters, especially those at the *Delta News*, dubbed him half-jocosely.

When the steamer with the Great Man's insignia was spotted approaching the city from the delta, cries of joy rose over the streets.

In the meantime, two horsemen galloped down the road, two fierce riders determined to win against all odds, racing the clock, two desperate men whose purpose was to reach New Orleans before anything irreversible happened in that city. They were half-mad from fatigue, their throats parched with thirst, their limbs numb. Their horses breathed heavily, expiring, the riders' superhuman determination being the only thing still making them gallop like two graceful arrows shot by an expert archer – eating up the miles. Their sides were bloody, tortured by the riders' spurs; they frothed at the mouths; their eyes were bloodshot.

One of the riders was a dark-haired, slender man of about forty, the other blond, handsome, powerfully built, and fifteen years younger than his companion.

"The relay station?" shouted the fair-haired one.

"Two miles," the dark-haired one shouted back. "Cheer up, Tim."

"My horse might not make it!"

The dark-haired one did not reply. His thoughts were grim.

Normally so resourceful, so logical, so optimistic, he was too fatigued to consider what might happen if they didn't make it in time. He did not want that kind of responsibility. No. They were going to make it. There was no other way.

He extended his hand, pointing. A little path to the right of their course led into the woods.

They galloped up that path and continued to travel at the same maddening speed until they reached a picturesque clearing. A log cabin stood playfully in the middle.

The dark-haired horseman, already apprehensive, yet hoping against hope, turned left, alighted, and led his horse to the stables behind the cabin. A terrible curse escaped his lips. The fair-haired one, seeing this, alighted also, taking out his watch with a trembling hand and shaking his head.

In the stables, avoiding each other's eyes, they gave the horses water and oats. The dark-haired one reached into his portmanteau, produced a flask and, opening it, was going to pour the contents over the oats when he realized the flask was empty. He cursed again. Silently they entered the cabin.

There was one table, two crudely made chairs, a stove and a cupboard, and two beds. The fair-haired one fell onto a chair and closed his eyes. There was not a muscle in his body that wasn't numb.

The dark-haired one went over to the beds and ran his palm along the surface of each. They had been slept in very recently. The covers were silk. Any other man would have gotten suspicious. The dark-haired man, however, had no use for *becoming* suspicious – he was so by nature. He crossed over to the cupboard. It contained a pitcher of water.

"Half-an-hour," he said.

"We'll kill the horses."

"I know. I don't see how we can help that. It's Pierce. It's all his fault."

"How?"

"He's the stingiest bastard I've ever met. I told him. I told him a thousand fucking times. Starve the spies, starve the police, let the army and navy go barefoot, but keep the relay stations going. You know, Sutton, I planned them myself, these relay station, selecting each spot with the greatest care, ordering lumber, choosing the horses, hiring attendants. Attendants don't want to work for free, though. When you don't pay them, they start feeling neglected and unloved. The fellow who lived here had a wife and two children. He was owed four months pay. I have it in my portmanteau."

"He couldn't wait anymore."

"That's right. I don't know what he got for the horses he stole, probably much more than was owed him, but can I blame him? No."

"No."

"Loyalty withers if you starve it, Sutton, loyalty hardly ever works on an empty stomach."

"I agree."

They had some water.

"Whoever's living here now," the dark-haired man concluded, "is not the person we seek, but might turn out to be someone we could use."

"That's possible."

They were silent for quite a while.

Suddenly there was the sound of voices outside. The two horsemen stiffened. No hooves struck the dry ground. Whoever it was seemed to have arrived here on foot.

***

Manny's dear old mother was freed by the great and terrible Guillome, one of the wealthiest Louisiana planters, along with Manny himself, shortly after Monsieur Guillome's unfortunate death by a sword thrust in the ominously romantic shadow of the Dueling Oaks. The man who delivered the thrust was none other than the illustrious fencing teacher Pablo Vasquez. He had never killed anyone up to that point, and would never kill again. The police looked the other way; the Mayor expressed his commiserations and ordered to open the prominent citizen's will. The latter decreed, among other things, that all of Guillome's children born into slavery were to be freed on the day of their father's funeral – and that the children's mothers, too, were to enjoy liberty, such as it was. Two hundred dollars came with the freedom. Manny pocketed the money.

His mother, a peevish and stubborn woman, occasionally vindictive in a petty, more or less harmless way, and absurdly thin, insisted she still wished, after thirty years of absence, to return to her native African Village of which she claimed to have vivid and sweet memories. Manny, who wished to go into business for himself as a shoemaker, and who looked a great deal like his father – in that he was tall, broad, and ash-blond – and a little like his mother as well – the stubborn thick lips, the chiseled flat nose – resented the idea of traveling but was eventually persuaded by his mother to make the trip. She assured him that once she was among the people she loved –who would doubtless love her dearly in return – Manny was free to do as he pleased, jump out of a tree and break his stupid neck, for all she cared. But it was his damn duty as a son, she insisted, to take her where she wanted to be taken.

So he did. It was easier than listening to her lamentations every day. It took some time and hardship to traverse the Atlantic and then more time and more hardship to find the village. They got lucky – paying an impoverished Dutch traveler a sum of money and becoming his servants for the duration of the ocean phase of their journey. Once in Africa, Manny, who spoke none of the local dialects, found a guide. His mother, who claimed she knew most of the dialects, turned out to be completely helpless. The guide, a lean, very dark-skinned fellow who would have been shunned by Manny's mulatto friends back in New Orleans, flirted for a while with the idea of selling them to a New Englander he knew but Manny, who was wiser than his mother when it came to human nature, prevented the sale by offering to take the guide apart limb by shaking limb and feeding the resulting bloody mess to the crocodiles. The guide agreed there were going to be no further stupid fucking tricks.

On they traveled. Manny had two pistols, a very good hunting knife, some spare clothes, and a volume of Alexandre Dumas the Father, among other things, in his backpack. His mother carried some stones and shells in hers she claimed were from her native village and which very obviously traced their origin to one of the beaches on the Golf of Mexico.

The part of Central Africa they journeyed through was no longer the health hazard of yesteryear, when any non-native was likely to die very unpleasantly in three days' time. Many poisonous and toothy animals were already extinct, and dangerous plants were on the decline. Nevertheless, inhaling the air and listening intently to the neighborhood's sounds, Manny realized that danger was in excellent supply here still. One had to stay alert at all times around this place.

Every night, he tied the guide to a tree, securing his hands behind the trunk and sleeping nearby so as to be awakened by the slightest disturbance. His mother protested feebly, claming that a wayward snake might come calling against which the poor tied-up man would be defenseless. She knew about snakes, there were some back in Louisiana. Manny, who also knew a thing or two, said that all one had to do was avoid movement. He also offered to tie *her* up if she didn't stop badgering him soon.

***

"Tell me, Sutton," the dark-haired man said, sipping his tea and fingering an unlit cigar with some disgust. "What am I missing? Something's definitely wrong with the admirable picture, but what is it?"

"Someone wants to provoke someone."

"Yes, and they tip off one of my men, and, miraculously, the telegraph is working. By the way, why was it working? That line had been defunct for months."

"Someone repaired it."

"Yes. Someone who wanted to make sure we got the message. Someone with inside information. Someone who does not sympathize with the Southerner.... Someone who does not like the Northerners either. Right? Someone who actually knows that I exist! And what my job is. Possibly my wine preferences as well. A well-meaning Yankee living down South would try to contact the officials first."

"Fifth column."

"Sort of. There's definitely a third party here, Sutton, and they definitely want to stay incognito. Who are they?"

"Take your pick."

"Oh, yes. Let's see... There's the Spanish gang with that silly wretch who wants to be King of America..." He laughed. "Now, there's the Gallic Faction, but they don't care much, and anyway they've been dormant for ages... There's the mixed population – the *homme de coloures*, as they so pretentiously style themselves...

And there are also French, British, Prussian, Austrian, and very possibly Russian spies as well. Now, the Russians are definitely on the Union's side... but there aren't enough of them to penetrate... to discover the most obvious. The Frogs are still making up their minds as to whom they should support... The Brits... the South will blackmail them into activity sooner or later, but not yet... The Spanish fop is a cretin, he won't take an opportunity unless it actually speaks to him from three different continents in seven different languages... The men of color... That, in fact, is a possibility, but it's unbelievably far-fetched. Although I do like far-fetched... I adore farfetched..."

He nodded, his eyes closing involuntarily. He awakened himself with a start, clenching his teeth.

"That just about concludes the list," Sutton said. "Let's get some sleep."

"No, not yet. Not just yet, Sutton. Pardon me, my good fellow, I'm just thinking aloud... I'm not sleepy at all. Anyway, the men of color is one group in which I have no contacts. None. Believe it? Hiring someone off the street would be pointless. When you're starting from scratch, you need someone you could trust. Not to mention the trust has to be mutual. Some reciprocation is most certainly in order, Sutton. Where does a white man in my profession find a mulatto he can trust – who would also trust us? Huh?"

"Tell me."

"I thought you knew."

"No."

"Fantastically enough, neither do I. Why aren't you a mulatto? I'd send you in right now. Right this moment. It would be a great consolation to me to know I've done one positive thing today. It's frightening, Sutton. After what happened today... After what we failed to prevent... The next President is definitely going to be a Northerner. When that happens, all hell will break loose... Excuse the platitude, I'm very tired... But I'm not sleepy. Sit down, don't hover like that. Can you imagine what a civil war would mean to this country? Goodness gracious, they have those new... whatchamacallit... rifles... yes, with threads inside the muzzle. A musket that kills at two hundred paces. Three hundred! So many people will be slaughtered, it's mind-boggling. Unimaginable. And all of it will be on my conscience, all of it."

"On mine too."

"No, Sutton. You have nothing to do with it. I'm the one responsible, my lad, they send *me* messages and orders. I'm not a monster, Sutton. I've killed people, sometimes indiscriminately. Never gratuitously, though. I'm not a monster."

Sutton regarded his superior with dark skepticism.

"Don't give me that look!"

"Get to the point."

"I need a man, Sutton... a man... in the *homme de coloures* group. I need to know who their leaders are... their plans... their capabilities..."

"Here, or..."

"Here. Right here in New Orleans. No other mixed community is as organized, as intelligent, and as powerful – and they are powerful, Sutton. Twenty-five thousand souls who refuse to take sides. Who disdain blacks and whites – equally... Who deem themselves superior to all, unless I'm terribly mistaken."

"You are."

"No, no, Sutton, please. I've given it more thought than I'd care to admit even at gunpoint. On and off, I've been thinking. Oh, and did you hear that fellow speak to me earlier? Dignity, form and coldness. One would think I was an Injun and he a good-natured, condescending member of the proud *Conquista* come to civilize the ignorant but well-meaning savages. For all I know, if there's a war, it might be decided by a single factor, which will be – whose side are they going to take? And if they *don't* take sides, the war might go on for generations, Sutton."

He threw the unlit cigar away and leaned back in the chair.

"There are things I need to know, Sutton," he said hoarsely. "Oh, and whoever the next President is, I have to get to him early, before anyone else does. I could afford to take my time with Buchanan, but... Our office is not exactly official, and each Commander-in-Chief has to be introduced to us, and..."

He fell asleep in mid-sentence.

Sutton rose, went unsteadily to the coat rack, and slipped his hand into his jacket pocket. He retrieved the letter he had received two days earlier. He unfolded it.

"*I don't know whom else to turn to,*" Manny wrote. "*I desperately need money – just enough to get back to New Orleans. I'm married – to a girl whose innocence defies description. I'm responsible for her, although...*"

The letter had been sent from Marseilles. Sutton pondered. His superior needed a man... someone he could trust...

He tried to remember Manny, whom he had seen four or five times in his entire life. The features... the build... He assumed that Manny, a local and very much a member of the community in question, would fit in perfectly in his boss's plans.

Watch for more from Richard V. Hamilton

Richard V. Hamilton has been producing novels and screen plays for more than a decade. Enders' Family Publishing is working with Richard to bring you those stories.

The Kept Women of New Orleans
Coming to you in spring 2003

If you'd like to recieve Richard's next novel at 15 % off the cover price, send a note to the publisher to be added to the mailing list for Richard V. Hamilton, snail mail or email.

Enders' Family Publishing
PO Box 37
Gilbert PA 18331

or

mail@endersfamily.com

Let us know if you'd like to be added to our general mailing list or if you want to be notified only when Richard V. Hamilton releases a new book. Send us notice now to lock in your reduced rate for Richard's next novel.

Introducing Angels Among Us

The Angels Among Us™ are those everyday heroes who, as a matter of habit, help others change their lives for the better. They are people who live in your neighborhood, without celebrity and probably modest about what they do for others, those genuine neighbors who, a century ago, our great grandparents were taught to emulate, to look up to and to respect as the pillars of the community. These are the people we should try to be like, the true heroes in our society so often overlooked for the sake of today's superstar worship.

> *I think you're on to a winner. The raw material is not going to be too hard to come by, your subject matter lends itself to excellent promotion potential in all media wherever you go and - something everyone secretly yearns for - it's all so upbeat!*
> — Neil Marr, 35-year veteran journalist
> and editor of BeWrite.net

Scheduled to begin release in January 2003, Angels Among Us™ is a book series published by Enders' Family Publishing. Roughly 100 to 150 pages in length, each Angels Among Us™ book is the life story of an everyday hero who causes others to effect positive changes in their own lives.

Angels Among Us™ books are high-quality paperbacks printed as this book, on acid-free paper that will not yellow with age. Add them to your personal library and share the stories with your family, friends, whomever.

The cover price for each book is $5.95 USA. (Occasional blockbuster-sized books may have a higher cover price.) The cost for a one-year subscription to the Angels Among Us™ book club reduces the cost to you by more than 15 percent, and each title is mailed directly to your home as soon as it's released. You can also purchase gift subscriptions.

Angels Among Us™ Book Club subscriptions will be available for purchase beginning in September. If you purchase a book club subscription as a gift for the December holidays, we'll send a holiday greeting card announcing your gift. Gift subscriptions will also be given priority treatment, shipping in December before other orders are filled.

If you would like to receive an email notice when the Angels Among Us™ Book Club becomes available for purchase, send an email requesting notice to Angels@endersfamily.com. You can also subscribe to the Angels Among Us™ Newsletter free to keep posted on the latest book club information by sending an email to subscribe@endersfamily.com. Each newsletter brings you a short story about a local angel.

For more information and to learn about our other offers, visit the Enders' Family Publishing web site, http://www.endersfamily.com/.